Pride and Joy

Sophie's Log

Thoughts and feelings in poetry and prose

by Sophie Large

Foreword by Dame Judi Dench

FOREWORD
by Dame Judi Dench

Although I never knew Sophie, I didn't hesitate when Stephen and Cherry Large asked me to be patron of Sophie's Silver Lining Fund. I was so moved by the tragedy that ended Sophie's young life that I wanted to do what I could to help.

Sophie's Silver Lining Fund has been set up to help gifted and determined young actors and singers, and this book will help to raise funds. This collection of Sophie's work is just one aspect of her wide range of talents.

I urge you to support Sophie's Silver Lining Fund so that something positive can come out of the sad loss of such a unique young woman.

Judi Dench.

Praise for Sophie's Log

This is an extraordinary and moving anthology. It gives courage to the young who, like Sophie, have set their hearts on a special and difficult path in life.
Joanna Trollope

Teenage dreams that touch the soul – her writings are a way into her mind and heart. She speaks directly to our own adult memories of what it is like to be a teenager. That's why her book is so important.
Susan Hill, The Mail on Sunday

When a 19-year old girl died in a car crash, her family found her private writings. Her haunting words will touch the heart of every reader.
Jane Kelly, Daily Mail

Sophie's ambition, breathless excitements, disappointments and despairs, the lists of her successes and reasons for happiness… recall the young Sylvia Plath.
Gillian Clarke, The Times Educational Supplement

Sophie lives on in poetry and prose. Her writings are helping other talented youngsters to fulfil their ambitions.
Katherine MacAlister, The Oxford Times

In this collection we see Sophie developing her own voice – a voice which sings.
Juliet Townsend

That poem 'Sunglasses' is amazing. It reassured us that we weren't the only ones who felt like that.
Sophie Jennings and Kate Golledge, 17

Thank you Sophie, for showing me how to live life to the full.
Lizzie Cotton, 19

Sophie

"How can the End be the Beginning Again when All seems Lost?"

a play by
Bryan Willis

Based on the writings of Sophie Large

"Moving, funny, true"
Sue Roberts, BBC Radio

Praise for Sophie, the play

Moving, funny, true.
Sue Roberts, BBC Radio

A definite must-see.
Zoe Green, The Scotsman

Surprisingly funny, touching without being sentimental, thought-provoking... I was sorry when it was over.
Susan Carrdus, The Banbury Guardian

...Vital, touching and poetic.
Vivien Devlin, Rampant Scotland, Festival Fringe Review 2002

I would like to dedicate this story
as a tribute to the inspiration of

My unique daughter – my precious little princess Sacha who is a constant source of amazement and joy and the most wonderful treasure God could have given to me. Life is one long Sacha and Mummy adventure. Also I would like to thank the staff at the Trinity Street Surgery and Norfolk and Norwich hospital for helping my daughter and me through two very difficult years.

My dear friend and best-selling author, Katie Flynn – for her belief in me as a novelist. Her phenomenal capacity for research and prolific writing has always been an awesome inspiration, particularly when I was a teenager and she was my writing mentor.

Mum and Dad, Eleanor and Bernard Rose, for constant love and support. I remember as a teenager, burning the midnight oil and still writing. Often, my Daddy would come down in his pyjamas and with gentle exasperation, tell me to go to sleep. I love you and miss you, Daddy.

Cherry and Stephen Large, mum and dad of Sophie, and Dame Judi Dench, Patron of Sophie's Silver Lining Fund – for encouraging support and for allowing me to use Sophie's emotive words in my story. In appreciation, a percentage of the net proceeds from the sales of my novel will go to the charity.

My test readers: Carol Crouch and my spiritual sister, Ruth Chesney. Both deeply Christian, special needs and junior school teachers. These lovely ladies are unknown to each other, but both responded with almost identical positive reviews.

Pride and Joy

DAWN ROSE

Pride and Joy

ENGLISH ROSE

English Rose
PO Box 3176
Norwich
NR2 2WX

ISBN   978-0-9554352-1-8

Printed in Great Britain by
Creative Print and Design Group

A Haiku

This is a haiku, or short poem with a deep meaning.

> How can the End
> Be the Beginning again
> When All seems Lost?

Don't read on for a minute, I'll tell you what it means on the next page –

Have you thought about it?

Because if you haven't, don't read on.

It means that when something dreadful happens, like someone dies, it seems the end, and yet it is the beginning of coping without. See?

Sophie Large – aged ten.

WASN'T always this happy – as happy as I feel right at this moment. I thought I was, but when I found true happiness, I realised what I had been missing for all those years. Happiness isn't about what you have or what you are, it comes from within and it can only happen when you truly learn to like yourself.

I have just had my twenty-first birthday and in the following twenty-one chapters I would like to tell you about my own journey of self discovery. It began seven months ago, on the first day of spring – my favourite day of the year.

You can't expect life to be perfect, you just have to make the best of what you have and enjoy it to the full, but just when you feel safe, life has a habit of throwing some unexpected surprises at you. You cannot run away from the past, no matter how hard you try, and you cannot live a lie. You certainly can't even hope to find happiness if you can't face up to the truth. I've learned that now, but facing up to the truth about yourself is painful.

When I lost everything – all the security in my life that was so vitally important to me – I felt scared and very much alone. I felt that I had nothing to live for. I had no identity, no personality. I was no-one special and I chose not to have friends. A very dear nun gave me a book, *Sophie's Log*, which changed my entire perspective on life. The giver had become my replacement mother and I loved her far more than I ever had the original. My life was also shaped by those who loved me. I just didn't realise it!

I have now discovered that pride had always blinded me to the truth, in any situation, and created deep-rooted prejudice. I thought I was helping others, but really, they were helping me.

Sophie Large has helped me to open my eyes and see the truth. I wish I had known her. I feel as though she is my best friend, sharing her very private thoughts with me, knowing it will help because when she tells me about her life, I feel that I am on the outside looking in on my life and so I understand, much more.

To thank Sophie for her profound words, which inspired me to find the courage to learn who I am, I would like to tell my story and introduce each chapter with quotations from Sophie's verse and prose that will show you how very much my life has mirrored hers!

A Sniff of the real me

Somewhere floating above reality,
In time and space and place,
I exist. The real me
Stretches, and yawns, waking
Like a cat from oblivion,
Or an animal from hibernation.

The real me swirls and wavers,
Like a half remembered memory
Or a tune, once heard, now forgotten.
I move silently across my mind;
Behind my eyes, under my nose:
My ears hear me acutely.

I, me, myself, am real, alive, here.
I enjoy the feel of life under my hand,
The shouting and screaming,
The mad abandoned laughter of one
Who has let go of the parts of her mind
That hold the real her prisoner.

Feelings I want to feel
But would never dare to admit
Fill me up and drink me in like wine:
Sensual, sweet, intoxicating,
And I wallow in their rays,
Basking in the delight of release.

People ask her personal questions,
And smilingly she lies. But the real me
Cannot lie: I feel things, experience things
Too potent and wonderful to be wrong,
And my mind screams out the truth

While
My mouth smiles,
My head shakes,
My lips are still.

Sophie Large – aged seventeen.

Chapter One

REVELLED in the feeling of the soft sand moulding to the shape of my body as I lay on the beach. The still cool sea breeze caressed me, gently lifting tendrils of my hair so that it tickled my face. I took in a deep breath of that wonderful, early morning air. It had a crisp freshness to it, like putting your face against cool, freshly laundered linen sheets. The flag on the mast nearby even made that snapping noise in the breeze, like when you shake a fresh sheet out of its folds to spread it over a bed.

My hands played with the cool softness of the sand. They dug and lifted little heaps and my skin tingled as the sand poured back again between my fingers in rivers of granules. The coolness of my natural bed was in delightful contrast to the early morning sun which was beginning to warm the day in the cloudless blue sky.

I felt that the world had been freshly laundered and at that moment, it was a great big bed, encouraging me to lie-in and savour the feel and aroma of it, then rouse myself and enjoy the delights of nature. Even the sounds of the birds and the waves gently rolling in to the shore had a freshness to them that would be lost later in the heat of the day. This was a moment to truly savour.

I lifted my head and shielded my eyes from the sunlight with my hand to see if I was the only one savouring this moment. I was. Others had their own mode of pleasure. I was wearing khaki shorts and a men's shirt. Beside me, Lisa, my best friend, was still wearing her winter jeans and Arran sweater. She had spread the latest society magazines on the sand. I couldn't see her face because, head bent, her dark hair fell like a curtain as she devoutly studied the latest gossip, style and fashion tips.

A few feet away from us, adorable Annie, Lisa's daughter, was squealing with delight as she played the chasing waves game. Her cute little toddler jeans and the sleeves of her teensie Arran sweater were rolled up. Her gorgeous, baby perfect skin was shining wet as she jumped and splashed and her damp hair had formed a halo of large brown curls. Holding her bucket and spade, she ran, laughing as the flow of the wave chased her but didn't quite manage to catch her before it was sucked back as the next little wave broke. The foam hissed as it spread over the smooth sand and made another effort to try and catch her.

A little further along the beach, a man was throwing a stick into the sea and a collie dog was retrieving it. There were also two older children, trying to play badminton in the breeze and laughing at the wayward shuttlecock.

Nearby, two fishing boats were still tied to their moorings, like twins, tipped on their sides on the sand, after the tide had gone out. There was no-one else on the beach as far as I could see for miles in either direction. The sea had come in during the night and left a clean and smooth, perfect beach. Wherever the few of us had trodden this morning, we were making fresh footprints and we could feel like the pioneers of old, making our mark on an unexplored new land. It was such a good feeling.

I lay back and closed my eyes as I let the sun warm me. No, it was just me, enjoying this moment in this way. I took another deep breath and held it, then let it out again in another long sigh of contentment. The warmth of the sun was like a snuggly, cosy blanket. The soft breeze brushed my skin, carrying the sound of distant children's laughter and I drifted off into a deep sleep

SPRING – Easter Day

Easter Egg hunt

A silver glass of water.
Each puts a tear of water to their
eye, youngest to oldest.
I cry for the pain You suffered
And I thank You for loving me.

Sophie Large – aged nine.

Chapter Two

SOMETHING was tickling my nose. In my dream I woke up, a younger version of me, and looked into the eyes of a boy. His head was bent over me, his face just above mine. I gasped in shock and my reaction seemed to startle him.

His eyes searched my face and then held mine, intensely. We both seemed to be holding our breath. He had a mop of thick, wavy black hair which fell across his forehead, but it was his eyes that held my attention. In sharp contrast to his tanned face, thick black eyebrows and framed by the most amazingly long, thick black lashes, his eyes were a vivid blue. They were like two huge pools and I felt a curious desire to dive into them and swim around for ever.

"Ça va? Quelque chose ne va pas?" he whispered.

He seemed concerned and appeared to be asking me a question. I shook my head and frowned in confusion.

"Vous êtes Anglais, non?" He was still whispering and seemed in awe as he stared at my face. "Vous avez un visage angélique. Étes-vous une déesse?"

I shook my head again. "I don't understand." My voice was barely audible even to my own ears. A smile touched his full mouth, briefly and then he became serious, again. "Je suis désolé... I'm sorry... Are you English?" he whispered, with a heavy accent that was now obviously French.

I nodded.

"Can you breathe?"

"I don't think so," I whispered back, illogically, but it was how I felt. Something seemed to be wrong with my breathing. When he spoke, my eyes were again drawn to his mouth. I had never seen a mouth that was made like that before. It was entirely different to any other boy's mouth that I had noticed. In fact, I had not ever even considered a boy's mouth before. Perhaps they made them differently in France.

"Me also," he said. "Le charme."

I shook my head again.

"Have you put a spell on me?"

I frowned in confusion, "I'm not a witch."

"No, you are a goddess. I am a Catholic. I have not met a goddess before."

I began to laugh. "I think you are mistaken. I'm not a goddess."

"I don't know what you are," he said softly. "I was walking along the beach and I saw you lying here by the water's edge. I am tall for my age and I have never seen a girl as tall as me or as beautiful as you are. You are long and slim and your wet clothes are almost as pale as your skin. If it wasn't for your long waves of red hair you could be almost invisible against the sand. I thought that you might have been washed up on the shore and I didn't know if you were alive or dead or a goddess sent to play tricks on me, so I found this feather and tickled your nose with it to see what would happen."

His eyes were truly mesmerising. I smiled. Being so close to him was giving me a lovely, tingly feeling like little electric shocks, making my skin prickly. "Why would you think I am a goddess?" His eyes were suddenly serious and they made me melt like a box of chocolates in the sun.

"Because my father took me to an art exhibition once, in Florence, and my favourite painting since then has been 'The Birth Of Venus,' by Botticelli. Venus is the goddess of love. The symbol of mystery through which the divine message of beauty came into the world. She had just been conceived by the sea and risen out of the waves. She stands on a large shell, which is being blown in to the shore by the cherubs of the wind so that she may just step off. She appears as a gift from heaven, amidst a shower of roses and she is hailed with daisies, primroses and cornflowers to celebrate her birth and the birth of spring."

"You seem to know a lot about her," I whispered. Normal speech didn't seem possible.

"I keep a postcard picture of the painting. She is the absolute definition of beauty. A nymph is waiting at the shore to wrap her in a beautiful, purple cloak." His eyes were intense. "I wish that I had a purple cloak to wrap around you. You could be her. You look the same and today is the first day of spring. You must be Venus."

He stood up and held out his hand as he bent over me. I put my hand in his and he kissed it, his eyes not once leaving my face. Then he gently pulled me upright until I stood before him.

"They say that Botticelli's Venus is so beautiful that you do not notice that he has made her neck and limbs too long and yet here you are. You see. You are as tall as me. No girl is as tall as me. How old are you?"

Something told me that he wouldn't like my answer. He was wearing shorts and flat sandals on his bare feet. My feet were just bare. Perhaps it was his blue shirt that made his eyes seem an unusually vivid colour. I drew myself up to full height, my eyes level with his. "I am ten and a half."

He was astonished. "I have just had my fourteenth birthday! You are a goddess. No girl can be as tall and beautiful as you are."

I shook my head. "I'm just a normal girl."

He shook his head back at me. "There is nothing normal about you."

I felt suddenly shy and I wanted to change the focus away from me. "What are you doing on my beach? You seem to be French. Have you just landed and intend to invade my country?"

He looked left and then right along the coast. Miles of golden sand and no–one but us on it. "My mother is ill and I am staying with her at the beach house belonging to the convent school, just a couple of kilometres up there."

"I know it," I said. "My mother used to attend there and I'm due to start in September. I'm sure you are causing a stir with all the girls who are boarding there. Are you joining in their lessons?"

His eyes looked huge and worried. "Sister Ruth says they will eat me alive so she keeps me a secret from them and brings school work to the beach house for me, every day."

I smiled at him. "Yes, you are tasty…" I gasped and felt my expression freeze in horror. What had I just said? Why did I say that? My mouth opened and closed like a goldfish. I felt myself blushing and I didn't know what to say. "I… I mean…"

He was frowning, as though he was mentally trying to check his translations. "You mean that you like me? No?"

"No…I mean, yes… yes," I said quickly. I shrugged my shoulders to try to seem casual. "You… you seem to be a nice person."

"Je vous aime bien, aussi," he said, quietly. He looked down to the sand on my right. "Is this your castle?"

I nodded, and let out my breath with relief that he had changed the subject. I just felt uncomfortable because he was too close, too beautiful and too different to any other boy I had ever met.

"Is it finished?' he asked, tactfully. I shook my head as I sat down, glad of the distraction.

I had enjoyed many years of practice and I was a perfectionist. I considered my castles as masterpieces but I was surprised by how good he was at helping to build the ultimate castle. Of course, it had to have a moat and a drawbridge and a long channel down to the water's edge so that when the tide came in it would fill the channel and fill the moat, but not overwhelm the castle. That would be an inevitability to happen much later.

"Je suis curieux… so why is this your beach?" he asked. "Is this not a public beach?"

I was concentrating hard on building the perfect drawbridge, in order to make the castle 'keep' completely protected and secure. I paused to look at the boy. He was looking at me with that intense, curious expression again.

I pointed to the sand dunes behind us. "You see that path there, where there is a fork to the left and right?" He nodded as he followed my gaze. "The left-hand of the fork in the path goes over the dunes and to my garden."

He looked at me, and his beaming smile seemed to illuminate his face. "The right-hand fork of the path, that leads to my castle."

I frowned at him now in total confusion. "You have a castle?" He shrugged and smiled as he looked at the path. "Sort of. At least, it used to belong to my family and, one day, I am determined to get it back and then it really shall be mine."

It was my turn to smile at him. "So you really have just sailed from France and landed on my beach to invade and take back what was once yours!"

The pleasant scents of spring

When I was very, very small,
I swung upon a swing,
And slid quick down the old stone wall
In the pleasant scents of spring.

When I was relatively small
I succeeded, with a sling
That got me onto the trapeze tall,
In the pleasant scents of spring.

When I was younger, six and all,
I loved the great old field
Where horses graze until the call
Of the pleasant scents of spring.

And now I'm older, ten and all,
I long for trapeze and swing,
And the old stone wall, and the field of green,
In the pleasant scents of spring.

Sophie Large – aged ten.

Chapter Three

SOMETHING tickled my nose, again. I tried to brush it away. Suddenly I woke from the shock of a punch so hard to my stomach that it knocked all the breath out of me. "Annie, no!" I heard Lisa's shriek at the same moment that I opened my eyes.

"Joy, I am so sorry! Are you alright?" Lisa was kneeling by me and looked concerned.

"Boo!" said Annie, her big brown eyes sparkling with mischief as she beamed at me with a white, baby-teeth smile. She was waving a long feather.

I instantly played the game that Annie wanted and pretended to be cross. "You little monkey. Ooh, I'm going to get you, just you wait until I catch you!"

Annie squealed and laughed as she stood up on her little legs and ran towards the sea. I clapped my hands and pretended I was going to chase her. "I'm going to get you, you little monster!" Annie squealed again and laughed.

"Auntie Joy," Annie called as she splashed in the water, and then she squealed with the anticipation of me chasing her as I pretended to be cross again and pointed a finger at her. I collapsed back on the sand, panting.

"Not now, Annie," Lisa called out to her. "Auntie Joy is feeling tired and needs a rest. Why don't you do some more work on the sandcastle and Auntie Joy can help you later."

"Are you alright?" Lisa asked worriedly. "Can you breathe?"

I looked up at the cloudless blue sky and was struck by the similarity of its colour to his eyes, an intense, glorious blue. He had seemed so real that I could still almost feel and smell his nearness. "La couleur de ses yeux s'estompera. Sa voix, son odeur, son visage," I whispered. Echoes of my dream returned. "Can you breathe?" That's what the boy had asked me. My heart was pounding.

"Joy!" Lisa said, impatiently. "Will you stop it!"

I turned to look at her. "Quoi? Qu'y a-t-il?"

"Joy, what is the matter with you? You were asleep."

I shrugged. "J'ai fait ce rêve, dont je ne me rappelle pas bien."

"Joy, you are talking in French!"

"Vraiment? Je suis désolée…" I gasped. "I… I mean… sorry." I shook my head in wonderment. "Was I? What happened?"

"You were talking in your sleep and Annie was tickling your nose with a feather to wake you up. When that didn't work she decided to do a knee-drop on to your stomach before I could stop her."

I held my breath in panic. "What was I saying?"

Lisa shrugged and sat down on the sand again. "I don't know. Don't you think it's weird that you were dreaming in French? What were you dreaming about?"

"I can't remember," I lied. Dont je ne me rappelle pas bien. I heard the French translation in my head.

Lisa was intrigued. "If you're so fluent in French, does that mean that you think and dream in French?"

"I wasn't aware that I did," I said, softly. I was still thinking about the boy. I could still see his face, his eyes.

She turned the page of a magazine. "If you like speaking French, there's a gorgeous Frenchman in here who's available."

"Lisa," I complained, trying to forestall what was coming next. "Those are not shopping magazines for a prospective husband."

I closed my eyes and tried to recreate my previous mood of perfect relaxation but my equilibrium was now shattered and my blissful moment had gone.

Am I awake this time? Am I thinking in French or English? I feel like David in 'American Werewolf in London,' when he kept waking up in the hospital but each time, he hadn't really woken up and the scary things that happened were still in his dreams – although, they were actually a premonition of things to come.

I mentally tried to shake off the weird feeling of disorientation. Perhaps if I went back to sleep I could wake feeling relaxed again. I didn't want to dream about the boy, but I couldn't quite quell the feeling of disappointment that I had been woken too soon.

"Remind me why I'm sitting here on a freezing cold morning when I would rather be sitting at your kitchen table, eating your chocolate chip muffins by a lovely warm Aga."

Lisa interrupted my thoughts and I *tried* to get back to normality. "It's not freezing! It's a beautiful morning," I said defiantly. "This is the first day of spring, my favourite day of the year and it's my tradition to lie here and soak up all the beauty of it. This is the day when I put away my winter jeans, put my shorts on and let the sun see my skin until my birthday in October and then I put my winter jeans back on. I have never known the weather to not be good on this day."

I looked at Lisa and she shrugged indifferently. I tried again to win her appreciation of my special place. "Don't you think that it *feels* like the world has been freshly laundered and we can capture the essence of nature here on a beach which is practically our own? This is a moment to savour, early in the morning on the first day of a new season, celebrating God's gift of spring. Spring is the birth of *everything*, including Jesus, actually, because there were lambs at his birth and they don't come in December."

"I'd rather be celebrating on a beach in Miami," Lisa said irreverently.

"On a crowded beach, where in July and August, you can't even set foot out of your house because its one hundred percent humidity and one hundred degrees? Ugh! No, thank you."

"They just open the sliding doors of their living rooms or bedrooms and dive right into their pools."

I had a fleeting impression of the boy's eyes, like pools which I had wanted to dive into. I fiercely pushed the thought aside. "Pools which are surrounded by bug netting and alligators at the bottom of their gardens. They are practically prisoners in their own homes or offices and have to stay there because their home or work air-conditioning is the only way they can survive," I argued back "and they need it in their cars to get from one to the other."

Lisa was not to be beaten. "Wouldn't it be wonderful to get out of bed in a morning, open the sliding windows and dive right into your own pool, then shower in your en-suite before sitting on the terrace, next to your pool to enjoy a breakfast of fresh, local fruit, like Florida oranges? Mmm."

"You do shower in your en-suite," I said gently.

"In my caravan!" Lisa complained as she glowered at me, fully aware that I was teasing her.

I grinned at her. "Okay, we can't open our bedroom doors and dive into pools and we don't grow oranges but it's just a very short walk to the beach and you could swim and then enjoy Cley smokehouse kippers for breakfast with fresh, local strawberries and asparagus, the food of kings, for dinner, with Cromer crab, Blakeney lobsters, Morston mussels followed by freshly caught fish or duck with wild mushrooms, apples and our famous mustard, then sleep on a pillow filled with local lavender. This is Norfolk – the land of plenty. Mmm,' I closed my eyes and sighed, licking my lips as my imagination explored the prospect of such a wonderful menu.

"But this is England! We're known for our bad weather!"

Lisa was goading me. She knows how much I love living here. "This is the larder of England because we have more sun and less rainfall than anywhere else in this country." I pointed behind us. "That flag says we have the highest European award for our beach and look, there's almost no-one else here! Not much more than a stone's throw away is a vast network of rivers and huge, open water in the Broads. We're famous for them! You can drive all day through the country lanes and not see a bit of water, yet if you follow that mysterious sign in a village that says, 'To the Broad,' it's like you're suddenly in the Lake District. This is heaven!"

Lisa made a disagreeable expression. "Yes but who would want to *live* here? I wish I could afford a holiday abroad. You could travel if you wanted to. Why don't you?"

"Where would I go that is more beautiful than here? We have no need to go away on holiday, because we *live* in a holiday area. Millions of tourists come here but our countryside is so big that we barely even notice them! They dine at a host of renowned little waterside pubs and restaurants. The owner of the Michelin Star Morston Hall recently said on television that his success is because he uses local produce from our land of plenty and celebrates his quality ingredients."

This was a familiar debate between us. "It's still the back of beyond," Lisa grumbled.

Lisa failed as always to convince me. We usually ended up agreeing to disagree, basically because Lisa could not accept my winning arguments. "You'll never win, Lisa. We have everything we could possibly wish for on our doorstep."

"Such as?"

I racked my brain to ream off a list of reasons why Norfolk is so wonderful. "London is only two hours away by train. We have a fantastically convenient little international airport, if you did *want* to go anywhere. You know the phrase, "Fly via NIA." We have a Premier Division football club, owned by the nation's favourite television cook. The PGA hold their European Golf Championship here annually. The city is one of the greatest centres for the arts in Europe and every West

End show comes to our major theatre. There is a profusion of theatres, outdoor festivals, drama and dance schools, art schools and galleries.

There is a fantastic community spirit and low crime rate. Norwich has one of the rarest city centre permanent markets in the UK. Stunning modern architecture complimenting classical. You can skate outdoors in winter. There are two major television centres. They're building yet another shopping mall. Olympic standard sports facilities at the UEA… which has also produced some of the most popular authors…" I paused, gasping for breath.

"Okay, okay. Enough! I just think that living in Miami or Beverley Hills would suit me better."

"Those people are there for their work but they don't actually *want* to live there. The rich and famous are surrounded by intrusive press whenever they go out so they actually *prefer* to live somewhere out in the back of beyond, where no-one will bother them. I'm sure they would love to live here."

Lisa was studying her magazines again. "Don't you *want* a different life?' she asked.

I took a deep breath of the wonderful air and then expelled it very slowly, willing my body to relax and seep into the sand, like pouring a bucket of sea water into a sand hole. "I'm very happy with the life I have, thank you."

"You know, in those pale clothes, that skinny length of you practically disappears into the sand. If it wasn't for that mass of red hair you'd be almost invisible."

Oh, no! Déjà vu! I just knew what was coming next.

"You look like that famous painting, except that she's in the nude and standing on a shell."

"Botticelli," I supplied.

"Pardon?"

"Botticelli. He's the artist. You're talking about 'The Birth Of Venus.' She's the one standing on a shell."

"You see, you know!" cried Lisa, triumphantly. "You've been told before, haven't you?"

"It has been mentioned," I murmured. "Lisa, I'm just normal."

"Sweetie, you are not normal, no matter how hard you try! I just don't get it!" Lisa was intent on pursuing this. "You look like a goddess! Even some of these supermodels don't look like goddesses! Yet you try and hide it by wearing men's shirts and jeans in the winter or shorts in summer. You don't wear make-up. The only vanity you allow yourself is your fabulous mass of hair but even that you try to hide sometimes by putting it in plaits and then you look like a fourteen year old, except that there are no fourteen year old giantesses." Lisa gave me a searching look. "Why?"

"Because I want people to like me for who I am, not what I am or what I have."

"*Are* you happy?"

"Joy is my name. Of course I'm happy," I said with careful determination.

Lisa was still staring at me. "Yes, but are you *really* happy?"

Help! My discomfort was starting to get worse. I took a deep breath. "When my best friend asks me if I'm *really* happy, that means that she doubts that I am actually happy and having to defend my state of happiness throws a question mark on my happiness. Yes, Lisa, I *am* truly happy." I closed my eyes, trying to relax.

"Truly?"

"Yes," I said firmly. "When I woke up this morning I was in a state of perfect happiness with the world. My life is in total order. Everything is just exactly as I wish it to be and there is nothing in this world that I could ask for that could make me happier than I am right at this moment."

"What about a man?"

She wasn't giving up this morning. "I have a man."

"Your father!"

I opened my eyes and looked at her. She was animated, like a dog gripping a bone. She just wouldn't let go of it. "Yes! I don't need another man. I look after him and we are totally happy."

"What if your father was to fall in love and want to marry again?"

I sighed with exasperation. "My father will be seventy in November. That's hardly likely to happen."

Lisa was obviously puzzled. "You have such a simple life and you don't ask for anything. Don't you want a career, money, your own home and a family?"

"I don't need money," I assured her. "I work for my father and all the money goes into the business. My father *is* my family. We live and work together and I love working for him in the antiques business. We've got the little bed and breakfast and the tea room and the holiday caravan park with the little shop. I love my life and I don't want it any other way."

"And if something happened to your father?" Lisa asked gently.

This was something I didn't want to think about. "God forbid anything should happen to my father and I know you cannot avoid the inevitable, but, when the time comes, then I shall just carry on as I am. This is the life I want, Lisa." Lisa was looking at me like I was the saddest creature in the world.

Lisa put her magazine down and gave me a long, hard look, like she was trying to look inside my head. "You are the sweetest, kindest, most unselfish person I know. You work so hard and you do so much for other people but you take *nothing* for yourself."

"I don't *need* anything," I assured her. "The Catholic meaning of my name is Jesus-Others-Yourself. My pleasure is to give pleasure to others."

"I worry about you," Lisa said softly. "You run the business, make all that wonderful food, no packet stuff ever crosses the threshold. You keep a spotless, stylish home that could be featured in any of those magazines that you keep in your shop. You've even made one room into a stunning nursery to keep Annie happy while we're working. It's all utterly perfect, but there just one thing that's missing! A man!" Lisa looked lovingly at Annie. "Annie adores you. Don't you want your own little patter of tiny feet?"

I looked at Annie, who beamed a beautiful smile back at me as she patted the side of her sandcastle and I felt a twinge inside me, but I was determined to put it aside. I waved at her and she waved back, then carried on, busy with her work on the mound of sand. "Yes," I replied to Lisa's question. "But that would require a man and I don't want any man other than my father. I am happy with my life. What about you? Why do you read those magazines, yearning for a life that can never be yours?"

"I can dream can't I? Okay, my life isn't great and the future doesn't seem to hold much for me, but there is always hope and dreams can come true, right?" Lisa sighed. "I know it's my own fault, well, Gary's as well. If I hadn't got pregnant the first time we *did* it, I wouldn't have had to quit school to have Annie and Gary wouldn't have had to quit school to get a job as a builder's labourer, in order to support us. If you and your father hadn't kindly offered the caravans to us and the rest of the bunch of young couples who can't afford their own homes, and if you and your father hadn't offered me a job, allowing me to bring Annie to work with me… I don't know where we would be! I *know* I made a mistake!"

I looked at Annie, busy digging sand and filling her bucket with spade-fulls that mostly fell off before she could get it in. "I know you shouldn't have done what you did, but you can hardly call Annie a mistake," I said softly.

"That's what I don't understand," said Lisa. "I don't have a choice but you do. You could be in these magazines, earning a fortune and have the pick of any man you want *and* your own little patter of tiny feet. What is so wrong with having your own man and your own home, living a life of luxury, rubbing shoulders with the rich and famous?"

"Enough, Lisa. Why are you so obsessed with those magazines?"

Lisa refused to be beaten. "I want to *know* what's going on in the rest of the world," she said adamantly.

"Lisa, those people don't live in *our* world. In fact, they live on a different planet and you're reading the latest intergalactic news!"

"Speaking of news!" Lisa's face lit up suddenly with great excitement. "Did you know that they've sold the old castle over there?"

"What?" I shrieked and sat bolt upright before I could control my reaction.

"I thought you'd be pleased." Lisa looked puzzled. "Why are you so upset? Being an antiques restorer with a love of old houses, I thought you'd want someone to buy the old place and do it up. Perhaps they may even ask you to help them restore it and maybe find some antiques for them."

I struggled to control the rising panic inside me. I tried to sound nonchalant but failed, miserably. "Who's bought it? How did you know it's been sold? I hadn't heard anything."

Lisa continued to flick through the pages of a magazine. "Josie's dad grazes his sheep there and he's been informed that the ownership is in the process of changing but he doesn't know who's bought it yet."

Lisa lifted her head and beamed at me. I could see the cogs working in her head as she put two and two together – the magazines and the mysterious new owner.

"Hey, wouldn't it be exciting if a movie star bought it or someone really rich and famous!"

"Lisa!" I protested. "Come back down to earth! Who would want to live there?"

"But you just said…"

"Never mind." I didn't like the way this argument was going and I tried to calm the terrible upset that was building inside me. Something I thought I had put away in a box, on a shelf, a long time ago was now 'off the shelf' and the lid was open! "We don't want a movie star living next door with all the nuisance paparazzi. Just imagine how inconvenient that would be. You wouldn't be able to move in the country lanes because they would be everywhere, like swarming ants. Besides, someone rich and famous is going to be someone who travels all over the world for their work and they're hardly going to want to live in an out of the way, inconvenient place like this."

Lisa was now frowning at me in bewilderment. "Huh? What has got into you? Who rattled your cage? In fact, what gets into you every time we debate about my magazines? What is it with you?"

I was rattled. I tried to regain a foothold on the crumbling slope of our argument. For once, Lisa had the upper hand and she was enjoying it. "Let's agree to disagree, shall we? Annie, come on, let's build this castle. Shall Auntie Joy make a nice bridge across the moat?"

I avoided looking at Lisa and gave my full concentration to working on the castle. This was something I was good at and I find building sand-castles very rewarding, particularly when doing it to please an adorable toddler.

I worked hard with a delighted, chattering Annie, leaving Lisa free to study her magazines in depth. This was fun and I didn't want to think about anything else right now. We dug the moat to make it deeper and dug a long channel for the water to come in. The castle 'keep' was well-protected, with a deep moat and high walls. I always love making the drawbridge – the link between 'safety' and the outside world. It hadn't escaped my attention how similar this castle was to the one in my dream.

"You know, there's a huge similarity between you and that castle."

Lisa interrupted my thoughts and I was thrown off balance, yet again. What was wrong with me, today? The day had started out so perfectly. It was obviously a mistake to ask Lisa to share my special day, even though Annie was enjoying it. Without them, I could be lying here in perfect peace and harmony with nature.

"In what way?" I asked politely and carefully.

Lisa was studying me, intently. "You are my best friend, but sometimes I think that I really don't know you. It's like you have walls around you. You give so much out, but you won't let anything in, and if something upsets you, like talking about the rich and famous seems to or men, the drawbridge instantly goes up and the shutters come down on the windows and I really don't know how to get in." She sighed, not taking her eyes off me and shook her head in bewilderment. "How did you get to be such an enigma by the tender age of almost twenty-one? You adamantly refuse to consider having any man in your life, other than your father, when as far as I know, you've never even been kissed and you have this weird barrier that goes up at the mere mention of the rich and famous? Tell me why you don't want to marry a rich and handsome Frenchman."

I groaned. "Oh, no! We're back to the Frenchman!"

"Tell me why you wouldn't want a man like that," Lisa insisted.

"Tell me why I would," I countered.

"Okay. I'm eighteen, married, with a little girl, so there's no chance of me ever being photographed with movie stars at one of their extravagant parties or having lots of attention as a bridesmaid for Lord and Lady *So and So*, but if I was in your shoes, I could and he would be my ideal man."

I went over to Annie. "Can you just dig this bit out here, for Auntie Joy? I need to go and put your mum straight on the facts of life. Then we'll go for an ice cream, shall we on the way home?" I went and sat beside Lisa. "Alright. Let's have a proper debate about this. The one who loses buys the ice cream, right?"

"You're on."

I looked at Lisa's spread of magazines which so fascinated her. "Okay. You tell me the why's and I'll tell you the why not's. Agreed?"

"Definitely. This time, I'll win."

"You never do," I reminded her. "Why the Frenchman?"

Lisa positively glowed with confidence as she put forward her case. "He is one of the most gorgeous men in the world and he is heir to one of the richest. He has a wonderful name, Richard de Bowes-Lyon, and he will one day inherit the title, Duc de Lyon. He and his parents, the Duke and Duchess are not only aristocracy, they are practically royalty in these magazines. They are pictured in almost all of these magazines at various parties, but in this magazine there is a big feature about them. Look, they're celebrating because the Duke has retired from running the business and handed over the reins to his son, who is already rich, and there's a photograph here of them at Richard's twenty-first birthday. His father is handing over an elaborately jewelled box. The box itself is said to be worth around two hundred thousand pounds but inside, is Richard's birthday present. It's a cheque for twenty million pounds. Can you imagine being that rich? Mind boggling isn't it? The money and title make him a prize catch but he's totally desirable!"

I concentrated on retaining my composure. "So what makes him *available*?"

"He's not married, but he wants to be." Lisa was positively drooling.

"What about Gary? How would he feel, if he knew you were having heart palpitations for another man?"

"I love Gary but this is just dreamtime, as you said. It's not like I'm ever going to run off with him."

I felt a stab, like someone was sticking a knife into my stomach, but I tried to keep a straight face. "Waste of time, if you ask me. How do you know he wants to be married? If he's announced his engagement to someone, then he's not *available* is he?"

Lisa kept turning the pages, insistent on showing me all the various photographs of the 'Happy Family.' "Oh, no, he hasn't announced it yet. He has just let it be known that he wants to be. The press can't work out which of the numerous dates he has is going to be the one he will actually marry. He's keeping them guessing. He's seen out with movie stars, models and society heiresses. He could have any of them but he doesn't let on which one it is. He is certainly a man with the world at his feet. Young, rich, devastatingly handsome, heir to a title." How could you say no to him?"

"Very easily," I said quietly. "If he wants to marry, it would only be because his father is putting pressure on him to produce the next in line to the title. Aristocrats do that, don't they? And a man who is that rich and that handsome would always be offered temptation. Women would be throwing themselves at him and be his for the taking. How could you ever trust a man like that? He couldn't keep a promise to you. He couldn't be faithful. You would always worry where he was and who he was with and just imagine, if the press had a photograph of him with someone else, there would be public speculation of him being unfaithful to you. That would just eat into you and cause a terrible rift between the two of you, even if it wasn't true, which lots of this stuff isn't." I looked at the photographs. "They're all happy and smiling, but what goes on really in their lives?"

"His wife would have lots of money to console her though, wouldn't she?"

"Exactly. What sort of a life is that? These people wouldn't know genuine love if it slapped them in the face. They're not capable of being honest and faithful. I mean, just look at these headings. This movie couple were having problems in their relationship because he wanted children and she didn't, then he has an affair with his next movie co-star and leaves his wife because his new love wants to have children. Then the distraught ex says, "But I wanted to have children!" This one had an affair with his PR, that one had an affair with his children's nanny and then publicly apologised to his *girlfriend*, who is the mother of his children. Honestly, Lisa, just look at this stuff. They're not capable of being faithful and if the press aren't printing stories about them, they're giving interviews and washing their dirty laundry in public. Who would want to live like that?"

"What a life, though." Lisa, it seemed, was not to be deterred. "I mean, the Duke and Duchess and Richard are just *everywhere*. They seem to be invited to every party and premiere and award ceremony, even royal weddings."

"So when do they ever work?" I commented. "Do they spend their whole lives partying?"

"Mmm, what fun." Lisa was beyond redemption in dreamtime. "And shopping!" she suddenly said. "They must spend the rest of their time shopping for clothes, particularly the Duchess, because you never see her in anything twice. Isn't she gorgeous? I mean, just look at her! She's fabulous! Actually, come to think of it, she can't be Richard's mother because she's too young. She must be the Duke's second wife."

I bit my lip. I didn't want to be having this conversation.

"She's so beautiful, and so stylish, don't you think so?" Lisa enthused. "She must spend a fortune on clothes."

"I expect she dumped her former husband and married the Duke for his money and title," I said, scathingly. "Money is all that matters to them and, actually, the richer people are the less they spend on clothes because its good publicity for designers if such people are wearing their clothes so they just give them, don't they?" I asked. "You've read that recent best seller about the lives of these people. Why are you so interested in them, Lisa? They're just fakes! So shallow and false."

"Mmm," Lisa sighed. "They would certainly want to have her wearing their clothes. She's a legendary beauty of our time. An international icon. She is 'A' on the 'A' List. These magazines have the top one hundred richest, the top one hundred most invited, best dressed, celebrity style. They're always there in the top ten and, often, she's number one in the style list. She's a gourmet cook as well. She does those television programmes and she's often being interviewed. How can she possibly eat with a figure like that? She's like a tiny, delicate bird."

"And who would want her as a mother-in-law?" I said, coldly. "How would you ever compete with that?"

"That book isn't really true you know. It's fiction."

"Written by a girl who is living the life of the character and is pictured in these magazines herself, Lisa. She knows exactly what she's talking about. When she talks about girls snubbing you if you are not wearing next season's shoes, it's probably true. Imagine the pressure of having to say and do and wear the right thing! Nightmare! I wouldn't want to live like that. Whether you're a movie star, model or society heiress, you're in fierce competition to get the next important role, husband or to be first with a new look! What do your magazines say the latest look is?"

"White, particularly white crochet," Lisa said knowledgably.

I was defiant. "When did anyone last wear crochet? When will they ever again after the end of this season? If white is in now, guaranteed it will be black next season and you'll be snubbed at the ball if you've been on holiday and arrived to find that the world has flipped in your absence and white is now way out!"

"The Duchess has survived it. She is the number one style icon and she seems to thrive on it."

"Exactly," I muttered. "She must be tougher than the rest and she'd be a nightmare mother-in-law. Nothing you did or wore would ever be right or good enough. What would you do, have your mother-in-law tell you what to wear and how to cook?" I looked directly at Lisa. "I think I've won this argument. Richard de Bowes-Lyon is the most undesirable man you could wish for because of his nightmare step-mother!"

Lisa sighed as she looked wistfully at the pictures of Richard.

"Lisa, have you noticed that Richard is not photographed anywhere

here with the same girl twice? He must go shopping for girls as often as his step-mother goes shopping for clothes! Now can we go for an ice cream? You're paying."

"You know, I've always said that the Duchess, Elizabeth de Bowes-Lyon, uncannily looks like you. I mean, if she were a foot taller, and just a little younger, you could be sisters. Your faces and your colouring are almost identical. In another life, you could be her!"

"No thank you," I said firmly. "Annie, ice cream time!" I turned back to Lisa. "Have you finished with these magazines?"

She made a rueful expression. "Okay. You win. You can put them in the recycling bag. I feel depressed. As its quiet would you mind if I go shopping in Norwich, this afternoon, as it's *so* convenient!" she said with mild sarcasm. "Will you look after Annie for me?"

I hugged Lisa. "Of course I will. Just don't go wishing for your dreams to come true. If you're not careful, they just might."

"You are my best and *weirdest* friend," Lisa said emphatically as she hugged me back tightly.

All's well

Darling Mum and Dad,

I am at this moment in time sitting on my bed in my box (study/bedroom). It's dark outside so I've drawn the curtain. In the background I can hear Eric Clapton playing quietly and mellowly on my tape recorder and my room has the faintly untidy look that accompanies me – and every Saturday afternoon – after I've been to town. And you know what? I am utterly happy. I'm happy. I'm happy with myself, my life, you, my darling parents, my brothers, my work situation (almost), my box, my friends, my teachers, er, and lots of other things.

I really feel that at last, last, last I've found my niche and established myself properly. Of course I have my little grumbles - don't we all - but I rather enjoy them, strangely. I mean, I am doing pretty well here. I've got lots of friends and I'm a music scholar and an academic scholar.

Sophie Large – aged seventeen.

Chapter Four

I PARKED the pushchair on the little paved area by the kitchen door. The flagstones had been warmed by the sun and they were worn with age.

Annie was in a deep sleep, slumped over with her head on her shoulder, in that wonderful way that children sleep. It just makes you love them more, because they are so innocent, so vulnerable and so trusting. They are so totally reliant upon you, their carer, to look after them, especially when they are comatose.

God's nature is very clever. When a child is asleep, their need for your care is greater, the bond is strengthened and you love them more. Lisa is right. I do have an inordinate love for Annie and I would love to have my own patter of tiny feet, but the way my life is, I have just come to accept that it is not something that will be possible for me. You have to love a man who will love you back and I just don't think that is going to happen for me.

I took the magazines out of the deep pocket of the pushchair and put them on the kitchen doorstep. I carefully undid the little plastic fastens to release Annie from her protective straps, and I lifted her in my arms. Its funny how, as a woman, you automatically do the hip thing when you hold a small child. Men don't do that. They just support them in the crook of their arm. Perhaps it's something in your genes that tells your body what to do. You don't even have to think about it. You just lift the child and your pelvis immediately contorts out, to that side, like a shelf, so that you can support the child on it, their legs wrapped around you, as you hold them. God's nature! Wonderful!

I love the feeling of Annie, asleep in my arms, her head on my shoulder, against my neck. Can it be wrong to love another person's child this much when you cannot have a child of your own? I do love it when Lisa leaves me to baby sit, because then I can be a make-believe mum, just for a little while.

As I held Annie, I turned to enjoy my perfect garden. I love my Norfolk home because we actually *live* in such a wonderful environment. The deep walls of the farmhouse and barn are protection from the winter weather. In the local tradition, they are flint, which is the name for covering walls with local pebbles, making defined patterns with different shapes and sizes, so that the walls themselves are a work of art.

The internal walls are half-timbered, with beamed ceilings. It has always fascinated me that the wood used to make houses at that time came from old oak ships' timbers. What ships had those timbers belonged to and where had they travelled, at a time when people still thought that the world was flat and you could sail off the edge of it? Had they discovered new territories? Had they been in battle? They had probably sailed from the nearby ports of Great Yarmouth and Lowestoft. How old were those trees before they became ships and where were the forests where they had stood?

The roofs are made of thatch, harvested locally in the Broads and created by local craftsmen. Each has his own style of doing a roof in a particular pattern which is like their personal signature. The texture and feel and smell of everything is wonderful here. I'm sure Lisa really does love it, no matter how much she grumbles. She just wants to explore the rest of the world, which I can understand. I just feel that I don't want to because everything I need is here, in this house and garden.

On the left-hand side of the garden is the boundary wall between us and the huge estate belonging to the castle. Part of the wall is hidden by a large clump of shrubs which have been deliberately left to be overgrown. At the end of the garden there is a little gate and the path leading over the sand dunes to the beach. I love the old flower beds and the clumps of daffodils around the trunks of old fruit trees on the lawn and, particularly, my vegetable and herb sections. Everything around me is old, worn and wonderful, basking in the early spring sunshine and soft sea breeze.

I pressed my thumb on the big iron latch and as it lifted, it made an echo in the kitchen. The heavy oak door creaked as I pushed it open. I bent to pick the magazines up and put them on the huge, oak kitchen table that stood on the smooth, aged flagstone floor. It was worn, like everything else around here. Worn means aged and aged means history and I just love having the honour of being a part of the history of this ancient farm house.

The house was quiet. I walked on the flagstones along the hallway, Annie, a comforting weight in my arms.

I opened the latch on the oak door of my father's study. He was fast asleep, his huge frame snug in his big old armchair by the fireside, his head comfortably pressed against one of the high wings. It is his favourite chair. He has been sleeping a lot, lately. The logs made a nice little crackling sound in the grate. There were papers spread over his big oak desk. I assumed that he must have been busy with paper work and then decided to have a nap. I closed the door as quietly as I could.

The smooth, polished oak creaked as I went up the narrow staircase and along the landing into the nursery.

I laid Annie down on the cot bed and took off her tiny shoes, little Arran jumper and jeans. I changed her nappy for a fresh one and took some Winnie The Pooh pyjamas from the chest of drawers and carefully put them on Annie, then covered her with the duvet. She was still completely fast asleep, her pretty head snuggled against the pillow, almost overwhelmed by images of Winnie The Pooh on the bedding. She loves to have me read the stories to her and she loves the characters.

I looked, reflectively, around the room. Lisa is right. I am terribly house-proud and I am pretending to be a mum. I do everything I possibly can to make my father's life wonderful. This is a very special home, which I have worked hard to create and maintain. I know she is right. All that is missing is a man, but I will never admit that to her.

I went back to the kitchen and picked up the pile of magazines and then went into the sitting room. Apart from the kitchen, where I love to bake, this is my favourite room. I love the low beams, the whiteness of the plaster between the timbers on the walls, but I particularly love the big inglenook fireplace which goes from floor to ceiling and the cosy rug in front of it.

Dad must have lit the fire in here while I was at the beach. There isn't a grate. The fire was simply on the brick floor of the inglenook. In winter, you can burn a large section of tree trunk on it, but today, there was just a little fire to take the chill off the room. I took a couple of small logs out of the willow basket and put them on the fire. They soon crackled as the flames caught the fresh wood. We don't have any overhead lighting in our old house, so I switched on some table lamps.

I opened an old door of a cupboard, which had been built into the depth of the wall. I took out a box and put it on the rug, then removed a large scrap book from a pile which I had carefully hidden at the back of a shelf, behind a pile of assorted books.

I set everything out in front of me and began to work. This is my secret project. The box contains glue, scissors and pens. I took the magazines and began to carefully cut out pictures and, sometimes, entire pages. The Frenchman smiled at me, his arm around the new starlet of Hollywood's latest big hit movie.

"If Lisa ever finds out about this," I said to him, "she will kill me."

I worked quietly and with a great deal of concentration. The only sounds were the satisfying crackle and shift of the fire as it consumed the logs and coal and the ticking of the old grandfather clock against the wall.

I was so busy concentrating that I didn't hear the door open. "Joy," a voice said, softly.

I gasped as I looked up to see my father towering above me. He is six feet six inches and quite broad. He seems to fill a room when he stands in it. My dad is a gentle giant.

I looked down in dismay at the array in front of me. Caught in the act! I looked helplessly at him.

He sat down in the nearest armchair and smiled. I just love his blue eyes. His crinkled smile lines and grey hair make him so, sort of, distinguished, in a way that women can never be as they grow old. It isn't fair is it? Some men just look better and better as they get older, whereas women just get old.

"I…I.." What could I say?

"Don't worry, Precious. I can keep your secret," he said softly. He has a lovely kindness in his eyes. He is just so gentle. I have never, ever known him be cross. "Actually, I've known about it for quite a long time, because a few years ago, I was looking for a book that I thought I had lost and I accidentally discovered your little pile in the back of the cupboard. It's alright, don't worry," he reassured me.

I smiled awkwardly, still feeling very sensitive and embarrassed. It was a bit of a shock that he had known about a project that I thought I had taken great care to keep a secret.

I suddenly noticed that he was biting his lip anxiously and it was actually my dad who was now looking uncomfortable. I don't know why, but something twanged inside me.

"Dad? What's the matter?"

He tapped the arm of the chair and looked at me for a moment, and then pulled a letter out of his shirt pocket. "I think you ought to read this." He handed the letter to me.

The paper was headed with the address of the local doctor's surgery. The more I read, the more the panic rose inside me, until I had to stop myself shaking to keep the paper still. When I had finished reading, I looked up at him. There was a terrible tightness around my chest and my eyes were a well of tears.

The letter was referring to an illness that my father has, which I have known nothing about, and was giving him a list of the options available to him for treatment. It mentioned that there was a pioneering treatment possible at a research hospital in New York.

I was totally dumbfounded. Suddenly the tears burst their dam and flowed down my cheeks. With an anguished cry I covered the short distance between us and buried myself in his arms. I was shaking. Dad hugged me tightly and we stayed like that for a while, not speaking, just hugging and tearful.

Eventually, I took a deep, shuddering breath and spoke, my words muffled against the now wet collar of his checked shirt, "Why didn't you tell me? You should have told me."

He held me tightly in that wonderful, big bear hug. "I didn't want to worry you until I knew for sure."

"How long have you known?" I asked, my voice still muffled and tearful. I loved being in the security of his arms. I had always felt so safe there and protected. Now, I felt vulnerable and frightened.

"For about six months. I was hoping the local hospital treatment would work but the specialists there have now said that it's beyond them."

I felt a large lump in my throat. "Does that mean it's serious?" I didn't really want to hear the answer.

He hesitated and squeezed me tightly. "Yes," he said, quietly.

Something stabbed in my chest. I could barely speak. "What is to be done?" I whispered. "The letter mentioned the possibility of treatment at a research hospital in New York which is pioneering a new drug. That sounds expensive."

He sighed. "It is. We have some money saved but it isn't enough for the complete treatment. I could mortgage the farm or we could sell the farm and the business…" He hugged me when I gave a muffled cry. "The thing is, it isn't my money to use."

I kneeled on the floor between his legs and looked up at him. "It's your money."

He shook his head. "You've been working in the business for a long time, now. It's also your money *and* your home, if we choose to sell it."

"Dad, no," I cried, vehemently shaking my head. "We're not going to mortgage and we're not going to sell. We will get you better and I will just work harder to earn the money."

His smile was so loving. "Sweetheart, we don't earn very much money. The antiques, the bed and breakfast, the tea room and the holiday camp are a lot of work but they don't bring in that much money. We have enough money to start the treatment and the summer season will be starting soon and we'll see how we go. A mortgage is probably the best option and then sell everything, if that doesn't work, but, Sweetheart..." He hesitated and looked carefully at me, again. "I can't have this treatment if it is going to break us financially. That wouldn't be fair of me and there is no guarantee that this treatment will work. It's just that the medical press say that this hospital has had some success with it for this type of illness. I'd be a sort of guinea pig, taking a calculated risk and hoping that it works for me."

"What happens if you don't have this treatment?"

His eyes held mine, sadly. He shook his head and shrugged.

"You are going to have this treatment and you are going to get better," I said defiantly, feeling some sort of strength building inside me. The sort you read about when people face inevitable disaster and have to be brave. The only chance they have to survive is to give it to God and let his strength fill them and carry them through. "I don't care how many extra hours I have to work, I will find the money for this. When are you supposed to go?"

"As soon as possible is best," he said quietly.

"You can't travel alone. I'll have to apply for a passport and come with you. Oh, this will be so awful. I'll have to work here to earn the money and you'll be there, all alone, having to go through this terrible ordeal with no-one familiar there to hold your hand." I was so concerned for him. This was an unbearable predicament.

A strange looked crossed his face and he took a deep breath as he looked at me. He ran his fingers through his hair in an agitated sort of manner. I had an awful dread. "Dad, what is it? Is there something worse that you haven't told me?"

He sighed. "Sort of. It's just...well."

"What is it?" I urged.

He took another deep breath. "Well, now that you know the worst, I think its time that you knew the rest."

My face froze in horror. "The rest?" I said faintly.

His hands rubbed my shoulders and he still seemed to be searching for words and then he took the plunge. "I won't be alone in New York. There is someone coming with me."

I frowned in confusion. "Who?"

"You remember Miss Penny?"

"Moneypenny?"

Dad smiled then. "That's right. You remember that she's Miss Penny, but because she owns the post office, when you were a child you used to take your money to put in a savings account and you decided to call her Moneypenny."

I smiled. "Yes, she's a nice lady. I still think of her as Moneypenny, but why is she going with you? Doesn't she have to run the post office?"

"She's putting a manager in charge so that she can take the time off work to be with me. She's paying her own costs."

I frowned in amazement. "Wow. That's very kind of her to go to such trouble in order to keep you company."

He looked thoughtful again. "Joy," he said carefully.

"Yes?"

He took another deep breath and said, "You know all those church meetings I used to go to?"

I smiled. "Yes, you've worked so hard for the church over the years. I don't know anyone else who has attended so many church meetings."

"Well, I apologize to God and I apologize to you. I didn't actually go to any church meetings."

I stared at him in confusion. "Where did you go to, then? Several times a week, you would go out and you said that you were going to church meetings!"

"Umm, well, actually, I met Moneypenny. I mean, Miss Penny."

The penny still hadn't dropped with me. "Why?"

"Because, Sweetheart, I've been having a relationship with Miss Penny for the last nine years. She consoled me after we lost your mother and... well, it just sort of happened. Apparently, she's always had a soft spot for me but didn't let on and I've always rather liked her, since before I met your mother but... I was always a bit shy. After we lost your mother, Ruby, that is, Miss Penny, was very kind and supportive and... we talked and, sort of discussed everything and it... just happened."

It had dropped now! I stared at him, dumbstruck. "Does anyone else know?"

He shook his head. "Of course not, Sweetheart. We've been very careful. I think that some people suspect that we have a close friendship but no-one knows any more than that."

My mouth was suddenly dry. "Why didn't you tell me? Nine years?"

His eyes held mine and they were ever so gentle and worried. "You were so upset about losing your mother and you've worked so hard to make life wonderful for me. We haven't known how to tell you and, well, what has happened now has sort of brought everything to a head. When you're facing the worst, you may as well know the rest."

"I'm stunned," I whispered. I swallowed hard, trying to take in the shock. "I had no idea."

"There's something else," Dad said, gently.

"More?" I gasped.

"It's not bad," he reassured me. "He seemed to be suddenly relieved and he was smiling with happiness. "The thing is, Sweetheart... well, you're nearly twenty-one now and, well, now that you know, I wanted to tell you that, if I survive this, when we get back, Ruby and I would like to be married and she will move in here, if that's alright with you?"

I was shell-shocked! What could I say? I was utterly stunned, but the least I could do was congratulate my father and his prospective bride.

"Wow! It's a shock but, congratulations, Dad. You will get better and you will get married! Seems like it's about time after nine years, doesn't it?"

Dad beamed at me and kissed my cheek as he pulled me into his arms. "Thank you, Precious," he said, his words muffled in my mass of hair. "Your approval was what we needed."

My flat

My flat would be lovely. It would have planks on the floor. I would have borrowed some old rugs from home and bought some cheapo ones for it. There would be a chest of drawers for my clothes and a bed I had picked up in a junk shop. All the chairs would be painted a tasteful green colour and would be all different shapes and sizes, being cheap bargains from auctions, etc. I would have bought some brown, fiver a throw, cushions and covered them with nice material.

The walls would be white and I would have hung pictures of varying impressiveness on them. I would have one or two book cases stuffed with books and plays and things. There would be candles in candlesticks dotted about.

The cutlery in the kitchen would be all that cheap tin ware, except the mugs, of which there would be loads of different shapes.

There would be interesting oddments – like nice lamps and cruddy lamps and all my soft toys and my little writing desk. There would be a typewriter on the floor.

Out of the window I would have window boxes for my cooking herbs. I would have lots of green plants on the window ledges too. It would be great fun cooking interesting meals for one pound each, etc. Somewhere near my home would be a market and on Saturdays I could go and get my fresh vegetables and bargains – rugs and plates and things for my mobiles. I would have gone to Ireland and collected shells to string up in mobiles and as wall decorations.

I would have a bicycle with a big basket on the front. I might get the urge to go to Hyde Park for a picnic with a friend, or to the cinema or something.

I might wake up early and walk to a patisserie, and buy pain au chocolat and eat it when I got home with coffee.

I'd go to auditions when I wasn't working – perhaps as a secretary, perhaps as a waitress. It's debatable.

Sophie Large – aged fifteen.

Chapter Five

FROWNED with concentration as I leaned over the antique mahogany table, rubbing it with a soft rag that was damp with liquid.

I dipped my rag into the jar of my home-made concoction and gently rubbed the area again. This was my dad's special secret recipe for bringing new life to faded old wood and it worked beautifully. I made and bottled it so that we always had a supply to use.

I have a glorious feeling of satisfaction when I do this. There is a special kind of magic as the long forgotten glory of the original colour replaces the drab dullness.

Normally, this kind of condition is caused by a table being left in sunlight, perhaps beneath a window, and it loses all its colour. To those lacking in knowledge, the table is ignored at a sale because they think it is beyond redemption, but, if you have an eye, and the recipe for a certain liquid, the table can be re-born and then people fall in love with it all over again.

I was in the workshop, which is next to our antiques shop at the front of the house. My head was in a whirl and the only thing I could think of doing that would block everything out was this. It required total concentration and was completely absorbing. It stopped my head even considering what was going on in my life today.

Events were happening that I could not face up to right at this moment. Earlier, I could have sworn that I heard the cracks as the walls began to crumble in my carefully built fortress of defence.

The day had really warmed up. Dad left earlier to go to tell Ruby that

I now knew all and had given them my blessing. No-one else was around, so I had removed my shirt and I was just wearing my shorts with a skimpy camisole vest top. I don't ever wear a bra because I don't have sufficient breasts to require one. They are there, just, very small. It was so hot and there was no-one around to see me as I worked.

Yet again that day, I was in such a deep concentration that I didn't hear the shop door open.

"I always loved watching you do that," said a soft, deep male voice.

I jumped in fright and looked up.

"Je suis désolé," he said, quickly. "I… didn't mean to startle you. There was no-one in the shop and I realised you were in here."

I stared at him in shock. My castle suddenly came crashing down around my ears and I stood there, completely vulnerable, scared and defenceless. I couldn't say a word. I just stared at him. Déjà vu! My premonition had materialised in front of me. I closed my eyes and opened them again, hoping it was my imagination and that when I opened my eyes again he would have disappeared.

I was suddenly conscious of my skimpy top, stretched over my small breasts. When he had walked in I had been bending over the table in my shorts, revealing, possibly, a hint of cheek. My face suffused with colour.

He was wearing jeans and a dazzling white, immaculate shirt. The shirt was obviously an expensive, designer's creation which on other men may have looked effeminate, but he wore it with an stamp of masculine authority and the unbuttoned neckline showed a tantalising glimpse of black, curled chest hair. I was conscious of my disarray. My hot, smeared clothes and messy hair compared to his aura of cool, relaxed sophistication. Even in jeans and an understated shirt, he looked like a rich man. He looked like a different class of person. I stared at him in awe. Speech was impossible.

My heart was pounding and I was suddenly experiencing a difficulty in my breathing. It was rapid and shallow. The boy had gone and in his place was a man who was threatening me just by standing there. It wasn't that I felt he was going to attack me with a knife or anything. It's just that he was too male, too beautiful and too kind of predatory. He was very much a man and even in that moment, I knew that it was my heart that was in danger.

I thought of the press quotations about him. They said that he had a sort of animal attraction, that women found him irresistible and the physical effect of meeting him made them go weak at the knees. They had seemed ridiculous quotes but I now understood the reality of them. My knees felt weak and my legs were unstable but this was different. My experience went back ten years and standing face to face with him was more than a shock; it was a bombshell and my ears were ringing with the explosion.

His eyes held mine, like two huge, blue pools. Richard de Bowes-Lyon stood before me. We stared at each other. The air almost seemed to be pulsing with a charged electricity around us.

I could see why women found him attractive. It wasn't just his features. He was a mass of contradictions. His expression had an aristocratic reserve and yet at the same time seemed to have a boyish openness and vulnerability. He was very tall, somewhere near the height of my father, but although the breadth of his chest and powerful arms were perfectly balanced with his height, he was also slim and didn't appear to carry a spare ounce of flesh. His stance indicated an unconscious elegance in the way he held himself, yet mixed with a sort of confident indolence. All these observations whirled in my head. I could easily see how he could blow a woman's mind and sweep her off her feet. He was a very, very dangerous man, far too appealing, far too male and far too close. Alarm bells were ringing in my head and my throat felt dry. Such a man could never be trusted, I reminded myself. I was aware that I was still staring at him, but I couldn't help it. I was stunned to find him standing in front of me and the very fact of his undeniable attraction made me nervous and defensive.

"Salut, Angélique. Ça va?" His eyes were such a vivid blue, against the tan of his skin and the white of his shirt. They were still in shocking contrast to the thickness of his black eyebrows and lashes, beneath a flop of shining black, wavy hair that made my fingers just itch to ruffle and rake through it. I tried not to look at his mouth as he smiled at me. It was way too sensual.

The pounding of my heart was drumming in my ears. "Richard," I gasped. I still couldn't speak properly.

"C'est moi." His eyes held mine. "Vous êtés magnifique." he said, softly. He was still so very French. So very *gallant*.

I began to laugh and realised that I was shaking. "As if!" I put my hand on the table to support myself. "What..." I frowned at him. "What are you doing here? Did *she* send you?"

He walked towards me and cupped my face in his hands. His eyes were too close, too intense. I felt faint and gripped the table harder.

"Don't you think that *I* would want to see you?"

"Pourquoi?" I said, helplessly.

The world seemed to turn into slow motion as he kissed my left cheek, then my right and then my forehead. I was conscious of his height. There were few men who were taller than me and it was unusual for me to feel small and so very vulnerable. His eyes held mine and I was like a rabbit, mesmerised by car headlights. I couldn't breathe.

He raised his eyebrows. "I said I would come back for you."

"Il y a longtemps," I whispered. "A very long time ago." I really was shaking now, but I tried to control it.

"Its time to reunite."

"No," I gasped. "No, Richard. Please, no."

His mouth was devastating. I tried to concentrate on his eyes but I was drowning in a sea of emotion and feeling weaker with each passing minute.

"You have to face up to it," he said gently. "You can't run away from it any longer."

I shook my head. "She sent you, didn't she?"

He paused, his eyes searching my face. "You look so much like her, though a lot taller, obviously. Its incredible how much alike you are."

His fingers stroked my hair and then traced the contours of my face. "It's good to see you." His eyes were following the path of his fingers, as though they were rediscovering some forgotten land. "I've missed you." He paused, and then said, carefully, "Your mother has missed you and she would very much like to see you."

"No!" I shook my head and managed to pull away from him. I moved, so that the table was between us and created at least some kind of barrier to keep him at a distance. "Please go," I said, shakily. "I don't want to see you."

"I'm afraid it's too late for that."

"Richard, it was a long time ago. You live in London, or wherever around the world you are now. Just please leave me alone and go."

"Je dois t'avouer quelque chose."

I stared at him, warily. "Quoi? Que veux-tu dire?"

He smiled. "I'm glad you've remembered your French. I've bought the castle," he said quietly.

"Quoi?" I shrieked.

He was grinning like the cat that licked the cream. "Je voulais que ce soit une surprise... aren't you pleased for me?"

The room was spinning and I leaned heavily against the table. I didn't know how many more shocks I could actually accommodate, today. "It is a surprise..." I struggled for words. "How did you manage to buy it?"

He was positively beaming and his eyes seemed bluer than ever. "My father has retired now, so I get paid to be Managing Director of the business and... well, for my twenty-first birthday, my father gave me some money and it was enough to allow me to pursue the purchase. It took a while to track down the owner. He had gone to live on the island of

Mustique and it was hell having to stay there, in glorious weather, while I tried to persuade him to part with the castle but, eventually, he agreed and I've just been sorting out the paperwork in London. I tried to make it up here this morning to catch you on the beach. Where you there?"

"Oui," I said faintly, picturing what Lisa's expression would have been when she was drooling over the photographs of Richard de Bowes-Lyon and could have looked up to find him standing in front of her. I shook my head to dispel the image and tried to concentrate on the present. "What do you intend to do with it?"

"Restore it to its former glory. I was hoping you would want to help me. Isn't it exciting that after more than two hundred years, I've been able to return it to the family?"

The prospect of helping Richard restore the castle shook me to the core but I desperately struggled to be polite. "Félicitations... that is an amazing achievement. I'm pleased for you. You wanted so badly to restore it to the family. What, umm, are your... plans for it?"

"Un foyer et une famille. I plan to marry and settle down there, have a family. I think it will make a wonderful home, don't you?"

My legs were almost buckling beneath me. I struggled to get the words out. "Are you engaged?"

He grinned. "Not yet."

"The press can't seem to work out who the lucky girl is..." Aghh! Why did I say that? I bit my lip, scolding myself for coming out with such a comment.

He looked really amused. "Well, you shouldn't believe anything you read in the press, anyway, so I'm just keeping them guessing. There is no way I want to spoil everything by giving a hint of who she is."

"Does she know, yet?" I couldn't stop myself from asking but I was somehow beyond caring what he thought of me, now. This was all too much to take in one day.

He smiled, wryly and, for a moment, he seemed like a young boy again. He was suddenly serious and shrugged. "I haven't asked her yet. I'm hoping that she'll have me."

"Richard," I tried to speak calmly. "I really don't think this is a good idea. I don't think I would be the right person to help you create a home for you and your family."

"You are my family," he said, softly.

"No, I'm not." I shook my head, vehemently, but then stopped because it hurt.

Richard stepped around the table and took my hand. He was much too close for my sanity. "You are my little sister." His mouth twitched with amusement. "Okay, not so little, but you *are* my younger sister and I need to reintroduce you back into the family." He frowned and looked around, and then back at me. "Speaking of family, where's your father? I would like to see him."

At the mention of my father, that was the last straw. My legs buckled and I would have sunk to the floor if Richard hadn't caught me. He swept me off my feet and easily carried me through to the shop. I allowed myself the pleasure of breathing in the smell of him. He smelled wonderful. I could feel the heat of his body and the powerful muscles of his arms through his thin shirt. The hint of dark chest hair that I had glimpsed earlier, now tickled my skin. I was conscious of my scant clothing and his flesh, so very close to mine. My head ached and the room seemed out of focus. I realised it was tears in my eyes.

Richard gently set me down in a big oak carver and knelt in front of me. "Mon ange, tu pleures?" He cupped my face in his hands. " Ça va? Quelque chose ne va pas? Dites-moi." He saw the tears in my eyes and I couldn't help it, they overflowed down my cheeks. I felt too exhausted to make any attempt to stop them. He looked so concerned and much, much too beautiful and he was much, much too close. He put his arms around me and I just sank against his shoulder, revelling in the feeling of being there, despairing in the pain.

"Angel, hey. It's alright. Don't be upset." He pulled a white handkerchief out of his pocket and gently dabbed my face. "I don't want to upset you. I didn't want to make you cry."

I looked at him through blurred vision because my eyes were swimming with tears and I bit my lip, as I shook my head. "Mon père…" I shook my head and took a deep breath. "It's not you, Richard. It's Dad." I took a great big gulp of air and blurted it out, quickly. "Dad has a serious illness and he's going to have to go to a research hospital in New York for treatment. There is no guarantee that the treatment will work but it's the only hope he has. We can't afford it and I'm going to have to work very, very hard to earn the money to pay for it and right now, I just feel ever so tired."

"Mon Dieu." Richard's expressive face showed his deep concern. "Angel, let me pay. It's the least I can do."

"What? No, you mustn't. That's a very kind offer, but you mustn't. You can't."

"Pourquoi pas? I can afford it? You're my sister. C'est ma famille."

"No," I shrieked. "I'm *not* family!"

Richard gently held my face in his hands and his eyes held mine. "You are and you have no choice."

I tried to shake my head. "No, don't you see, it would be like compensation money to my father for your father stealing his wife!"

"Then let me lend it to you, and I won't ever expect to have the money back. If you can afford it, then one day you can repay me if you want to."

"No, Richard," I said defiantly. I gulped air to try to regain some remnants of composure. "I have to do this myself."

He raised his brows, questioningly. "And how do you propose to do that? Tu as un plan?"

"I will work hard to earn it."

"Is there a possibility of doing that at the moment?"

I took a deep breath. "No," I said, firmly. "But, I will find a way."

"Then you have no alternative. J'insiste." Richard smiled.

I frowned in confusion. "Je ne comprends pas." His face was so close to mine. I could feel his breath.

"Let me put it simply. You need to work to earn the money to pay for your father's treatment in hospital in New York. I need you to help me restore the castle. I can pay you to do the work for me. I doubt if another contract that will earn you that kind of money is going to drop into your lap now, when you need it. In other words, you have no choice. You're going to have to do the work for me and then you can be secure in the knowledge that you can pay for your father's treatment."

My mouth opened and I stared at him in dismay. There would be no point in protesting because he was right, I had no choice. As much as it would be better for me if I never saw Richard again, I was going to be totally reliant upon him and, at the same time, he seemed quite determined to reunite me with my mother.

I felt like I was adrift in the middle of an ocean, without a paddle. Richard was now offering me the paddle which I could use to get me back to the safety of dry land.

Richard was frowning, his eyes narrowed. He seemed to be listening to something. He shook his head and listened again. "Is that...a baby I can hear, crying?"

I gasped. Suddenly, my ears were unplugged and I could hear it, too. "Sorry, I have to go. I'll be back soon."

I ran towards the door and realised that he was behind me. "Richard, I'll be back down, soon."

Richard was looking extremely puzzled. "Oh, no. This is something I have to see."

I had no choice. He followed me up the stairs and stopped in the doorway as I ran into the nursery and quickly scooped Annie up into my arms. She was reassuringly warm and snuggly. I took comfort from holding her. She put her arms around me and buried her face into my neck, almost burrowing into my ponytail, which had come loose.

Richard looked as though he was in shock. This time, he was the one struggling for words. "Am I too late? I... I mean, umm... is this inconvenient?"

It was his turn to be thrown completely off balance and I had a little time to regain my strength.

He stepped closer and looked at Annie. "She's beautiful," he said in a whisper. "Motherhood suits you." His eyes held mine. "I..." He paused, struggling for words. "I didn't know that you were married."

"I'm not," I informed him.

Richard visibly flinched. His face had actually gone paler. He obviously thought that Annie was mine and, for the moment, I let him.

"Umm... er... does her father live with you? Will he be coming home at any moment? Am I, er, going to meet him?"

"I'm not in a relationship with her father," I said, calmly, and saw him really jolt this time. He seemed deeply shocked.

"I... I didn't know." He ran a hand distractedly through his hair and my fingers itched. "Perhaps you're right. Perhaps I should go. You're obviously busy." He seemed to mentally shake himself. "Angel, how are you going to work all the hours that God sends when you have a small child to look after?"

At that moment I heard footsteps on the stairs. Richard glanced towards the doorway and then back at me. The thing was, that I knew they were not men's footsteps. There was only one person they could belong to.

Lisa breezed into the room. "Hello, have you been..." Her face froze mid-sentence, her mouth open in shock as she saw Richard and she just looked like one of the creatures in Narnia who had been turned into a stone statue by the Ice Queen. Nothing moved, apart from her eyes which were blinking, as though she couldn't believe who she was looking at.

I have never before seen Lisa lost for words. Richard was looking back and to between us, trying to work out the equation. I could understand why Lisa was dumbstruck. Not only had she come face to face with the image in the magazine she was drooling over, this morning, in the flesh he really was someone special.

His strong, well-toned body physically dominated the small nursery and he didn't stoop, as some tall men do, as if they are almost apologetic for their height. As he stood erect, with his elegance and a natural dignity that set him apart from other men, he appeared comfortable within his own frame and commanded respect and attention, without appearing to consciously do so.

However, it was not just Richard's physique that was striking. He was devastatingly handsome and had that kind of presence that some people have, such as movie stars, who can fill a room or a stage, just by standing there. I had to acknowledge that he was now a very impressive man and Lisa's awe showed the general affect he had on women.

The silence gave me a few moments to study him again and I realised just why I needed to maintain my guard with him. The total package was a potent combination. Physically, he was undeniably attractive and he probably was fully aware that he could have almost any woman of his choice. His strongest weapons were his boyishness and vulnerability and his gentle, charming manners, his French chivalry, which made him seem so approachable. His appeal would probably draw a response from even the most reserved and wary women, persuading them to drop their guard, disarming them with his charm. I reminded myself of his catalogue of photographs with famous and beautiful women. This man was far more dangerous than an obvious womaniser. A wolf in sheep's clothing.

I remembered my manners. "Richard, this is Lisa, who is my best friend."

Richard flinched again, as though my words had inflicted pain. "You are very fortunate," he said to Lisa. "I used to have that honour." He took Lisa's hand and kissed it in a theatrically *gallant* gesture. "Enchanté, Lisa."

Lisa still didn't move, unable to find any words. I decided to come clean with Richard. "Lisa is Annie's mother."

The realisation dawned on Richard. It was strange to see the mixture of emotions on his face. He turned to me. We often used to play tricks on each other and I could see that he was going to pay me back for this one.

Another realisation dawned on his expression and his eyes narrowed, speculatively as he looked at Lisa and then back at me. "Ah, I see," he said, softly. He stepped towards me and took my face in his hands, again, his eyes searching mine. "I think I'd better go. I think you have some explaining to do." He raised his brows. "Demain?"

He gently kissed my left cheek, then my right cheek and then my forehead. I bit my lip. I didn't want him to kiss the bit in the middle, but, at the same, I so very desperately wanted him to. I had the most agonising knot in my stomach.

"Bye, Angel," he said, softly. "I'll pick you up at midday, tomorrow. Okay?"

"Do I have a choice?"

He smiled, his eyes brimming with amusement. "Non."

He turned to Lisa, who still was standing there, gaping with amazement. She now held the record for the longest silence in her life. "Au revoir, Lisa."

He turned as he left the room. "A bientôt." He winked at me and then went down the stairs.

Lisa stared at the place where he had kissed her. "I don't think I am ever going to wash that part of my hand again," she said, faintly. She looked at me in bewilderment. "Do you want to explain this to me?"

"No," I said, quietly.

"Why did he call you, Angel?"

I bit my lip and hesitated. "It's... his pet name for me."

Lisa was still in shock. She closed her eyes and put her hand to her head. "I..." She looked at me. "With all due respect to my husband, I have just found you standing in my daughter's nursery with the ultimate man of my dreams... and he has a pet name for you?"

Footsteps pounded on the stairs. Gary appeared in the doorway. He was grinning with amazement. "I could have sworn that was Richard de Bowes-Lyon who just left here in that Aston Martin."

Lisa looked at me. "It was." She crossed the room and removed Annie from me and then gave her to Gary. "You take Annie and look after her for the night. I am going to pour alcohol down this girl's throat and she's going to tell me what's been going on."

I opened my mouth to protest but Lisa intervened. "And before you say that you only have one glass at Christmas and New Year, I don't care. Tonight, you're drinking!"

I quaked inside. My world had come tumbling down today. My Armageddon. The beginning of the end of my world. There was only one person I wanted to talk to right now, but that was not going to be possible because there was no way Lisa was going to let me out of her clutches.

"Lisa!" I opened my arms and looked down at my clothes. "I need a bath, just look at me."

"Okay. You have a quick shower while I get the wine. You prefer white, don't you?"

There was no escape for me!

Old family photographs

I got into a real mess this evening because I looked at some old photos of Mummy and Daddy. They really affected me. I think it's the idea of time running away, and seeing children – carefree children – on paper before you, and the old adults next to them. I could hardly get over it. I burst into tears and Becca, dearest Becca, seemed to understand and I just sat there for ages crying.

It's the idea of so many days gone that were wasted or that I don't remember – each second moving and never there again: and that some day Mum and Dad will die, and some day I'll die; it's years and years away, but quick as a flash those years'll be gone and all that will be left of them is a pile of photos.

Sophie Large – aged sixteen.

Chapter Six

I PUT another two logs on the fire and then sat on the rug. I felt clean and snuggly in my huge, men's bath robe. It's one of my few luxuries. The white towelling is so thick and so soft. You have to pay a bit more if you want a really good quality one and mine has to be extra large so that I can be swamped, like a little child in it.

My long mass of hair was damp over my shoulders but it would soon dry in front of the fire. Lisa hadn't said a word so far. She was quiet and thoughtful, as though she was still trying to take in what she had seen, earlier. She had removed her Arran jumper and she was wearing a sparkly gold top that she must have bought, today when she was shopping. I was glad of the silence. My heart was pounding with trepidation.

Lisa filled my glass with the pale liquid. The firelight flickered on the reflection of the glass. I took a sip of the cool, pleasantly dry wine. I held it in my mouth, rolling it around with my tongue and sucking on it, to draw out the extra flavour before I swallowed it.

Lisa sat down in the big armchair in front of me. "Well?" she asked.

I put my glass down on the hearth and stood up.

"You're not going anywhere until you tell me what's going on?" she warned.

I shook my head and looked at her, carefully. I chewed on my lip and then said, "There's something I need to show you."

I went to the cupboard in the wall and took some of the books off my once secret pile at the back. I took a deep breath and then carried them back to Lisa. This was something I had thought would never happen and

I braced myself for her reaction. I put them down in front of her and sat down again on the rug.

She frowned at me in confusion. "What's this?"

"Take a look," I said, quietly.

Lisa's frown deepened. She turned the pages of the books and then she came to the last pages in the unfinished, latest book that I had been working on this afternoon.

"These are the pictures that I was looking at in the magazines this morning!" She looked at me, accusingly. "I thought you put the magazines for recycling, yet here they are, going back over several years! You're even more of an addict than I am for this stuff. You've been hoarding them and keeping a celebrity scrap book!" She flicked again through the pages. "These pictures seem to be mostly of Richard de Bowes-Lyon and his parents. You must have had a crush on him for a long time. How did you meet him? Are you in a secret relationship with him?"

"Lisa, whoa." I put my hand up to stall her torrent of questions. "That isn't a celebrity scrap book…. it's my family album."

"You mean you're engaged to Richard? How could you not tell me? I thought you said he is the most undesirable man in the world because of his nightmare step-mother!" Her voice was rising.

"You know you've often commented on the likeness between me and the Duchess." I paused to take a deep breath and then took the plunge. "Well, she's actually my mother."

"What?" Some wine spilled from her glass as she jolted. She put her glass down beside the chair, on the polished oak floor. Her face was like a cartoon character registering shock. The truth had hit her like one of those huge balls on the end of a crane that are used to knock down old buildings. "And that makes Richard…"

I took a shuddering breath. "My step-brother," I filled in.

"You told me your mother was dead!" she shrieked.

I winced. "Actually, I didn't. I told you that I had *lost* my mother and you assumed that she had died. I actually lost my mother ten years ago when she left us and ran off with Richard's father."

"But your father is almost seventy!"

"And she's more than thirty years younger," I supplied.

Her brown eyes were huge and wide with amazement. "All this time," she said slowly, obviously struggling to find her voice, "you have let me go on and on about film stars and celebrities and their super-rich lifestyles and how I dream of one day having a life like that… and yet you're one of them! Why didn't you say something, I mean… you're my best friend and I don't know you. I always thought there was something that you seemed to be hiding from me but… this!"

I shrugged. "I don't really like to talk about it.

"How... how can she be your mother. I mean, you're almost twenty-one and she's..."

"She was eighteen when she had me," I said, quietly. "You remember that you said to me this morning that you are eighteen and married with a daughter of almost eighteen months..." I raised my brows as my eyes held hers, meaningfully. "You said that there was no chance of you ever having that kind of lifestyle now, with your current situation, and I said, don't go wishing for your dreams to come true because they just might. My mother's did and I will never forgive her for it!"

Lisa blinked, her face a picture of confusion as she tried to take in the facts. "You have this... family album, and whenever the subject of these people and their lives has been discussed, your barriers have gone up and you've been so secretive, yet, you are one of them. You have a life that I don't even know about! When do you see them? Where do you go to? What clothes do you wear? How have you managed to keep a super glamorous lifestyle a secret from me for so long? It's so unfair of you, letting me go on and on about these magazines! I want details!"

"Lisa, I *don't* see them."

"But... they're you're family!"

I shook my head, vehemently. "No, they're not. I haven't seen them for ten years and I never wanted to see them again."

"But..." Lisa looked down at the open pages on her lap. "These... family albums. If you don't want to see them, why have you collected these pictures?"

I looked down and watched my fingers tracing the pattern on the rug. "I don't know." I shrugged. "It's just something I feel compelled to do, but I never wanted to see them again. I was happy with my life, until today. Everything was in order and exactly as I wanted it to be. Now, it's all changed." I didn't want to tell Lisa everything so I was going to have to be careful what I said.

"Is Richard the reason why you speak French so fluently?"

I jolted. Lisa was watching my nervous reaction. "Richard taught me to speak French."

Lisa beamed. "I'll bet he did!"

"Lisa!" I complained at her obvious innuendo.

Lisa wasn't letting go of this train of thought. "I'm sure I would have swooned at his feet if he had taught me in French and I would have learned more than just his language."

"We are not in a relationship," I insisted, but Lisa obviously didn't believe me.

"So, why was Richard here, this afternoon?"

I chewed on my lip again, and then said, "He's bought the castle."

"Wow! I told you, I said that someone rich and famous might buy it. That means we'll probably get glimpses of ultra gorgeous, famous people passing through. In a castle, there's probably room for big parties and weekend guests." She paused as she looked at me, suddenly concerned. "How does that make you feel?"

"I wish he hadn't," I whispered.

Lisa lifted her glass and took a large gulp, then put it down again. She studied me, carefully. "Is Richard planning to live in the house?"

"Yes."

"And, does that mean that his parents will be visiting?"

I sighed. "Probably."

"So, will there be a family reunion?"

I took another sip of wine before I answered her. I cupped the glass in my hands and suddenly remembered Richard cupping my face in his hands. "No!" I said defiantly.

Lisa was looking at me with raised brows. "If she stays next door, won't there be a possibility of bumping into her? She may even call in here to visit you. Being a mother, surely she would want to see her daughter."

"She knows that I never want to see her again." I took another sip and concentrated on the taste of my wine. "Richard is intent upon reuniting us but I don't want to see her. I didn't even want to see Richard."

Lisa was thoughtful. "If that castle has been empty for as long as anyone can remember, it must need a lot of work to turn it into a home. Who's going to do the work?"

"I am," I said quietly.

"What? How? Who's going to do all the labour? There must be one heck of a lot of work to be done? How are you going to do it?"

I took a deep breath and licked my lips, tasting the remnants of wine. "I don't know, but, I'll find a way."

Lisa looked at me thoughtfully, as she sipped her wine and then lowered her glass. "If you don't want to have any contact with them, why are you going to do the work on Richard's home?"

I hesitated, consciously careful of how much I was letting out. "I discovered, today, that Dad has an illness. Apparently, it's very serious and there is no guarantee that he will recover." I felt tears stinging my eyes again and I wiped them away and took a deep breath. "There has been some success with a new type of treatment that is being tried in a research hospital in New York. It's as expensive as it sounds." I traced my finger around the rim of my glass of wine. "We can't afford it but, if I do the work for Richard, he will pay me and then we'll be financially okay. So... I have no choice."

Lisa was still watching me, intently. "So, you are caught in a trap," she said, softly.

"Put it like that, I suppose you're right. A trap is exactly what it is and I cannot get out of it."

"So, inevitably, Richard will re-introduce you to your mother."

I shrugged, not wanting to think about the prospect of facing my mother again after all these years.

"Do you hate her?"

I jumped at the question and my eyes shot up to Lisa's face. She looked intrigued.

"I don't hate her," I said carefully. "If you hold hatred, it eats into you, like a poison, and destroys your life. Jesus said that we have to forgive people, most especially our enemies, but I can't forgive her. I just give it to God and it's up to Him to judge her. I let Him deal with it."

"If the family are French, are they Catholic?" Lisa suddenly asked.

"Yes, they are."

"But, you're family aren't, are they? And the Catholics don't like divorce."

I was careful with my answer. "No-one likes divorce. You don't have to be Catholic to marry into a family today, but their family are traditional so my mother probably converted after she was divorced."

"What exactly is it that you dislike so much about the rich and famous?"

I tried to make Lisa understand. "Like you, she probably always dreamed of a life of luxury and, when the opportunity came along, she seized it. She's beautiful and artful. She uses people to get what she wants. Those sort of people in your magazines are like that. They are not genuine, sincere people. They only care about their bank balance or how something can benefit them."

"You're scared, aren't you," Lisa said, softly.

I was alarmed. "Of?"

"Them! Those people in the magazines. You're worried that you won't fit in with them."

"Firstly, I don't want to! Secondly, how will I ever fit in with them anyway? Nightmare!"

Lisa drank the remnants of her wine, then picked up the bottle from beside her chair and refilled it. "Top up?"

I shook my head. I had barely drunk from my glass.

"Talk about a slow drinker. No wonder you only get through one glass in a night," Lisa muttered.

"The difference between us," I retorted, defensively, "is that I savour every mouthful and you consume it in quantity. We're just different."

Lisa observed me, thoughtfully. "Sweetie, you don't have to worry about *them*. You're more than a match for them. You're stunning *and* you're a brain box. You have heaps of qualifications."

"Not in handbags and shoes!"

Lisa looked interested. "Is there one?"

"No, but if there was a degree, they would have it!" I implored Lisa to understand. "They speak an entirely different language. They *live* on a different planet."

"Your mother is the Queen of society. The Duke and Duchess de Lyon. You can't get a much better qualification than that!"

"Exactly. The Family of Lions! The King and Queen of the jungle! The King and his Lioness!"

Lisa began to laugh. "Golly, you have got it bad"

"Lisa, it's not funny!" I glared at her. "What am I supposed to do, have my mother dress me and take me to the hairdresser and beauty salon and tell them what to do with me? Those girls were probably weaned into their own sense of style, aged six!"

Lisa was trying to keep a straight face. "Oh, Sweetie, poor you. You have got a raw deal. Your mother is one of the most beautiful and stylish women in the world, your step-father is one of the richest men and your step-brother is one of the most gorgeous and you don't know how to fit in. What a predicament!"

"Lisa," I said crossly. "It's a jungle! They'll eat me alive and I don't want to be part of all that rat race, anyway! I just want a quiet life, here..." I almost said, "in my home," but I stopped myself. Soon, this wasn't going to be my home.

I took another sip of my wine and felt the alcohol begin to relax me.

"So, what are you going to do?" Lisa asked, tentatively.

I sighed. "I don't know and I don't want to think about it, right now. I feel absolutely shattered. It's been difficult enough to face up to things I thought I had successfully put away. This morning, my life was in order, now it's a wreck. I don't want to have to deal with it, yet." I looked at my glass of wine. "It would be nice if this could take my pain away, but I'm not that sort of person. Hopefully, because I feel so exhausted, this will help to put me into a deep, dreamless sleep and then I won't have to think about things until tomorrow."

Lisa suddenly remembered. "Richard said that's he's coming back tomorrow to pick you up. Where are you going?"

"To the castle, I presume. I expect that he will want me to take a look at it with him."

"I just hope you haven't bitten off more than you can chew."

"So do I," I agreed, but my meaning was entirely different. I wasn't sure that I would be able to survive what I had just taken on!

All my life

All my life I walked in shadow
Of my mother's good and worth,
"Follow in your mother's footsteps"
Said the vicar at my birth.

I tried, I tried to match my mother,
But I failed when I began –
To follow in your mother's footsteps
That is easier said than done.

She was lovely, I was plain.
She smiled and laughed, I thought I should.
I could not follow in her footsteps –
But my sister could.

She came later; one year gone,
My mother loved her more each day.
She followed well in mother's footsteps,
I was left alone to play.

Some day I will match my sister,
And I'll match my mother, too.
I needn't follow in their footsteps –
I'll follow dad's, that's what I'll do.

Sophie Large – aged fourteen.

Chapter Seven

NEVER, in my life, have I been as glad to go to bed as I was that night. I collapsed on to the mattress, feeling completely shattered, and pulled the duvet over me.

I buried my head into the sweet smelling pillows. I was grateful that I had made my bed this morning with fresh linen and had put a handful of lavender, from my precious garden, inside my pillowcase to celebrate the first day of spring.

Soon, this wouldn't be my garden and soon, this wouldn't be my home. *If* my father recovered, then I would have to find a new home. I didn't want to think about that, now. I reached under my pillow and grasped my rosary beads, which were hidden there. I fervently said my prayers. I always say please and thank you to God, every morning and every night, but I needed him more than ever now. The only one person I desperately needed to talk to was Sister Ruth, the Head Teacher of the convent school, but that was going to have to wait.

I closed my eyes and willed God to help me. "Please let me sleep until morning, God, and please, no thoughts, just sleep." I repeated these words as a determined chant, willing myself to fall into a deep, dreamless sleep but I was unsuccessful. The moment I fell asleep, I dreamed that I was on the beach again, ten years old, with the French boy. We were running as fast as we could along the shoreline, splashing and getting soaked, but it didn't matter. We were laughing as we each tried our best to outdo the other, but we were perfectly matched.

Eventually, we stopped and stood with the shallow, cold water, lapping around our legs and each wave rose against our thighs, making our shorts even more wet. We were panting and laughing, trying to regain our breath.

His smile was wide and illuminated his face. "I have never known a girl like you," he said. "Who are you?"

I rose up to my full height and raised my chin, suddenly coquettish, although I didn't really know what I was doing. "I am Joy Bennett."

"Joy," he said softly, his eyes holding mine. "How very apt. If you are not a goddess, then you must be an angel. My angel of joy."

My heart missed a beat and I was suddenly struggling for breath again. "And you are?"

"Forgive me," he said, bowing low, with an exaggerated spread of his arm. "I am Richard de Bowes-Lyon, heir to the Duc et Duchesse de Lyon. I am at your service."

"Wow!" I said, impressed. "What a name! And what a bow. All you need is one of those French hats and you could be one of those dashing musketeers."

He grinned and raised his arm, pretending that he was holding a sword. "For truth, honour and freedom! I swear to protect you, milady!"

I laughed. This was fun! "You are so different to any other boy I have ever met!"

He frowned with interest. "Why?"

His hair was damp and windblown by the sea breeze, but it somehow made him look even more handsome. For some reason, my fingers itched to touch it. The thought made me blush.

"The boys I know don't want to play with girls. They just want to talk about cars and football or play cowboys and Indians."

Richard's brows raised in surprise and he looked at me, intently. "Then they are very foolish. What could be better than enjoying the company of a beautiful girl?"

I blushed again and sought to change the subject. "Are you hungry?"

"Ravenous," he replied immediately.

"Do you want to come to my home for some lunch? I'm sure my mum wouldn't mind and she is a very good cook."

He bowed again in a theatrical manner. "Lead the way, mademoiselle."

Richard had been running barefoot through the waves. We stopped to pick up his sandals, which were by the sandcastle, and then walked towards the dunes. There is something deeply satisfying about pushing your feet deep into the sand as you walk through the heaviness of it, spraying sand around you as you lift your feet. You feel the coolness of the underlying sand, as your foot digs into it, and the tingle of the granules on your skin.

Something suddenly occurred to me. "I found a set of keys when I was digging my flower bed in the garden." I stopped and looked at him, earnestly. "They are really big and really old. You know that you said your family used to own the castle. Well, there is a big stone wall between our garden and the castle estate. Hidden by a large shrubbery is an old door and, when I tried one of the keys, it fit. The lock was a bit rusty and I secretly used some of my father's oil to try to make it work, but it did! The key turned in the lock and I was able to open the door a bit. It's a bit overgrown, but you can squeeze through."

Richard had stopped and was looking at me, his eyes huge with amazement.

"If one key opens the door in my garden wall, do you suppose that the other one might open a door in the castle? It would be exciting if it did. Do you think that the key might have once belonged to your family?"

Richard was visibly excited. "Have you tried the other key in any of the locks at the castle?"

I shook my head, vehemently. "Oh, no. It was as much as I dared do to open the door in the wall. I daren't go on to someone else's land or to someone's home."

His hand grasped mine and his eyes were mesmerising. "I think that God intended me to meet you, today. My father said that no-one has lived in the castle for about two hundred years. There was a bitter argument between my family and another and the castle has remained, sealed up, all this time. My father has been trying to buy the castle but the other family won't let him have it. The feud runs deep. They don't want it, but it gives them satisfaction to know that my family cannot have it. Joy, can we use your keys and visit the castle this afternoon? What an adventure!"

I was alarmed. "I'm not sure. It's a bit scary to go trespassing on the land of a family who hates your family."

"But, they don't live there. Let's do it!" he urged me.

I thought about it as we climbed the sand dunes, feeling the satisfying ache in my legs. I ran down the other side, with Richard running beside me, down the steep slope, winding our way between the clumps of long grass, which scratched my legs. I turned to him at my garden gate. Somehow, doing something scary could feel exciting. "Okay. I've hidden the keys but I'll get them. We'll have lunch and then we'll go, but not a word to my parents."

He raised his arm and grinned. His eyes were vivid with anticipation. "I swear."

When we went into the kitchen, Mum was busy, baking. My mum is a wonderful cook. "Mum, this is Richard. We met on the beach. Can he have lunch with us and then we're playing outside again, this afternoon."

Richard stepped forward and kissed my mother's flour-covered hand. "Enchanté, madame. May I say that your daughter is as beautiful as you and you look more like sisters."

My mother was visibly delighted. "French! What brings you here?"

"My mother is ill and we are staying here because she wanted to be by the sea." My mother smiled. She is a beautiful woman. Richard stood taller than her and he was obviously dazzled.

"Of course you can stay to have lunch. I am very pleased to meet you, Richard. Do sit down."

I sat down as well and took one of the freshly-made chocolate chip cookies.

"Joy, I'm surprised at you. Look at the state of you! Why are you not wearing a dress?" my mother scolded me.

I blushed scarlet to have been so deeply embarrassed by my mother, in front of Richard. "I don't wear dresses when I'm playing, Mum. They would only get spoiled."

"Then you shouldn't play like a tom boy! For goodness sake, go and change into a pretty dress and look like a girl for once. A handsome French boy comes to play and you look like a boy! Your hair is all messy and I'm fed-up of seeing you in jeans and shorts. I buy beautiful dresses for you. Go and put one on."

I was fuming! How could my mother embarrass me in such a way in front of the *handsome French boy?* I was humiliated. I was determined to not give in. "Mum," I pleaded. "How can I possibly *play* in a dress?"

My mother was not to be deterred. "Like a girl! Now go and get changed and show Richard how pretty you can look."

I was wishing that I hadn't asked Richard to come back for lunch. This was total humiliation! This was the first time I had brought a boy back to the house. How could my mum do this to me!

Richard leaned over and whispered quietly, "Pour moi, s'il te plaît." I looked at him and his eyes held mine. He reached under the table and squeezed my hand with gentle reassurance. "You are beautiful in boys' clothes, but let me see you in a dress, my angel of joy."

I looked at my mother, whose back was to us as she took a batch of steaming, freshly baked cakes from the Aga oven. I looked back at Richard. "I'll only do it for you," I whispered back. "Not for my mother." I shot a really angry glance at my mother's back. He squeezed my hand again tightly and then I left the table without a word.

When I walked back into the kitchen, freshly washed, my hair brushed and wearing a blue dress with a full, floaty skirt that moved in folds when I walked, Richard's eyes showed his appreciation. I kept my hands behind my back.

My mother turned. "That's better! That's my girl. You know, sometimes I doubt that I have a daughter under all that boys' clothing. Don't you think she looks pretty, Richard?"

I felt my cheeks blush, scarlet.

Richard seemed amused. "Elle est très belle et charmante, madame."

I sat next to him and concentrated on eating my lunch, my eyes lowered. I was feeling very cross with my mum and very uncomfortable in the floaty creation. It wasn't me at all, but my mother bought the dresses, determined that I would wear them, at least for special occasions, which she obviously thought this was! The first time her daughter had brought a boy home! I ate in silence.

My mother chatted with Richard. After a while, I said, "Richard and his mother are staying in the beach house belonging to the convent school."

My mother was delighted. "Really? I know the nuns so well! Perhaps your mother would like me to visit her, to keep her company."

"I'm sure she would," Richard said. "I think she will like you."

An idea occurred to my mother. "I could take some baking to cheer her up. Do you think she would like that?"

"I'm sure my mother will enjoy your cooking as much as I am, madame. Your food is very tasty. Exquis."

Richard winked at me and I blushed scarlet again as I realised that he had fully understood the meaning of my comment to him on the beach. This was far more humiliation than I could cope with.

"Is your mother very poorly?" my mother asked.

"She is dying," Richard answered.

Both my mother and I gasped as we looked at him. "You didn't mention that," I said, in horror.

Richard shrugged and looked down at his plate. I thought I saw tears in his eyes.

"My parents think that I don't know how seriously ill she is but it is not hard to work out." He paused, reflectively and then sighed. His long fingers played on the tumbler in front of him. "She has cancer and has been ill for a very long time. My father works in London and he spends as much time with her as he can, but she has had to have a separate room, with special medical attention for a long time. My father comes to visit as often as possible and although my mother would love to be in France, she will not return there without him." He looked very sad. "I think that she felt a need to be by the sea and the nuns offered to look after her at the beach house. I think that she probably does not have very long to live now." He bit his lip, as though trying to stem the flow of tears that were welling in his eyes. He took a deep, shuddering breath. "They haven't told me but,

I don't think it will be very long. I do my studying in the morning and spend time with my mother, but in the afternoon, she sleeps. She falls asleep sometimes in the morning now, also."

"Oh, my dear boy!" My mother rushed across the room and hugged Richard. "You poor thing, having to go through this. What a terrible ordeal for you and your father. I'm sure your mother is being very brave but she must be upset at the thought of leaving you."

Richard couldn't speak. He just nodded.

My mother squeezed him, tightly. "I'll go and visit her and take some baking, if you think that would be the right thing to do."

Richard found his voice and gave a faint smile. "I'm sure she would appreciate your kindness."

My mother put some dishes in the sink and I dug my elbow into Richard's side. He looked at me in surprise and I indicated with my eyes for him to look in my lap. I was holding the big, old set of keys and a torch. The spark of interest returned in his eyes.

"Mum, can we go back out to play, now?"

Mum turned and gave me a beautiful smile of pride. It obviously meant a lot to her to see me looking like a girl. "Of course, my darling. Have fun. I'll probably see you again, then, Richard."

"I'm sure, madame. Au revoir," Richard said as he bowed gallantly and then we escaped out into the garden.

"Phew! My mother!" I exclaimed. "That's the first time I've ever asked a boy to come to my house. What a fuss she made! I'm so sorry."

Richard took my hand and kissed it. He was so wonderfully different from any other boy.

"I'm honoured." His eyes were intense. "Your mother is a very beautiful woman and she obviously wants to be proud of a daughter who is as beautiful as her."

"She should love me for what I am, not what she wants me to be," I said petulantly.

"I'm sure she loves you very much," Richard said, gently. He turned and looked around the garden. "Now where is this door?"

"You tell me," I challenged, grinning with sudden excitement.

His eyes narrowed as he surveyed the layout of the garden. They followed the line of the huge, old boundary wall and then studied the large, overgrown shrubbery.

He took my hand and then glanced at the house. "I think we'll go this way." He began to lead me towards the shrubbery.

I glanced at the house as well, to make sure that neither of my parents were watching.

It was a bit of a struggle to get through the natural, little passageways within the shrubs, without tearing my dress. I held the long folds of skirt close to me, trying to protect it. It was a few minutes before Richard found the door.

"Here it is," he said, with great excitement. He turned to me and looked at the large keys in my hand. "Puis-je?"

Richard tried the first key and then the second. He turned the big, old key in the big, old lock and the heavy, oak door creaked as he pushed it with his shoulder. It would only open a small amount because the ground was so overgrown on the other side.

"Mind the nettles," Richard warned as he squeezed through and I followed him.

We were at the edge of a wood which stretched as far as we could see in either direction against the boundary wall.

"If the door is not visible from either side, then probably no-one knows about it," Richard said. "What an adventure, starting with a secret door!"

"Which way do you think we ought to go?" I asked. "I've heard about people getting lost in woods for days because they quickly become disorientated. They think they are walking in one direction and then discover that they have gone in a complete circle. It's a bit scary."

"This is fun!" His eyes were full of mischief.

"Richard," I gasped in horror. "I've just thought. How do we find our way back?"

"It's alright." He squeezed my hand to reassure me. "I have a plan. The boundary wall is our landmark. From where we are standing, and your garden, we know that the beach is that way, so we'll head straight across this way. When we come back, all we have to do is find the wall and walk along next to it, until we find the door."

I took a deep breath. "Okay, o great explorer! I'll follow you and I just hope no-one catches us! I just don't want to think about what your feuding opposition would do if they found us."

We wound our way between the trees towards what I hoped was the estate parkland. Where the trees and shrubs were too overgrown, Richard forged ahead and held the branches back to allow me to follow, keeping close behind him. I thought he was mad but he was right, this was fun. My heart was pounding with fear and excitement.

We stepped out of the wood on to the edge of open ground. The sight took my breath away. The grounds were beautiful, so green and flat, with a scattering of majestic, huge old trees and small copses.

In the distance was a castle. It was very small for a castle, more like the size of a large manor house. It was so much like the sandcastles that I love to build. It stood close to the edge of a large expanse of water. This was part of the Broads network. A channel ran from the Broad to feed the wide moat of the castle. A gatehouse and a drawbridge controlled the only access from dry land. The walls of the castle rose straight up from the moat and the shutters of the windows were high, denying access to all, except by the official entrance of the gatehouse, which was elevated and accessed by a slope of ground, so that it was level with the gigantic wooden gates of the castle.

"Regarde. Quelle vue fantastique," Richard said in awe. He was obviously so overwhelmed by the scene that he sat down on the grass, at the edge of the wood, and I sat beside him. "Regarde le paysage. Il est superbe."

It was a truly memorable scene. The castle was like a crown jewel set in a glorious emerald parkland. The castle basked in the warm sun, with the flint walls of the towers and castellated ramparts mostly overgrown with ivy.

Richard was stunned. "Mon Dieu, c'est étonnant, ici!" he said, softly. He turned to me. "Look at that! "Isn't that the most beautiful place you have ever seen in your life?"

"It's awesome," I agreed. "I've lived next door all my life, next to that wall, but I didn't know this was here. It's like a wonderful secret."

Richard turned to me urgently. "This seems to be a place that has been forgotten. Swear to keep it a secret?"

He held my hand and his eyes held mine. "I swear," I whispered. I looked again at the castle which was surrounded by a vast parkland.

Richard was looking at the castle with his intense expression. "Un jour, j'achèterai ce terrain," he said, softly.

"Are you sure no-one lives here?" I asked, nervously.

Richard was still staring at the castle. "Elle est abandonnée. Personne n'y vient plus." He turned to look at me and I noticed the sadness in his eyes. "It was abandoned a long time ago."

"Why did your French family used to own this piece of England?" Richard smiled as he looked again at the spectacular view. He seemed as though he was rooted to the spot, never wanting to leave. "It's a long story."

I looked at the castle. "It's a long walk."

Richard turned to me. "The lives and loves of the Elizabethans and the Georgians are not for a child's ears."

I bristled. "I'm almost eleven!"

Richard kissed my forehead and looked at me questioningly. "Do you really want a history lesson?"

"I do," I breathed.

"Okay, you asked for it. Leçon numéro un. I'll edit it, tactfully, for you.

There are some things a girl your age just shouldn't know about." He stood up and took my hand to help me up.

We walked in the direction of the castle, the skirt of my floaty, long dress spreading as we stepped through the long grass.

"How old is the house?" I asked.

"Elizabethan," Richard said, quietly, not taking his eyes off the castle. "My ancestor built it for the young Queen Elizabeth."

"What?" I stopped and stared at him in shock. "Did she live here?" It was astonishing to think of someone I had barely related to in my history class, having a connection with my next door neighbour.

Richard took my hand and we began to walk again. "Allons. I'll explain. What do you know about Queen Elizabeth the First?"

I racked my brain, thinking of my inattentiveness in my history classes. "She was the daughter of Henry the Eighth. He divorced or beheaded most of his wives. He wanted a divorce from his first wife because he wanted a son and she was only able to give him a daughter. The Pope wouldn't agree to a divorce so Henry broke away from the Catholic religion and set up the Church of England. He became very powerful and wanted to be independent from the Pope and when Elizabeth became Queen she followed the path that her father had set. She was very cold and she didn't marry and she became a very powerful Queen. Like her father, she had lots of people beheaded if they crossed her. I think she was jealous and spiteful."

"She was young, innocent, beautiful and passionate when she became Queen."

"Why did she change, then?" I asked, intrigued.

"For the same reason that my family lost this castle," he answered, quietly. "Love, religion and politics arouse a fearsome passion. Like Queen Elizabeth the First, my family had all three of these. The history of my family is very much in line with the history of your country. It has been very complicated and, often, scandalous."

"I thought history was something distant and boring, that you read in books," I commented, "but you make it sound interesting."

Richard smiled at me and spread his arm at the view. "We are living history, right now."

I frowned. "Do you mean that you and your family are a part of the history of this country?"

"Absolutely, but life is not as traumatic in modern times as it used to be. At least, not for us, but it seems that religion will always cause conflict in the world."

"And what does God do about it?"

Richard sighed. "The best that He can. He is there for those who seek

Him, but the point about religious conflict is that it is man-made. God does not welcome assassins who kill in his name. Such a person is not truly religious. It is man's interpretation of religion for his own ambition, that causes the problems. God just wants peace."

I considered this. I was awestruck that I could be walking through a field next to my house, with a person who seemed to be a living part of history. "Why did your ancestor build this for Queen Elizabeth?"

"Because he was in love with her, and it seems that she was in love with him, but she had to keep her affection for him a secret."

"Why?"

"She had big problems. Elizabeth did not directly inherit from her father. She wanted to honour her father, but others came first and it was purely by chance that she became Queen. People forget about the three in-between."

"Three?"

"Oui. Henry the Eighth did actually have a son and he became King when he was only nine years old. Because he was so very young, others ran the country and continued the work of Henry's separation from the Catholic religion. You know that you have the English prayer books?"

"Yes, we have them at church."

"All prayer books used to be in Latin."

"Latin?" I said, horrified. "I've never learned to speak Latin."

"Most people haven't now, but when the country was being run by others, the first prayer book was written in English by one of the first Archbishops of Canterbury and you still have it. It is sad that the young king died when he was only a little older than me, aged just fifteen."

"Fifteen?" I was shocked. "How did he die?"

Richard shrugged. "Pneumonia or tuberculosis or something like that."

I was amazed. "How do you know so much about the history of my country?"

"I begged Sister Ruth to teach me and I'm learning a lot. I want to know all about the connection between my family and your country."

"You said there were three people?" It seemed weird to be talking about history as we were walking hand-in-hand through a field towards a forgotten castle on a gloriously sunny afternoon. I felt disorientated, like I was walking back in time.

Richard looked at me, carefully. "Have you ever heard the name of a drink called a Bloody Mary?"

I shook my head.

"It's a mixture of vodka and tomato juice."

I pulled a face. "Ugh! That sounds disgusting."

Richard smiled. "Some grown-ups like it! It is named after Queen Mary the First. She was gruesome and cruel."

I felt my eyes widen in shock. "Why?" I asked faintly. "Was she worse than Elizabeth or Henry?"

Richard nodded. "There have been many cruel monarchs and she was one of the worst. She wasn't originally to have been Queen but, she was actually the first child of Henry the Eighth. Her mother was a devoted Catholic and when they were banned from public life, her mother successfully poisoned her against Henry and his regime. Before she could be Queen, she had to get rid of another one."

I frowned at him. "Who?"

"It's really sad. These people were probably innocent. The controllers of the country did not want it to revert to being Catholic, which it would under Mary, so to protect its inheritance, they made the daughter of a man beheaded for treason, Queen. She was Lady Jane Grey." He paused and looked at me. "You know we are here in East Anglia?"

I nodded.

"Mary was somewhere in this area, which was strongly Catholic, when she heard about the proclamation of Queen Jane, when Mary's half-brother died. Mary immediately rode to London and took the throne for herself. She had Jane, who was only seventeen, and her husband put in the Tower of London after only nine days of Jane's reign and then she had them beheaded. Then her days of gruesome persecution began."

I grimaced, horrified, but fascinated. "What happened?"

"She immediately overturned her father's policies and reverted the country to being Catholic."

"What difference did that make?"

"She had anyone beheaded who was in opposition to her and she began the policy of publicly burning at the stake anyone of the Protestant religion that her father established. The burnings had to be guarded to prevent the people being rescued by the angry crowd. The first was at Smithfield which is famous now as a meat market and a big exhibition centre in central London."

My jaw had dropped in shock. "How ghastly! Ugh!" I couldn't imagine the horror of those poor people. "So, how is your family connected with all of this?"

Richard looked ahead, his eyes focussed on the castle as we neared it. "My family is French Catholic. We have had a lot of to-ing and fro-ing across the channel. It's strange how history works. There are a lot of *ifs*. If Henry's first wife had given birth to a son, this country would still be Catholic and your royalty would be allowed to marry Catholics."

"Aren't they?" I asked.

Richard shook his head. "Non, this is still deeply rooted. If the next king hadn't died when he was still young. If Mary had been able to have a child."

"Wasn't she?" This was fascinating. Much more exciting than boring history books.

"Non. She married King Philip the Second of Spain. He had already lost one wife and he was, obviously Catholic, like the rest of the Continent, but after marrying Mary, he found her repulsive and went back to Spain. She thought she might be pregnant but it turned out to be a stomach tumour and she died, so Elizabeth, the half-sister she hated, became Queen."

I was totally absorbed. "Why did she hate her?"

"Because she represented her father's religion and was the beautiful daughter of Anne Boleyn, the woman Henry had taken as a wife after divorcing Mary's mother."

"So why was Elizabeth cruel?" We were nearing the gatehouse to the drawbridge and it loomed in front of us.

Richard stopped and looked at me, his face animated with all that he was trying to explain to me. "Visualisez-là, maintenant. You are a princess, only two and a half years old. Your father did not even come to your christening because he was so upset that you were not a boy. He has now declared you illegitimate and had your mother beheaded because he wants to replace your mother with another wife, who might give him a son. When you are twenty-one, a rebellion takes place against your half-sister. You are not a part of it, but she has you arrested and put in the Tower of London. Her officials try to get you to confess. They want you dead because if you survive and become Queen they will be vulnerable for supporting Mary's cruel Catholic regime. Your blessing is that you are completely innocent and they cannot make any charge stick. They still try to persuade Queen Mary to sign your death warrant to have you beheaded but Mary knows that the effective murder will look bad on her so she doesn't and you are released. Four years later you become Queen when she dies. That means that since your father's death, eleven years earlier, your country has had a king and two queens."

I was mesmerised by his eyes. Awestruck, that I suddenly felt that I was the young Queen Elizabeth.

He cupped my face in his hands and I was very, very still.

"Do you realise that not only are you the image of Venus, but you are also the likeness of Elizabeth who had blue eyes, pale skin, a glorious mass of red hair and she was considered to be very beautiful."

I was transfixed. I could barely speak. "Couldn't I have peace when I was Queen?"

Richard shook his head as his eyes held mine. "Many wanted you dead and you and your throne were weak and vulnerable."

"Why?" I breathed.

"You were Protestant, of your father's religion. The Catholics were terrified of the Protestant backlash. You wanted to keep the peace between the two but people were trying to force you to choose. The courtiers who had supported the previous Queen and wanted you dead were now your advisors, particularly, the Duke of Norfolk. You couldn't trust anyone and your life was in danger. There were lots of offers of marriage but if you accepted one, then you would upset another."

I gulped. This was terrifying but, somehow, exciting. "Who should I marry?"

Richard shook his head. "You can't marry anyone. The fact that you are young and beautiful is a bonus, but they only want your country and you would be a puppet queen, without power or authority. The French have declared war on you and are grouping in Scotland. You were tricked into sending an army into battle, but you didn't know that it was made up of young, inexperienced boys because the bishops didn't want England to defeat the Catholic French. You were defeated. You and your throne were embarrassed."

"Why didn't I have a proper army?" I said softly.

"Your father had confiscated all the land and wealth from the Catholic monasteries. The Catholics feared for their lives. Your father created a great army and navy and became powerful. When you were crowned, you were also, officially, according to England, Queen of France. But, because of a child king and then a Catholic queen, when you became Queen the treasury was empty and you didn't really have much of an army or navy because they had been practically disbanded. Probably, Queen Mary gave all of England's wealth to the Pope in atonement for her father's behaviour."

My jaw was now well-dropped. "Can't I marry?" I asked, faintly.

Richard raised his brows, questioningly. "Who? Philip of Spain wants you as his third wife. France wants you to marry the Duc d'Anjou, who is the nephew of the French woman waging war on you. You choose neither and decide to honour your father so they all declare war on you. The Pope has issued a decree to reward anyone who assassinates you and given his full blessing to the Duke of Norfolk to take your throne and suggests that he marries your cousin, Mary Queen of Scotland."

I was enthralled and I knew my eyes were huge. My mouth was dry. "What do I do?" I was very aware that I was standing on the soil of Norfolk.

"You have one devotion amongst all the confusion, and that is to your father and his legacy. I believe that you wanted to prove yourself worthy to the father who didn't want you. There is only one person who, luckily for you, you can trust. He was devoted to your father and feared by many. He is your assassin, your spy and your protector. Only because of him can you survive. When you took the throne, he was able to return from exile on the continent and most people in this country hated him. He is your only hope. His name is Walsingham and he rounds up your opposition, including the Duke of Norfolk, and you have them beheaded for treason and their heads displayed on stakes to deter others from rebelling against you."

I was in shock and actually shaking now. "Who was your ancestor?" I seemed to have taken on the role of Elizabeth now.

"He was Robert de Bowes-Lyon, the same name as my father, Duc de Lyon."

"Did he own this land?"

"As Norfolk is a very religious area, it is likely that this land was part of the vast wealth of the Catholic monasteries and estates. Your father probably confiscated it and then I think that you gave it as a present to Robert de Bowes-Lyon."

"Why is Norfolk so important?"

"This was the land of the wealthy. Everyone wanted to control its resources but I think it was sentimental for you also, because your mother was born here, on one of the wealthiest estates. You wanted to please the man you loved. What better present could you give him?"

"But, Robert was Catholic," I whispered.

"Yes."

"Was the story of our relationship, romantic?" I could hardly breathe. I was rooted to the spot, wanting to know more.

Richard's eyes narrowed. "In the same way that any great historical romance is truly tragic."

"Why?" I was vaguely aware of the warmth of the sun as I stood before Richard.

"Robert loved you and built this castle as a home in your honour. You only visited it once. You were both in an impossible situation. You had chosen the path to dedicate your life to your father's legacy. You could not marry a Catholic. Robert wanted you to convert, become a Catholic and marry him. You wanted Robert to relinquish his religion and marry you. Your devotion to your throne and your father ran too deeply and Robert's family devotion to the Catholic religion was too all-consuming. Robert would not give up his religion for you and you could not forgive him. You felt that if he really loved you, he would give up his religion."

"What happened?"

Richard studied my face, carefully. "You remained single and became one of the most powerful women the world has ever known. One day, you discovered that Robert had married one of your ladies at Court. You were so enraged, you had him arrested and beheaded on a charge of treason. His wife feared for her life and was able to escape to France. She was carrying a child and when he was born, he became Richard de Bowes-Lyon, Duc de Lyon."

My mouth was dry. My heart was pounding in my ears. "Is that when you lost this castle?"

Richard shook his head and led me down the slight slope to the edge of the moat. The water was not stagnant because of the flow of the Broad it was connected to. The edge of the water had a thick growth of bulrushes. We walked to a place where the water came right to the edge of the grassy slope. Richard sat down and reached out to put his hand in the cool water. I did the same. It was a refreshing feeling. I waited for him to answer me.

Eventually, he said, "My family lost this castle at another bad time in history."

"Another conflict?" I asked.

He smiled, ruefully. "My family has had to flee between my country and yours several times. Hopefully, no more. Under Henry's rule, it was unsafe here for Catholics. With Mary, Catholicism was restored, but she was Queen for only five years. With Elizabeth's reign and all the problems, it was unsafe to live here again and there were many other times, under certain monarchs, when it was dangerous to be a Catholic in this country. On the other side, it was mostly safe until the French Revolution when the aristocracy, anyone suspected of having a rapport with the English, and even Catholics were persecuted. That was in the Georgian and Regency eras. My family could therefore be three times accused. They had to flee from their French estates to this one."

"It was lucky that you had estates in both countries," I breathed in awe. This was more, fascinating history. "My father has antiques in the shop which are Elizabethan, Georgian and Regency but I don't know much more about history than that. I know that Jane Austen was a writer in Georgian times and I love her stories. They are very elegant!" I took my sandals off, pulled my dress above my knees and dipped my feet in the cool, running water.

Richard laughed. "What a good idea!" He did the same.

I frowned in puzzlement as I looked at him. "You are so very French but you seem to know so much about English history and you speak English very well."

Richard bowed his head in his gallant way in acknowledgment of my compliment. "Merci. I was born in France but because my father chose to spend most of his working life in England, I have attended schools here. At home, we only speak French so," he shrugged, "I am still very French. Sister Ruth has been my favourite teacher and I am learning so much from her. I enjoy English literature. There have been so many wonderful, English writers. I prefer Elizabeth Gaskell to Jane Austen."

I lay on the grass, looking up at the cloudless blue sky. "Who is she?"

Richard lay beside me. "She was one of the greatest Victorian writers, and she is my favourite."

"Why?" I was mesmerised by this boy and I loved hearing him talk, with his heavily French accent, and I was absolutely hooked on every word he said.

"She was obviously successful and recognised for her work in her era by her friends who included Charlotte Bronte, Charles Dickens and William Wordsworth. Jane Austen was a vicar's daughter but perhaps it was because Elizabeth was a vicar's wife that she showed such a social conscience and because they were apparently wealthy she was probably able to experience all social levels. They travelled in this country and on the continent and she wrote about what was actually going on in the world. Her stories show that she really understood people and their situations. She seems so perceptive about how people relate to one another and the vast difference between the wealthy and the poor. Also the enormous social division between the people in the north and south of England. It was the time of the industrial revolution. The working classes didn't understand each other and were trying to start up unions to protect their jobs and incomes for their families. A wealthy mill owner might have been a self-made man who created his own success to become acknowledged as gentry in his town and master of his workers but because he worked hard to make his business earn money, the southern aristocracy viewed him as a tradesman, not a gentleman, and no better than any shopkeeper they looked down upon. Elizabeth Gaskell wrote 'North and South' and it's the best story I've ever read."

I was fascinated. "Why was it different with Jane Austen? She wrote about people and families, didn't she?"

Richard was silent and thoughtful for a moment and then he said, "Jane Austen wrote about the elegant life that she lived. She was obviously very intelligent, witty and observant of the society she lived in, but she must have either not been aware of the ugliness of late Georgian, early Regency life, or she chose not to write about it. I feel that if Elizabeth Gaskell had been writing in that era, she would have shown much more depth and understanding of what was happening around her. Did you know that Jane Austen was exactly of the era of the French

Revolution? Actually, there was a hint in Pride and Prejudice. It was barely mentioned, that the reason for the soldiers camping in the local area was in case of a French invasion, and then they moved on to Brighton. Jane Austen was actually a favourite of the Prince Regent. Apparently, she dedicated 'Mansfield Park' to him. Perhaps if she had lived longer, her writing may have shown more honesty about what was really going on around her."

"When did she die?"

"She dedicated the book to the Prince in 1816 and a year later she died, when she was just 42. She had only just begun to be famous as a novelist."

I was stunned. "How sad! Richard, you are so clever to have learned so much!"

"I give all credit to Sister Ruth. She is a wonderful teacher. There was one invasion by the French which was the last on this country. Do you want to hear about it?"

"Yes, please!" I was still hooked on every word.

"Well, there is a place called Saint David's, on the south-west corner of Wales. One thousand four hundred men landed. They were mostly French, but led by an Irish captain, because the Irish didn't like the English either. It was seventeen ninety-seven, exactly of the period I've just been telling you about, but they were not real soldiers."

"Who were they, then?" I asked, captivated by him.

He was grinning. "They were actually a group of convicts and no-goods who had been rounded up to be soldiers. When they landed they went in search of food. Now, there had just been a wreck of a Portuguese ship and, inevitably, it was carrying a lot of port and brandy. The local homes were at that point fully stocked from the wreck, so the pretend soldiers, on finding the alcohol, got completely drunk."

"What happened then?"

"When the local militia arrived, who were mostly made up of women, the drunken pretend soldiers couldn't see properly and mistook the ladies' traditional Welsh tall hats and red capes to be the uniform of English soldiers and promptly gave themselves up, just forty-eight hours after they had arrived!"

I could imagine the scene and I almost cried with laughter. "Oh, Richard, that is so funny! And you are very good to make fun of your own countrymen!"

"They're not countrymen I am proud of. I love that story, too, but, going back to Jane Austen, it seems that she chose to look at family life through a microscope, rather than give the whole picture of sordid Georgian life in Britain. As you say, her work was elegant and enduringly popular. Perhaps if a diary of hers had ever been found, we would have had a clearer picture."

"Sordid?" I asked faintly, becoming suddenly serious.

Richard bit his lip. He paused, and then said, "Okay, I'll put it this way. The Georgian and Regency eras sort of run into each other because George the Third was seriously ill and pronounced clinically *insane*. The Prince was Regent for nine years, until his father died, and was then King George the Fourth for only ten years, but it was a significant time and there were significant people. Are you sure you really want to hear this? Haven't you had enough history for one day?"

I shook my head, totally fascinated.

He took a deep breath. "Okay. I'll try and be brief about this in a way that is, er, not too shocking."

My eyes, I knew were huge and intent on his.

"You are aware of Princess Diana, who was Lady Diana Spencer before she married?"

Now I was confused, but intrigued. I nodded.

"Well, the sister of her great-great-grandfather was the equivalent in beauty and influence on fashionable society as the Diana Spencer of modern times. This lady was Georgiana Spencer and she was born in 1757. She was just two years younger than Marie Antoinette, who became a close friend."

My jaw had dropped again. Now he had my attention. This was awesome and I almost forgot to breathe.

"Lady Georgiana became the Duchess of Devonshire when she married the Duke. She could have become a wonderful example to society, as Diana has been, but, society wanted to follow whatever Georgiana did and, unfortunately, she was influenced by the worst traits of Georgian lifestyle in the upper classes. She became both a victim and a perpetrator. There was a lot of good in her but, she reacted badly to what went on around her and, being hailed by the country as its foremost fashion innovator, she could have had an influence to steer Georgian society away from its worst excesses."

"Didn't she?" I asked, quietly.

"She jumped right in and was one of the worst," Richard replied.

"Oh!" I was puzzled. "In what way?"

"The Duchess and her close friend, the Prince of Wales were symbolic of the era. Society had a vast wealth, but they were bored, self-indulgent and far-removed from the plight of the greater population of poor people, just the same as in France, where Marie Antoinette and King Louis the Sixteenth were also criticised. They were, politically, bad times. Violence constantly threatened to explode over here so the government were fierce. The death penalty was given for those found guilty of petty theft, forgery and even poaching. These were all seen to be crimes that affected private property and the government was determined to protect the ranks of society. At the same time, as in Georgiana's case, which was typical, as soon as she was married, she discovered that her husband only wanted her because she was the right sort of person to bear him a son of the right sort of blood lines. She was passionate and feisty and she rebelled against him. They soon hated each other. He had girlfriends, she had boyfriends, and she drank, took drugs, gambled and lost a fortune. An entire estate could be lost in one game of cards."

I stared at him, dumbstruck, with a sudden enlightenment. "Are you saying…" I could not say the words.

Richard nodded. "Yes. Stupid people." He found a stone beside him and threw it into the moat. It made an angry 'plop.'

I stared at him and touched his arm. "No wonder you are so resentful. What a waste!"

He shook his head, as if in disbelief, to be sitting here, looking at the estate that his family had lost.

"What actually happened?" I ventured.

He took a deep breath and held on to it, then let it out in a long sigh. "My family was grateful to Georgiana for her help. She used her contacts and her influence to help many to escape. She couldn't help everyone. She couldn't help her friends, the King and Queen of France, although she used all her political influence on the British government and French officials. She was devastated when Louis was taken to the guillotine in January of 1793 and then her dear friend, Marie, nine months after her husband. It was tragic. The aristocracy in this country was very scared so I suppose they just sank further into their indulgences."

"What happened to your family," I asked in a whisper.

Richard's eyes were far away, deep in thought. "They left almost everything behind in France and carried only what they could, when they were helped to escape. Their homes were ransacked and confiscated. They came here and immediately fell into the Regency lifestyle and excesses. Perhaps they were relieved. Perhaps, like people over here, they were still scared. My father had a relationship with a woman who was already married to another Duke. This ancestor of mine was called, Antoine and his wife was Annette. The Duchess Annette was devastated. They already had two daughters and she was expecting again." Richard paused again and threw another stone into the water, as though aiming at Antoine. "The other Duke found out about the relationship they were having and challenged the Duke Antoine to a game of cards – winner take all."

"What did Annette say?"

"She tried to stop it, but the Duke Antoine would not listen. At that time, society had lots of house parties and gambling was quite normal for them. As I have said, entire estates were lost in one game of cards or throw of the dice. L'esprit de jouer. Vous avez perdu votre patrimoine au poker."

"How could they rationally do that?" I was horrified.

"That's the point, they were not rational. They drank to excess, they took some kind of drugs, and if they lost money, they would gamble even more to try to win it back and, inevitably, lose more. There were terrible bankruptcies and divorces. Often, men hated their wives so much that they had their girlfriends and children they were father to, sharing their home with their genuine wife and children. It was just awful." Richard bit his lip. "Stupid Antoine was no different. He was probably off his head with drink and drugs. He lost everything and then, when he sobered, and realised what he had done, he tied a sack of stones to his feet and jumped off the drawbridge, probably, just about there!" Richard threw a stone with great ferocity, as though he was aiming it at Antoine's sinking head.

I was truly stunned. I didn't know what to say. What a family! What a history! What a different life they had! I felt very boring in comparison. I felt I had to break the ice, somehow. It was still a beautiful, sunny afternoon and it was still the first day of spring, my favourite day. I had to break Richard out of this sombre mood. We had come here to have fun and now he seemed depressed about his family. Perhaps it was the shock of seeing the castle which he had obviously dreamed of seeing for so many years.

A thought occurred to me. "What happened to the Duchess Annette? She had lost her home in France and her home in England. She had children and she was expecting another. What did she do?"

Richard seemed to recover a little. "The Duke took pity on her. He did allow her to keep the convent estate and the nuns looked after her and the children."

"Convent estate?" I asked, faintly.

"Yes, I didn't tell you. When it was safe in this country for Catholics to live here again, after Elizabeth the First died, my family established a convent here in memory of Robert de Bowes-Lyon, who would not give up his faith, not even for love. The Duchess Annette and the children lived in the beach house and were looked after by the nuns. The Duchess was careful to keep her children away from Regency society. During the time of the French Revolution, the nuns cared for those who fled from France, including other nuns, who were being persecuted. My family was allowed to retain ownership of the convent estate but the castle estate was a bone of contention. Throughout the generations since, that Duke's family have dangled it at mine. They don't care about it, apart from as a symbol of the feud. I think that it is just an item on their list of assets and they don't want it but won't let it go."

"Phew!" I exclaimed. "Golly, what a history! You should write a book about it."

Richard smiled. "Maybe I will. Do you realise that you are in one of the most important areas in England?"

I frowned. "I am beginning to. Why?"

"So many famous people have come from your county. You've heard of Nelson, who defeated the French at the battle of Trafalgar?"

"Of course!"

"Did you know that he was born in Norfolk and that's why you have a copy of Nelson's Column that is in Trafalgar Square in London, on the sea front, further down the coast from here at Great Yarmouth? His girl-friend was Lady Hamilton. He was another Georgian example of a man taking another man's wife?"

I thought for a moment. "I think I've heard about that."

"Did you know that Lady Hamilton was also a close friend of Georgiana?"

I gasped. "Was Georgiana friends with lots of famous people?"

Richard nodded. "She was the most notable English woman of her era and every famous, gifted, person wanted to be her friend, because she was beautiful and fun and because of the influence she had which may further their prospects. Many famous, aristocratic families have Norfolk estates, including the Spencers and, also, the Queen."

"But why is Norfolk so important?"

"Before the agricultural and then industrial revolutions, this was the larder for your country. It was known as the land of plenty and was the most densely populated area outside of London, and, therefore, the richest and most powerful. In fact, the Duke of Norfolk was probably richer than Queen Elizabeth the First. This area supplied the rest of the country with fuel and the finest quality produce. It provided food and work. When your country was invaded, they landed here first so, unfor-tunately, your people were the first to feel the effect of the murdering conquerors. During the more modern times, when the Second World War was happening, your entire county was one huge American air base, from which the planes took off for their missions in Europe."

"The Germans took France!" I suddenly remembered. "Did your family have to leave their home again?"

Richard nodded. "Yes, they had to seek sanctuary at the convent estate, yet again, and leave behind what they could not carry. The Germans ransacked the entire country and, luckily, my family were able to smuggle out some of their treasures and works of art, which were stored in the vaults of the convent. The Germans were persecuting the Jews then but it was not safe for anyone to live in France."

I stared at Richard in awe.

"Did you know that your leader, Winston Churchill, used Norfolk as one of the greatest deceptions the world has ever known?"

I frowned and shook my head. "Did he?"

"The Germans expected the allied army to invade from England but they didn't know where. Churchill wanted to throw them off the scent so he made them think it was going to be another part of the French coast, by pretending that the invasion fleet was grouping on the coastline of Norfolk."

"How can you pretend something like that?" I asked.

"He had life-size models built of planes and ships. It was all just a sham, like theatrical props, but it convinced the Germans in their spy planes, so, when the invasion happened in a completely different place on the French coast, the surprise gave the allies the advantage. The Germans were just not expecting it. Of course, there were many injuries in the war, so the convent became a hospital and the nuns became nurses. After the war, my family and the nuns decided to turn it into a girls' school."

I shook my head in amazement and looked down at the ground. "I don't think I will ever look at history in the same way, again. You have certainly opened my eyes."

"And what beautiful eyes you have," Richard said gallantly, as he kissed my hand. He pulled me gently to my feet in front of him. "Shall we try the key now to see if it fits?"

I hesitated and looked around the estate. I had forgotten to keep a lookout. There was no one else in sight. I turned back to Richard. "Alright, we've been lucky so far. I suppose it wouldn't hurt to push our luck a little further."

We walked, hand in hand, up the slope and stopped in front of the gatehouse. I suddenly thought of something. "I forgot to bring any oil!"

Richard smiled at me and surveyed me from head to toe "And spoil that pretty dress! Are you a tomboy?" He winked at me.

Next to the gigantic, iron gate, was a relatively small oak plank door with iron studs. It was obviously for access by the staff. Richard tried the first key, which was a distinctively different shape to the one which had worked in the door in the wall. It fitted! We both gasped and looked at each other in amazement. I held my breath. Would it turn? It was obviously an extremely old and rusty lock. Richard fiddled and fiddled, ever so patiently and then it began to turn and… he was able to put his shoulder against the heavy door and it opened! We couldn't believe our luck now.

Richard looked ahead. "One down, one to go. That door in the castle wall seems to match this one. Do you think our luck will stretch far enough for the locks to be identical?"

I shook my head in wonderment and licked my suddenly dry lips. I was trembling, but I think it was more with excitement than fear now. Our eyes were locked. "Only one way to find out," I breathed.

We crossed the drawbridge, our footsteps making a soft thud on the creaking old timber planks. I could see the water below us through the gaps. We hurried to the second door and Richard was equally patient. Eventually, the same thing happened and he was able to open the door. We quickly closed it behind us and found that we were almost out of breath, as if we had been running a long distance, instead of standing there, not daring to breathe.

Richard's eyes were almost glittering with excitement. "We're in! And no-one knows we're here!"

"I'm stunned," I said, hoarsely. "I didn't think we would make it this far."

Richard cupped my face in his hands and kissed my forehead. "Merci beaucoup. Tu es mon ange porte-bonheur. I told you, you are my angel of joy. God wanted me to meet you, today! You are my fortune! Shall we explore, mademoiselle?" He bowed low and extended his arm in the direction of the arch way which opened on to the castle courtyard.

We walked through the huge arch way into the sunlit courtyard and I stopped and exclaimed, "This is just like the square at the cathedral in Norwich! The part that used to be the monastery!" I had the same feeling that I had at the cathedral. I was so far disorientated in time now, that I would not have been at all surprised to hear monks singing and see them walking, in their brown robes, hands folded in prayer along the passageways that edged the central square.

"That part of the cathedral is probably much older than this," Richard said in awe, "but it looks the same, only a double layer!"

We turned around and around, trying to take in the spectacle. It was fantastic! The grey stone had been carved into a double layer of pillars and arches. The upper and lower levels were deep, with their wide walk ways and they edged the courtyard. Huge, French style glass double doors opened from the surrounding rooms onto the walk ways. It was the most incredibly secret and exciting place I had ever seen or could even have imagined. The shutters on the outside kept the world out and even if anyone had flown over here in a plane, the deep walkways were hiding the glass doors which were visible only by standing in the courtyard. It appeared to be a complete secret!

We wandered along the overgrown paths in the square. "I think these must have once been flower beds and I think there are some herbs here, as well," I commented as I bent down to inspect a plant which I thought was rosemary.

Richard began laughing with delight and I looked up to see him running through the passageway, jumping on to the little boundary walls and swinging around the pillars between the arches.

"Richard, we shouldn't be doing this!"

He grinned as he swung at arms length around a pillar. "Pourquoi pas? It isn't a holy place. There are no monks here to tell us off and no-one knows we're here!"

I gulped. I felt excited and nervous at the same time, as though someone was going to catch us at any moment.

Richard saw my expression and ran to me. He took my hand.

"Don't worry. This is our secret! Shall we explore inside?"

I was trembling. I really felt as if I was trespassing, now but we had come this far and it seemed a shame to go back without looking inside. I nodded. "Okay. Let's do it!"

Richard led me to a double set of glass doors. They were very tall. We couldn't see inside because the curtains were drawn. Richard pushed the handle down and opened the door towards us.

"It's not locked!" I exclaimed.

Richard laughed. "Why should it be? We are inside a fortified castle!"

He opened the door fully and parted the curtains so that we could step inside. What we saw made us both stop in our tracks. We turned to each other, totally stunned.

Wordlessly, we each took a curtain and fastened it with an enormous tie-back and turned to face the room. We looked at each other, both of us unable to speak.

Richard reached for my hand and held it, tightly. We couldn't breathe. We just stared.

Eventually, I said, "I was somehow expecting it to be Elizabethan and...empty." I was frowning because I couldn't believe what I was looking at.

"C'est incroyable," Richard whispered. He chewed on his lips and turned to me, urgently. "Et je pense... I... I think that the people who own this have never bothered to come here. They cannot know about... this! I think that we've opened a time capsule. I think that the Duchesse Annette walked out of here, threw away the keys and no-one has been in here since. This is a complete secret. I don't think anyone knows about this!"

"But why would she walk out and leave all of this stuff?" I was stunned.

"Remember that she was going to live on the convent estate. She was probably so disgusted by her husband's behaviour and society's over-indulgent lifestyle that she wanted to walk away and leave it all behind her."

"But why didn't the new owners ransack the place and sell it all off?"

"They probably thought that she had emptied the house. With their immoral lifestyle, they probably couldn't imagine that she would want to walk away from this and have a simple life at the convent."

We were still rooted to the spot in shock. "But wouldn't the new owners be the least bit curious and want to look inside?" I whispered.

Richard turned to me and his eyes held mine. "Think about it. The Duchesse Annette walked out of here, locked it up and threw away the keys. She probably threw them over the boundary wall and they might have landed on some rough ground. More than two hundred years later, you dig your flower bed and find the keys. I don't think the new owners had the keys. They must have thought the place was empty. Elizabethan houses were very unfashionable at that time and they were spending their considerable fortunes on the new Georgian and then Regency styles. They wouldn't have been interested in this place and it must have been practically forgotten, except as a bone of contention between the two families. It was just a pawn in the game."

"It's like a museum," I said, softly.

Richard shook his head. "It's more than that. This is exactly as it was when the Duchesse Annette walked out. It's a time capsule! From the outside and from the air, no-one would know what is here." He gripped my hand, tightly. "You have to swear that you won't tell anyone about this. It has to be our secret."

"I swear," I whispered.

"I feel like one of those children at the Caves of Lascaux," he said, quietly.

"Pardon?"

"It's in the Dordogne area in southern France. Some children were caught in the rain while playing in the hills at Lascaux, in nineteen-forty. They stumbled into a cave for shelter and discovered paintings that hadn't been seen for fifteen thousand years."

"Oh, my goodness! What a discovery!"

"It turned the entire, previous concept of ancient man on its head!"

"Shall we explore, now?" I whispered.

We opened the doors and curtains of each room, on both levels, so that we could see properly. It was a French, Louis the Sixteenth and Regency home, exactly as it was the moment that the duchess walked out, except that it was covered in a thick layer of dust and cobwebs. Everything was dry; there was no sign of damage from dampness that often affects old houses, which was surprising as we were surrounded by a moat.

Somehow, the thick dust did not detract from the beauty of the elegant furniture and sumptuous swathes of wonderful material. I was the daughter of an antiques dealer. I knew I was looking at something special.

We wandered in awe through the house, room after room of an elegant standard of living more than two hundred years old. This had been the home of French aristocrats who were probably close friends of the beheaded King Louis the Sixteenth and his Queen, Marie Antoinette. I had to pinch myself to believe that this was really happening and I had to remind myself that the boy who was with me was the heir to the family who had lived here. It was almost more than I could mentally come to terms with.

"Regarde!" Richard opened an armoire, which is a French-type wardrobe or cupboard.

My eyes opened wide with amazement as he took out a French lady's dress. It was extravagantly beautiful. The sort of dress you might have expected to see in the palace of the beheaded royal couple. My breath caught in my throat as I walked forward. I opened the other door and saw that there were several, hanging there. They were perfect. Stunning! Richard and I silently exchanged glances and explored further.

In another armoire were men's clothes that must have belonged to Antoine. That was a bit creepy, to find the clothes of a notorious man who had killed himself by jumping into the moat outside.

The armoires were full of clothes, so were the drawers. There were under-garments and even jewellery. The beds were made, beneath their romantic canopies that made them seem like fairytale beds.

This was a fairytale. We were standing in a frozen piece of history, surrounded by what would be priceless antiques if they were ever to leave this building. I grabbed Richard's arm. "Do you realise how much all of this must be worth?"

He shook his head in bewilderment and then his eyes fixed on mine as a thought occurred to him. "If the family who own this ever find out what is here, they will sell it and this… collection will be split up and sold all over the world. My family's wealth and inheritance will be dispersed. They must never know about this! I think that you have the only keys and, one day, I shall buy this castle and restore it and all of this to my family. C'est mon avenir. A récupérer."

It seemed almost an impossibility, to keep a secret like this from its owners, but if they hadn't bothered to investigate it for more than two hundred years and had almost forgotten about the place, perhaps

Richard's luck may hold out and he may be able to achieve his ambition. It seemed impossible, but, when God is on your side, that word doesn't exist.

We found a large leaded glass window on the lower level and the doors were heavy oak instead of glass. Richard turned the big iron handle and opened the door towards him. We stepped inside and both gasped at the same time.

"This was their chapel!" Richard said in awe. "Bien sûr, they were devoted Catholics and they would have had a chapel."

It was lovely, like stepping inside your own private little church. I felt somehow privileged to be there. This was still very much Elizabethan. The floor had large flagstones which had been worn by people walking over them. I felt like I was in the cathedral again, in Norwich. The oak pews were worn and had that lovely patina that my dad talks about. He had explained to me that it happens when dirt and dust and age and polish combine to give that lovely warm colour and shine.

I sat on one of the pews and looked around. I was in awe of the statue of the Virgin Mary and the baby Jesus and the enormous gold cross and candlesticks on the altar table at the front of the chapel. Also on the table was a large silver bowl and what seemed to be a painted carving of a group of figures. One of them seemed to be Mary. She seemed to have fainted and the others seemed upset.

There seemed to be writing on the walls. I shone my torch and gasped again. "Richard, look! What does it mean?"

Richard's eyes followed where my torch illuminated the high stone walls, pillars and vaulted ceiling. The walls were covered in a faded gold writing.

Richard's eyes narrowed as he studied them hard and then his face was illuminated by the realisation. "They are proverbs from the Bible!"

"Why are there so many? Why would someone go to all this trouble?"

Richard was amazed. "There are thirty-one proverbs in the Bible, one for each day of the month. They are sort of like a good thought for the day to keep you on the path of righteousness and virtue. I can't see a man having the patience to do this but, you remember that in that era it was very important for young ladies to learn the elegant skills of needlework, art and languages. They were described as being accomplished. Society wanted them to improve themselves so as to be delightful wives for their future husbands."

"That's a joke!" I interrupted him. "Considering what seems to have been going on!"

"Exactement!" Richard agreed. "Imagine if you were a young lady of society and found yourself caught in the awful trap of life that many felt they were in. If you were sad and lonely and did not indulge in the excesses that went on around you, who would you turn to for comfort?"

"God!" I exclaimed with enlightenment.

"I think that's what happened, here. The Duchess Annette, or possibly one of her predecessors, must have devoted their time to decorating the walls with proverbs. They are probably all here and they used a lot of gold leaf to decorate in those days so it's probably some kind of gold paint."

"Richard, there is a huge curtain behind the table at the front. Do you suppose there is a door behind it?"

Richard parted the long, heavy curtains and fastened them with the tie backs and then he went rigid with shock and stared at the painting he had just revealed.

There was such an odd expression on his face. "What is it?" I asked. He turned, slowly, to me, his eyes were huge and his face seemed pale. "What's the matter?"

"It's the painting. The one I told you about. The famous painting of Venus, except that she looks different. Someone seems to have copied the painting and added swathes of white material over her body that sort of, fan out behind her. She looks like an angel, now."

I went to stand by Richard and I illuminated the painting with my torch. It was exactly as Richard had described it to me this morning, except that, as Richard had said, she was sort of more demure now with a kind of robe. Was it only this morning I had met him? It seemed like a lifetime ago, now.

The painting was huge. It was on a canvas and the frame was heavily ornate and decorated with what was probably gold leaf. It was fixed against the wall.

Richard quickly took the torch from me. "Je suis désolé! Puis-je? I want to see what this inscription says." He crouched down and illuminated the plaque. When he looked at me, he had turned even paler.

I was concerned. "What's the matter?"

He didn't say anything for a while and just stared at me. Eventually, he said, "Look."

I crouched down next to him and looked where he shone the torch. It said, 'Angel of Joy.'

I gasped. "That's incredible! That's what you called me! But... who would have done such a painting?"

Richard now seemed to be on a mission. He used the torch and scoured every inch of the painting. It took him ages.

Eventually, he stood, completely still and said, "Goya."

"Who?"

"Goya! He's another famous painter." Richard was staring at the painting in awe. He walked backwards until his legs met the pew and he sat down heavily, still staring at the painting.

"Who is he?" I asked, still confused.

"I learned about him when I went to Italy with my father. Some of his paintings were being exhibited there at the same time as those by Botticelli."

"Why would this be here though? I don't understand. Why would he have painted an altered copy of another artist's work?"

Richard frowned. "I'm trying to remember." He paused. "I know that he painted during the time of all this!" His arm indicated back towards the rest of the house. "He was a society painter. He was Spanish. You remember I told you that all these famous artists and aristocrats all knew each other, even all over Europe! I remember that he hated what was happening in the world at that time. He was reliant on these people for his work but he became very religious and very bitter and disillusioned about society and its false pretences. When the problems in France calmed down he settled in the south of France and that is where he died."

"Are you saying that you think he visited here and painted this?" I was completely stunned.

Richard nodded, considering the facts. "He probably did. It would make sense. He was probably a friend of the Duchess Annette and found in her a kindred spirit. She was probably a very genteel, good person who was devoted to her religion and it is likely that he responded to that."

Richard got up and quickly covered the distance between us. He took my hand firmly in his. "Joy, we have to save this from dispersal. We cannot let that happen. We must keep this a secret and hope that one day I can be successful in buying it. No one must know about this."

"I promise, faithfully, Richard."

Richard turned to look at the painting and then looked at me. He held both of my hands, tightly. He seemed suddenly lost for breath. "Be my Angel of Joy, toujours… forever," he whispered. His eyes were so intense.

"I will if you never leave me," I whispered back, my heart pounding.

He kissed my forehead and then looked at the door. "The light is fading. We had better go. Let's come back tomorrow."

"Do you think we dare?"

"We must," he said urgently.

We ran all the way back to my home, careful to lock the doors behind us and careful to not let anyone see us.

We did go back the next day, just to confirm to ourselves that it wasn't a dream. We explored the castle, further. We stood in one of the bedrooms. Richard had put on one of the elaborate outfits that had probably belonged to his ancestor. He wore a long cape. It seemed to be made of a heavy silk. He had already found a sword that was displayed on a wall in one of the drawing rooms.

I giggled. "You look like a musketeer, and you have a hat!" He did his low, theatrical bow. "You are a musketeer," I said with delight. This was such fun!

"Now it's your turn," he said.

"What do you mean?"

"I'll step outside onto the balcony and you put on one of those dresses."

"Oh, I couldn't!" I protested.

His eyes held mine. "Pour moi?"

"Oh, very well. How could I refuse that expression on your face?" I pretended to be cross.

I put the dress on and called Richard. He came back in and helped to fasten me up in it.

He observed me, thoughtfully. "Turn around."

I did so and found I was looking at my reflection in the full length mirror. I looked at the reflection of his face to see what he was thinking. "Well?"

He was silent and thoughtful, then he said, with a lovely look in his oh so blue eyes, "You look like a beautiful lady who would grace the palace of Versailles. Il ne te manquè qu'une chose." He reached into a drawer and removed something, then put it around my neck, his eyes holding mine as he fastened it.

I shrieked when I saw what he had done and my heart pounded in my ears. "You can't! No, you shouldn't!"

He grinned. "Qui est la déesse, maintenant?"

It was an elaborate necklace made of diamonds and sapphires that were in tiers. They just looked like the sparkling blue and white of the waves breaking on the shore line.

"Pourquoi pas?" It suits you. You are Venus, are you not? My Angel of Joy, the lady of the waves." He studied the necklace. "Ton collier. Ces beaux diamants."

I gulped and looked at the dazzling beauty of it and then back at him. "How much do you think it is worth?"

He shrugged. "Who knows? And, let's hope they don't find out!"

I was panting, struggling for breath. I was quite overwhelmed. We were in a fairytale playhouse which was full of priceless treasures and it was a giant dressing up box!

Once I had overcome my nerves, we played around the castle. We went back the next day, and the next, and for the whole, endlessly long summer. It was bliss. Richard ran around, pretending that he was having sword fights with the imaginary guard of the evil Cardinal Richelieu in 'The Three Musketeers.' Richard, of course, was the young and handsome D'Artagnan, who hoped to become the fourth musketeer.

When he wasn't fighting them he was rescuing me from a tower and swearing to protect me for ever. It was wonderful.

My father had an antique wind up record player in his shop. We borrowed it and played it at the castle. We tried to learn to waltz. At other times, we would just lie in the long grass in the courtyard and bask in the warm sunshine. Richard liked to trace the contours of my face with a long stem of grass, as though fascinated. He also spent hours sketching me and taught me how to draw, with proper dimensions. I listened to Richard as he told me more about history. He taught me to speak French. I listened avidly as he read classical novels to me. Life was one long haze of blissful summer days and when it rained, we sat under the arched walkways, safe and dry, watching the spectacle of rain bouncing off the courtyard.

We were lying in the long grass one day, basking in the sun. Richard was lying beside me, leaning on his elbow as he traced my face with a long piece of grass.

I sighed. "You know, being here, wearing these clothes, borrowing their Georgian lifestyle, I feel I'm more Elizabeth Bennet in 'Pride and Prejudice' than Margaret Hale in 'North and South.' I admire Margaret so much for what she did. She was a true heroine, but I don't think I could have coped with leaving an idyllic country home to live in a smoky, industrial place like Milltown in the north."

"Remember that Margaret spent many years living in London, growing up with her cousin," Richard said, quietly.

"In absolute luxury. Not the relatively poor conditions they had to endure when they moved to a cold, damp, dirty town." I shook my head. "I would much rather be Elizabeth, living here."

"Then who am I?" Richard asked with amusement.

"Mr Darcy, of course!" I replied.

I was fascinated to watch Richard's throat vibrate as he laughed. "Bien sûr! You realise that it is a French name, but with an apostrophe... D'Arcy. Then I must be Monsieur D'Arcy!"

I closed my eyes, revelling in the warmth of the sun. "I love being here. I never want to leave."

"Jamais?" Richard enquired.

"Never," I assured him.

I was lying in the sun. I could smell the lavender. The sunlight was making my eyes itch. I rubbed them and then opened them. I had a shock to find myself back in my bedroom, looking up at the apex of half-timbered ceiling in the eaves of my house. Not, my house! I reminded myself with a jolt. The sun was pouring through one of the little windows in the slope of the roof.

I was completely disorientated. Since yesterday morning, my life had turned upside down and I wasn't sure which was a dream and which was reality. It seemed as though I had just relived six months of my life rather than slept through a few hours of it and I couldn't quite quell the disappointment in finding that I had woken up. Those were the heavenly days... before my mother ruined everything!

My head seemed ever so heavy and painful to move. I felt drunk. I thought back to the night before. I couldn't be drunk because even though I am not used to alcohol, I only had one glass! I turned over and breathed in the wonderful smell of lavender and fresh linen bedding. My head and neck ached. I must have been drunk with tiredness. I felt as though I had been tossing and turning all night.

I reached out and picked up my watch from the bedside table. "Aghh!" I shrieked in horror. It was ten o'clock already and Richard would be here in two hours!

"Oh, my God!" Another thought struck me and I quaked with trepidation. He was going to take me to the castle this afternoon, I was sure of it. I still had the keys and I didn't want to be with him when he explored it, for the first time, after ten years, but I would have no choice!

I remember...

The wind swept the long grass to the East,
It whispered in the leaves of the trees,
And rushed over the water in the stream.
It crept through the window where clean glass once shone, and
    through the roof,
Where slates had long since fallen and sunk into the once well kept
    soil.
'Oh to be young again!' the rotting boards sighed.
'Oh to flow free again!' the choked stream cried.
Only phantom footsteps fall along the path to the house now.
An imaginary door opens,
As no-one walks into the once welcoming hall,
And silently the no-clock ticks against the faded wall.
'I remember...' sighs memories, long since gone.

Sophie Large – aged fifteen.

Chapter Eight

I WALKED into the kitchen, feeling slightly better after a shower and wearing a fresh set of khaki shorts and shirt. Lisa and Annie were already there, having breakfast. The buttered toast that Annie was enjoying seemed suddenly very appealing to me and I realised that my stomach was rumbling with hunger.

Lisa looked up as I entered. "Good morning!" she said, cheerfully. "You appear to have had a good night's sleep."

"Sort of," I muttered. "Fresh toast and coffee smells good."

"Sit down, this is my treat. I'll pop another couple of slices in the toaster. Are you in an espresso or cappuccino mood?"

I sat down gratefully at the table. My legs still felt as though they couldn't support me this morning. "Mocha whip?" I asked, hesitantly.

Lisa beamed. "Certainly, madam. I'll make your favourite just as you like it."

I laughed. "You're not working in the tea rooms now!" My eyes almost winced when Lisa got up from the table. She was wearing neon pink trousers with a pink and purple jumper. "Ow, Lisa," I complained. "You're a bit fierce on the eye this morning!"

Lisa grinned. "Sorry! I bought these, yesterday in the sale. Do you like?" She did a twirl with her arms spread. Annie giggled at her mum.

"I think I'd appreciate them better if I was wearing sunglasses," I commented.

I turned to Annie, who was kneeling on a chair beside me, her little fingers clutching her toast. Do you have a kiss for Auntie Joy, this morning, Sweetie?" I leaned towards her and got a buttery kiss on my cheek, which I then had to wipe with a serviette.

Lisa was busy making my breakfast and then she set down a mug of mocha cappuccino in front of me, gloriously topped with a mountainous peak of whipped cream and chocolate dusting. She set another cup down in front of Annie which had just the cream and chocolate dusting, with a spoon. "There you are, Sweetie, just like Auntie Joy's."

"Thank you." I sipped the coffee through the cream and Annie giggled at my cream moustache as she tucked into her little mountain.

"I can't believe you had one of those machines put in the kitchen."

I shrugged and grinned. "What was I supposed to do, keep traipsing across the courtyard in my slippers to the barn tea room for my favourite coffee? Now I can have one at any time."

"Most people have to go out and buy one on their way to work," Lisa argued back. "They don't have a state of the art Gaggia in their kitchen."

"Where's Dad?"

Lisa put a plate of fresh toast in front of me and pushed the butter dish towards me. "He's busy doing some paperwork in his study. I took coffee and toast through to him earlier. He's says that there is quite a bit of sorting he wants to do before he leaves for New York."

I buttered my toast, thoughtfully. "It's going to seem strange with Dad not around."

I looked up and Lisa was looking at me, carefully. "How are you?"

"I'm fine," I said, breezily.

Lisa wasn't fooled. "You always say that. You had a lot of shocks, yesterday. Are you alright?"

I took a deep breath and looked down at the chattering toddler beside me. "I will be alright, once I've got through this afternoon. I'm not looking forward to it, to be honest, but it's a job I've had to agree to do."

"Your father told me he's getting married," Lisa said gently.

I concentrated on buttering my next piece of toast.

"You didn't tell me that."

I didn't answer.

"I think there is a lot you haven't told me."

I was aware of Lisa still watching me.

"If they live here, will you stay here? I'm sure they would ask you to."

I looked up at her. "I can't can I? I wouldn't fit in to their newly married life, would I? I'm the chick that hasn't had the courage to leave the nest yet."

"What will you do?"

I shrugged. "I don't know. Yesterday morning, I thought that my life was perfectly mapped out, exactly as I wanted it to be. This morning, I have nothing. I'm just going to have to take this one step at a time."

"Perhaps it's a good thing to happen. Maybe it's time for you to start living your own life and find out what makes you happy. Independence can be a positive step. You could be a model," Lisa suggested, tentatively.

I shook my head, vehemently. "No way. That is definitely not the life I want."

Lisa looked bewildered. "I would if I was you, but there is something that is holding you back and you're still not telling me."

Lisa was right. There was a lot that I wasn't telling her, but there was a lot that I wasn't ready to face up to, yet.

"I've been thinking about your problems."

My head shot up and I looked at her nervously. "Which ones?"

"Okay. For a start, you need help, lots of it, and you're going to have to learn to delegate. It will be an impossibility for you to carry on as you are now, working every spare minute to make life wonderful for your father. His life is going to change and so is yours."

My throat seemed to struggle to swallow the piece of toast. "What are you suggesting?"

"Well, what exactly is the sort of work that will be required to make the castle into a home?"

I thought back to my dream of last night. My world was weird at the moment and I was still feeling disorientated. Capsules of time seemed to be moving and switching. Was I awake now or was this yet another dream? And, in a short time, I would feel I was going back in time with Richard, yet again. Soon, he would be taking me back to the castle. I thought of those rooms, the fabulous furniture, priceless antiques and miles of sumptuous material covered in dust. The building was basically sound and the woodwork wasn't rotten.

I looked up at Lisa. "It's mostly labour. Some of it is general building maintenance, but a lot of it needs specialist supervision. It's a restoration project, really."

Lisa gave me a piercing look. "How do you know? Have you seen it, yet?"

I put my hand up to stall her. "It just is, okay? What is your suggestion?"

Lisa looked as though she was bursting with curiosity but knew that she couldn't get any further with me at the moment.

"Think about it. The large group of us that live on your caravan site, with your kindness, there are about thirty of us, in couples, so you have fifteen each of healthy and able young men and women."

"What are you saying, exactly?"

"Well, at the moment, the girls help you out during the season in the campsite shop and the tea rooms and the bed and breakfast, while the men are mostly cheap labour for builders. They are officially called apprentices, but they know their jobs and they are really just cheap labour. Work has been a bit slack for everyone lately and I'm sure they would jump at the chance of helping you. They're good, hardworking people, you just need to tell them what to do. What do you think?"

Lisa was glowing. She was obviously really pleased with her idea and, I suspected, a bit proud of thinking of it.

I smiled at her, "What a good idea!" Lisa beamed at me.

"Do you really think they would want to? Don't they have work commitments elsewhere?"

Lisa shook her head, she was obviously excited. "Not really. They are just attached to people who are officially qualified and given work as and when it is available. They could still go to night school to get their qualifications. I spoke to Gary about it, last night, and he thought it was a good idea. What do you think?" Lisa seemed to hold her breath, waiting for my answer.

"I think it's a great idea! But it will need some discussion and planning. I will need to know that they really are up for it."

"I thought about that too," Lisa said excitedly. "I was hoping you would say yes, so I've arranged that we meet the boys in the beach bar, tonight."

"Tonight?" My heart sank. I had planned on going to see Sister Ruth tonight! Now, that would have to be put off until tomorrow morning. "The beach bar? Lisa, I've never been into a bar!" I protested.

"Well it's about time you learned to live!" Lisa said triumphantly. "I'll call for you and we'll go and meet them there at seven o'clock."

I quaked. This was not what I had planned for tonight and I didn't even want to go into a bar, but Lisa was right. This was important and had to be discussed as soon as possible.

I looked down at Annie, who had finished her toast and the cream. "How about some baking, Annie? Do you want to help Auntie Joy make some biscuits? You can make them into shapes for me."

Annie's eyes lit up and she clapped her hands with excitement. There was so much I didn't want to think about at the moment, and busying myself cooking with Annie helped to block my other thoughts out.

I opened a drawer and took out an apron for me and one with a big bunny on it that I kept for Annie.

"Here we go, Annie." I took her little pink jumper off, so that she was just wearing her T-shirt, and tied the small apron around her.

We had fun. I always love baking with Annie. She enjoys it so much and likes the little 'jobs' I give her, such as rolling the dough and using the various cutters. Lisa helped by washing up for us.

"I still think you're scared," Lisa said.

My head shot up and I looked at her. "What do you mean?" I asked, carefully.

"You're scared of not fitting in with your mother's lifestyle."

I continued to supervise Annie as she cut more shapes out for me and I put them on the baking tray. We both had flour-covered hands and arms and Annie had flour on her nose and in her hair. She was chewing her little lip with great concentration as she worked. I imagined that I looked as equally flour-covered as she did.

I carried on working as I spoke. "I've never known my mother to get messy when she worked. This is my fun. I wouldn't fit in and I don't want to see her."

"I think Richard seems to be a man who gets his own way," Lisa said, softly.

I shrugged and didn't comment, pretending to be busy.

"I've thought about it and I think you are wrong to be worried. No-one cares what sort of background you have and you can develop your own sense of style."

I glanced at her, intrigued. "What do you mean?"

"Well, you're so fond of those old movies with Grace Kelly and Audrey Hepburn."

I was puzzled and frowned at her. "So? They were the glory days of Hollywood and I'm not planning on trying to become a film star."

"No, but the point is, they were two very different women with very different backgrounds."

"What are you saying?"

Lisa's face was animated as she explained her thoughts to me. "Grace Kelly was a beautiful, builder's daughter with the three m's."

"Which were?" I queried.

"She became a model, then a movie star then married a prince."

"You mean, two m's and an mp," I corrected her.

Lisa shot me a look. "Whatever. The difference was that Audrey Hepburn was the daughter of a baroness. She came from one of the wealthiest aristocratic families in Holland, but she played it down. One of the greatest roles she played was in The Nun's Story. She took her work very seriously. It was a true story and she wanted it to be completely authentic and *live* the part so, she became friendly with the actual nun and tried to understand her and her life. For the entire production of the film, Audrey lived like a nun with no make-up and a very simple lifestyle. Her portrayal was profound and very emotional, but most of the roles that were given to her were sort of rags to riches transformations. The reverse was true. She had the regal bearing of a princess but she wanted to be ordinary. She was made for those parts!

"Exactly what are you saying?"

"There are many similarities between you. Audrey had a controlling mother and she could never quite live up to her mother's expectations. Her mother was very critical of her. As a child, Audrey learned that if she wore the pretty dresses that her mother wanted her to wear, she would please her and she realised that she could please other people too. She had a wonderful personality but she didn't feel that she was attractive and never felt that she was good enough. She spent her whole life seeking the approval of others. She gave in every way possible to please and people just took from her. She had two very unhappy relationships with very selfish men and only found happiness in the last fifteen years of her life with a man who wanted to give back to her. He was seven years younger than her and totally adored her. It is said that when she was president of UNICEF, she gave so much of herself and found the situations she was put in so harrowing and traumatic that, because she really became deeply involved in whatever she did and was so sensitive, it actually shortened her life."

"And, in what way does this relate to me?" I asked, my heart pounding.

"I don't want to see that happen to you. You have devoted your life to pleasing your father and giving so much to others, but you haven't done anything for yourself. You've not even had a boyfriend. I hope that you can find happiness with a man who wants to give to you and cares about making you happy. Audrey gave such pleasure to others, but she didn't find happiness for herself until she was aged forty-nine."

I reeled, my breathing rapid and shallow. I sat down heavily on the nearest chair. "Okay, I get the picture. But, how does that relate to fitting in with my mother's lifestyle?"

"You have a choice!" Lisa said, urgently. "There are more similarities between you and Audrey. She is probably the greatest icon of beauty and style, ever, in history, but she broke the mould!"

"What do you mean?" I frowned.

"She was taller and skinnier than most women of that era. No-one looked like her. When she went to do her first film in Hollywood, no-one had ever heard of her. All the stars then were petite and curvy, with large breasts. Bosoms in jumpers! They looked more like me. She was very conscious of having no breasts, big hands and big feet. She looked like a boy, compared to them but she was like a coat hanger and she looked good in clothes. Her waist was less than twenty inches but her feet were size eight! She kept the same statistics for her entire life! Marlene

Dietrich said that a woman either looks good in clothes or out of clothes, never both and one of her most famous directors said of Audrey that this girl may single-handedly make bosoms a thing of the past!"

"So? I'm tall and boyish, too."

"The trick is, she developed her own sense of style and then everyone wanted to look like her and the reason that she is probably the greatest icon of all time is that she didn't follow fashion, she created it and the looks she created come back into fashion again and again, even fifty years later! Designers are constantly revisiting her look for inspiration."

"How am I supposed to do that, then?"

"Be yourself! Find what suits you best. Audrey didn't think that she was creating an all-time classic style, she just tried to make the best of the features she had and take the emphasis away from the bits that she didn't like, such as her hands and feet. For instance, she was conscious of being taller than almost any other woman around her and men were not that much taller, so she wore flat shoes or very low heels if necessary. She loved to dance so she liked clothes that she could move and feel comfortable in. She hardly drank and worked very hard. There have been loads of imitations, but no-one has ever really outshone or even matched her innate style."

"She was stunning," I agreed, "and wonderful in every way. She was so... different!"

"Joy, remember that you asked me yesterday morning about the latest fashions and the prospect of fashion victims having to be in the know about the latest look, otherwise they would get caught out if they were still wearing last season's fashion?"

"Yes," I said, carefully.

"Well, do you remember in Funny Face, the magazine editor had the brilliant idea of turning everything pink as a major concept to boost the sales of the magazine?"

"I remember the film. Audrey starred with Fred Astaire and she danced with him. It's one of my favourites."

"Think about it! Do you remember that the editor ordered everything that was moving or not moving to be decorated in pink and do you remember that when they were due to launch the magazine issue, she walked in and a comment was made to her that she was noticeably not in pink? She said that she wouldn't be seen dead in pink and she had a fabulous idea for the following issue that she wanted them to start work on immediately. You're right. No-one could ever keep up with that, and it is true! I read enough magazines! The point is that Audrey was above fashion, she didn't follow it. She created her own look that suited her and it just never dated!"

I sighed, feeling depressed. "I don't really want to do it. People would inevitably compare me to my mother and I don't want to be seen to be in competition with her in the style ratings. Even if I did, I wouldn't know where to start. I mean, how did Audrey do it? Where did she start?"

Lisa was eager to inform me. "For the role of her second film, she was sent to a designer in Paris. No-one had heard of her because I don't think her first film had yet been released. He was a young, unknown designer, named, Givenchy, who had been given the chance to do the costumes for the film. When he heard the name, Hepburn, he was thrilled because he was expecting the famous Kathryn Hepburn and thought that making clothes for her would help to make him famous and establish his fashion business. He was really disappointed when he discovered that the Miss Hepburn, was someone called Audrey Hepburn and he felt that the film studio had cheated him out of the prospect of making a name for his work."

I was amazed. "What did he do?"

"He tried to hide his disappointment. He thought that she looked like a fragile animal. He thought she was an adorable child with appealing, big brown eyes but had no further interest in her and was basically, dismissive of her."

I was in awe. "So what happened?"

"He told her the truth, that he was really busy getting his collection ready for his next show and did not have the time to spend with her. She pleaded with him and he relented and told her that she was welcome to look around by herself and choose anything that was of interest to her."

"What happened then?" I was hooked on the tale of this Hollywood princess, now.

"She chose several and he was actually impressed by her awareness of her positive and negative attributes and that she had chosen exactly what was right for her. The rest is history! They were both unknown but they made each other. Her look made her probably the most important icon the world has ever known and he established a fashion and beauty empire that is one of the most illustrious names in the business, right up there with Chanel! Companies still use images of Audrey to sell their products and Givenchy devoted the rest of his life to her as a designer and friend.

"Wow! How do you know all this stuff?"

Lisa grinned. "This is my life's work! Do you know what Audrey's mother said to her?"

"What?"

"Something to the effect that for someone with strange looks, who couldn't act, couldn't sing and couldn't dance, she had done rather well."

I was stunned. "But, she's a famous movie star who was particularly known for all of those things! That's awful! How could her mother say that?"

Lisa shook her head, sadly. "Mothers seem to be the root of a lot of hurt that people carry with them. Perhaps it is because they see their children as extensions of themselves and therefore, whatever their children do reflects on them, good or bad! I'm not saying that your mother is like Audrey's and I don't think that Audrey's mother intended to be cruel. I think that mothers say things sometimes, just to push their children to try to get the best out of them. They probably think it is for the child's benefit but in truth, they probably want to be proud and show off about what their child has achieved."

My heart was pounding in my ears. Lisa was making general conversation. She could have no idea how close to the mark she was about my mother. I felt outraged for poor Audrey. "That is so unfair! I would never be like that with my children."

"Wouldn't that be an impossibility, because to be in such a position would require a man?"

"Alright, I may never be a mother, but I'll make sure you never do that to Annie!"

"Oh, I won't. We live in an enlightened age of positive psychology. We're breaking the mould that our forebears set, although there are still some archaics around. Reward and encouragement are the standard nowadays. Positive thinking! If you tell children they are thick and stupid, which was the reverse psychology our parent's and previous generations used to get us to try harder, and constantly compare them, unfavourably, to others, they will actually believe that they are no-hopers. Encourage children with positive thinking and they will blossom."

I was amazed by her knowledge. "And does it work?"

"Absolutely! Critical parents are totally on the wrong track. They feel that by telling children everything they feel is wrong with them, that the children will transform into what they want them to be. Instead, what happens is that the children feel that they are a constant disappointment to their parents and feel unworthy, or, if they have an in-built strength of character, they feel that their parents should love them for who they are, not who they want them to be. Ugh! They've had it their way for long enough! We have to right the wrongs of the past!"

This felt like a body blow to my stomach and I gasped in astonishment.

"How do you know all this parent psychology stuff?"

Lisa beamed. "We learn it at my parent and toddler group. Negative psychology is a myth that never worked. The problem was that people thought that being a parent was a job description that meant they had to be critical of their children in order to make them more successful than they were themselves and it was an adoptive behavioural role they immediately fell into. Parents should support their children, rather than always trying to find fault with them, but if you try to explain that to a parent who is ingrained into that role, do you know what their usual response is?"

I was intrigued. "Tell me."

"They will say that they are not always wrong and that you can't take any criticism. How are you supposed to argue with that? It leaves you floored and you can't win! Ugh! It's like Harrison Ford in the Indiana Jones series. He's your ultimate heart throb, dare devil hero who always gets the treasure and always gets the girl, right?"

I frowned with confusion. "Yes."

"Don't you remember, in the last episode, Sean Connery is in it as his dad, and he calls him Junior and treats him like a useless child. It just shows you that no matter how successful you are, critical parents who undervalue you can do damage."

"What about those parents who don't make any effort to do anything for their children?"

"They are not supporting and encouraging them either so they are equally to blame and don't form any bond at all with their child. If parents were able to have a good relationship with their children, then when the children grow up they can have a good relationship with their parents and we would all be happy. At least Elizabeth Bennet broke the mould with her mother."

Another body blow! "What do you mean?" I asked, faintly. My legs were definitely feeling weak now.

"Elizabeth Bennet, in Pride and Prejudice!" She was looking at me, oddly. "Why, who did you think I meant?"

I took a deep breath and then explained. "My mother!" It was Lisa's turn to look puzzled. "The Duchess Elizabeth... and... Alfred Bennett!"

Enlightenment dawned on Lisa's face. "Oh, I see. So, you think she was like the original Elizabeth Bennet?"

"No way! She is the exact opposite. In fact, she is more like the archetypal Mrs Bennet. Elizabeth most certainly broke the mould with her mother and was, just like you said, a constant disappointment to her. It was no wonder that Mr Darcy suggested to her that she wouldn't want to live too close to her parents." I frowned in confusion at Lisa. "I thought you didn't read classics!"

"I don't; they're too boring to read but I like watching them on television."

"You should try them some time," I suggested.

"Sounds like school work!" Lisa's face showed her distaste for the idea and she carried on with her argument. "The difference being that Elizabeth's mother couldn't control her and liked her least because she was her father's favourite, of all the daughters, and her father only wanted her happiness. He loved Elizabeth and her genteel older sister, but thought the younger ones were as silly and stupid as their mother. Excuse me, but I am not saying that your mother was silly and stupid. Why have you got that funny look on your face? I know you don't like your mother but she can't have been that bad!"

"There is a great likeness between them. My mother was obsessed with appearances and must be still if she is ranked as a world icon!" I said, scathingly.

"But Mrs Bennet's obsession with appearances was only matched by her lack of tact, and I'm sure your mother isn't like that."

I thought back to the first time Richard had come into this kitchen for lunch, and my mother's behaviour towards me. "Oh, she is," I said quietly. "Anyway, she in no way compares to the greatest heroine, Elizabeth Bennet, who was intelligent, witty and very sensible."

"But the basis of the story," Lisa argued, "is that Elizabeth and Mr Darcy cannot be together until they overcome their pride and prejudices against each other."

I thought of Richard's favourite classic, 'North and South,' by Elizabeth Gaskell, which Richard had described as 'Pride and Prejudice' with a social conscience. He had felt that Margaret Hale was a greater heroine because she had fought for social justice. "The same was true of Miss Hale and Mr Thornton," I said, quietly.

"Pardon?" Lisa was staring at me.

I shook my head and held up my flour-covered hands. "Never mind. Okay, you win that one!"

Lisa grinned. "I only won because of your prejudice against your mother."

I pinned her with a look. "My mother deserves it, so what is your point?"

Lisa was studying me. "All you have to do is be yourself."

We stared at each other. "Right now, I don't even know who I am!" I said, bleakly.

Lisa smiled. "Well, that sounds like a good start. You are open to the possibilities. Life starts now!"

"Auntie Joy!"

I looked down to see Annie's flour-smeared face and appealing, big brown eyes staring up at me.

"I've finished, Auntie Joy."

I pulled myself together, quickly. "Wow, so you have! Well done, Annie. Let's get those into the oven, shall we? Do you think I'd better check to see if the last ones are ready?"

Annie nodded very seriously. I beamed at her. I couldn't help it. She really was just so adorable, but inside, my stomach was in knots and my chest felt so tight that breathing actually hurt.

I took the tray out of the Aga oven and replaced it with another. I turned to Annie. "I know what Annie would like for lunch! Would you like some pizza? Shall we make a pizza?"

This required more flour and more water, which made more mess on the kitchen table and, by the state of Annie, I could only guess at what a mess I looked.

We were deep into our kneading when there was a knock on the door and Richard walked in, then closed the door behind him. He stood there and surveyed the happy domestic devastation.

I almost yelped with shock. "You're..." I looked up at the kitchen clock.

"On time," he said with obvious amusement. "Bon matin."

I had been so lost in my conversation with Lisa and having fun with Annie, that I had completely lost track of time. I seemed to be doing that a lot, now.

"We're making pizza for lunch," I said, lamely.

"It looks like you are lunch! Very tasty!" He winked at me.

My breath caught in my throat. He remembered our pun and it threw me completely off balance.

I attempted to recover and tried to deflect his attention. "Umm you...er... met Lisa, yesterday."

Lisa glowed. She seemed to take a deep breath. "Hello, I have my voice, today. Sorry about yesterday, it was a bit of a.. er... shock to see you."

Richard's eyes held mine. "I can imagine," he said, meaningfully. He turned his attention back to Lisa and walked towards her. She rose from her chair and Richard visibly flinched at the sight of her. "Mon Dieu, I... think we could see you in the dark!"

Lisa looked down at her neon trousers and then apologetically up at Richard as he approached her. "Sorry. I think fashion should be fun. I just wanted to be cheerful on a dull, spring morning."

Richard took Lisa's hand and kissed it in his wonderfully theatrical fashion and smiled at her. "Enchanté, Lisa. You would brighten any man's day!"

Lisa gasped, obviously thrilled with her first, proper introduction with the man of her dreams who, until yesterday, had only been a picture in her magazines. She was still clearly trying to come to terms with seeing him in the flesh. "I'm delighted to meet you," she said, sweetly.

Richard turned, "And this is Annie?"

"That's right," I confirmed. "Annie is my helper and she does some very important jobs, don't you, darling?" I looked down at Annie and she beamed up at me. I was glad of her distraction because I felt uncomfortable seeing Richard again. I glanced back at him. "We're going to have pizza for lunch soon. Would you like some?"

"Mmm. That sounds good. May I have one of these first?" He looked at the spread of baking on the cooling trays on the kitchen work surface, which were giving off a wonderful aroma.

"Help yourself," I offered.

He took a bite of a chocolate chip muffin and cupped his other hand underneath to save the crumbs. "Warm and delicious. You're a wonderful cook! Just like your mother." His eyes held mine as he watched for my reaction.

I jolted and tried to keep a straight face. "I presume you will be wanting to visit the castle, this afternoon." I was looking into his blue eyes and I could hardly breathe. He looked very handsome, in a dark blue jumper and jeans. His white shirt was in stark contrast to the jumper and his tanned skin.

"Are you ready to come with me?" he asked, softly.

I looked down at the mess I was obviously in. "I'll need to freshen and change."

Lisa was looking from one to the other of us, as though she was trying to work out what the underlying currents were that seemed to be darting across the room between us.

"Is your father here today?"

"Yes," I croaked. "He's in his study."

"Why don't you go and change and I would like to speak with your father. Is that okay?"

I nodded.

"Would you like some coffee, Richard?" Lisa asked.

Richard took a deep breath of the wonderful aroma and glanced at the coffee machine. "Real coffee! Oui, s'il te plaît. French people love coffee but you don't normally have the same standard in English homes."

"You don't normally get coffee machines in English homes," Lisa commented as she glanced meaningfully at me. "Espresso or cappuccino?"

"Espresso... please."

"I'm not the only person to have a coffee machine in my kitchen," I said, defensively. "Coffee machine sales are now greater than deep fat fryers."

"Yes, but they're not Gaggia, ultimate Italian engineering, normally supplied to the best coffee bars," Lisa retorted.

Richard smiled as he seemed to enjoy the sparring between me and Lisa. "Merci," he said as Lisa handed him a steaming cup-full. He breathed in the aroma and took a sip. "Exquis. You are a talented barista, Lisa."

Lisa watched him, thoughtfully and then briefly looked at me, again. "My boss has high standards and buys only the best equipment. Shall I bring some pizza into the study for you both while Joy is upstairs?" Lisa was clearly intrigued by the glances between Richard and me.

Richard gave Lisa a smile which made her blush to her hairline. "Wonderful." He looked at me, again. "A bientôt." He walked down the passageway towards my father's study.

I was shaking and sat down, heavily. My legs felt very weak. I really didn't see how I was going to go through with this.

Lisa's eyes were fixed on me. "What… is going on?"

I looked at Annie instead of Lisa. "Nothing," I said with forced brightness. "Come on, Annie, let's get this pizza in the oven."

Annie accompanied me outside to pick some fresh herbs and then we went back into the kitchen and finished making the pizzas. Annie's was just tomato, cheese and ham. I used the blender and did a simple recipe that I had learned from one of the famous television chefs. He makes a puree out of sun dried tomatoes and tops it with some mozzarella and fresh basil. When it is cooking, the juices of the tomato mixture just seep into the pizza base and it is absolutely divine, so I knew that Richard wouldn't be disappointed when he tried it. I mentally checked myself. You are not in competition with your mother!

I quickly ate a piece of pizza and went upstairs, still savouring the flavour. Once you have made your own pizza, there is no way you can ever eat a bought pizza again. It tastes like cardboard in comparison. It was the same with my baking. If Lisa and I are in Norwich and have a coffee, I have a complete aversion to cakes unless they are genuinely home-baked.

I went back into the kitchen wearing yet another pair of my favourite summer khaki shorts but I had put on a men's white shirt and a navy fleece because, as Lisa had said, it was a bit dull today. My trainers were suitable for exploring the castle.

"What on earth is taking them so long?" Lisa asked. "They have been talking for ages! They were deep in conversation when I took the pizza in to them. Your father clearly seems to like Richard."

"Richard is very much in admiration of my father and is very fond of him. When Richard spent time here, we would often help Dad in the workshop. Richard liked helping to restore the furniture."

"It was fun!" Richard spoke as he walked in to the kitchen, carrying two empty plates which he put in the sink.

I jolted and my heart missed a beat.

He looked at me with a raised eyebrow. "No dress?"

I stared at him, my mouth gaping.

"She doesn't possess one," Lisa intervened, with obvious enjoyment.

I shot her a murderous look.

"Vraiment?" Richard's eyes locked onto mine and he seemed amused. "Vous venez?"

I nodded and put my hand in my pocket, feeling the large keys pushed deep down there. I had a box of matches in my other pocket. We wouldn't be needing a torch, today. I licked my suddenly dry lips. I was absolutely quaking with trepidation.

"Viens avec moi" He turned politely to Lisa. "Au revoir, Lisa."

"Later, Richard." Lisa was obviously still trying to get used to the idea that he was here, in front of her.

Richard opened the kitchen door and held it for me, then closed it behind me. He took my hand and led me onto the lawn. He turned to me, his eyes the same vivid blue that I remembered from my dreams.

"Stop fidgeting," he commented as he frowned at me. "Qu'y a-t-il? You seem to be nervous."

"I'm not," I lied, trying to control my shaking. I ran a hand distractedly through my hair. "I'm fine!"

He was studying me, intently. "You don't look fine, you look uncomfortable and you are fidgeting. What is wrong?"

"Rien," I lied again, trying to control the panic that was rising in me. "It's… been a long time, c'est tout!"

He was looking at me, keenly, obviously trying to work out what was going on in my head. He squeezed my hand, tightly. "Shall we, for old time's sake?" He looked towards the shrubbery.

My throat felt really dry and I was dreading this. He frowned and led me towards the shrubbery. I panicked. "What if someone see us?"

"It doesn't matter now, and Lisa obviously has," he commented.

I looked towards the kitchen window and saw Lisa standing there with a comical look of bewilderment as Richard led me into the depths of the shrubbery.

"The path seems clearer. Have you trimmed it?"

I didn't answer. I couldn't. We walked through the path that was hidden from the garden but now neatly trimmed, like a secret maze through the overgrown shrubs. He held my hand and led me. He was looking at me, curiously.

When we got to the gate, he said, "Puis-je?"

I took the keys out of my pocket and gave them to him. The keys were in good condition. They fitted in to the well-oiled lock and turned perfectly. Richard didn't need to put his shoulder against the big, heavy door. The hinges were oiled and the door opened easily and fully, because the ground on the other side was neatly trimmed.

Richard raised an eyebrow at me and I looked down at the ground. We didn't say a word. The path ahead was obvious. It was neatly trimmed and easy to follow. I was aware of the intensity of his eyes, but I couldn't look at him. He took my hand very firmly and silently led me until we were close to the edge of the clearing. Only then did he have to push the bushes back which hid the path from the other side.

He turned to me. "Do you come here, often?"

I shrugged, trying desperately to appear casual, but I couldn't look at him. This was just awful! "Sometimes," I lied. I looked up then, to see him drinking in the view before him. It must be a pretty amazing feeling for him to achieve his lifetime's ambition of owning this. I looked at the castle. The sun had just broken through a small gap in the clouds and the castle was briefly bathing in sunshine.

Richard's eyes locked onto mine and he studied my face, then, without another word, we walked towards the castle. I really felt uncomfortable, now. I felt like a guilty child who had been caught out.

We walked up the slope to the castle gate and the smaller door beside it. Richard used the other key and the same thing happened. The lock and hinges were well-oiled and the door opened, perfectly. We crossed the drawbridge and it was the same with the next door. I kept my eyes down as we walked into the overgrown garden of the central courtyard.

Richard turned to me. "Do you want to tell me what has been going on?" I shook my head. "Has someone else been here or is this you?" he asked, quietly.

I scuffed the rough ground with the toe of my trainer and took a deep breath. "Okay, guilty. I wanted to protect your inheritance, so I came here to keep an eye on things."

"How often?"

I chewed on my lip. "Most days." I felt like a trespasser. I had escaped here to relive my time with Richard, over and over again, but I couldn't let him know that. I had only been reliving a distant dream. I hadn't expected this moment to ever become a reality.

"Did you pray in the chapel?"

My stomach turned over and I couldn't speak. I nodded.

"Shall we pray in the chapel now, to give thanks for this moment?"

My breath caught in my throat and I was unable to speak. He walked towards the chapel door and I reluctantly followed him.

Richard turned the huge, heavy oak door and then opened its twin to let light into the chapel. He walked in, his footsteps echoing on the flagstone floor, and then he turned around, his eyes firmly fixed on me. "This is just a guess but, do you have any matches on you?"

I swallowed hard and dug deep into my pocket for the box of matches and handed them to him. Silently, he went around the chapel, lighting the huge, relatively fresh candles until the entire chapel was fully illuminated. He surveyed the immaculately clean pews and floor and the shining gold of the candlesticks and cross. The polished silver of the large bowl and the painted, carved wood of the figures. Mary and Jesus were dust-free and Mary smiled down benevolently on the entire scene, but it was the walls that drew Richard's attention. The pure gold lettering glistened in the flickering candle light. The proverbs which covered the walls were immaculate, not faded as they had been when he had last seen them.

"You've kept the faith," he said, softly. He shook his head in amazement, his eyes scanning the walls. "How long did this take you?"

I cringed with embarrassment. "Most days for ten years," I admitted, quietly.

I looked up and saw that there were tears welling in his eyes. He bit his lip. "Come here."

He opened his arms and I walked into them. I was really shaking now. He pulled me close to him and hugged me, tightly. I was drowning in the delight and despair of breathing in his wonderful smell and I could feel the pounding of his heart against mine because he held me so close. This was obviously an emotional moment for him. For most of his life he had dreamed of standing in this castle as the proud owner.

He suddenly held me back at arms, length, the emotion burning in his eyes, making them seem like incredibly blue oceans. My heart was hammering in my ears. I was sure that he could hear it.

"How often did you pray?" he asked, quietly.

I was drowning in his eyes. I gulped. "Every day," I admitted.

He shook his head and smiled at me, his eyes studying my face. "Then it is you who have done this. Your faith made it happen," he said softly.

He cupped my face in his hands and my heart missed a beat as he kissed my left cheek and then my right cheek and then my forehead. There was a very deep ache inside me and I was struggling to breathe.

His eyes held mine. "I told you that you are my Angel of Joy. Thank you. Bless you. Shall we pray and thank God?"

I nodded and he led me to the altar. We kneeled on two little needle-point cushions which I had found and left there.

Richard crossed himself, in the Catholic way, and I did the same. He looked at me oddly and then turned back to face the altar.

We prayed, Richard holding my hand tightly the whole time. We thanked God for blessing this castle and for restoring it to Richard and his family after more than two hundred years of being in the hands of people who didn't care about it and Richard asked God to close that chapter of history and open a new one for the castle now. Then we silently prayed, each feeling close to God.

I asked God to please, please help me through this ordeal so that I could successfully help him to restore the castle into a wonderful home and manage to survive the emotional trauma it would be for me.

Richard squeezed my hand and turned to me. "I am forever in your debt." His eyes were brimming with excitement. "Shall we explore now?"

I took a deep breath and nodded.

We blew out the candles and walked back outside. The sun had burst through now and it was a lovely sunny day, but still a bit chilly.

I followed Richard and he opened both of the double French glass doors. "Let the light in. Let's open all the doors. Do you remember how we explored on that first day and the shock of finding what is inside?" he asked.

I nodded. I remembered only too well.

"I have dreamed about that so often," he said, softly. He was so excited and looked almost like a boy again. "We had such fun, didn't we? This wonderful play house! Do you suppose that beyond these curtains it is still the same? Did we dream it?"

I shook my head in wonderment. It was impossible to believe that we were really standing here, doing this. I was completely confused by my life now. Which was dream and which was reality? It all seemed to be mixed up.

I touched Richard's arm and he turned to me. "How did you manage to do this? I mean, how did this time capsule manage to survive in secret for so long and then become yours? It's beyond the realms of possibility. This is a fairytale and we must be dreaming, now!"

Richard smiled. "With God, anything is possible. You just have to give it to him and have faith as you did."

"But why didn't anyone come here?" I indicated with my arm and my eyes took in the aged beauty of it.

"The family had no interest in it. I eventually managed to persuade the owner that the feud was just a silly nonsense, to be still continuing something that was more than two hundred years old, and I said that we just ought to put the past to bed. Officially, this place is classed as a historic monument. People have looked at it from the air and from outside and they just thought it was an overgrown castle. Some thought it was a folly. It was just left to pass its days quietly in the middle of a field. Sheep graze here and no-one took any notice of it."

"The family will be livid when they find out what is inside." I grimaced, imagining their anger.

"Tough luck! We didn't know what was inside did we?" Richard winked at me. "I just thought I was buying an empty old castle," he said with affected innocence. "The owner told me that I will have a struggle breaking the locks, because there are no keys." He grinned at me, looking so very boyish. "Shall we open one of the windows with its shutters to let the light flood into the room, just to see what it looks like? It won't be so easy to open them without your can of oil." His eyes were full of amusement.

Richard tied back one of the curtains and I tied back the other and we stood there, surveying the awesome secret that we had first witnessed ten years earlier which now, amazingly, belonged to him.

I shook my head, stunned by what Richard had achieved. "Ce n'est pas possible."

Richard squeezed my hand and whispered, "C'est mon destin, n'est-ce pas?" He turned to me. "It was my destiny to meet you that day."

"A lot of things happened because of that day," I said quietly.

Richard kissed my hand and then frowned. "Do I smell moth balls and lavender?"

"Guilty." I put my other hand up in admission. "I wanted to protect your inheritance as much as possible and it didn't seem that anyone else was going to come here. At least, I prayed that they wouldn't."

He smiled. "Thank you, Angel." He looked around the room and at a set of curtains on the far wall. "Shall we?"

We tied back the gorgeous folds of extravagant material and revealed the glass windows. They were tall and leaded, still of Elizabethan style as they were original and set into the very deep castle walls. They opened towards us and we saw that the heavy, oak shutters had iron fittings with an oak plank holding the two halves firmly together. Richard and I lifted the plank from its slot and the big shutters creaked as we opened them. The sunlight poured in and a breeze licked us and ruffled the edges of the curtains and the pelmet.

We stood, side by side, silently drinking in the view from high up in the walls of the castle. By leaning over the deep window sill, you could look down at the moat, sparkling in the sun and rippling against the castle wall. Beyond the wide moat, the channel led through the sloping green field to the Broad. The view was stunning, with the large expanse of water lapping against woods and fields into the distance.

We opened every set of French doors on each level and then, slowly wandered through room after room in the house, opening drawers and doors.

In one of the elegant bedrooms, Richard turned to me. "You're very quiet."

I shook my head and looked around the room. "I'm lost for words. I think that you and I are both obviously subdued."

His eyes narrowed. "Ça veut dire quoi? Tell me how you feel."

I took a deep breath and tried to put my deep rooted emotions into words. "I believe that when you have been chasing a dream, sometimes the thrill is in the chase and when you get what you want, it is an anti-climax."

He raised an eyebrow. "Is that what you think this is? Why my heart feels so... heavy?"

I shook my head. "No. This is different. When we were children we discovered a fairytale and we wanted to live the dream. We had fun in a giant play house that was a dressing up box, but it didn't belong to us. We were only borrowing it, in secret. Our thoughts and dreams were filled with the ambition of you owning this and now..."

"Quoi? Que veux-tu dire?" he urged, gently.

I looked at the elegant carving on the Louis the Sixteenth bed and its sumptuous bedding, the headboard theatrically higher than the foot and set against the backdrop of the intricately carved and gilded panelling on the walls. The detail of the ornate plaster and spectacular fireplaces, which were in each room, apparently by Robert Adam. The elaborately, painted depiction of heaven on the high ceiling. The stunning, gilt framed, floor to ceiling mirror, adding light and another dimension to the room, and the sunlight catching the gold thread in the dramatic drapery that framed the tall, delicate, glass-panelled double doors, which opened onto the balcony and the central courtyard of the castle.

"Did we dream it?" I asked, softly.

Richard didn't answer. He opened a drawer and took something out. It was his sketch book. He showed it to me and flicked through pages of drawings of me as a child.

I gasped in astonishment. "This is a real-life fairytale, and we're going to have to pinch ourselves to realize that we are not dreaming. You have it. You've achieved it, but the reality of it, this... phenomenal collection, is almost more than we can comprehend. Priceless! It's beyond imagination!"

Richard opened a door in the armoire and took out a dress. He looked at me and I began to laugh. "No, Richard, I am not dressing up today, not even for you, so you can take that sweet, puppy dog look off your face! Besides, they won't even fit me now."

Richard put the dress back and closed the door. "Is it true that you do not possess a dress?"

"I don't need one," I said, defensively. "I don't even have a handbag!"

He laughed. "You've been reading that book."

I rounded on him. "They are obsessed with shoes and handbags, aren't they?"

He shrugged in acquiescence and raised his arms. "Okay, I fail to understand it but most of the young ladies I know do appear to be obsessed with the subject."

Richard opened another drawer and took out a diamond necklace which caught the light and made reflected patterns on the walls and the ceiling. "What shall we do with all this stuff?"

I sneezed, suddenly. The room smelled musty and the dust and the gentle breeze must have affected my nose. ""Je suis désolée," I quickly apologized to him. "I think I need some fresh air."

I walked out on to the balcony and took a few, deep breaths of the cool air. I could still feel the dust, tickling the inside of my nose. The breeze gently brushed my face. It smelled salty, from the sea which was so close. I looked down at the overgrown garden. From here it was easier to see where the paths had been and how it would have looked. An elegant pattern that ladies could wander through, stopping to enjoy the aroma of a rose or some lavender or rosemary. I realized that Richard was now standing beside me.

I sneezed again. "Sorry, I think the breeze must have lifted some dust."

"A little dust won't hurt." His arm indicated back into the bedroom. "Well, what shall we do with all this stuff?"

"You," I corrected him. "It's your stuff."

"We," he said firmly. "I need your help."

I sighed as I looked around. In that moment, I decided to pull myself together. I must give Richard my support and be happy for him to have the castle. I must help him to restore it and then leave him to it. I turned to him. "What do you want to do with all of this? Do you want it to be a museum or do you want to live in it?"

"I want it to be a home," he said quietly, his eyes holding mine, intently. "I want to live in it. It was designed as a home by a man who was in love. It should be lived in because life goes on."

I glanced around at the open doors of the rooms, each holding their wealth of secrets. "Okay. When we discovered it, we opened a time capsule, as it was the moment that the Duchess Annette walked out of it. Now you own it. You're right, it has to be saved and, therefore, every item has to be restored or stored because you want it to be a real home that you can live in. At this moment, it is a collection and feels like a museum. We have to do it, but... at the same time, it seems such a shame to touch it. You were so afraid of the possible dispersal sale of your family's heirlooms. We won't let them be sold, but it just does feel as if they are being dispersed because everything here is about to change. You cannot live in what effectively is a museum."

Richard was thoughtful. "I feel that it should be my home but, at the same time, we never really own these homes. They long outlive us. For our brief lifespan we are mere caretakers. Just a chapter in its long history, that will continue long after we have gone. What do you think that we should do with the collection?"

I chewed on my lip. "I have been thinking about it. This is of tremendous historical importance. I feel that I should contact the V and A, and ask them to send an expert to look at it all, before we move it. I believe that we should take each room, one at a time, empty it, restore the walls, floors, windows and drapery, restore everything that we take out and decide what we want to put back in. Someone once said that when you restore a house, you should do one room at a time, take it slowly, be polite, introduce yourself, and let it introduce itself to you."

"I like the sound of that. It's a very good plan." Richard was obviously considering the prospect.

"We will need an electrician to surreptitiously fit in a wiring system," I continued, my mind well into its thought process now, "and we will have to carefully choose appropriate lighting and electrical fittings. We will obviously need a plumber as well! I think that we need the V and A person to come here before anything is touched and we need to take their advice on correct cleaning methods."

Richard nodded. "Good idea." He leaned on the balustrade and looked down. "Do you think they might want to do an exhibition of it? I've attended all sorts of opening nights of exhibitions at the V and A, even Princess Diana's dresses and the clothing collection of Versace."

I laughed. "The difference between us is that you have attended those evenings. I have only read about them in magazines. I feel positive that the V and A would want to hold an exhibition of items from the castle. I have a feeling that they will suggest it."

Richard grinned. "Then you will get the invitation to attend an opening night at the V and A yourself!"

A light bulb switched on in my head and Richard was obviously puzzled by the change in my expression. "I've just thought of something!" I said excitedly. "Much as I would have loved to go the V and A party, I have a much better idea!"

"Go on," he said, intrigued.

"Norwich is one of the greatest centres for the arts in Europe and the city is dominated by its central castle which has a museum and art gallery. The castle was built by the Normans, more than nine hundred years ago, as a Royal Palace. Norwich is much easier to get around than London and the entire city is like one big arts and cultural centre. It would be perfect to have an exhibition in the castle and I'm sure they would be interested. This is local history which is of national importance." I didn't mention that I would feel more comfortable if I came face to face with my mother on my own territory.

"What an excellent idea. Good thinking, Angel. You should be able to get expert local help and the stuff won't have to travel too far. I think it would be perfect!"

I looked down at the garden layout. "I have been itching to get stuck into that garden and recreate the rose beds and the herb sections, but I daren't touch it, fearing that someone would notice the difference from the air. It's not like the Secret Garden. They didn't have planes then, so they could keep their secret."

Richard followed my gaze. "Now you have the opportunity. The transformation is all down to you."

I turned to him earnestly. "Won't your wife want to participate in creating your home? The home that you will share together?"

Richard's eyes held mine and he smiled. "I am sure that she will trust your judgement and your skill as much as I do."

I flinched and quickly looked down at the garden. It felt like a knife had just stabbed my heart. I took a deep breath. I had to get through this! "But you haven't proposed to her yet?" I said, quietly.

Richard was leaning on his cupped hands, with his elbows on the balustrade, his attention on the garden paths in the courtyard. He shook his head.

I chewed my lip, and then said, "Does she have any idea?"

Richard shook his head again and took a deep breath, still looking down on the courtyard. "She doesn't know. I think she may suspect that she is the one, but I don't want the speculation to spoil my moment, so I have said nothing."

"Richard," I said softly, and he turned to look at me. "Why do you want this house as a home? Your family have numerous homes. You work in London and you travel all over the world. I know that you wanted this house because you wanted to restore it to your family. That was so important to you and it's incredible that you have been able to achieve a life-long ambition, but why do you want to live in it? Why not somewhere else?"

"Family honour," he said and saw the look on my face. "Not for the feud; that is past." He clasped his hands together and rested his chin on them, his eyes focussing on the garden again. "My great-grandfather was able to buy the chateau, in the Loire Valley, and restore it back to my family. It has a very large vineyard. He was renovating the house and creating a good name for the wine, when the Second World War interrupted him. They had to escape and live on the convent estate for a while. At least, my great-grandmother stayed here and her husband went off to fight for the allies to try to save his country."

"More history!" I said in awe.

Richard smiled, his eyes distant. "After the war, they returned to the chateau and my great-grandfather continued the work he had started. Unfortunately, he died when his son, my grandfather, was just a teenager. My grandfather devoted his life to achieving his father's dream. He replanted many thousands of vines and created a wine label that became famous. The wine is considered to be of the very highest standard. He was then disappointed when my father grew up and didn't want to run the wine business."

"What did he want to do?"

"Something for himself. He wasn't sure what, but he felt a burning ambition to achieve some accolade for himself. You see, after Antoine, and Annette going to live on the convent estate, the family had a title but no money. My ancestors gained a little, but nothing significant. What my great-grandfather and grandfather did made a start, but it was actually my father who made the family very wealthy, again."

"How did he do that?" I was fascinated.

"He bought a publishing company before the huge revival in interest in literature. His original investment was small and the business was just ticking over. When the boom happened, my father, having such a good business head, was able to make decisions that put him ahead in the market. He was on the ball and astute enough to take advantage of the right opportunities that came along. He bought out other companies and got the newly popular, really good writers on board and he had some really good marketing strategies. The top writers became so phenomenally successful that they were soon millionaires. That basically means that when the company prints books its almost literally printing money for itself, with its share of the cover price. My father simply kept reinvesting all of that profit so the business is hugely successful and very valuable."

"Wow! That's amazing. He must be a clever man."

"He is." Richard took a deep breath. "And I've been given all that responsibility so I have a lot to live up to, now that my father has retired."

"And the wine business?" I enquired.

"Oh, that's running well for us, too. My father being a good businessman, when his father died, he inherited the vineyard and put in a really good management team, which he used to supervise. That's down to me now, too."

"So it isn't easy, being successful in business," I said, softly.

Richard shook his head. "No, it takes a lot of dedication and a lot of working hours."

"But you always seem to be at parties," I said, before I could stop myself.

Richard looked at me and was obviously amused. "So, you have been following our progress in the press!" He grinned. "Parties are work! That is where we do most of our networking or marketing."

"You realize that you are now a multi-millionaire in your own right because of all this!"

Richard shrugged. "I cannot even contemplate its value, therefore I cannot think of it in terms of value. It is just history, a part of my family that will never be sold. The Inland Revenue will be very keen to talk to me, but I'll have to negotiate something with them. How can I be taxed on a treasure that is beyond value?"

"But why do you want it as a home, when your family have so many other homes?"

"That is exactly right. Those homes belong to my father and your mother. One day, they will be mine when I inherit, but I am twenty-four. I could not continue to stay in the nest. I needed to fly and make my own nest."

I almost choked and looked away from Richard, at the pillars and arches surrounding the courtyard. Anywhere except at him. This was a conversation I was having with Lisa, this morning. I was much too raw. This was much too painful.

"What will you do, now that your father is marrying again?"

My breath caught in my throat and tears stung my eyes. Richard took hold of my shoulders and turned me to face him. "Hey, what are these tears for?" He took a handkerchief out of his pocket and gently dabbed my eyes. "What is it? Are you not happy for your father?"

I took a deep breath and struggled to regain my composure. I forced a smile. "Of course I am happy for my father! It's wonderful news!"

He ran the fingers of his other hand through my hair, caressing and soothing my aching head. "Your father told me that you were completely unaware of his illness and his relationship until yesterday afternoon, and then I turned up, out of the blue, so you must have felt a little shell-shocked."

I certainly had, but I tried to appear natural. "It was a day full of surprises." I tried another forced smile to throw him off the scent.

"Angel, I'm worried about you."

Uh, oh! Alarm bells! "I'm fine," I said breezily. "Why should you be worried about me?"

"Have you ever had a boyfriend?"

Ouch! "Richard!" I gasped. "That's none of your business." His eyes held mine, his brow raised in a questioning manner. "I've been too busy, looking after my father and I have no interest," I said, defensively.

His eyes burned into mine. "From what I have seen in the last couple of days, you have been a replacement wife for your father and have spent the last ten years in devotion to him. You keep an immaculately wonderful home, and you are a wonderful cook. You work for him in the business. You also seem to be a stand-in mother, with a perfect nursery for a little girl you obviously adore as though she were your own child. On top of that, you have come here every day and made this possible for me with your devotion and your faith."

Ouch, ouch, ouch! It was hurting to breathe again. I tried to hold his gaze. "Your point being?"

"Where is your life? Where is your happiness?"

Bulls-eye! I gasped as I felt the now familiar body blow to my stomach. I struggled to breathe. "My happiness is in giving pleasure to others. That's my name, Joy! Jesus-Others-Yourself."

Richard looked very serious and my heart missed a beat. "When the chicks are ready to leave the nest, if they don't go of their own accord, the parents push them out and they die or fly. Of course, they fly and they learn to soar and have a life of their own. But they don't know that when they have that first leap out of the nest. They don't know what they are capable of and, therefore, don't know what they really want to do with their life."

I gasped and pulled away from him. I began to walk along the balcony towards one of the towers. "Enough!" This was too much to bear! "I need some more fresh air."

Richard accompanied me. We walked up the spiral stone steps in the tower. At the top, I opened the heavy oak door and stepped out onto the ramparts. Being so high up there, I immediately felt the blast from the sea breeze and welcomed its invigorating force and freshness. We walked around the ramparts in silence. I trailed my hands along the stone wall, feeling its roughness with my fingertips. The granules in it sparkled in the sunlight, like grains of sand.

I stopped and drank in the view. The wind was blasting my hair out in a fan behind me, brushing through it, like Richard's fingers had. Beyond the wide moat below, beyond the parkland and the woods we walked through to get here, over the top of the trees, I could see the sea and its distant horizon. I couldn't see the sand dunes, because the trees were higher, but I had the most glorious sight of the sea beyond. In the opposite direction, the Broad stretched for as far as I could see, into distant trees. This was a spectacular location and I felt privileged to be standing there. I let the wind almost force its way through me, dispelling my tumultuous emotions. Richard was beside me, taking in the view as well.

"Can we please just talk about the job?" I kept my eyes on the distant horizon of the North Sea. This was the land of Queen Boudicca – the land of plenty! The invaders had come over that horizon many times in the past and landed here. The Vikings, from Denmark, the Angles and also the Saxons, both from Germany, the Romans, the Normans, from France. Norfolk and Kent had been exposed, their first landings, and had borne the brunt of the horrifyingly cruel invaders almost every time and now Richard had landed and taken back what was his.

"Okay! Tell me your plans for the job. How will you do it? Who will help you?"

I took a deep breath. This was safe territory. "Lisa came up with the idea of getting the local labour force to do the work. We have thirty young people who live throughout the year on our caravan site. Obviously, tourists come in season, but my father and I let this group live there all the time."

Richard was curious. "Why would they do that?"

I closed my eyes, relishing in the wind, blasting me. We were having to speak loudly because of it. "Lisa and her husband are young. They have Annie and they couldn't afford to buy a house to set up home. It was going to be difficult for them to live with either set of parents and there was a bit of family friction, anyway, because of Annie arriving when they were so young, so we offered for them to live on the caravan site and then discovered that there were quite a few young couples in a similar situation and they soon made their own community. The girls help out with seasonal work for us and the boys are mostly apprentices to builders."

"I have noticed that your business seems to have expanded in the last ten years. When I knew you, you only had the antiques shop. What happened to change that?"

I smiled then and looked at him. I was starting to feel better. "The tourists came. They liked our shop and, obviously, we are quite a bit out of the way, so when they asked if there was anywhere local to have a cup of tea, I would make one for them and give them some cakes and biscuits. Suddenly, it seemed like a good idea to convert the barn into a tea room. People also started to ask where they could stay. Some had caravans and we let them use our fields and others, as we had empty rooms in the house, we let them stay overnight. Suddenly, we found that we had a caravan site and a bed and breakfast business. Lisa laughs at me. She says I'm like Cinderella, up in the attic, but I like my room up there. It made a nice-sized en-suite for me and, apart from Dad's room and Annie's nursery, the rest of the bedrooms were then free for the tourists. It's been fun!" I realised I was getting onto dangerous territory again, so I steered the conversation back to the labour force. "Lisa says that the group are really keen to do the work on the project here, so I will have plenty of willing hands. It will be perfect actually because, apart from the plumber and the electrician, the rest is mostly labour."

Richard's smile was warm and affectionate as he looked at me. "I'm sure you will adapt easily into the role of supervising everything here. I will set up an account for you so that you will have access to any funds that you need for the work. You can pay for any labour directly out of that."

I nodded. "Thank you." I deliberately focussed on the prospective job. "I have some restoration knowledge that I have learned from Dad and the apprentices actually know their jobs quite well, it seems. I will also need to do some research and have some specialist advice, but I think we'll manage."

"There is a huge amount of work to do," he commented as he walked over to the wall behind us that looked down to the courtyard from such a high level.

I joined him, feeling comfortable again.

"What is your plan of action?"

I breathed easily and relaxed. Apart from the emotional thing with Richard, I was looking forward to the actual task ahead. "I think the castle museum people should see it first, before we do anything. They will probably want to take pictures. This is quite a discovery!"

"I imagine, if they exhibit it they will call it the Discovery of the Century!" Richard commented.

I smiled at him. "They probably will. I think they will find it as over-whelming as we do. The labour force will come in handy because there will be a lot of packing and every item will need to be catalogued, researched and identified."

Richard was intrigued. "If they do that, then they should identify the date that the Duchess Annette walked out of here, because there would be nothing beyond that date."

"You're right!" It suddenly hit me, too. "It will be interesting to find that out! The nearest discovery in recent years was a house in the north of England. The last in line of the family died and the house was put up for sale. When the estate agents went in there, they were stunned. The family had somehow continued to live an Edwardian lifestyle. Their home had remained unchanged over the years and they were literally living in what effectively was a museum."

"I dread to ask," Richard ventured, "but what happened to the house and contents?"

"It was horribly sad. The house was stripped and sold. All contents went in a massive dispersal sale. They had a marquee arrangement in the garden and the sale took several days."

Richard shuddered with revulsion. "That is what would have happened here."

"But it didn't!" I wanted to lift his mood and turned to him, mischievously. "You do realise, Monsieur de Bowes-Lyon, that you are now King of the Castle! Lord of all you survey."

He grinned. "That's true."

I felt a little stab in my heart, again, and tried to concentrate on my subject. "There certainly is a lot of work to be done!"

"Do you think you can do it by the thirty-first of October?"

"Quoi?" I almost yelped with shock. I looked at him in disbelief. "Que veux-tu dire? Why the thirty-first of October? You can't be serious!" I waited with an agitated breathing for his reply. He must be joking!

"Do you think it is not possible by then?"

I struggled for breath. "I... I suppose it could be. Are you really serious?"

"I want to be settled in before Christmas. That's what everyone says when they buy a house, isn't it?"

I gasped. "Yes... but this isn't just a normal house. Why... the thirty-first of October?"

"Ton anniversaire!"

I looked at him in horror. "And?"

He grinned. "So, I thought it would be a perfect opportunity to have a three-fold celebration. A big party!"

I was quaking and leaned heavily onto the rampart for support. "Three-fold?"

"Oui! C'est parfait." He seemed really excited at the prospect. "We could have a party to celebrate your twenty-first, a house-warming and I can announce my intended engagement."

My chest suddenly convulsed so tightly that I could hardly breathe. It felt like a knife was stabbing me and I felt faint, suddenly. I tried to concentrate on my breathing. It was excruciatingly painful. I felt like someone who has to focus on their breathing as they try to recover after they have had a severe body blow.

Richard looked worried. "Do you think it is too much to ask?"

Yes, I jolly well do! I thought, but my sensitivities were nothing to do with him. He had a new home to look forward to and a prospective engagement! I fought to get the words out. "It's a bit of a shock, but I suppose that it could be achieved. We'll have to work really hard."

Richard still looked worried. "I'm asking too much, am I not?"

"No," I said with forced lightness. "I can take the challenge. I'm not afraid of hard work, and with more than thirty people on board I promise you shall have your party." I began to walk around the ramparts. "Let's go and assess the work."

As I walked towards the nearest tower, I noticed the overgrown drive that went straight across the parkland from the drawbridge to the gap in the wood. I stopped and pointed it out to Richard. "That was for horses and carriages more that two hundred years ago. You'll never get your Aston along that!"

He laughed as his eyes took in the rough and overgrown gravel. "You're right!"

"I think you should borrow our old Land Rover if you come up here."

"Thank you, I think that would be a good idea!"

He was looking at me now and I turned to look at the stunning view that was in every direction and I thought about the treasure chest beneath our feet. I turned to Richard earnestly. "I would love to have my father see this before it all changes."

Richard smiled. "Why don't I bring him this afternoon? You can stay here and I'll go back and get him."

Richard really was so kind and such a gentleman. I smiled gratefully at him. "Merci."

"You know, I've been thinking…" He frowned.

"What?" I was suddenly nervous, again.

"Well, it's difficult to say this, but…"

My heart was hammering. "Go on," I urged with trepidation.

Richard's eyes held mine, gently. "It seems that you haven't been away from this area that you love so much. I imagine that you don't have a passport."

I was confused. "No, I don't."

"I think that, with your father's impending trip to New York and the… rather, delicate matter of it, you should apply for a passport and keep it with you, just in case you need it. We'll pray that there isn't an emergency but, in such a situation, you cannot entirely rule it out."

My stomach turned over. He was right. Everything hung in the balance at the moment and I felt like I was standing at the edge of a cliff, not knowing what was going to happen next. I summoned a grateful smile. "You're right. I should. Thank you for suggesting it." I turned and walked towards the tower.

We explored the rooms again on our way down. Richard found the cape, hat and sword that he used to play with. He was really pleased. He put them on and they still fit.

"The trousers would be much too small, but these will do!" He laughed and had a few practice thrusts with the sword, as he used to. He was enjoying reverting to his childhood again.

We wandered through room after room and Richard carried his sword, not wanting to be parted from it. There was a ballroom with a marble floor, magnificent crystal chandeliers, floor to ceiling gilt-framed mirrors, ormolu wall lights with multi stems for candles and oval mirrors set into the panelling behind them to maximise the light. It must have been magnificent, with the candlelight illuminating the dancers, sparkling on their jewellery, the crystal, the mirrors, frames and white panelled walls with gilt decoration and stunning painted ceiling.

There was a kitchen with a big inglenook fireplace, bread oven, huge iron range and gigantic tables. There were walk-in cupboards. It was fully stocked with enormous copper pans and shelves of utensils, cutlery and dinner services.

I turned to Richard. "The only other treasure-find I can think of to match this was when they found the Titanic. Even after its catastrophic crash and years at the bottom of the ocean, the explorers were stunned to find the panelled décor so easily visible. They were incredulous to see the furniture, cutlery and dinner services, so much of which had amazingly, remained intact. It was a huge treasure chest at the bottom of the sea!"

Richard's eyes widened in recognition. "You're right. It's exactly the same phenomenal treasure find. All those poor people in the lower decks but, above them, the most lavish lifestyle and the richest people in the world, with all the treasure that they couldn't take with them on the lifeboats, the few, that is, who managed to get to one and survive!"

"The explorers felt that most of what they found should be left, so that it was almost like a museum and a memorial to those who died, but now, the ship is deteriorating so fast that they are going to have to move as much as they can. I mean, just think about what you have here in this castle. There are Sèvres, Limoges and Dresden dinner services, apparently complete! Meissen porcelain. Even Louis the Fifteenth pots pourris bowls. Ming vases and dishes. Medici and Borghese vases. Furniture from Louis the Fifteenth and Sixteenth, George the second and Third, and Chippendale. Let alone the paintings by Rembrandt, Gainsborough, Canaletto and Sir Joshua Reynolds. It's mind boggling!"

Richard laughed. "You've been studying this, haven't you?"

I felt myself blush. "I've had ten years to research it. This is standard stuff in the homes of families like the Rothschilds, Devonshires, Spencers, Marlboroughs, Westminsters and even the Queen. This is the elite in the antiques world. The difference being that the other families have lived with theirs and had to negotiate with the Inland Revenue when an heir inherits. This is a forgotten treasure chest."

We walked along the flagstone floor of the passageway and opened the door in the wall of the dining room with its vast table, panelled and mirrored walls and painted ceiling, similar to the ballroom. It was all so spectacular.

Richard ran his fingers along one of the Chippendale dining chairs. "People in the era of Georgians, Regency and Victorians wanted modern. They wanted to celebrate the latest architectural and furniture designs. Now, we don't want modern of our own age, because we think that their taste was better. Luckily for you and your father, being in the antiques business."

"You're right," I agreed. "After the trouble in France settled down, the latest fashion in England became all things French. I suppose fashion will always have a favourite style but classics do remain."

Richard turned to me. "What style do you think that this should be for a home?"

I laughed. "Yours is a grander home than most but it does need to be comfortable to live in. People like the Westminsters and Devonshires have formal areas but they also have their private areas where they can relax, put their feet up and enjoy a simple supper such as scrambled eggs. They don't want to live like royalty all the time, the Queen included."

He smiled at the thought. "What do you suggest, then?"

I took a deep breath, trying to concentrate on my task, not the handsome heir who stood before me. "Okay! I will admit that I obviously have thought about this in dream time, over the years I have been in this house and I had my vision of how it should be."

"Go on," Richard said, gently.

I felt embarrassed, but this was now my job so I had to explain my theory. "I feel that it should celebrate its French origins. French homes have an air of faded elegance, which are at the same time, grand and homely. Unlike this country, they don't care about faded or chipped paintwork. I feel that a good clean-up exercise and gentle restoration, with a few more comfortable pieces to go with the elegant will make a wonderful home." I blushed again. "I know I'm telling this to a Frenchman, but it's what I've read in magazines and its how the market feels at the moment. People want to live with the old and celebrate aged comfort rather than immaculate condition."

Richard nodded. "You have just described French homes. It's a shame that you haven't ever seen one for yourself."

"I want to show you something," I said quietly.

We walked across the expanse of polished floorboards to the double French doors and Richard followed me along the covered walkway to the next room, which was a typical French salon. It was as spectacular and extravagant as every other room in the house.

I stopped in front of a painting by Gainsborough. It was of a beautiful young woman in a fantasy landscape, as was the tradition, with classical ruins. She appeared to be of a gentle nature, with a simple, unaffected beauty. "The timescales fit. I believe we are looking at the Duchess Annette."

Richard was stunned. He was rooted to the spot. This was the woman who had consumed him with a desire to restore the family with its rightful inheritance. This wronged woman was no longer a figment of his imagination. He was standing, face to face with her. It had been a shock to me too, when I had realised who she was in my secret visits here.

"Elle est vraiment belle," Richard said softly. "Exactly as gentle and sweet as I thought she would be."

"There are more, over here." Richard followed me. "You remember that we ignored all these dominating portraits when we were young and just played?" I paused and watched for his reaction. "I believe that this painting by Gainsborough is of Antoine, when he was a child and there is another of him, when he is a young man."

Richard was now really shocked. "I… I hadn't ever considered that I would come face to face with the man who threw away the family's inheritance." Richard was obviously looking for some hint of self-centred, careless, ignorance in the young man's face.

"The shock is, Richard," I said in a whisper of awe, "he looks so much like you. Take away the time difference, you could be brothers."

Richard shook his head, trying to take in the shock. "I hadn't expected a family resemblance." He aimed the tip of his sword at Antoine's throat, not quite touching, his eyes narrowed as he studied Antoine's.

I led Richard away from the pain of seeing himself in the portrait. "I believe this is another portrait by Sir Joshua Reynolds, of the Duchess Annette with her two young daughters. It was painted before the French revolution and Sir Joshua died in seventeen ninety-two, during the height of it. I believe it was probably before eighteen hundred that she left here."

I studied Annette's face, and her enchanting daughters. There was pride in her expression and the girls appeared to equally adore their mother. They had wonderfully elegant and elaborate costumes to compliment their curls and cherub faces. They appeared to be so happy, but what was really going on behind the Duchess Annette's eyes?

"A quoi tu penses?" Richard prompted, gently.

"What a simple, idyllic life they had, and how very traumatic and tragic, too. I was thinking about the women and what you used to tell me. They obviously had luxuries beyond the imagination of the common man, but they were very sad and lonely. If they were not in London or having house parties, they felt very trapped. The privileged ladies of society didn't actually have any privileges, because they were owned by others. They were no different to prisoners, really. Their marriages were mostly arranged, to improve the bloodlines or finances of a family, and then they were in a life sentence with men who often didn't even like them or have any interest in them, apart from procuring an heir. A woman was unable to deny a man his marital rights and she could be taken by force, whenever her husband felt inclined to do so. As daughters, they belonged to their parents and their parents decided whom they should marry and, once married, they became a possession of the husband, and that was legally so. A man was entitled to beat his wife, smacking her if he felt it was necessary, just as the law today allows the smacking of children, but it is a fine line between that and beating. If the law allows, there will always be people who will take advantage of it, just as the men did in that era. Some were downright cruel. The ladies must have felt so scared sometimes and so trapped, because no one could help them. It's no wonder I suppose that Georgiana rebelled. She entered into marriage thinking that she would have respect and companionship but she soon learned that she had neither."

"I have to right the wrongs of the past," Richard said quietly, as he gazed in awe at the Duchess and her daughters. "It was important to end the feud between our families, regain the house and put history straight."

I was thoughtful. "You can't mend everything."

"I have a compulsion to try."

"Does that include reuniting me with my mother?" I enquired, guessing the answer.

"Yes, I want to repair the damage and bury the hatchet." He noticed my expression and began to laugh. "Not in my head!" He became serious. "Have you still not forgiven me for leaving you or for not running away to come back to you?"

I made a point of studying the painting, rather than look at him. "For a while I didn't, but I was only ten years old. When I was a little older, I realised that a fourteen year old boy is not in control of the decisions when his father chooses to run off with another man's wife. Why are you so insistent that I should reunite with my mother? You should just leave it alone."

"I can't!" He turned me to face him and his eyes burned into mine. "This has to happen, Angel. You cannot keep running away from the past."

I shook my head. "It's not possible to bridge the gap. There is a chasm between us. You live on a different planet! We are literally world's apart. This is your world, with priceless family portraits looking down on you and a dinner party with a fifty foot long table and Sèvres dinner plates."

"Can't you forgive her?"

"She didn't even say goodbye!" This was starting to physically hurt again, but Richard was holding my shoulders and he wouldn't let me go.

"She didn't know how to explain it to her ten year old daughter. She felt that saying goodbye to you would be too awkward and too painful. She left it to your father to explain, once she had gone, and then she expected that she would see you again after that, but you refused ever to see her."

I suddenly felt the anger of the past. "Why should I see her?"

"She still loves you," Richard said, gently.

"Can you forgive Antoine?" I asked fiercely, shaking with emotion.

"No." His eyes were blazing, so close to mine. His mouth was firmly set.

There was anger in both of us now as I stood up to him and I was conscious of being almost as tall as him, our eyes almost level.

"Then why should I forgive my mother and your father?"

"That's different."

I shook my head. "What is so different about your father stealing my father's wife and my mother running away with him for a luxurious lifestyle with a rich man? The sort of lifestyle she might have always dreamed about but dumped my father and took the opportunity when it came her way. Okay, Antoine threw away his inheritance at the gaming table, but what is so different about the affairs that society had then and what my mother and your father did?" I felt really angry now and tears welled up in my eyes.

I pushed myself away from Richard and walked outside into the sunshine. I was shaking. I walked through the overgrown garden and then lay down in the long grass, staring up at the shapes of the clouds as they moved across the blue sky. I took deep breaths to try to calm myself down.

Richard sat beside me. "I'm sorry, Angel. I didn't want to cause you pain."

He reached out and squeezed my hand. I sighed. "I just don't see how the damage can be repaired. We're too far apart!"

Richard was quiet for a while. He lay down next to me and stared up at the clouds as well. We lay in silence.

Eventually, Richard broke the silence. "Did you ever ask your mother and father if they really loved each other?"

"That's hardly the question a child of less than eleven asks," I commented.

"And you have not ever mentioned it to your father, since?"

"I don't discuss her with him," I said firmly. "We were better off without her if she didn't really love us."

"I can absolutely assure you that your mother still loves you very much and is very keen to see you. Can't you consider it?"

After a few minutes of silence, I said, "The Duchess Elizabeth is one of the most talked about women in the world. She is ranked as a legendary icon, married to one of the richest men in the world, with a fabulous lifestyle. I have seen you and your family featured in many magazines. You appear to be on the most wanted list of guests for any party or event. The Duchess is constantly in the society news, but she has never admitted to having a daughter. Can you imagine what the press would do with that story! They are always looking for a juicy story of intrigue and scandal. Think how they would get their teeth into that one! I may not like her and I may not want to forgive her, but that revelation would cause her huge embarrassment. It would be very painful for her and I wouldn't wish to do that to anyone!"

"We can work it out," Richard tried to reassure me.

"Not only my mother, think what it would be like for me and my father, with his illness and impending marriage. Our lives would be under the microscope. The press would descend and camp at the garden gate! It would be horrible!"

Richard sat up and put the sword he had been carrying to his chest, the blade in front of his nose. The sun caught the sharp blade as his eyes held mine. "I swear to protect you, milady," he said, very seriously.

I laughed, shakily. "You can't protect me from everything, Richard!"

He put his sword down on the ground, his eyes still holding mine. "Oh, yes I can," he said, softly.

"Including the beautiful, callous and scheming, Countess de Winter?"

He raised a brow, his eyes gently scolding me. "Your mother isn't that bad!"

He lay beside me, propped up by his elbow. He plucked a piece of long grass and traced my face with it, as he had when we had lain here ten years ago. I was so conscious of the length and breadth of him beside me, so very close. His powerful arms.

"I saw a game show, recently, and it's one of the most awful things I've ever seen."

He frowned. "Pourquoi?"

"Americans have a weird taste in voyeurism for entertainment. The show organisers basically tricked a girl into participating. She was the most perfect girl you could imagine! Beautiful, kind, gentle and so sweet. She was looking for love with the man of her dreams. She was invited to a ranch in the middle of nowhere and thought that she was on some kind of TV blind date. All she knew was that she was to spend some time there, along with fourteen, equally perfect men, and hopefully, one of them would be the man of her dreams that she would fall in love with."

"Doesn't sound too awful to me."

I shook my head. "There was a catch!"

"Uh, oh!"

"She was sitting at the head of the big table, with all of these wonderful men and she was really enjoying, getting to know them. Then, after the meal, one of the production team came in and told her why she was really there. The men had been told the day before, but had been told not to say anything to her."

"What was the catch?"

"If she fell in love with one of the men, they would share one million dollars."

"Wow!" Richard grinned. "That's quite a catch!"

"That wasn't the catch," I said, quietly. "The poor girl was told that she and the man would only share the money if he was a straight guy. If the man she chose to fall in love with was gay, then he would get the entire million dollars for himself."

Richard's eyes narrowed. "What did she do?"

"She was devastated and began to cry as she sat there at the table, looking at all the men. The men didn't know who was gay and who wasn't and she couldn't believe that some of the men there, that she had become friendly with that day, had been lying to her and were out to trick her. I mean, it's just awful, the television company playing with people's emotions like that. It was no longer a simple case of finding love. She had to work out who was trying to use her to get the money and she simply couldn't tell!"

He looked at me, steadily. "What is your point, Angel?"

"Some people are just out for what they can get. They will use people for their own personal gain, and then move on, just as my mother did with my father. That programme showed that you just can't tell who is out to trick you in life."

"That's not the way your mother is," he admonished, gently.

"Richard?"

"Mmm?"

I paused and then said what was in my heart. "How do you know that you will be faithful? So many marriages don't seem to last. How can you be sure that yours will?" He continued to trace my face with the head of the grass and it tickled. It felt like a dream and at any moment, I would wake up again.

"Because, I will only marry for love. Je suis vieux jeu."

My heart missed a beat, but I had to have this conversation with him. It was painful, but I felt the need to know the truth. "Are you very much in love?"

"Oui."

My breath caught in my throat and I swallowed, hard. "So why haven't you proposed?"

"Because I need to be sure that she really loves me and that we are right for each other. It's a big decision to spend a lifetime together. I have to know that she really loves me as much as I love her."

Ouch! Ouch! This was really hurting, but I had to go on! "She's a very lucky girl."

A smile touched the corners of his full and sensual mouth. "Why do you say that?"

"A proposal from a man who is generally considered to be gorgeous and is heir to one of the richest titled families in the world!"

He raised an eyebrow. "I thought that material things were not important to you!"

I almost choked. "I… mean that you are considered a good catch! That's what they generally say, isn't it?"

He laughed, softly, showing a glimpse of his white teeth against his tan. "That's just nonsense. You and I both know that is not what is important in life."

A knife was stabbing in my chest and it really hurt to breathe. ""Are you really intending to have a big party here on the thirty-first of October?"

"Yes. We will have a wonderful celebration of the renaissance of this home and your coming of age."

"A party means a room full of people that I don't know. The only people I know are the nuns and Father David, at the convent school, and Lisa and Gary and the rest of the crowd who are going to help with the restoration of the castle." It is a rather odd feeling to realise that you do not have many friends, but I value the people I do know."

"Then you must invite them!"

"And you still intend to announce your engagement?" He nodded as he watched the grass trace my face. "Can you be certain by then?"

He was quiet and then said, "I'm hopeful."

He suddenly broke out of his thoughts and looked at his watch. He sat up. "Why don't you stay here and relax? I'll go back and get your father and then you can greet him when we arrive."

"Richard."

"Oui?"

He looked down at me. My heart turned over. "Je n'y arriverai pas."

Richard smiled and took my hand in his. "I would like to see your family rift mended. Don't look so worried, Angel. I'll hold your hand and we'll do it together." He glanced around at the castle and then back at me. "Après ce qu'on a vécu… we could not have achieved this if we were not a successful team. You should be part of the family."

He kissed my forehead and then left me lying there with my thoughts. This was going to be so very difficult and I didn't see how I was going to survive until the first of November.

To Grandmother

A bright light all around me,
And a deep happiness filling me.
I laugh, I jump, I sing, I shout for joy.
For this is a joyous place and God is with me.

Calm, still lake of water, all still and like glass.
The sun peeps over the hills, and a brilliant light
Shines over the water to me, laughing for joy.
For this is a joyous place, and God is with me.

Waving green grass, on a hill,
I lie in it and think, looking in to the blue sky.
Joy is all around me, and time flies.
For, Grandmother, this is a joyous place, and God is with me.

Time, here, is like nothing on earth,
And I am soon with my loved ones.
I am happy, free, and clothed in white.
For this is a joyous place and God is with me.

Happy, Forever and Ever, Amen.

Sophie Large – aged twelve.

Chapter Nine

IT TOOK a surprisingly short time for Richard to arrive back with my father. I had decided to wait on the castle ramparts for them. I really needed time to think. The sun was warm and even the sea breeze now had a soothing, mellow warmth. I leaned on the castle wall and looked out to sea. The wind had whipped up the white-tipped waves and some yachts were taking advantage of the weather conditions. Further out, an oil tanker was crossing the horizon. In another direction, I could see some wind turbines and a windmill, new and old features of the Norfolk landscape, further down the coast.

I walked around, drinking in the view in each direction. I loved being here so very much, but I didn't see how I could stay. I couldn't be part of Richard's family, as a sister, and see him marry someone else. I couldn't live as a neighbour to him and his new wife, and – there was a stabbing again in my heart – see him settle down and have a family with little Richards running around.

I couldn't stay at home anyway, as my father was going to marry again and I would be like a cuckoo in the nest. I didn't know where I would go or what would happen to me. I so very desperately needed advice from Sister Ruth. She would be able to tell me what to do, but I was going to have to wait until tomorrow morning.

I walked, lost in thought, trailing my fingers along the top of the rough stone wall. Suddenly, I saw the old Land Rover emerging through the gap in the distant trees and progressing along the rough track.

I waited, watching as it neared. I saw that Richard was driving and my father was in the passenger seat. Richard parked the Land Rover close to the huge gate house and they both got out. Richard put his hand up to acknowledge me and then pointed in my direction and spoke to my father. Dad looked up and waved. I made a huge wave, back. I noticed for the first time, how really frail he looked. He was leaning on one of his carved walking sticks. He had lost a lot of weight and I hadn't even realised, until now. It hit me again, how ill he was and how close I was to possibly losing him.

I ran as fast as I could down the steps of the tower and across the courtyard to the oak door. I opened it as they were crossing the draw-bridge. I hurtled across the distance between us and threw myself into my father's arms. Unfortunately, I was such a missile that I almost knocked him over, forgetting again how frail he was. There were tears in my eyes.

"Hey, hey. Steady there," Dad said, as he recovered from being slightly winded. He is one of few men who are taller than me and I buried my face in his neck, tears wetting one of his checked shirts for the second time in two days. I breathed in his comforting smell and realised I was shaking. His arms gently enfolded me and I held on tightly, needing the security of feeling like a child in his comforting warmth.

"I'm not going yet you know," Dad said softly against my hair. "Not until tomorrow morning."

I stepped back and looked at him in horror. "Tomorrow?" I gasped. "You're going so soon?"

His hands gently stroked my arms. "The sooner the better. I have to go, Precious."

I gulped and tried to bite back the tears. "Yes… yes, you must, but… how is it happening so fast?"

Dad smiled and turned to Richard. Richard was looking at me with concern and affection.

"Richard made a few calls and it is all arranged. The sooner I get to the hospital, the sooner I can start the course of treatment and, hopefully, get better."

There were tears brimming in his eyes too, and I realised how fright-ening the experience must be for him. He was leaving and didn't know if he would ever return. This was just one of the traumatic events that were going on in my life at the moment.

"Richard has arranged for us to be collected and Ruby and I will fly out from Norwich airport, tomorrow morning."

Tomorrow morning! I thought faintly. That would mean having to postpone seeing Sister Ruth yet again!

I frowned in confusion at my father. "Flights don't go direct from Norwich to New York. You will have to change."

My father actually grinned and seemed excited. "Not if you are going by private jet. Just imagine! Ruby and I will be travelling in the luxury of a private jet and then, when we get to New York, Richard has very kindly arranged for Ruby to stay in their New York penthouse. What about that? Ruby living like royalty and Richard has arranged transport so that she can come and visit me every day!"

I stared open-mouthed at Richard. I was lost for words. Stunned! Yet again, I was going to be indebted to him for the care of my father and also his fiancée, and it would be churlish of me to be resentful, but I so very much didn't want to be any further in his debt or subject to his generosity and kindness. I couldn't say that I didn't want him to go to so much trouble for us, because it was obviously the best care that my father and Ruby could have.

I struggled to find the appropriate words. "Richard, that's very generous of you."

Richard smiled. He was so kind and such a good person. "My pleasure. It was really no trouble to make a few phone calls and have the jet waiting at Norwich tomorrow morning. The hospital will be waiting to admit your father immediately on his arrival and it will be much better for Ruby to stay in a fully-staffed apartment and have transport at her disposal, rather than stay in a hotel and be reliant upon taxis. I'm sure the whole experience will be emotionally exhausting for her, as well as your father, so they need the best support they can get." He read my worried expression. "The apartment will be empty for a few months anyway, except when I have to pop to New York on business, so it really is no trouble and it is the best way of doing this."

I shook my head at him in disbelief. "Tu es étonnante!" I shyly kissed him on the cheek and caught a whiff of his wonderful aroma. "Merci beaucoup."

"Now," said Dad, "are you two going to show me this secret you've been keeping for ten years?"

I looked up at Dad. "I'm sorry I couldn't tell you."

He smiled and squeezed my hand. "It's alright. Richard has explained. It was a secret that couldn't be told because it didn't belong to you until now." He looked at Richard. "Well done." He turned back to me and linked his arm with mine. Now, lead the way. I want to see this treasure chest."

I squeezed Dad's arm and Richard followed us as we crossed the drawbridge and I couldn't help feeling that my life was still crumbling to the ground, bit by bit.

Richard pushed back the oak door and I led Dad into the courtyard. Dad looked at me, with a fondness in his eyes that I love him for.

"I suppose you can't wait to get stuck into that garden?"

I smiled because he had so easily read my mind. "That is going to be a herb and rose garden. There will be quite a transformation by the time you come back." I mentally prayed that my father would return to see it.

We walked through open French windows into one of the salons, which is the French equivalent of a drawing room. My father stood on the threshold and gasped in astonishment, in the same manner that Richard and I had ten years before.

He looked at both of us and then his eyes scanned the room again, in disbelief. He shook his head. "You said, treasure chest but this…" He looked at both of us again in turn. "I don't know how you managed to keep this a secret. It's astonishing. I always used to wonder where you two disappeared to, to play, but I didn't imagine this!" He shook his head again. "What a pair you are!" He began to walk around the room and put his hands on the furniture. "I've visited Chatsworth, Blenheim and Waddesdon Manor, to see their collections and, although this is smaller, it is of exactly the same standard. It is truly amazing." He looked at both of us. "What a truly remarkable opportunity you have to restore all these beautiful items!"

"S'il te plaît," Richard said, "feel free to pick up and hold anything you wish to." He glanced at me and then back at my father. "We trust you."

"Have you researched any of this?" Dad asked me.

I nodded. "Quite a lot. The quality is overwhelming. Do you see the portraits?" My father turned and looked at them. "They are by Gainsborough and Sir Joshua Reynolds. The rest of the collection in the house includes Rembrandt, Canaletto and Goya."

Richard and I exchanged glances. My father still seemed lost for words. He walked towards the magnificent Robert Adam fireplace and held the mantle shelf for support.

He lifted a piece of porcelain and looked at it in his hands. "I've been an antiques dealer, practically next door, for fifty years. I didn't believe I would ever hold such a thing in my hands," he said reverently.

"Why?" I asked quietly, watching the awe in which he was exploring this room – and this was only the first room!

The piece he was holding so carefully was of an oriental figure, sitting in a garden arbour. It was very delicate, with a lot of openwork. The man was holding shells, one on his lap and one above his head, and he was admiring the glory of the profusion of flowers.

"The first piece I pick up! It's Meissen and it's priceless, and it's just sitting there on a dusty mantelshelf. What a houseful! What a joy it is to look at something like this. It's almost too much to take in!"

"I know what you mean," Richard said. "Come and see more."

We took my father on a slow exploration of the house. He kept stopping to admire the furniture, pick up a piece of porcelain or delicate glass that was just sitting on a dusty table or sideboard.

In one of the bedrooms, he just kept walking around, touching the furniture in total astonishment, muttering to himself in wonderment.

"I have to say, this is the pinnacle of my career as an admirer of antiques. Just to be able to stand in a room like this and touch this furniture. Do you see that?"

He pointed to a semi-circle satinwood and marquetry commode, its flat side against the panelled wall. It was a piece, obviously by the finest craftsmen who had celebrated their skills in this work of art. It was elaborately inlaid, with lots of panels and ovals with beautiful, painted scenes of mythical figures and landscapes.

"It's George the Third. Beyond price."

He walked over to the French secrétaire. I always loved to think of the Duchess Annette, writing at that ladies' desk. The sloping front was faced with pictorial scenes in an imitation of Chinese lacquer in shades of gilt, black and red. It was glorious.

Dad opened the front to reveal the three sections, perfectly fitted with inlaid drawers and doors and tiny little handles. "You really get a feel for how they lived. You are right, Richard. It's like a time capsule."

"Look at this." Richard indicated for my father to join him and he opened some of the drawers in a chest to show my father the contents.

"It's astonishing!" Dad said, his eyes growing wider with awe as Richard showed him undergarments, clothing and jewellery. "Just forgotten!"

Richard opened the door to an armoire and Dad stood, rooted to the spot in shock. Richard took out some of the fabulous dresses which were hanging there and then replaced them and closed the door. My father was still standing, staring at the armoire.

"What's the matter?" Richard asked.

We all looked at the gold lacquered armoire, with its ormolu galleried, coved frieze and ornate decoration of musical instruments and swagged shells, scrolls and foliage. Some of the relief work had been painted in delicate shades of blue and green.

"It's French, Louis the Sixteenth! May I touch it?" he asked in awe.

Richard glanced at me in gentle amusement and then looked at my father, with obvious fondness. "Bien sur, go ahead."

Dad walked slowly towards it, reached out and traced his fingers over the relief of the elaborately ornate design. "I can die a happy man, now."

I gasped and Dad quickly turned to see my expression of horror. "Sorry, Sweetheart! I didn't mean in that way. I just mean that it is an honour to be able to touch such a work of art." He shook his head in bewilderment. "Among so many works of art! I feel like a child in a sweet shop! I don't know which one I like more, and then you show me something even more wonderful. What a treasure!"

We walked through the rooms slowly, because my father wanted to appreciate everything. In the library he looked around the room, at the walls lined with bookshelves, the pair of George the Second giltwood window seats and the George the Third library staircase with its two flights and half-landing.

He walked towards one wall. "How old do you think these books are?" he asked as his fingers traced along the spines of them.

"Not younger than the year eighteen hundred, I think," I informed him. "I expect there are a lot of first editions there."

Richard winked at me. "The Georgians loved their reading and felt that young ladies should do a lot of it to improve their minds."

"Instead of being obsessed with handbags and shoes," I returned, and he laughed.

Dad threw a curious glance at us and then paused to admire the enormous and elegant mahogany settee. "Is that George the Second?"

I nodded.

"May I ?"

"Of course, as long as you don't mind the dust," I commented.

Dad sat down. Obviously trying to take it all in. "You're a very fortunate man, Richard."

"Oui. Je le sais," Richard said softly. I realised that he was looking with affection at me. "I don't believe it would have been possible without Joy's faith. She has visited here almost every day for the last ten years and it is her devotion that has made the dream come true."

I felt like something had grabbed hold of my stomach and was twisting it into knots. I went and sat at my father's feet and he put his arms around me. I was considering something that Richard had said earlier and it had to be said now, while I had the chance. Dad would be going away tomorrow and there was no guarantee that I would ever see him again. "Dad?"

"Yes, my darling?"

"Did you and Mum love each other?"

My question took Dad completely by surprise.

"I'll leave," Richard said, quickly.

I looked at Richard. "No, stay. That is, if it's alright with you, Dad?" I looked at Dad and he was smiling at me fondly, but also frowning in puzzlement.

"I'm happy for Richard to stay. Why do you ask me that now, after all these years?"

I chewed on my lip, my eyes searching his face. "It is something I have not ever asked you."

Dad was thoughtful for a while, as though I had opened a door and he was now looking at the past. He squeezed my hand. "I loved your mother, very much."

"And did she love you?" I asked in a whisper, not sure that I really wanted to hear the answer.

"I wasn't the greatest love of her life, but she did love me in a different way."

"In what way?"

He smiled, gently, as his eyes became distant. He was looking back through time. "I was a sort of father figure that she needed in her life."

Suddenly, I desperately needed to have answers. Richard was right. I needed to know. "So, why did you marry?"

"She swept me off my feet!" He laughed at the expression of confusion on my face. "She was the dearest little thing. Like a tiny, beautiful, fragile bird. Almost exotic. So delicate but she had the heart of a lion and the dominating, mental strength of an ox, yet with such sweetness. She was so beautiful and she needed me so much. I was just overwhelmed that such a creature could want to be with me. It happened so fast that, before I really knew it, she had taken control of my life and we were married."

"Why were you forty-seven and unmarried when you met Mum?"

"Well, I'd always been rather shy. Not very good with the ladies, if you know what I mean. I had never actually had a girlfriend and I had just become deeply engrossed in the business of antiques and restoration, which I love so much. Time went by and I didn't expect that I would ever have a relationship. I had always been quite keen on Ruby, but I was too shy to ever ask her out and it seems that she felt the same way as me but was too shy to make her feelings known to me. Its just one of those things, I suppose. When Elizabeth came along like a whirlwind and suddenly I was married, it came as a huge shock to Ruby and she never married. It was only after your mother left, when Ruby was so kind and consoled me, that we talked and the past all came out."

"Were you and Mum happy?" I whispered, my heart hammering. It was pounding in my ears so that it seemed the whole room was vibrating.

"I thought so."

"And Mum?" I almost daren't hear the answer.

"I think she was at first. She was like a burst of sunshine and she brightened every day. She had a childlike enthusiasm for everything. She loved helping me to restore the antiques and she loved baking for me and making a wonderful home."

I was so scared of asking the next question, but I had to. "What happened?"

He squeezed my hand and looked at me carefully. "You."

I went rigid with shock. "What do you mean?"

Dad stroked my hand, as though to soothe an injury. "Your mother and I married and she must have become pregnant on the first night. When she became large with carrying you, she couldn't help me with the furniture and she couldn't do much around the house and then she had a difficult labour."

"Why?" I breathed.

He looked at me indulgently. "You were a very large child for such a tiny person to give birth to."

I was stunned. "Did that make her not want you?"

Dad shook his head. "No, it wasn't that. At first, when you were born, your mother couldn't really help me with the antiques because she was looking after you, but she made the home lovely and she adored you. You were like her very own, live doll. She loved dressing you up and playing with you and baking with you. Then things changed."

I was shaking with trepidation. "What changed?" I asked carefully. I glanced over at Richard. He was sitting on one of the window seats, listening quietly.

"Well, little girls love their daddys, don't they? It just seems to be a funny trick of nature that little girls adore their daddys and want to spend time with them and please them." He was still stroking my hand and his expression seemed to be trying to urge me to understand. "It wasn't your fault. You didn't mean anything by it. It's just what little girls do. And you still loved your mother."

"What did I do?" I croaked, not realising that I had done anything to damage my parents' relationship.

"You just wanted to please me and do things for me, that's all. You baked with your mum, but you did it for me, to impress me. You spent time with me, restoring the antiques because you loved to see the transformation and you wanted to help me. You kind of idolized me, in the way that your mum had, and you sort of took her place and she felt left out and redundant."

Tears stung my eyes and I couldn't believe what I was hearing. Had I really caused so much damage to my parents' relationship?

Dad saw my expression and squeezed my hand again in reassurance. "It wasn't your fault. You weren't to know. I didn't realise either. I thought we were all happy and I thought that it was normal, family life. Your mum didn't really let me see how unhappy she was. Then, when Richard came along..." Dad looked up and exchanged glances with Richard, which I couldn't read. "Your mum found a role, caring and baking for Richard's mum and consoling his father. I didn't see what was happening. I was busy with the shop and restoration. You two were busy helping me when you didn't disappear off to play. I just didn't see where it was leading."

I gulped, tears now flowing down my cheeks at the sheer realisation of what I had caused as a child. The damage I had done by simply being born and then growing up to adore my father and take my mother for granted, rebelling against her wanting to treat me like a doll!

My voice came out as a hoarse whisper, now. "Were you devastated when she left?"

Dad's eyes became distant again as he reflected on the past. "At first, but you made such a tremendous effort to make up for her loss and you basically filled the void. You did everything you possibly could to fill my life and my home as a wife would have done. When I thought about it, I realised that your mother had always been too good for me. I did love her and I was happy for her to go on to greater things, to a lifestyle that she was obviously born for. A lifestyle I could not ever have given her. She was wonderful, but she was too wonderful for me and it all made sense when I got together with Ruby. She and I have a very different kind of love. It just took us a very long time to realise it." He took a deep breath and patted my shoulder. "Now come along. Enough about my past. I want to see more of the past in this house!"

Suddenly, Richard was beside me. He too, patted my shoulder in an effort to comfort me, and then we both helped Dad to stand. He was a little unsteady, and we continued working our way through the house until we climbed the stairs and stepped out onto the ramparts.

Dad stood looking down at the moat and the incredible view in every direction. "You know, it's amazing how this treasure chest has remained intact for all these years. Just, forgotten. At Waddesdon Manor, their collection is similar to yours, but larger, in a huge French chateau sitting in the Buckinghamshire countryside. They have collections of dinner services, just like yours, but they have entire rooms full of glass display cases with complete collections. At least, they were. It broke my heart to hear that after I had seen that wonderful collection, thieves had broken in and stolen fabulous pieces."

Richard and I exchanged glances. We were equally horrified.

"How did they get in?" Richard asked.

Dad shook his head. "It's beyond belief how they could have got away with such a crime. Somehow, they had scaled those high walls and got in through a glass section of the roof. I can't remember how much they took, but how could they have carried it? They couldn't have carried entire dinner collections, but they broke the glass cabinets and removed items.

Whatever they took was from priceless collections. That kind of history and collection can never be replaced. The thought of it made me feel sick."

Richard's expression was a picture of alarm. "Right, I will immediately arrange for security to guard the site."

I looked at the peaceful grounds. Life was about to change already. Now there were going to be security patrol guards with dogs.

I noticed Dad. He seemed short of breath. "Are you sure you're alright? Is this too much exertion?"

He shook his head in denial, though he was obviously struggling to regain his breath. "I'm fine, Precious. Don't worry about me. I just needed to see this before I go."

Go where? I thought. Leave here or go to New York and not come back? I trembled with fear. I put my hand in his and he squeezed it, tightly as we stood looking at the view.

Richard put his arm around me and kissed the top of my head. "Don't worry, Angel. Your father will be back to see this, won't you Alfred?"

Dad took some deep breaths of the stimulating air. "I certainly will."

I looked at the distant horizon of the sea as tears stung my eyes. I only hoped they were both right.

About myself

I have nothing interesting to write, but, because I have nothing very interesting to write about, I shall write about myself.

It is hard to describe oneself truthfully, I find, because some truths we do not like to admit. I am not the stereotype teenager. I do not make or maintain many friends easily, being too deep. I like my own company and have a fascination for the 'old way,' (the romantic side) i.e.: candles, dip pens, sealing wax, shells, home cooking, herbal cures, dried flowers and secret passages.

I am one track minded – I get an idea set in my head and cannot change it. I am very disorganised and scatty. I cannot take practical jokes unless in a particularly good mood. I can be very bitchy without meaning to be. I can be very stubborn. I am musical, and can sing very well and act very well. I love reading, getting away from reality.

Sophie Large – aged fifteen.

Chapter Ten

ISA was already in the kitchen, waiting for me, when I walked in. We looked like chalk and cheese. She was wearing a white, mohair jumper and white jeans, which were tucked into fur trimmed, white flat boots. In complete contrast, I was wearing white shorts, a white men's shirt, with a navy men's jumper around my shoulders and flat, tan shoes with no socks.

Lisa looked me up and down. She looked very pretty, wearing lots of make-up, lots of pink lip gloss, and her dark hair was casually worn up, held in place by a huge, silver clip. My waist-length mass of wavy, red hair was just washed, brushed and down and I don't wear any make-up.

Lisa stood, with her hand on her hip, eyebrows raised. "Is that the best that a step-daughter of one of the wealthiest men in the world can do for her first visit to a bar?"

I pulled a face at her. "Don't talk nonsense. This is me."

Lisa grinned. "I'm not sure how much longer you are going to manage to stay looking like you, but come on, let's go and crack open a bottle."

"I'm not drinking," I protested. "We have some serious issues to discuss! I'm only having a Perrier. I need a clear head."

"Sweetie, if anyone else was in your shoes, right now, they'd go out and get blind drunk! I know, I know, don't give me that look. You don't have to get drunk, but you do need at least a glass of wine on your first visit to a bar, even if it takes you all night to sip it. Who knows, you may enjoy the experience and join our community every night. Gary and I take it in turns to baby sit Annie, but we have fun. They're a good crowd. Katie is looking after Annie tonight, so Gary and I can both be there."

I took a deep breath. I was feeling nervous, as anyone would be, doing something for the first time. I knew the group because they lived on our caravan site. The girls did seasonal work for me but I had only had a brief, passing conversation with any of the young men and, although I wouldn't admit it to Lisa, I was actually feeling a bit shy. However, if they were going to work for me, I had to get to know them. "Okay, let's get this over with."

Lisa was enjoying my discomfort. "Don't worry. They won't bite!"

We went outside. The light from the kitchen window was illuminating a large area of the garden. There was a full moon, thankfully, and that illuminated our journey as well. We crossed the garden, climbed and descended the sand dunes, and began to walk towards the twinkling lights of the beach bar. The moon was reflected in a broken circle on the sea as the waves rolled in and lapped gently on the shore. There was a light breeze that lifted my hair as I walked.

Although I have never actually been to the bar at night, I do love to walk on the beach at night, or even just sit there, enjoying the soothing sound of the breaking waves, the moonlight dancing on the momentum of the water and the stars, twinkling above in the vast sky. I love lying on the cool sand and staring up at the staggering spectacle of a clear sky and millions of stars. The more you stare at it, the more you can see. I lifted my head and looked at the sky, enjoying the cool breeze on my face.

I looked at Lisa. She had been quiet and thoughtful so far. I had taken my shoes off the moment I stepped through my garden gate. I revelled in the cool, tingly feeling of the sand on my bare feet.

I looked up at the bar as we neared it. The white lights were strung around its frame. It was like a large wooden shack and had a thatched roof. It had been a large boat house, fronted by huge double doors. Technically, it still belonged to my father, but when Phil had suggested that it would make an ideal bar for the tourist season, my father had helped to convert it and let Phil have the use of it. The building was now fronted by a veranda, so that people could just step off the beach and sit at one of the sets of wooden tables and chairs. It was very casual. It looked idyllic and could honestly be situated on any stunning beach front in the world.

I was feeling nervous again. Lisa had often asked me to come here but I had always said that I was too busy doing other things, like looking after Dad. I also, secretly visited the castle and often went to see Sister Ruth. I didn't talk to Lisa about those parts of my life. Now, I had no excuse and also a reason to be here.

"Well?" Lisa asked. She was looking at me. "Are you going to explain to me why you and your gorgeous step-brother held hands and furtively disappeared into the bushes for hours? I didn't see you come out again and I daren't go near the bushes for fear of what I might see. I didn't see you but, later, Richard suddenly walked into the house and then drove off with your father in the Land Rover. Are you going to try and tell me that you and the handsome Frenchman are not lovers, because if you do, I won't believe you! Are you getting married?"

"We are not lovers, Lisa." My heart missed a beat as I said it. "It was children's stuff that you saw."

"Making babies?"

I laughed. "No! We played together as children and, well, as you know, the castle is next door."

"So?"

"We used to sneak onto the estate to play and there is an old door in the wall that is hidden by the overgrown shrubs. That is all you saw!"

"That's not all I believe went on! You were rolling around in the long grass, weren't you?" Lisa refused to be deterred. "I've seen the way you look at each other. You are completely in love."

Ouch! Ouch! I blushed, glad that Lisa couldn't see me in the darkness. I had been lying in the long grass with Richard, but that was different. "No, Lisa, you've got it wrong. Richard is fond of me and thinks of me as his sister. He wants to reunite me with my mother and mend the rift between me and his family."

"But he sees you as more than a sister," she insisted, like a terrier holding on to a bone.

I shook my head and looked at the beach bar as it loomed in the night. "He wants me as his sister and he's marrying someone else."

Lisa squealed. "When? Is there going to be a big wedding at the castle with lots of famous people? Will you be a bridesmaid if you are his sister?" She was suddenly fired up with interest.

Ouch! I hadn't thought about that! That was another stabbing pain. I took a deep, shuddering breath. "I don't know the details. Look, we're here, already. I'll explain more, later." I suddenly thought of something. "Lisa, there are actually some antiques in the castle and if people are going to help us, they are going to have to be totally trustworthy and reliable. Do you have any doubts about them, because, if you do, I need to know. There must not be any problems in that respect."

Lisa stopped suddenly and raised her hand. "I swear, Joy. I know how important this job is to you and we won't let you down. They are a really good crowd. We will do everything we can to help you."

I smiled and hugged her. "Thank you. This is all just so difficult and I really value your support."

The bar seemed to emanate a welcoming atmosphere. It was starkly lit inside, with a simple, rustic charm. Through the windows, I could see the girls grouped around some tables. There were opened bottles of wine and there was a comforting buzz of chatter and laughter. In the corner was a television with a music video playing.

The young men were on the veranda, sitting at the tables and drinking beer. The dangling string of white lanterns illuminated the group. I could hear them chatting about cars and golf. I was surprised because I expected them to be talking about football, but some were in deep discussion about handicaps, which went right over my head because I totally fail to understand how the handicap system works!

"Hi, guys!" Lisa said as she stepped out of the darkness and into the pool of illumination in front of the bar. I had stopped to put my shoes on. There was a raucous greeting and then silence as I stepped into the light and joined her on the veranda. They were all staring at me and I began to feel uncomfortable.

"Come on, boys. Say, hello. You all know, Joy," Lisa commanded, encouragingly.

It was Gary who spoke first, but, of course, I knew him better than the others. "Hello, Joy."

"Hello, Gary, hello, everyone," I responded with a smile. There was a gush of greeting from the others and then silence, again.

"Come on, Joy, let's get a drink. It looks like this lot aren't capable of conversation at the moment." Lisa opened the door and I followed her in.

"Well, hello," came a loud greeting from behind the bar. It was Phil.

The girls looked up with smiles on their variety of pretty faces. There was a general gabble of, "Hello, Lisa, hello, Joy!"

"Hello!" I responded and smiled at the faces I knew. I felt much more comfortable being with them. Outside was alien territory! I just hadn't mixed with boys, apart from Richard, but he was so very different and now I was going to have to learn because my life seemed to be changing, fast.

"Come and join us!" said Alice, who was a cute blonde. The girls grabbed another couple of chairs and pulled them into their group.

"Thanks," said Lisa. "We just need to buy some drinks first."

"No need," said Phil as he approached us, taking us by surprise. "In honour of you bringing our lovely lady of the land for her first visit, the drinks for you ladies are on me!"

"Thank you!" I smiled. He was smiling at me, most appreciatively. "That's very generous of you."

"My treat for a special occasion," he said.

"Phil has given us these bottles of wine," said Alice, "so we're having a good night. We're glad to have you join us!"

"In your honour," Phil said, rather proudly, "I went out and bought some very special plonk. Its the label of your friend who has bought the castle. Lisa tells us that you are going to have the task of restoring it."

"With a little help," I said tentatively as I glanced at the girls.

"We're definitely up for it," said Louise, a short-haired brunette.

Phil picked up a bottle and showed it to me, holding it carefully, as a wine waiter would. "It is the Lyon de Loire," he said in an exaggerated French accent. "Lisa says that you don't drink much but you may as well get used to the taste if you are going to be mixing with those people. There is red, white and method champagnoise, I think they call it, because they're not allowed to call it champagne now, unless it comes from that region, with the new European rules."

"Come, on," Alice said, eagerly. "Sit down and try some! It's good stuff and it's because of you we're drinking it!"

I glanced gratefully at Phil. "Thank you," I said as I sat down amid the gabble of girls.

Phil positively beamed at me. "My pleasure." He put wine glasses in front of Lisa and me. He was still adopting the manner of a wine waiter, with a linen towel over his arm and he bowed slightly. "White, red or sparkling?"

I began to relax. "Sparkling, please, but just a little if I am to taste test the three varieties."

"You should come here more often and then we might get used to this standard," said Louise.

I sipped the cool, golden liquid. The white and sparkling were in ice buckets of the table. The bubbles fizzed at the back of my throat and went up my nose a little. The first sip twanged the corners of my jaw, like the sharp taste of strawberries when you take the first bite. I took another sip. It wasn't often that I had tried champagne, which was effectively what it was, and this was delicious.

"Well?" Phil was waiting for my verdict.

I smiled, gratefully. "Delicious. Thank you, very much."

Phil beamed again with pleasure and returned to the bar.

"Wow, we are honoured with this service," Lisa commented. "I told you, you should come here often."

"Tell us about the work," said Alice. "Is it going to be difficult?"

I sipped the wine again, enjoying its flavour, and then put it down to concentrate on the conversation. I shook my head. "Not really. You would be like glorified cleaning ladies."

"Like making beds for you in the bed and breakfast," Louise intervened.

I smiled, thinking of the difference between the farmhouse bedrooms and those at the castle. "Sort of, it's just going to be a massive clean-up operation with lots of sorting and packing. There is rather a lot of stuff in there and it's covered in dust. The castle hasn't been lived in for more than two hundred years and it's going to be a major job to turn it into a home by the thirty-first of October. We are going to need all the help we can get."

"Why the thirty-first of October?" Lisa asked, frowning.

"Richard wants it to be completed by then so that he can have a big house-warming party."

"But isn't that your birthday? You'll be twenty-one on that day!"

I felt a churning in my stomach. I sighed. "Yes. Richard wants it to be a celebration for his new home and a coming of age party for me." I looked at the faces which were all staring at me.

"Party?" Lisa asked. "With... famous people, like... movie stars?"

I shrugged. "Probably. And you're all invited."

There was a moment's silence and then almost deafening shrieks and screams of excitement. I had to put my hands over my ears. I noticed that the men were looking through the windows, obviously wondering what on earth was going on. They shrugged, realising it was girlie stuff, and went back to their conversations.

"Is this reliant upon you having the place ready by then?" Lisa's face was a picture of incredulity and excitement, which was mirrored by the others, who were now totally focussed on me.

"Yes. It will be a lot to achieve in a short time."

"Don't care," gushed, Sophie, who was another sweet-faced blonde. "We will work our socks off!"

"What do you need?" Lisa asked.

"Lots and lots of labour. There is some specialist cleaning, which I will have to research, and I'm going to get some expert advice. Every room will need to be emptied and then I have to decide what goes back and what goes into storage. Actually, there is some stuff there that the castle museum in Norwich may want to exhibit." I didn't elaborate on this point. I didn't want to explain that yet. "Obviously two hundred years ago, they didn't have running water, flushable toilets, electricity or telephones, so I'm going to need the necessary experts there. The drive was only used for horses and carriages and now it's way overgrown and in need of repair. There'll be some masonry and carpentry work as well. What do you think?" I asked, worriedly.

"I'm up for it," Lisa yelled, and the others did likewise.

"Me, too! Me, too!"

"Sophie's dad is an electrician, Louise's dad contracts for a road works company and Amy's dad is a plumber."

"We can do it!" Alice yelled. "Between us, we can do it!"

I chewed on my lip. "I still have to keep the business going at the same time. The shops, the campsite, the tea rooms, the bed and breakfast and then there's all the cooking and organising for them."

"We can do it!" Lisa said, brimming with confidence. "I told you, girl, your life is going to change and you're going to have to start delegating. What about it girls? Are we up for the job?"

There was another deafening crescendo which drew the men's attention, yet again and they were frowning in puzzlement.

"Okay," Lisa said, triumphantly. "Looks like you have a team!"

"We haven't asked the other halves, yet," I commented.

"Oh, they'll be up for it," said Louise. "We'll make sure of that, won't we, girls?"

There was a general mêlée of agreement. I felt that a burden had been lifted from my shoulders. For the first time in my life, I now felt the support of a team. I was so exceedingly grateful for that comfort. I smiled. "Thank you, girls. We'd better go and ask the men though. Lisa?"

"I'm coming. Don't forget the drink," she said as she handed me a bottle of red and picked up an ice bucket with the white. "See ya later, girls!"

We left the girls, who were suddenly totally devoted to the subject of what they were going to wear to the party. They were almost bursting with excitement.

As we walked away from the table, Lisa said to me, "I don't imagine your step-brother will let you get away with wearing shorts for your twenty-first!"

I glowered at her. "Don't start!"

Lisa was positively grinning from ear to ear like the Cheshire cat. "This is going to be fun!"

I opened the door and we stepped outside into the cool sea breeze that was wafting along the veranda. The rollers were gently pounding the beach just a short distance away.

The men fell silent again. They were staring at me.

"Come on, boys," Lisa said. "Give a girl a break."

"May we join you?" I asked.

Immediately there was a scraping of chairs and suddenly there were two spare chairs in their midst.

Lisa and I sat down. "Thank you," I said. I took a deep breath. "Hello, everyone. I think I know you all, by sight at least."

There was a murmured greeting back.

"What's going on in there?" Gary asked, glancing through the window at the excited babble and occasional squeal.

"You've been volunteered to work for Joy, to help her renovate the castle."

"We know," Gary said. "That's why you've brought Joy down here." He raised his half-empty beer glass. "Nice to have you join us!"

I smiled. I felt more comfortable with him than any of the others. "Thank you. Are you all keen to do it?"

"Absolutely," said one, who I think was Stephen. "But what's all the excitement about?"

Lisa was bursting to tell them. "You've got a deadline! The thirty-first of October!"

Gary frowned. "Why?"

Lisa's face was animated. "Because Richard de Bowes-Lyon wants to have a house-warming party on that night, which coincides with Joy's twenty-first and we're all invited!"

One of the others groaned and covered his face with his hand. "Don't tell me! They're talking about clothes. We'll never hear the end of it now!"

"Well, it makes a change from you lot talking about golf!" Lisa returned.

"Why are you so interested in golf?" I asked. "I must say that I am surprised. I expected your favourite subject to be football."

"We're nuts about golf," Gary admitted, "but you have to be – in our line of work."

I was confused. "Why?"

"Most of us are apprentices to trades people," he explained, "and they all play golf. All the trades people in Norfolk seem to know each other because they all meet up on the golf course and that's where they do their networking. I have yet to meet a Norfolk electrician, carpenter, plumber or whatever, who doesn't play golf! If we want to get on in our careers, it's essential and, once you have the bug for golf, you're hooked!"

"And sliced!" Lisa said, scathingly. "Heard about golf widows, Joy? This lot can't afford a set of golf clubs between them, but it still doesn't stop them going off to practise on the local course whenever they can. No wonder we girls talk about clothes! We hardly ever see you!"

I turned to Gary. "There's a lot of work to be done at the castle, mostly labour in various trades. Can you spare the time between golf practice? We've been given a pretty tight deadline."

Gary turned to the others. "How about it, boys?"

They all raised their glasses and heartily gave their agreement. Then they fell silent again. I sipped my glass of bubbly and tried to concentrate on that but I felt uncomfortable, because they were still staring at me, particularly, my legs. I felt myself blushing. Eventually, I could no longer stand it.

"They are just legs!" I said calmly. "Everyone has them!"

There was a general coughing, scraping of chair legs and sipping of beer. One young man was still staring in awe at my legs. I found the confidence to look straight at him and he jumped when he met my gaze. I think he was called Adam.

"Sorry!" he apologized quickly. "It's just... well..."

"They've never seen legs like yours," Gary intervened.

I frowned at him in puzzlement. "Why?"

"They're just so... long," said Adam. He looked embarrassed.

"The only time we see legs like yours are on the models in the girls' magazines," said another, "and... well, you are a stunner. When we happen to see you in passing on the caravan site, it's always a bit of a shock and you haven't joined us until now."

I chewed on my lip, feeling my cheeks turn scarlet. I took a deep breath. "Well, get used to it! They are just ordinary legs, I'm an ordinary person and I'm going to be working with you from now on."

"There's nothing ordinary about you," said Adam.

Lisa exchanged a glance with me that said, I told you so!

I stayed there a little longer and the boys and I started to relax as we got over the awkwardness of being in each other's company.

I left Lisa with them and walked home alone. I needed to let the wind blow through my hair and try to calm down. The fast-changing pace of my life was difficult to keep up with and I was not looking forward to tomorrow. I only hoped that I could sleep because it was going to be a difficult day. The trauma of being parted from my father.

That night, I did sleep, but I tossed and turned all night. I dreamed that I was adrift on a boat in the middle of an ocean, in a raging storm, and Richard was calling out to me. The waves were pounding my boat and he was trying to reach out to get me to the safety of his boat, but couldn't quite cover the distance between us.

Catkins

Catkins, hanging in the sun,
Pollen enough for everyone,
Will you still hang there when I'm gone,
When your job is done?

I wish I were like you, small and light,
When I die I think I might
Soar and fly through the night,
'Till my job is done.

Sophie Large – aged nine.

Chapter Eleven

I KNOCKED on the door of Dad's study.

"Come in!"

I opened the door to see Dad, sitting in his favourite armchair. Beside him was a very small, black canvas holdall.

I closed the door behind me and walked towards him. "Are you packed?"

Dad glanced down at the bag. "Yes, it's all there!"

I knelt on the floor between his legs and he put his arms around me. "You are joking!"

Dad smiled and shook his head. "Think about it! I won't need much where I'm going. Just a toothbrush and a bathrobe. I'm going to have a draughty bottom for a few months. I don't know why they have those confounded back fastening garments that don't effectively cover your behind, but I have no choice."

I leaned into his chest and breathed in his lovely, comforting smell. He held me tightly. "Oh, Dad, I'm going to miss you so much. Having to say goodbye to you is just too awful!"

Dad stroked my hair with a gentle, soothing hand. "If you're working hard on that project, time will fly and before you know it, I'll be back."

I took a deep, shuddering breath. I looked up into his kind face. The face I loved so much and had adored for all my living memory. "How long?"

He shook his head and smiled. His blue eyes had become watery. "Soon. Just pray for me, okay?" He stroked my cheek with the rough skin of his well-worn hand. "Keep that faith going, Precious. You're very good at that. God smiles on you and he seems to work miracles for you."

I could feel tears pouring down my cheeks and I gulped to try and catch my breath. "He's not smiling on me now! This is too painful, Daddy. I need you!"

I hugged him fiercely, not wanting to let go. We sat like that for a few minutes in silence. Each holding on to the other. I imagined that my father's thoughts were in line with mine. "Please come back to me, Daddy," I whispered.

"I will, my darling. I will."

He hugged me more tightly and my head was on his knees. I was silently praying for his return.

There was a knock on the door. Lisa opened it. She looked at us and her face showed her concern. "Sorry to disturb you. I just thought that you ought to see this."

I wiped the tears from my wet face, knowing that my eyes would now be very red. We followed Lisa through to the antiques shop at the front of the house and what we saw made us stop in our tracks in amazement.

We turned to each other and couldn't help laughing. Both of us, tearfully, but it was such a sight!

A huge, white stretch-limousine was manoeuvring and then parked in our car park at the front of our farm house.

A uniformed chauffeur got out and then came around to open the door. Richard stepped out and then turned to assist Ruby to get out.

I gasped in shock!

Dad laughed. "Well I never," he said, softly. "What a send off Richard is giving us! First class luxury, door to door!" He shook his head in disbelief.

I just stared, feeling rooted to the spot. My life was changing faster than I could keep up with. I wasn't going anywhere to look for a luxurious lifestyle. It had presented itself on my doorstep. Or at least, the doorstep I had at the moment. I would have to hide my misgivings. How could I be ungrateful when Richard was giving my father the finest send off anyone could have!

I clung to my father's arm. Lisa had popped back to the study and picked up Dad's holdall. She handed it to me.

"Is this all?"

I nodded. I couldn't speak. It was so small and so light. He was taking almost nothing with him. Would he be coming back? Would I ever see him again? I felt the tears overwhelm me, but I didn't care. This was just too awful to bear!

I stepped forward and opened the shop door. Dad followed me and stepped outside, using his walking stick for support. My legs felt weak. I felt that I needed him for support but he was the frail one.

We met Richard and Ruby on our gravelled yard. Ruby covered the ground between us. "Oh, my poor child. Come here." She enfolded me in her arms, against her ample bosom. I couldn't help it. The tears just flowed and I was shaking. She stroked my hair and I just let her comfort me, like a large mother hen. "It will be alright," she said, quietly. "He'll be coming back and I want you to know that you can ring me any time to see how he is. Okay? Promise that you will ring me!" I nodded, mutely.

I found the strength to step back and gave her an attempt at a smile. "Thank you." I breathed deeply, trying to get through this.

"Richard said that he will give you the contact numbers and then we can keep in touch and have some nice little chats. Yes?" Ruby looked at me with concern.

I nodded. "Thank you. Yes, I will call you. Richard will have to remind me of the time difference though! Otherwise I'll be calling you at two o'clock in the morning and you won't thank me for that!" I tried to laugh but it wasn't very successful. I was struggling to breathe.

Richard turned me to face him. He hands were gently on my shoulders. "Ça va?"

I couldn't speak. My lips were just pressed together and I shook my head. My chest was so tight, I almost couldn't breathe.

Richard pulled me against the length of him and I just collapsed into his arms and let him hold me, I didn't have the strength to hold myself up. I breathed in his aroma and felt I was in a whirlpool. I drew shaky, unsteady breaths. The ground seemed to be rising and falling, like the waves in my dream last night, but he held me tight and spoke softly against my hair.

"Come on, Angel. Your Dad needs to know that you'll be here, giving all your strength to praying that he comes back. He will. Your faith will see to it. It hasn't let you down before, has it?"

I couldn't answer him truthfully, so I just shook my head.

"Are you coming with us to the airport?"

I took a few deep breaths and tried to regain my strength. I looked into Richard's kind face. "I couldn't."

I turned and went to Dad, while Richard picked up Dad's holdall and then helped Ruby into the car. The chauffeur just stood by the door, waiting patiently, without a word.

I looked at Dad through my blurry vision and we hugged again. I held on and I held and I held on. I didn't want to let go.

Richard gently stroked my head. "We have to go, Angel." I looked into his eyes and they burned into mine. "You will see your father again." He kissed my forehead and then helped Dad into the car.

I just stood there watching them. Richard's eyes held mine again, and then he got into the car and the chauffeur closed the car door. I didn't wave because I couldn't see them through the blacked out windows. I didn't move as the car disappeared out of sight. I felt that my heart had just been torn out and I wondered if I would ever see my father again.

Lisa touched my arm. "Hey," she said, softly. "Are you okay?"

I glanced at her and shook my head, my lips pressed firmly together. I couldn't speak. Suddenly, I realised that I needed to be in the only place where I could feel close to Dad.

I ran into the house and hurtled through the rooms and corridor until I reached Dad's study. I closed the door behind me. My heart was pounding, my breathing in ragged gasps. Suddenly I noticed that Dad's favourite old jacket was still over the back of his oak desk chair. I hurled across the room and fell on my knees by the chair and buried my face into the material of the jacket. It was tweed. Old and well-worn, with leather patches on the elbows. It smelled of Dad, and I clung on to that aroma.

I breathed in the smell of him and sobbed and sobbed until my heart literally ached, and I repeated over and over again, "Please come back to me, Daddy. Please come back to me."

I cried until I was exhausted, and just lay silently, holding on to the material and stroking it, as I held on to the hope that I would see him again.

On being alone, outside, on a summer night...

The warm treacle day dissolves,
Mellows to ruby red Port wine.

The night glides and smooths
In deep contented dreamings

I drift into the garden folds,
Lie still in cool moist grasses. Now

The finite world around me stirs,
I seep within its slow rhythm;

The air flows clear; is full
Of serene, boundless stillness. Yet

My eyes search high heights, through leafy
Boughs of darkened summer trees.

The whole sky soars down to me,
Droves of streaks of invisible.

My mortality aches in me,
Stretches sobbing to its core

Before this vast weeping space
My smallness smalls and crumples more

The skies are mourning for me
With countless white tears!

Running limbs flicker in the moonlight,
Grasses part and swish and crackle.

Something turns – some cavity
Deep within lets free its captive

Those thoughts reluctant from me
Break away, away in night breezes

Grieving black, of a sudden,
Return to air, retracts its lull.

My mind, deceptive slow, snaps back –
The red wine of my being thrills –

Behind me trail strange wonderings
In darkness lonely, unconfessed.

My whole being mirthful rings.
Not yet, I say. Don't mourn me yet!

Sophie Large – aged eighteen.

Chapter Twelve

DECIDED to walk along the beach to the convent school. I needed Sister Ruth's comforting reassurance now more than ever. The sun was shining, and I wanted the warm sea breeze to blow through my mind, pushing out all the pain. I was determined to be calm and controlled when I saw Sister Ruth. I needed her advice about the strange turn that my life had taken. I needed her to tell me what to do.

I left the beach and took the path over the sand dunes. I drank in the peaceful atmosphere as I walked through the immaculate, landscaped gardens. Some nuns were working in the garden in the distance and they waved when they saw me. I waved back at them. I always feel at home here. I love the beautiful little church, the fountain and the white stone statue of Jesus, which faces across the car park, to the imposing entrance of this very grand building. It is like a huge, elegant manor house.

I turned the brass knob of the extremely tall and wide oak door. I always feel like the shrunken Alice when I walk through the door and it is just bliss to see the uniformed children pass through here.

As I closed the door, the two nuns who were receptionists looked up and their expressions burst into broad smiles as they greeted me.

"Is Sister Ruth available?" I asked tentatively.

"I'll just find out. It's so good to see you!" Sister Elizabeth said as she picked up the phone. She had a brief conversation and then put the phone down. "Sister Ruth is expecting you. Do go through."

"Thank you." I smiled at both of the delightful nuns and then opened another giant, internal door that led into the central staircase hall. All the dimensions of this building are vast. I walked along the flagstones of the very wide corridor and then knocked on the polished oak of the door to Sister Ruth's office. It had a wonderful patina and I thought of Dad. I took deep breaths, determined to be calm.

I heard Sister Ruth acknowledge me and I opened the huge door and then closed it behind me, with a quiet click. Everything here is hushed.

Sister Ruth was already half-way across the huge room, with her arms spread, when I broke. All my resolve instantly dissolved when I saw her. The floodgates opened and I gave an anguished cry as I flew into her arms. I had to bend, because this tiny and wonderful lady is about a foot smaller than me.

I cried on her shoulder, making her habit wet with my tears, but she didn't care. She hugged me tightly and I was shaking.

"Oh, Sister Ruth, God is punishing me because I am the most terrible person in the world. I am a self-centred, selfish person and a thief. I have stolen from people and now Daddy is dying, Richard is marrying someone else and my world will come to an end on the thirty-first of October and I will die, and if I don't die, please may I become a nun and devote myself to God for the rest of my life to make up for my sins." It all came bursting out of me and I was racked with sobs.

"Whoa, whoa, whoa, there. Joy! Come, my child." She lifted my face with her tiny hands and her expression was full of love for me. "Let's calm you down first and then tell me all about it. Come and sit beside the fire."

I straightened and assisted this lady, who was so very dear to me, to sit in her favourite huge, high-backed chair, beside the enormous stone fireplace. I knelt on the rug in front of her.

Sister Ruth took a deep breath and held my hand. "Now, let's ask God to help you to calm down and then you can explain to me what on earth you are talking about. I think the Lord's Prayer and Psalm 23 are the most apt for this moment and then, I think, Psalm 46."

She placed her other hand on my bowed head and I felt God, through her, instil calmness into me. We prayed for several minutes and quietly recited the familiar words from the Bible. My breathing began to return to normal as her soothing words and calmness flowed through me. I felt her hand, gently stroking my head. I was aware of the stillness of the room, the vastness of it and the power of God in every inch of the high oak panelled walls and glorious detail of the plasterwork on the ceiling. I felt it in every cell in Sister Ruth's body through the folds of her robe.

"Amen," we both said, together, and then I looked into her face. If you have never looked into a nun's face, you cannot know the peace and serenity you will find there. They do not need artificial enhancement to create beauty. They have it, inherently, because it comes from within. A beauty they exude because God fills their lives and their devotion to him is complete.

I collapsed forward with my head on Sister Ruth's lap, and her hand gently stroked my head. "This is the one place in the world where I can truly feel peace. I wish I could always stay here," I said softly, feeling as though I was melting into her and all anxiety ebbing away. Anxiety was out there is the world, not where I was at that moment.

"Tell me what it is that troubles you, my sweet child."

"Please tell me about my mother."

Sister Ruth's hand paused for a moment and then she continued to stroke my head, instilling her calm. "You haven't asked me this before."

My voice was muffled by her robe. "I need to know."

"Tell me what you would like to know."

"Everything, Sister Ruth."

There was a pause. I imagined that Sister Ruth was thoughtful and reflective. She was obviously surprised by my request. "Did you know that she was an orphan?"

"No. I didn't know that. Before I was eleven, I didn't question my mother's background, and then, after she left, I refused to mention her." I could feel the warmth of her other hand on my back, through the cotton of my shirt.

"Elizabeth had very selfish parents. She was born to them, but they didn't care about her. They only cared about each other. She was left in London with a nanny. Her parents had been born into wealthy families but they spent all the money that came in to them on travelling the world and enjoying themselves."

"That is so horrible," I commented.

"It is how some people are. It is strange how there are people who are desperate to have children but can't and there are others who have children but have no interest in them. Elizabeth never really knew her mother. When Elizabeth was three years old there was a terrible plane crash, which was in the news. Her parents died. There was no money left, because they had spent it all. In fact, they left debts."

I was shocked. "What happened?"

"Her guardian paid the debts but he had no interest in Elizabeth and didn't know what to do with her. He rang me, and asked if I would take her. As you know, this is a boarding school for girls of the age of ten years and upwards, but I was so drawn by the plight of this poor child that I took her. She was the most beautiful, delightful child, and she had thirty nuns bring her up. We all adopted a motherly role towards her and, well, I'm sorry to say, you can imagine how spoiled she was."

I was intrigued. "Was she a badly behaved child?"

"Oh, no! Not bad, just full of fun and mischief and we all indulged her."

"Dad said that she was like a beautiful tiny exotic bird. Fragile and delicate, with the heart of a lion and the dominating mental strength of an ox, but also very sweet. He said that she was like a whirlwind and, before he knew it, he was married."

"You've asked your father about this?"

I nodded against her leg. "I needed to hear it from him."

Sister Ruth laughed softly. "Alfred has given a good description of her. That is exactly what Elizabeth was like and unfortunately we were to blame."

"Why?" I was confused.

Sister Ruth laughed again and I realised that she was looking back in time. "She ran rings around thirty nuns. We would do anything for her and she knew it. We loved her so much and, between us, it was impossible to instil any discipline into her. She was a free spirit, full of life and energy. She was so good but just found it impossible to concentrate on her lessons and didn't want to."

I was taking all of this on board very carefully. This was new territory. If I learned about my mum, maybe I could understand her. "How did she meet Dad?"

"Well, your mother was surrounded by nuns and she craved male company. She would spend hours playing chess or other board games with Father David and chatting to him in his office. There came a time when some of the pews in the school chapel were desperately in need of attention. I asked Alfred if he would take on the task of repairing them. Elizabeth was immediately drawn to him as another male companion. With all the females around here, Elizabeth really enjoyed having conversations with men."

"That wasn't a reason for her to marry my father."

Sister Ruth hesitated, and silently stroked my head. Eventually, she said, "Please understand, sweet child, that you were not a mistake. God intended you to be born and you are very special!"

"But?" I ventured.

She was silent for a short time and then said, "Your mother was in an unusual situation. She was orphaned, without a penny and the guardian who passed her to us said that he would fulfil his obligation to pay for her upbringing until her eighteenth birthday, but then he would absolve himself of any further commitment to her."

"So what happened?"

"She was seventeen when she met your father. Apart from Father David, Alfred became in Elizabeth's mind, the father figure that she had always yearned for."

"A father figure isn't a husband!"

"No," Sister Ruth agreed, "but Elizabeth believed that she was in love with him. She idolised him and he filled her thoughts. He was everything that she had ever felt that she needed in a man. With her eighteenth birthday approaching, and nothing in her life beyond that point, she didn't know what to do. She saw Alfred as the love and security that she needed for her future. We urged her not to marry him, because we felt that she was doing it for the wrong reasons. But, as Alfred explained to you, she had the dominating mental strength of an ox and a sweetness that swept him away. It was our fault that she was such a delightful, determined impossibility and we couldn't do anything except allow Father David to marry them."

"But if she married because she had no future, why didn't she become a nun?"

I could feel Sister begin to shake with laughter at the thought. "Elizabeth was like Maria von Trapp. She was so bursting with life and fun and mischief that there was no way she could ever have settled to becoming a nun. She grew up with us, but our life was not for her. She was a free spirit, waiting to spread her wings and fly, and now look at her, shining in the constellation of stars in this world."

"And then she had me," I said, dully.

Sister Ruth took a deep breath, as though bringing herself back to the present. "Now, what is it that brought you here in such a state? You mentioned that Alfred is dying. Richard told me that Alfred is very ill, but surely it is not certain that he will die."

Something twanged in my stomach at the mention of Richard and the realisation that he had been talking to Sister Ruth. "The specialists here were unable to treat him effectively and the only chance of survival that he has is if a pioneering drug, that has been used with some success, can work for him. He left this morning. Richard made all the arrangements for them and took them to the airport. Did you know that Dad is marrying Ruby, if he survives this? She is going to be staying in New York for the duration, to give Dad some moral support."

"Richard told me that they intend to marry. How do you feel about that?"

I shook my head feeling pangs of guilt again. "How can I not be happy for them?"

"But how do you feel?" Sister Ruth asked, ever so gently.

"Guilty!"

"Why should you feel guilty?"

"Because it's all my fault! I'm to blame for everything! I'm the most selfish, terrible person and I'm a thief!"

"Joy," Sister Ruth said quietly. "You are the kindest, sweetest, most unselfish person I know and I cannot imagine you stealing from anyone."

Sister Ruth lifted my face with her hands so that I was looking up into her lovely face. Her pale blue eyes were so kind but she was frowning with confusion.

"What is that is your fault? What did you do?"

"I was the cause of the break-up of my parents' relationship! I made my mother suffer and drove a wedge between her and my father. If I hadn't been born, perhaps they may still have been happy!"

Sister Ruth was very patient, obviously trying to grasp my meaning. "No-one can be at fault for being born."

I urged Sister Ruth to understand. "By having me, she couldn't devote her time to Dad as she had before. Besides which, I appear to have been conceived on their first night, so there was very little time to have a normal relationship, and my birth was painful for my mother because I was so large."

Sister Ruth was now smiling. "Still not your fault."

"She couldn't spend time with my father because she had to look after me."

"Yes, that's the joy of motherhood."

I shook my head. "But then I came to idolise my father, as she had, and I wanted to please him. I no longer wanted her to dress me, like a doll. I rebelled against her, dressed in boyish clothes and I wanted to spend time with my father, taking the place that she had before and she felt left out."

Sister Ruth was watching me carefully. "Go on."

"She became unhappy. Then I met Richard and took him home for lunch. I was the one who told Mum about Richard's mum. I was the one who introduced her to Richard and, therefore, his family. I gave her the reason to go to see Richard's mother and then she met Richard's father. I then spent the next few months, totally besotted with Richard. When we weren't spending time with Dad, we disappeared to play at the castle. I gave her the alibi and the space she needed to form a relationship with Richard's father and it was I who had driven a wedge between them to cause her to look elsewhere for happiness. If I hadn't been born, none of this would have happened!"

"You cannot say that any of this is your fault, Joy!"

"But that is exactly right, Sister Ruth. I thought I was Joy, Jesus-Others-Yourself, but I've been a Yoj all along! I have put myself first, but I just didn't see it."

I put my head on her lap, desperately needing her comfort as I admitted to all my sins.

"So what is it that you have done that is so selfish? I do not see it, Joy. You are completely unselfish."

I shook my head. "No I'm not, Sister Ruth. What I have done is so bad. I feel guilty that I met Richard and guilty about our friendship. I am guilty because I was the cause of the break-up between my parents, even though, at that point, I didn't even realise that I had been the cause of driving a wedge between them. I tried to fill the void in my father's life by doing everything for him that my mother would have done. I baked, I cleaned, washed and sewed. I worked so hard to make a wonderful home for him and I helped in the business. I devoted myself to doing everything for him, to the exclusion of almost everything else."

"And what is so wrong with that?" Sister Ruth asked softly as she stroked my head.

"Because I have now realised that I did it for me. I thought it was a duty to my father that drove me, but I now see that I was fulfilling a selfish need in me. I needed to do it for him, because by focussing on that, I was avoiding making any decisions about my own life. He didn't need it because in fact he wanted Ruby but couldn't be with her because of me. I was so focussed on myself that I didn't see the needs of others."

"Now I am confused. Explain that one to me, please."

"Ruby and Dad had always been keen on each other but were too shy to show their feelings. Ruby was shocked when Dad married Mum. When Mum left, she consoled Dad and, when they talked, everything came out and they wanted to be together, but they couldn't, because of me!"

"Did they give any indication that they wanted to be together?"

"No, they kept it a total secret, because they didn't want to upset me as I had worked so hard to make our home special. I should have been able to see it though."

After a short time, Sister Ruth said, "Right. So why are you a thief? What have you stolen?" She lifted my face again. "Come on, what have you stolen?"

I felt bleak with despair. "I stole Dad from Mum, by taking her place, then I literally created a role for myself as replacement wife for Dad, when really I was stealing him from Ruby. I have taken you as my replacement mother. I have taken the role of replacement mother with Annie, from Lisa. I stole from what is now going to be Richard's home, because I pretended that it was going to be my home with him and I covet him when he is in love with someone else. I have broken the Ten Commandments. I have stolen, I have not honoured my parents and I covet a man whose heart belongs to someone else."

Sister Ruth was very serious. "I see. And why is your world coming to an end? Why will you die?"

I drew a shuddering breath, trying harder to seek peace, and feel her comfort. "I'm facing my Armageddon. Two days ago, I woke up and my life was in perfect order. Now it has completely fallen apart, and on the thirty-first of October, Richard will host a house-warming party. He is determined to have me there, as his sister, celebrating my twenty-first, and he will also announce his engagement to the girl he is in love with and I don't think I have the strength to stand there and witness it because my heart will break and I will literally collapse and die. My life will be at an end because there will be nothing for me. No future and no hope."

"And why is there no future for you in this world?"

"Oh, Sister Ruth, don't you see? This is history repeating itself. I am a nothing and a nobody. I don't know who I am. I have stolen identities from those I am close to because I don't have an identity of my own. If Dad does not survive, I get everything, and that would just be too awful! If he does survive, I will have nothing. I have not ever made any choices for myself in my life. I have only worked for Dad, or done things for other people. I don't have a personality, a career, a home, any money. Lisa and Richard have both said that I'm the chick who hasn't left the nest yet, and even Dad hinted at that, when he said that as I'm approaching twenty-one, it's time I knew that he and Ruby want to share a home together. I am in exactly the same position as my mother. Her deadline was her eighteenth birthday and she had nothing beyond. Mine is my twenty-first. I don't want to be like my mother."

"Joy, look at me," Sister Ruth said, firmly.

I took a deep breath and sat back. I raised my head to look at her.

"You are nothing like your mother," she said carefully.

"I am! I am in the same position and I don't want to be like her. I look like her, and people behave towards me in a way that says that I am sort of special. She might have been an innocent orphan, but she discovered that she had a power and that she could use it to get what she wanted. She ruined everything! Because of her, I lost a mother. And my new best friend, who I was totally in love with, became my brother and she became his mother instead of mine! She uses people, then dumps them and they get hurt, like my father. I don't want to fall into that trap. I don't want to use people. If I do survive until the first of November, please may I become a nun?"

Sister Ruth's mouth twitched at the corners. "You cannot be a nun. That would not be possible."

"But I'm not a bad person! God wants to punish me, I know, for doing bad things, but please ask God to not punish my father and ask that my father recovers and returns home and then I can be a good nun and devote myself to God. I have spent the last ten years trying to make up for the guilt of causing my mother to leave my father, now I'll have to spend the rest of my life trying to make up for what I now realise I have done to others. Pride is a sin and it blinded me to the truth. It caused me to be prejudiced against Richard and his family. I forced them to be cut out of our lives. There is too much damage there to repair and I cannot live as Richard's sister. I'm a good Catholic, so please let me spend the rest of my life making it up to God."

Sister Ruth was looking at me with such kindness. "As you say, for the last ten years, you have lived in the obligation of duty because of your guilt. You became a Catholic, in secret, for the same reason. I have to tell you that your father knows you are Catholic."

I gasped in shock. "What? How? But… I kept it a secret!"

"I'm sorry, Joy, but because of the age you were, I needed to ask his permission. He watched the service, hiding up in the gallery."

"Another secret I don't have," I said faintly.

"Richard has had such a major influence on your life. If he hadn't filled your head with the stories of Annette, Antoine and Georgiana, and if you hadn't identified so closely with Elizabeth Bennet, adoring your father and seeing your mother as the insensitive, materialistic Mrs Bennet, I don't think you would have been so outraged about what your mother and his father did. If Richard hadn't filled your head with the drama of classical novels, telling you about the relevance to his family history, you wouldn't have been inspired to study French, history, geography, art and literature. Truthfully, he was one of the reasons you converted to become a Catholic. You are not like your mother. She was a social butterfly who could not put her mind to study. Because of your love for Richard and the hurt caused by your mother, you avoided social friendship and became a book worm. You advanced so far ahead of your class that I had to teach you myself. I know you very well."

As I looked at her beauty, I felt empty and lost.

"Joy, You have not lived. You have not made any choices. You have not seen the enormous world that God has created and you have not enjoyed the pleasures that God offers us, because you have been too busy feeling guilty. And, my dear child, you cannot marry one, when you are in love with another. We all wear bands of gold because we are married to Jesus. We don't live out of guilt. We live for the sheer joy of giving to God."

"Then what am I to do?" I beseeched her. "Why is God punishing me?"

She smiled and stroked my head. "I don't believe that he is punishing you. I believe that he loves you very much. You are very special and he has set you on a journey."

"Where will I go?"

Her face was radiant. "God will tell you."

I was confused. "How?"

"The greatest trust we can have is to believe in something that we cannot see and cannot touch. That is what God asks of us, complete trust. If we believe, we can *feel* Him. You must do what you feel is right. The way that it works for me is that I feel an overwhelming compulsion to do something. I question it again and again, asking God if that is what He really wants me to do. If the compulsion is still there, I have to act and do as He wishes. However, God only asks us to do good things. If the compulsion is to do something that will cause harm, that is another entity trying to trick us and, unfortunately, there are some who are lured into that course of action. That is how the other side operates, feeding on people's ignorance because they haven't given themselves to God."

"But I'm such a bad person," I said mournfully.

Sister Ruth's smile broadened. "You are not guilty, my dear child, and I am happy to absolve you of your sins."

"But…"

"Listen," she said, firmly. "It is true that I was a replacement for your mother, one of thirty. When your mother left and you came here, I did become your replacement mother. You did not steal from me. It was, and is, my pleasure. You were not the cause of the break-up of your parents' relationship. If they were having problems, it was up to them to discuss it and put it right, not for a child to take on the burden of blame. It was not you who prevented Alfred and Ruby from being together. If they couldn't talk about their feelings and then Ruby's nose was put out of joint by Elizabeth, and then they still couldn't openly admit their feelings for each other until now, well, that's their fault and not yours. As for the rejection towards your mother and your determination to make a wonderful home for your father, yes, I understand you needed to, but you were very hurt by what happened and felt that your mother had rejected you and your father."

"What about Lisa?"

"They were still school children when they had Annie. You have been very kind to them. You have given Lisa a job and created child care facilities. From what you have told me, she is a beautiful and responsive child and it is only natural for you to show your love for her."

"And… Richard?" I held my breath.

Sister Ruth held my eyes, and then said gently, "You've been in love with him for ten years."

"I was only a child. Surely it couldn't have been real love!"

"As innocent as it was, real love can strike even when you are ten years old, and you've been holding the dream since then."

"Does Richard think I'm in love with him?" I asked hesitantly.

Sister Ruth's expression was a gentle reprimand. "You know that I cannot discuss what each of you says about the other."

"What am I to do?"

"You take a leap of faith," Sister Ruth said quietly.

"What do you mean? How do I do that?"

Her face was so wonderfully serene and I just felt her peace. "You let go. Take your hands off the controls and give it to God. Let go of everything: your father, your mother, Lisa, Annie, Richard and even me! Let go."

"What about the castle? I have to supervise the work on it."

"Focus on the work you have to do and let God do everything else."

I pleaded with her to understand. "Why is God punishing me? Why is everything going wrong?"

Sister Ruth shook her head slowly. She was smiling. "This is not punishment. I believe that He is testing you."

"But this is so hard!"

"It wouldn't be a test if it wasn't hard!"

I shook my head in total confusion. "Why do we need to be tested?"

"A test stretches our abilities. We try harder and we learn more about ourselves and our capacities. God is testing us every day but we don't always realise it."

I felt bleak with despair. "Stretching me to breaking point. How will I be able to stand there and watch Richard become engaged to someone else?"

Sister Ruth squeezed my hand. "God will find a way to give you the strength to face what must be faced, and Joy, that includes meeting your mother because you cannot truly live if you cannot face up to your fears. What you must realise is that you are not in control. You tried to control your life by putting all these things neatly boxed on a shelf."

I looked at her in amazement. She smiled. "I know how your mind works. I know what you did, but you cannot live by pretending that things don't exist. What you must understand is that you are not in control. Not of your mother's behaviour, your father's health or Richard's future. They are not your decision or responsibility. Your father will die one day. Whether it happens now or not yet, you are going to have to face up to the loss."

I was bereft as I looked into her face. "I am lost! Richard and Lisa have both basically told me that I need to discover myself and blossom. How am I supposed to do that?"

Sister Ruth beamed. "God has demonstrated the same desire to see you blossom and fulfil your life. That is why He has torn down the false life that you created for yourself, so that you will listen to Him and follow the path that He has laid so that you can discover yourself. This isn't punishment, my dear child. This is proof that God loves you. You are a priceless treasure, a rare and beautiful orchid. You have lived your entire life in the undergrowth, deep in the dark tropical rain forest. No one has seen you, until now. You are about to be revealed to the world but that means living in a strange, new environment, and you need to be protected, to ensure that you can survive."

"I'm not special, Sister Ruth," I protested.

"I'm afraid that you are. You are a debutante, in every sense of the word. You are pure and innocent and you have lived almost in hiding. Now, Richard is intent upon reuniting you with your mother and presenting you to the world as a true debutante."

I groaned. Sister Ruth patted my shoulder.

Sister Ruth gave a slight jolt, and seemed to suddenly recollect something. "Ahh, now I see," she said, softly as she gave me a beaming smile and her eyes seemed lit from within. She picked up the Bible which was on the flagstone floor, by the leg of her chair. "That's what it meant." She turned the pages of the Bible, as though searching for a passage.

"Here it is. Now I understand." Her face was radiant. "Often, I close my eyes and open the Bible at a random page to see if God has a message for me. Sometimes, with all those thousands of words, the book will open at the same page until I understand what He is trying to tell me. This morning, it opened at Ecclesiastes 3, which is entitled, 'A Time for Everything' and I just couldn't get the message... but now I do. Listen."

Sister Ruth began to read the passage to me. "What do we gain from all our work? I know the heavy burdens that God has laid on us. He has set the right time for everything. He has given us a desire to know the future, but never gives us the satisfaction of fully understanding what He does. So I realised that all we can do is to be happy and do the best we can while we are still alive. All of us should eat, drink and enjoy what we have worked for. It is God's gift. I know that everything God does will last for ever. You can't add anything to it or take anything away from it. And one thing God does is to make us stand in awe of him. Whatever happens or can happen has already happened before. God makes the same thing happen again and again."

Sister Ruth's intense expression fell on me. This is confirmation of what I have just told you. The timing is not yours to choose and you are not in control of what is happening in your life. God obviously has a plan for you." She squeezed my hand with reassurance. "Joy, dear, do you see those two little books which are on my desk?"

I nodded. "Would you mind bringing them to me?"

I crossed the room and picked them up from the huge mahogany desk, and gave them to her. She gave them straight back to me.

"I need you to understand that from this moment on, you have to start living. I am giving these to you, because they will help you. I have discovered these books and I now give them to every one of my girls. I think that every female from nine to ninety in the world should read them. Boys can read them too, but they are most appropriate for girls."

I was intrigued. There were pictures of a teenager on the front covers, sitting apparently at a street café. She was beautiful, happy and obviously full of fun. "Sophie's Log," I read aloud, the title of one. "And the other seems to be a BBC Radio play. It says on the book's front cover that there is a foreword by Dame Judi Dench. It seems to be the girl's thoughts and feelings in poetry and prose." I turned to the back cover. "This critical acclaim for her work is top drawer. Joanna Trollope, the Mail on Sunday, the Daily Mail, the Times. Wow! This girl's work must be good."

I looked at Sister Ruth to see that she had a strange expression. "What's the matter?"

"Those are the private thoughts and feelings of that teenage girl and you feel honoured and privileged that she has shared them with you. The other is a play, based on the book. Look at me, an old nun, yet she taught me about God, accepting death and how to live. She taught me how to celebrate life. By the age of nineteen, she had achieved more in her life than most people do in a lifetime. She was an extraordinarily talented girl."

I frowned. "You said, *was*."

Sister Ruth watched my expression carefully. "She died when she was a year younger than you. Those are extracts from her private secret diary, found later and printed posthumously by her grieving family."

I reeled, feeling an intense body blow with a power that could have cracked my ribs. I gasped and looked again at the girl on the covers. Dead! A year younger than me! And a more fun-loving, lovely girl you couldn't wish to meet. Someone you would value as your best friend. I was stunned. "What happened?"

"Her family later pieced it together. The last poem in the book is what she must have written, sitting at her dressing table, on the morning that she died, so they know that as she left the house she was feeling utterly happy and content. They lived in a little village, close to where she was working. She got into her car and was driving through the country lanes, when a lorry met her head on and killed her. Just three days after she had passed her driving test."

My mouth fell open. "It will break my heart to read these."

Sister Ruth shook her head and smiled gently. "That's what I thought, and, yes, you do need a box of tissues when you read them, but what you need to understand, Joy, is that it is as much of a crime to take a long lifetime that has been given to you and do nothing with it, as it is for a young woman whose flame burned so brightly and then was snuffed out much too soon. God wants you to live and celebrate the life that He has given to you. Let this girl teach you about life. Open the book and read the first poem."

I did so. "How can the end, Be the beginning again, When all seems lost?"

"And the inside back page," prompted Sister Ruth.

"The end... or is it the beginning?"

I stared at the books in awe.

Sister Ruth patted my hand. "She will make you laugh and she will make you cry. They are only small books and it won't take you long to read them, but I know they will help. She will inspire you. And, Joy, remember that what you want in life, isn't necessarily what you get. You just have to trust because He knows what is best for you."

I looked at the sheer exuberance in Sophie's face as she looked at me from the covers. "Why would someone so wonderful be taken so young?"

"Sometimes, God needs those who shine brightest to be an inspiration for others. To save lives... or to give hope."

I looked up and caught Sister Ruth's meaningful expression. I clasped the books tightly to my chest with one hand and hugged Sister Ruth with my other arm. "Thank you. I needed your comfort. I needed your advice, and you have given me peace."

Sister Ruth kissed my forehead. "Bless you, my child."

As I walked back along the beach, I truly felt that all burdens had now been lifted from me. I relished in the blast of sea air, which was stronger now, and the big waves were breaking on the shore with much more force. I felt invigorated and... alive.

Back at the farmhouse, I took a comforting mug of mocha cappuccino, piled high with cream and chocolate dusting, a box of tissues and my books through to Dad's study. I put some more coal and logs on the fire, and then settled in his big armchair to read. I switched the tall lamp on behind the chair, so that it illuminated me and I read. I didn't stop reading until I had finished both books and it was dark outside.

I did need the box of tissues, but for the sheer pleasure and privilege of sharing her joy and her sorrow. I was enthralled, and what really struck home was that I was, in effect, reading about myself. We shared the same likes and dislikes, passion and concern, thoughts and feelings. She had put into words how I felt about my life and it gave me a perspective. As though I had the ability to view my life from the outside. I hadn't achieved all the amazing credits that she had by using her skills in art, drama, singing, poetry, teaching and directing, but on the inside we were almost identical.

There was a poem where she explained that she had tried and failed to walk in her mother's footsteps because she was in awe of her loveliness and could not possibly match her, so she had chosen to follow in her father's footsteps instead.

We had the same insecurities. She said that she was not a stereotype teenager and did not make or maintain friends easily because she was too deep. She preferred her own company and her romantic nature would rather do things 'the old way.' We loved the same things. Candles, dip pens, sealing wax, shells, home cooking, herbal cures, dried flowers and secret passages. She loved reading and getting away from reality. She also said that she was one-track minded and, once an idea was in her head, she could not change it.

She wrote about her thoughts on love. She wanted a man who would kiss her gently on her face and slowly, gently, inexorably draw her into a proper kiss, because she felt that this was the way men who really care kiss and how women want to be loved.

I was shocked to the core. This private diary would have remained private if she had lived, and yet I felt that she was sharing her thoughts with me, as a best friend would. We were identical. She was describing my life!

At the age of seventeen, she had made a plan for her life, from the age of eighteen to thirty-one, which included an option to attend the University of East Anglia in Norwich, and then go on to be an actress or a drama teacher. She died before her birthday in only the second year of her plan.

The difference was that she had lived a full and positive life, which was tragically cut short. The book was in three sections, which were: Childhood - aged nine to thirteen, Growing Up - thirteen to sixteen, and Maturing - sixteen to nineteen. That's it! The end, at nineteen! The most poignant part was that the poetry and prose she had offered as comfort to those suffering from bereavement were the words that would actually comfort her own family for her loss!

The one act play was awesome and emotive in its simplicity. It was such a clever concept and was also harrowing and yet comforting. At the end of reading, I had rivers of tears flowing down my cheeks and my heart literally hurt.

Sister Ruth was right. It was a crime to not take hold of your life and do something sensational with it. Life should be a celebration of literally being here!

I went to bed that night and clutched my rosary beads under the pillow as I breathed in the linen and the lavender and fell in to a deep, dreamless sleep.

The next morning, I woke with a resolution. I took my laptop computer and placed it on my father's desk and put the telephone and notepads and pens next to it.

Gary called in, as I had asked him to, and we worked out a list of all those available for labour, and their skills, and who the contractors were that I would need to contact. Everyone in the group was related to someone who was a contractor, so it seemed that we would manage to keep almost all the work within the confines of people that were known by the group. Hopefully, the familiarity would mean that the groups would work well alongside each other.

I had been given a challenge and I must focus on it. I didn't know what would happen to my life beyond the conclusion of this challenge and I no longer felt the responsibility of worrying about it. I just had to put all of my energy into this test and let God and Sophie's belief in Him be my inspiration.

Career Planning

I looked up careers choices all day today. I think what I would like to do at the moment is get an English & Drama degree, at Hull, Bristol, or U.E.A., then go to Drama college and try acting as a career. That's six more years of education. And then if all that failed I'd train as a drama therapist. So:

Year	Activity	Age
1997	A Levels	18
1998	Gap year	19
1999	University	20
2000	University	21
2001	University	22
2002	Working	23
2003	Drama college	24
2004	Drama college	25
2005	Drama college	26
2006	trying to succeed	27
2007	at acting	28
2008	Drama therapy course	29
2009	Drama therapy course	30
2010	practising drama therapist	31

Omigod. But I don't see how I can get round it.

Um. That's about all.

Sophie Large –aged seventeen..

Chapter Thirteen

FROM high up on the battlements of the castle, I looked down on my beloved city of Norwich and I couldn't help smiling. I had just had the strangest encounter. I had just had a meeting with the museum's Curator.

The secretary led me to an office and knocked on the door, then opened it. "Miss Bennett, Sir," she smiled briefly at me and then left, closing the door behind her.

The Curator smiled as he rose from his chair and walked around his desk to shake my hand, and then he stopped. His hand, holding mine, went rigid and his face registered shock. He blinked, again and again and swallowed nervously.

I was alarmed. "Is... something wrong?" I asked, frowning in confusion.

The Curator appeared to shake himself mentally and released my hand. He was still staring at me, though.

"I'm sorry, I didn't mean to be rude. Would you like to accompany me? I would like to show you one of our exhibitions that may interest you."

He took me through the museum halls and then we entered an area where some school children were working on their projects. They turned to look at me in surprise as well.

"Are you Queen Boudicca?" a little girl with blonde plaits asked me, with obvious awe.

I smiled at her and shook my head. "Why would you think I am?" I asked her.

She pointed to a display.

"I think you need to see this," the Curator said quietly. He led me over to an area. "Dare I say, meet your double?" he ventured.

I was stunned! I was face to face with a waxwork model that was almost identical to me.

"This," the Curator explained, "is Queen Boudicca, also more commonly known as Boadicea, Warrior Queen of the Iceni tribe, which ruled here in East Anglia and led the rebellion against the Roman occupation, sixty years after the death of Jesus. This model is based on the ancient description we have of her by the Roman historian Dio Cassius"

I couldn't help thinking of Richard. He would have died laughing if he had been here with me now. Richard had always likened me to Venus and Queen Elizabeth the First, and now here was another legendary redhead.

The Curator continued to educate me. "At the time of the Roman conquest of southern Britain, Queen Boudicca ruled the Iceni tribe of East Anglia alongside her husband King Prasutagus, and when he died and her daughters were raped and flogged, her retaliation led the rebellion."

I was staggered. "What a woman!" I exclaimed as I stared at her.

"Boudicca was a striking-looking woman," the Curator continued. "She was very tall, the glance of her eye most fierce; her voice harsh and a great mass of the reddest hair fell down to her hips. Her appearance was terrifying and she was definitely a lady to be noticed! Not... that you are a terrifying prospect," he added gently as he smiled.

Seeing what was almost my double, wearing almost nothing, riding a re-creation of an Iceni warrior's chariot, with her hair fanning out behind her, I couldn't help but agree. Children were enjoying riding a virtual re-creation of the Queen's chariot charge.

"Would you like to see more before we discuss the reason why you have come to see me?" the Curator asked.

I nodded. "Yes, thank you. I would love to." I could barely take my eyes away from my double. It was bizarre to look at a model that looked so like me.

The Curator kindly gave me a guided tour of the museum and art galleries. After admiring the breathtaking displays of Iceni gold, we then walked through the Anglo-Saxon and Viking hall to see what life was like when the Romans left, including Viking treasures. Then we went even further back in time into the Egyptian tomb with its ancient mummies.

There was also an impressive display of the famous Norwich silver. The Exhibition that made me smile the most was 'Shoes: The Agony and the Ecstasy,' which was a celebration of the craft of shoemaking, looking at the craft and the creativity of the designers, past and present. It seemed that shoes had always been a 'must have' fashion accessory and a status symbol!

Later, back in the Curator's office, it had been my turn to shock him with the details of the treasure at Richard's castle. To say that he was stunned was an understatement.

When he shook my hand as we parted, he was literally shaking with excitement and held on, almost as long as he had when we had first been introduced. Again, he was staring at me and blinking in amazement.

"A treasure you say? A time capsule? I can't wait to see it. May I visit you tomorrow?"

I smiled as I imagined his reaction on actually walking into one of the rooms for the first time. Richard and I had been stunned. He would probably have to sit down in shock.

I stood on the battlements and let the sun warm me after the coolness of the exhibition halls. I walked around the perimeter, drinking in the view. This land, that had seen all those centuries of bitterly fought battles for domination over its resources, was a mass of contradictions. It was still one of the most remote regions in the country, in terms of road, rail and air links, and one of the most beautiful and unspoilt areas, and yet it was one of the richest.

As I walked around, I looked down on the evidence of the city's wealth. Millions had been spent on new architecture, which amazingly complimented its treasure of classical beauty.

Many misunderstood this castle and felt that it was a wedding cake of relatively modern architecture, such as Victorian, crowning the hill which was the highest point in the centre of the city. Because it was so incredibly immaculate, few realised that nine hundred years ago the Normans built it as a Royal Palace. Later, it became a jail.

Beside the castle, built underground and into the hill, so as not to detract from the castle, was the Castle Mall shopping centre. On the other side, way down the slope of the land, nestling picturesquely in the curve of the river, was another stunning, classical building. Norwich cathedral was one of the most awesome works of art in the country and had one of the tallest spires. So tall, in fact, that even though the castle was built on considerably higher ground, I was still looking up at the pinnacle of the spire – the actual highest point in the city.

In the distance, near to the Victorian station, and the circumference of the river, was the modern architecture of Carrow Road football stadium, home to Norwich City. It was evident to any visitor just how much the people of the city support their team. There was a carnival atmosphere because the team were doing well and the city buildings were decked with the team colours of green and yellow. Even the balcony of the City

Hall was decked with a giant team flag and the most enormous inflatable canary – in honour of the team's nickname!

Below the City Hall, in the central square, was the country's largest open air market, but even that had been given an expensive face-lift so that she could show off proudly to the tourists. The original, but tatty, striped awnings and metal framed units had been replaced with an artistic, architectural interpretation.

Some stall-holders had complained, because they preferred their draughty, make-shift originals but, after the difficult blip of the revamp, the market was thriving and the stylised effect was beautiful. The units, with their striped roofs, now almost look like seaside huts.

I basked in the sun, enjoying the warm breeze. In the heart of the city, it still felt like a sea breeze, because the coast was only fifteen to twenty miles away in most directions.

Along one edge of the market square was St. Peter Mancroft church. It was so huge and so beautiful that many visitors mistook it for the cathedral and then were staggered when they saw the enormity of the Anglican cathedral. A short distance behind the City Hall was the Catholic Cathedral which, because of its size, was also sometimes mistaken for the Anglican – but that was Norwich! A surprise, but an even bigger surprise waiting for you around the corner.

An indication of the religious strength of the city lay in the countless beautiful little churches. Whether that bore any relation to the countless pubs, I couldn't say – every back street corner seemed to have one.

Beside St. Peter Mancroft was Millennium Plain – a glorious celebration of modern architecture to mark the occasion. The focal modern building, the Forum, was home to the BBC, the library, an interactive visitor centre and restaurants. The giant metal and glass structure didn't detract from the glorious church it was facing, because it was reflected on it!

Behind Millennium Plain was the Assembly House, in Georgian splendour, where the likes of Jane Austen's characters would meet at dances.

There were still intermittent remains of the original flint wall which used to surround a city that was once the second largest in the world, after London.

I looked down to the street below me and saw Waterstones book store. I suddenly remembered that I had promised to meet Lisa and Annie in the Costa coffee lounge, there. I was reluctant to leave my position of Royal dominance, but the thought of a mocha whip with a chocolate flake and yet more chocolate dusting was now very tempting. Lisa sometimes teases me that I am a chocaholic and I happily admit to that sin! Now, an exhibition in the museum about the history of chocolate making would definitely attract me, rather than shoes!

I glanced at the clock tower of the City Hall and realised that I was going to be late. As I walked away from the battlement wall, I glanced at the Chapelfield, which stood close to Millenium Plain and behind yet another church. I had once counted twenty shoe shops in there. I couldn't imagine why a shopping centre would need that many shoe shops, and that was not counting the department stores. It had been the site of the Mackintosh chocolate factory but now it was yet another modern, layered shopping centre and the only reference to its history were the story boards and granite wheels, which used to crush the chocolate, at its entrance.

I'm not sure exactly what the metal sculpture was on top of the Chapelfield. It looked like a space rocket, and frequently changed colour at night. I supposed that, because of its supporting structure, it was a modern interpretation of the tower of St Peter Mancroft nearby, but interpretation is down to the observer. That's what you get for living in one of Europe's cultural arts centres.

The more I thought about it, the more it felt right to exhibit Richard's castle treasures in Norwich. It would be yet another tourist attraction for a phenomenal city.

I crossed the road and walked into what actually was the second level of Waterstones, in front of the stairs that went down to the lower level. The ground was lower on the other side of the shop. I walked through to the Costa lounge. I had thought I was late but, knowing Lisa and shopping, she was probably going to be a while yet. There were more than enough shops in the city to keep even Lisa happy.

With its burgundy, cream and brown colour scheme, the café was distinctive and restful. Ideal for a coffee break for tourists and professionals. The comfortable leather armchairs and sofas were very inviting and the canvas story boards of the history of the achievements of the Costa family added antiquity.

I stood on the threshold and observed those already enjoying the atmosphere. There were professionals in suits who appeared to be having intense conversations, mums and grandmas with pushchairs, taking a break, but those who drew my attention most were the book worms.

What a lovely idea! To take your shoes off, curl up in comfy furniture, and drink in the literary atmosphere with your hand holding a mug of contentment and your head in a book, transporting you and your imagination into another dimension. How absolutely fabulous!

I decided to do the same. I wandered among the shelf browsers and opted for a new copy of 'Pride and Prejudice.' I hadn't read it for years and right now, with the unfolding events of my life which were happening with such speed, I felt breathless. I felt the need to relax with the glorious wit of Elizabeth Bennet. I decided to buy a copy of 'North and South' – Richard's favourite - for Lisa. If I gave it to her as a gift, she might read it.

I also spent some blissful minutes browsing through the imaginative and colourful children's section. I was spoiled for choice. Eventually, I decided upon 'The Little Red Train.' As I turned the pages, it made me laugh out loud, so it had to be good. Annie would love it and I looked forward to reading it to her.

In the café I chose a settee by the window that looked down on the little old pedestrian street. I did as others around me had done, and snuggled into a big sofa. Soon, I was lost in the chemistry of Elizabeth and Darcy and the sparring of their arch rivalry for attention.

"Hello, you look cosy!" said a familiar voice.

I looked up and smiled at Lisa and Annie. "Hello, want to take that sofa?" I indicated to the vacant one on the opposite side of the low coffee table.

"Looks like you've had a feast," Lisa remarked, eyeing my empty mug, with tell-tale signs of cream lining its inside, chocolate crumbs on the saucer and white cake crumbs on the plate.

I grinned as she unfastened Annie from the restraining straps. "Delicious. I'd highly recommend it, particularly the lemon and white chocolate chip muffin. Divine! When I get home I'm going to have a go at making them. It you try one and then taste one of mine, you can tell me if I've succeeded."

Lisa raise her eyebrows meaningfully as Annie climbed up beside me. "Your food is always, divine! Why do you think I spend so much time in your kitchen?" she joked.

I smiled affectionately at her. I really do appreciate her friendship. I rose from the settee as Lisa was searching through the pushchair pocket for her purse. "My treat! I insist, and I know what my best little helper would like!" I focussed on the adorable angel who was looking up at me with her expectant, big brown eyes. "You would like one of those bottles of orange that you have to shake and a cup of cream and chocolate. Am I right?"

Annie gave me a huge, white baby teeth smile and clapped her hands as she nodded. "Yes, please, Auntie Joy."

As I stood at the counter, the owner was serving and his face seemed to light up with pleasure when he saw me. He is one of the rare men who are taller than me and so he is always noticeable. He stood head and shoulders above his other staff and he also was a man who did not stoop in apology for his height. Long, slim and handsome, he was distinguished by his silver hair, which seemed to compliment his burgundy apron.

"Hello, how are you?" he beamed a smile at me.

"Fine, thank you. How is your new coffee lounge in the Chapelfield doing?" I asked.

"Excellent. Really busy. I'm so lucky to have such a fantastic location." He looked really proud, as he should be of two such successful and lovely coffee lounges.

"Mmm," I agreed. "I always feel so privileged, sitting on the balcony, under a big umbrella, looking down on the mall, with the sun shining on me through the glass roof. I lose track of time and place."

He grinned. "I am so very lucky, and its always a pleasure to see you. What would like?" I gave him my order and paid for it. "I'll bring all this to your table when it is ready."

The owner soon brought the laden tray and placed it on the low coffee table. His smile took in Annie and Lisa, but lingered on me. "Bon appétit!" He straightened back to his great height and left us.

"He's nice!" Lisa remarked, meaningfully.

"Behave," I warned her.

"He obviously likes you."

I ignored her and concentrated on the darling little toddler. "Now, you be careful, Annie darling, because this is hot. Why don't you snuggle up with me and let Mummy enjoy her hot drink."

As Annie tucked in to her treats, I reached into my store bag and brought out their presents. "Now this is for Mummy!" I handed the book to Lisa.

She opened her mouth as she saw the classical cover. "But..." She saw my pleading expression and closed her mouth again. "Thank you." She studied it. "Okay. I promise I *will* read it and I will *try* to enjoy it! I appreciate the thought."

"And this is for Annie!"

Annie took the book from me with her tiny clutching fingers and looked at the brightly colourful cover picture.

"What do you say, Annie?" Lisa prompted.

"Thank you, Auntie Joy," Annie said, still totally absorbed in the book.

"Would you like me to read it to you, Sweetie?"

Annie nodded, still not looking at me, and I slid her across the leather and put my arms around her so that I could look over her head and turn the pages.

"How did your meeting go?" Lisa asked.

I looked up from reading to Annie, while she looked at the pictures.

"Great! Really well. The poor man was so excited when I told him about the discovery that he was literally shaking when I left him and he's actually going to come over tomorrow with a team to take a look, because he can't wait another moment."

I omitted to tell Lisa about my being mistaken for the reincarnation of a tribal warrior Queen. I would never hear the end of it!

"You should visit some time. You could spend a day there and even Annie would enjoy the activities. There were lots of children enjoying the interactive exhibitions." I hesitated. "There is one exhibition you may particularly enjoy."

Lisa took another bite of her cake. "You're right about this cake. I love it! Umm… sorry…" She wiped her mouth. "What exhibition is that?"

I watched for her reaction. "Shoes!"

"What?" Lisa face lit up and then she frowned in confusion. "Shoes… in a museum?"

"Shoemaking and design, past and present."

Lisa squealed. "Let's go." She jumped up, drawing attention with her excitement.

"Calm down," I said, quietly. "The exhibition is on for ages, yet, and I told you that you would need a day to properly enjoy it all." Lisa sat back down, looking disappointed. "The next time we come into the city, we'll spend time there. Annie would like to go to a big castle, wouldn't you?" Annie nodded, but she was still too engrossed in the exploits of the Little Red Train to answer.

As we walked back to the car park, we ambled through the glorious Royal Arcade, dazzling in its original Victorian architecture with plate glass and shining marble. On the corner, at its entrance, was another Waterstones book store, eyecatching in its period detail, with quirky, mysterious depths, inviting both serious readers and children to explore its shelves with clever window displays.

Colman's Mustard, the famous family company, was still in its original shop, celebrating its heritage and still taking its supply from acres of Norfolk mustard fields. The pace of life in Norfolk is slow and very little changes. Further on, Annie was mesmerised by a traditional toy shop.

As we emerged at the other end onto the market square, there was a visiting French market, with striped yellow and white awnings that added to the festive, Easter atmosphere. The stallholders looked smart in their white shirts, blue aprons and neat straw boaters. Annie thought that the giant canary on the balcony of the City Hall was an Easter chick.

At the corner or the square stood the stylish Jarrold, looking like a mini Harrods. It is one of the rare family-owned department stores to survive against the multi-conglomerates in this country.

Thankfully, time seems to pass much more slowly here, and the city has retained many of its period features, escaping the large scale 'out with the old, in with the new,' madness which other cities have suffered.

We wandered though the French stalls and I bought a hand-made Easter bonnet for Annie, which looked incredibly cute on her. I couldn't help but think that we had been invaded by the French yet again, this time to sell their produce.

Another thought struck me as I caught a glimpse of my reflection in the Jarrold store window, towering like a giant above petit Lisa and Annie. The blazing sunshine had turned my hair into a burning mass of curls that tumbled over my shoulders and down my back.

I remembered the Curator's description of Queen Boudicca: a great mass of the reddest hair fell down to her hips... she was definitley a lady to be noticed.

Queen Boudicca, Queen Elizabeth the First, Venus, my mother: they all had it - a fiery beauty that captured the imagination of men and their hearts. They were iconic, legendary beauties with the power to captivate and dominate men. Such an awesome power could be abused and that was precisely why I did not want it.

Surprise A Level results

11 am.

I get my A Level results back in one hour. Oh my God. What is going to be the outcome? Were any of my papers worth an A Grade? What if I get B's and C's? Then where will I be? And what will the B be in? Theatre Studies? If so, what a wasted opportunity. Or even English, considering the paper was so poor.

12.30 pm.

Four A's!
I don't know what to think! I mean, first of all I think how incredibly lucky I am. There were papers I did that I should not have got A's for. The General Studies must have been so easy to pass!

Then I think, my God! The world is my oyster! I could go to Oxford, I can take a gap year and to do all those things I want to do – get a computer qualification, some work. Then disappear off around Australia or something, maybe America, and afterwards go to Oxford or at least Bristol. I mean, I can do anything now that I have got the grades! I feel like the hugest weight has been lifted off my shoulders.

Sophie Large- aged eighteen.

Chapter Fourteen

STOOD on the ramparts and surveyed the scene. It was like a set from a James Bond movie. At any moment, a grappling hook would find its mark on the wall beside me, and James Bond himself, would climb over, remove his black cat suit, and present himself to me, dressed in his immaculate black tie. I had to shake my head to dispel the day dream, but what I was looking at was real.

I found it hard to believe that I had already achieved so much. The work was progressing really well, in every aspect. I had come up here to take a quick breather, and to survey the work.

I wasn't able to do any actual work myself, even my beloved gardening, because I was too busy supervising. I had been forced to delegate all of the jobs and I was constantly on call for advice or opinion, to everyone. It was like a snowball. The first few flakes were the notes that I had made and the initial booking of the various contractors. The first small snowball had been formed, when I had put it all together, organised the various teams and set the ball rolling when we started work here. The snowball had gained momentum and it was staggering how much had been achieved in so short a time. We were now in June, twelve weeks into a thirty-two week deadline, and the transformation was taking shape.

I walked around the ramparts and looked in all directions. The road works contractors had carved a scar on the landscape with the JCBs. They had started on the drive by the drawbridge and were working back, towards the entrance onto the estate. It would be to the highest modern specifications of durability and drainage, but finished with a fine gravel, such as the finest stately homes have. I love that satisfying scrunch of wheels or footsteps on fine gravel. They had also carved a very large oval, which would be the head of the drive and turning area, by the draw-bridge.

The old stable block was being restored and Richard's cars would be accommodated there. It was close to the estate entrance and surrounded by a wood, so as not to mar the view of the parkland. The gentry were very fastidious about their landscapes. Entire villages had been obliter-ated and the occupants moved elsewhere if his Lordship felt that it spoiled his view.

We were also 'Going Green!' With the advance of technology, although it cost a fortune to install, it was possible to be entirely energy efficient and have no domestic bills, so it would pay for itself in the long run *and* protect the delicate environment that we lived in.

Below, to the left, a huge sewerage system was being created with a cavernous cesspit. At an equidistant radius, another channel followed the line of the moat and then forked off towards the Broad. This was a tradi-tional style of ha ha wall. The area within the space would be a formal garden.

The Victorians loved their ha ha's. From the formal garden, there would be no visible boundary to the parkland, where animals would graze, but, if you ventured to the edge of the formal garden, you would find a sheer drop, shored up by a stone wall, that was in a deep, channel, with the ground slightly lower on the park side. It came as a surprise to the unknowing, hence, ha ha, if you came upon it! The channel was wide and deep, to prevent animals crossing it, but from the garden, the landscape was seamless.

I had worked with landscapers on a design for the formal garden that would surround the moat and slope gently down to the edge of the Broad, focussing on the water channel between the moat and the Broad as a feature and a wooden bridge was being created to cross it.

In the distance, forestry work was being done to recreate the woodland paths and rhododendrons were being planted. In the era when this was a home, the gentry amused themselves with the activity of taking gentle strolls through their spacious parkland and woodland walks were a favourite pastime. There was a village of air-conditioned marquees on the parkland and security patrols with dogs everywhere, twenty-four hours a day. Because of the timescale, which was a tight deadline, I had decided to empty all contents from the house. They had been packed and trans-ferred to the marquees, where a production line cleaning operation was in full swing.

The Curator from Norwich castle had been so overwhelmed by the quality and enormity of the project that he had called in their reserves, which were an army of volunteers. Security was high. Everyone had to walk around wearing an official pass.

All the fabulous items, paintings, drapery, bedding and everything, had been carefully packed. In the marquees, it was being systematically unpacked, cleaned, photographed, labelled, listed and re-packed. The curator was then going to organise the research and create a catalogue of the treasure. It was a phenomenal amount of work, but it was steadily progressing.

The ivy on the castle walls had been torn down, revealing the old flint walls. The stone masons were busy repairing and pointing the mortar, both outside and inside the walls. The huge oak shutters were now open and they and the leaded windows were being cleaned and restored and so was the drawbridge. The courtyard garden was the design I had long dreamed of. The central feature was a white lilac tree with its branches spreading over a circular seat and path. This was surrounded by four segments of garden, which were being planted in themes of salad, culinary, aromatherapy and medicinal. Around the circumference of these would be four circular lavender beds and four long curves of rose beds, with standard roses as their spine, flanked by low roses and each arched avenue to the central feature was to be trained with fruit trees, as was the fashion with previous generations of aristocracy.

Along the curved arches of the double layer of walkways surrounding the courtyard, I planned a wisteria to start on one side and spread in either direction, and glorious bougainvilleas on the other half.

Admiral Louis de Bougainville, lived during the reign of Louis the Sixteenth and Marie Antoinette, and brought the tropical beauties back to France from his voyage to Brazil. I felt that they would be appropriate for a Frenchman's home and should provide a spectacular show. Wisteria has a slow growth but can be trained to spread over a long distance in its long life and would be spectacular in the future also.

The entire courtyard would therefore be the most wonderfully aromatic vista to wander through, and provide some useful herbs, plants and fruit. I deliberately focussed on the work in progress and nothing more. There were people everywhere, because Gary and the gang had rounded up everyone they knew, to help out in any way possible.

Suddenly, my attention was caught by a helicopter travelling along the coastline. It then diverted straight towards the castle. I felt annoyance. I wondered if someone from the press had heard what we were doing and hired a helicopter so that they could come and inspect us.

With a helicopter in the scene now, it looked even more like a set from a Bond movie. The helicopter had a front like a giant goldfish bowl. Its body was white, with blue and silver stripes. It circled around the grounds and then around the castle. I was really beginning to feel annoyed, when it hovered directly in front of me and practically bowed. I was astounded!

It bowed again and I realised that Richard, wearing sunglasses and a headset, was waving at me from the pilot's seat. My heart plummeted into my shoes, like a lead balloon, when I realised that an attractive young woman, who was also wearing sunglasses and a headset, occupied the passenger seat. She was waving at me, too. I took deep breaths to try to make the stabbing pain in my chest go away. I reminded myself that Sister Ruth had said that Richard's future is not my responsibility. I leaned heavily on the ramparts and tried to calm myself. I am being paid to do a job for him and he is marrying someone else. His life is nothing to do with me and I must learn to live with that.

The helicopter had caused a ripple of interest in the working teams and they paused to watch it land. When the engine had quietened and the blades had stopped spinning, Richard got out and then walked around to the passenger side to help the young woman to get out. The first glimpse I got of her was of slender, perfect legs in a mini skirt. This did not help to ease the stabbing pain in my chest and it certainly aroused the attention of the work men, although they were well-behaved and did not make any audible comments.

Richard looked up and waved again. I put my hand up to politely acknowledge him but I did not hurry down to greet them, as I had when he had arrived with my father. In fact, I took my time and they were standing in the courtyard when I joined them. My heart was hammering, but I willed myself to deal with this. Richard marrying someone else was one of the fears that I had to face up to.

Richard gave me his usual, warm and wonderful smile. "Hello, Joy. I have brought Amelia to meet you." He was handsome and, as always, had an air of understated wealth, even in his jeans and white shirt. Amelia was petite, with a pouting, soft mouth, big dark eyes and a shining mane of dark hair. She was very pretty, with well-defined cheek bones. Her navy mini skirt was balanced with a navy crop top which revealed a perfectly toned and tanned midriff. She oozed quality and class from her immaculate eyebrows to her leather white and gold plaited, peep toe sandals and matching bag over her shoulder. Her fashionably large, designer sunglasses were pushed back on her head. I wasn't surprised by the upper class accent when she spoke. She was definitely the confident Sloane party type I had read about, and I felt sure that I had seen her in the society pages. Probably with Richard's arm around her! Ouch! Ouch!

"Joy, hello. I'm delighted to meet you."

"Hello." I couldn't muster anything more polite than that and let her take the initiative. I felt dominated by her personality.

"What a job you have, here! Richard has told me that you are in charge of the project. What a responsibility! How is it going?"

She was sophisticated, charming and confident and I didn't know how to relate to her. I was at sea without a paddle and felt at a definite disadvantage. I tried to smile at her. "Very well." I couldn't think of anything else to say. I looked at Richard for help. I was very conscious that he was behaving differently with me in front of her. He hadn't called me, Angel, and he hadn't kissed my cheeks.

"Amelia is a party organiser. You know, those sort of parties that are often featured in the society pages. Amelia is very experienced."

Amelia didn't look old enough to be experienced. She must have jumped into the top drawer straight out of a Swiss finishing school. She was probably an excellent skier. I looked at Richard, helplessly. How was I supposed to behave towards this creature, who probably was the love of his life!

She was exactly of the mould of the girls at my school. As one of the few day girls, I had managed to mostly avoid them and bury myself in work.

"Joy is an expert on antiques restoration and interior design. Her home is like a showcase."

I was taken by surprise by his comment. "Well, I wouldn't say that."

"You're just being modest, as all impeccably mannered young ladies are. I have told Amelia, that the entire design of this site is in your hands and therefore you are also to be responsible for the decisions about the house-warming party."

Amelia pulled a face and linked her arm with Richard's. "Couldn't you change the date, darling? Halloween is a bit of a tacky theme for a party."

Richard smiled at me. "That's up to Joy. She may not go for a Halloween mood. If I remember correctly, you don't celebrate Halloween, do you?"

I shook my head. "No, it isn't to my taste. I have not ever done the trick or treat thing."

"The party to celebrate the rebirth of the house will also coincide with Joy's twenty-first, so I think we need a big cake to match your theme," said Richard, indulgently.

"Ugh! Poor you! What a date for a birthday." She turned to Richard and looked up at him with obvious adoration. "Who is coming? How many guests do you plan on having?"

Richard smiled at her. "Oh, the usual crowd. About three hundred. I'm sure that Joy will have some good ideas."

Joy didn't have any ideas! Amelia was looking at me speculatively and I felt I was being checked out. Did she seriously consider me as competition? She was surreptitiously giving me rather odd glances. I'm not anywhere near her league! She was born on a different planet and now that her planet had collided with mine, I had been knocked off balance.

"Oh well," she said, "there's room for possibilities then."

I looked at Richard. "Do you want a guided tour of the work in progress? I can arrange for someone to show you around. I'm rather busy at the moment."

Richard's eyes held mine. "I would prefer to have you show us around and then you can discuss ideas with Amelia."

Why was he doing this? He was being so unfair and actually seemed, by the glint in his eye, to be amused by my discomfort. Amelia was beautiful, poised and immaculate, whereas I was in dusty, dirt-smeared, khaki shorts, men's shirt and a baseball cap. I was site manager and I decided to throw myself into that role. I became a works tour guide and tried to mentally distance myself from him.

The rooms seemed vast now that they were empty. There were teams of workers everywhere, cleaning the intricate moulding and carving on fireplaces, panelling and every little nook and cranny. Electrical wiring and plumbing were being fitted, floors polished and every room was a hive of activity.

"It's a shame that you have come at this time, Amelia, because all the contents of the house are in the marquees so you can't get a feel for the design, but, as you can see, the background in each room is spectacular. The emphasis is on conservation, rather than restoration, so it will really feel like a comfortable home. Faded, French elegance of a bygone era is the theme." I looked down at her delicate sandals. "I'm afraid that your footwear won't take you across the parkland to see the actual contents, but they are very good quality Georgian, Regency and Louis the Sixteenth era." I had been trying to hide my expression beneath the peak of my hat, but I noticed Richard's mouth definitely twitch with amusement.

"I have an idea," Richard said. "I would like to see what is going on in the marquees. Amelia, why don't you go around with Joy and you girls can come up with some ideas for the party. I'll catch up with you, later."

Amelia looked very disappointed and Richard's steady gaze told me that he knew he was dropping me in it.

I took a deep breath. Okay. I can handle this. I endeavoured to take the lead in the conversation. "Amelia, if you do parties, I'm sure you would like to see the kitchen, dining room and ballroom. The kitchen is obviously a mess at the moment, because of the modernisation work, but it will give you an idea. This house lends itself ideally to a party because, as you can see, all rooms open onto the walkway surrounding the central courtyard with their huge double French doors."

Amelia didn't seem too keen to be alone with me, but she was making an effort to be polite. "What are you planning in this garden?"

I explained the design and planting. "So you see, in this courtyard and, when the doors are open in the house, there will be a wonderful aroma wafting through. I plan on everything about the home to be tactile and aromatic. Therefore, it will be blissfully relaxing. A wonderful retreat for Richard, from his busy life."

Amelia wasn't hiding her resentment of me now. She was most definitely checking me out and I could see her hackles rising.

"Richard seems to have a great deal of faith in you and your skills. How long have you known each other?"

I shrugged. "Oh, we've been friends for a long time."

Amelia was peering at me curiously. "It's strange that he hasn't mentioned you."

I made a tremendous effort to smile from beneath my peak. "I'm sure Richard has many friends."

"I'm surprised he has given you so much responsibility."

"He trusts me," I said simply. "Now, here is the dining room. Unfortunately, the gigantic table has been removed, but I don't think you're going to get three hundred people around it for a meal. You could arrange the room with trestle tables as well, I suppose."

"Oh, no, we don't sit down to eat nowadays, not at the best parties!" Amelia positively cooed with delight to get one over on me.

"Do you have a buffet?" I asked faintly. "I suppose the table would work for a buffet."

Amelia glowed with enjoyment of her superior knowledge and laughed. "Absolutely not! We have gorgeous young waiters constantly walking around filling up your glass and offering finger food. The food must be tiny, tiny. Only one little mouthful! Everyone will be there to have fun, not be stuck holding a plate or stuffing their face, when they are having a conversation. We obviously know what everyone will be drinking at a Bowes-Lyon party."

Ouch! Points to Miss I Know More Than You Do! I was rattled. I had to get on top of this. "Come through to the ballroom."

I took the time to collect my thoughts. Richard had said that it was up to me to decide upon the theme and ideas for the party. Me! I had never been to a party in my life! I had simply avoided them, particularly my own birthday which was Halloween. The celebration of darkness.

Suddenly, I had the seed of an idea, which began to germinate in my head. The more I thought about it, the more it felt right.

Amelia could not fail to be impressed by the ballroom with its vast dimensions and myriad candle light holders. The carpenters were busy creating a stage to my specification.

Amelia looked at it. "That's quite useful," she commented.

I tried to get onto solid ground in this unspoken battle between us. "I felt that it would appropriate. For dances, plays and performances of any kind. I think this could be quite a fun entertainment room."

"Of course, Richard will probably use the occasion to announce the engagement. He is so secretive and plays his cards very close to his chest. It will be interesting, because no doubt there will be more than a dozen other girls in the room who will have their claws out, hoping to grasp him." I found this a rather odd comment from someone about the usual crowd of people at their parties, who would, presumably, be friends. Perhaps their friendship factor was different to mine.

Amelia turned to me with a brittle smile. "What are your ideas for the party then?"

This was an interesting turn. The transformation of the house was my territory and the party planning was hers. I was being put on the line to plan what I would like for a party. I racked my brain and the plan was coming to fruition there.

"Thank you for your suggestion about the food and drink. That will be ideal and help the flow of the party through the house and courtyard. Obviously, we have a ballroom, but, with a courtyard out there and the doors open, I imagine that people will overflow and dance outside. There could be illumination with white lanterns," I was thinking of the beach bar! "strung across the courtyard from the ramparts. Actually, thinking about it, people would probably want to wander up there and take in the spectacle." I was thinking as I was talking. "Yes, that flow of people would be nice. The gardens and walls will have some ground illumination anyway, you know, like they do with historic monuments, and with the wonderful aroma from the garden, that would provide a really good atmosphere."

"And everyone in black Halloween fancy dress?" Amelia suggested caustically, now clearly on edge. She was obviously fighting for her territory.

I smiled, feeling better with the confidence of my idea. "No. Everyone in white."

"Pardon?" She was taken by surprise.

I chewed on my lip, still considering the ideas that were starting to flow through my brain. "We will have a Light Party!"

"What is that? I've never heard of one."

I beamed now. It all seemed so right and the inspiration came bursting out of me. "Halloween is a celebration of darkness and bad spirits. Who wants to celebrate that? Yuk! Halloween is the point at which the barrier to the other side is at its weakest. When all those who secretly worship the dark side use all their influence through their rituals to bring the bad spirits through."

Amelia frowned. "Does that witchcraft stuff really go on?"

I smiled, ruefully. "More than you think and worse than you can imagine. Unfortunately, the innocent and unknowing use their children to unwittingly assist that process through the celebration of Halloween and the children dressing up as witches and whatever. They do it because they think it is fun, but it has serious repercussions. The Christians, however, try to stop the damage by holding Light Parties. They hold candles, sing and have tremendous fun celebrating the light that shines from God, which the dark side hates."

Amelia's pretty face grimaced. "I didn't realise this stuff was so serious."

"More than you know," I advised her.

She shuddered. "So, what is your suggestion? How do you have a Light Party?"

"By celebrating everything that is light and wonderful. I think the garden should flow into the house with aromatic white flowers and drapes and music should flow out with a traditional orchestra for the arrival of the guests, followed by a band for some more modern music to dance to. You see all these wall light fixtures, there are also glorious crystal chandeliers which are in the marquees being cleaned at the moment. They hold a myriad of candles. Because they obviously didn't have electricity, which is being installed at the moment, we can still maintain the traditional quality of the house for a party by illuminating the rooms with hundreds of candles. All the flowers should be white and scented and everyone wearing white. With the chandeliers and the mirrors, everything will sparkle."

Amelia considered this. I had scored a point and earned her respect, even though it was grudgingly given, because she could not deny that it was a good idea.

"Yes, I can see how that could work." She looked around the room and up at the high ceiling, which needed no adornment. "Okay. I could create arbours in the room, flowing with white roses, lilies and freesias, with posies of lily of the valley lying around the room and trails of white silk with cascading flowers from the chandeliers. Yes, I can picture it. Sparkling, reminds me of some parties that we have. I notice that you already have a high security around here. Sometimes, a jewellery store will support a party by allowing the female guests to wear their fabulous pieces and the party literally sparkles with all those diamonds."

"That seems to be a spectacular idea, but why would a company do that?"

"Publicity, of course! The parties are always featured in the magazines, let alone the guests deciding to buy some of what they are wearing. It's a huge marketing ploy for the company."

"I see." Ouch! She scored that one against me. "You mentioned three hundred guests. We don't have room for that many to stay."

Amelia laughed and shrugged. "Oh, we normally bus them in to a er... remote location."

I took that shot face on. We were in the middle of nowhere, but this was my territory. "In that case, there are some really lovely country house hotels nearby which wouldn't be too far for a bus journey." It seemed amusing to me that some of the most famous and celebrated people in the world could be grouped together and transported by a trail of buses from A to B. "You could book out Morston Hall, if its available, and the majority could stay at Sprowston Hall.

Amelia raised an immaculate eyebrow. "Are they up to standard?"

I smiled, pleasantly to reassure her. "Morston is Michelin Star and Sprowston hosts the annual European Golf Championship, so I think they can cope with a few celebrities for a night." I was pleased that we could boast a Michelin Star chef on our doorstep and an international event.

'Michelin Star? Hmm, I suppose I could enquire if they would like a catering contract for the evening. At least we could be sure that the food would be good, if that's the case.' I could see the cogs of her brain working.

She gave me a dazzling smile. "Golf sounds interesting. Richard plays golf with quite a few of our friends. Golf has always been a big hit with movie stars. Bing Crosby even died on a golf course! Their wives are catching up though. They are fed-up with being golf widows so the biggest female movie stars are now taking it up themselves, instead of seeing their tennis coaches every day."

More points to Miss I Know More! I didn't know that Richard played golf. I took a deep breath, determined to be remain pleasant. "Among those movie people, is there anyone who could arrange some period theatrical costume?"

"Of course, why?"

"I have an idea. What could be better than to transport everyone to the gates of the estate and then have them brought up to the castle by numerous coach and horses, with liveried footmen and waiters in white, period French clothing and powdered wigs! That would be a grand and traditional method of arrival and departure, and perhaps there could be a firework display to illuminate the sky at midnight. They do that, don't they?"

"Set to music, yes they do. I can picture the whole thing. The fireworks, being part of your Light theme."

"Are you ladies having fun?" Richard asked as he joined us.

Amelia positively draped herself over his arm and gazed up at him, flirtatiously fluttering her long lashes. "Darling! At last you've come back to us. Yes, I have some wonderful ideas for the party and you are simply going to love it. Everyone will adore the theme!"

It was notable that I was not given any credit in the matter, but I didn't care. I just wanted them to leave so that I could get back to work and get this project over with. I was reminded of how my father had described my mother. A whirlwind of dominant sweetness. Amelia was artfully reclaiming her territory with Richard and who was I to challenge her? Perhaps my mother had an influence on Richard's upbringing and he was obviously drawn to that type of woman.

Amelia was definitely stamping her possession on Richard as we walked outside and she chattered about the plans. He was indulgently listening, like a perfect gentleman.

"Amelia, why don't you start to walk those pretty shoes back to the helicopter and I'll catch up with you. I just need to discuss some matters with Joy."

Amelia pouted her disapproval and then recovered her manners to speak to me.

"Well, it's been lovely, Joy. I'm so pleased to have met you. I'm sure we'll see each other again soon. I'll start work on arranging the party." She looked up at Richard with sweet kitten eyes, her body language showing her attraction for him. "You will love the ideas, my darling. I'll tell you all about it on the way home." She turned back to me. "Goodbye, Joy."

"Goodbye, Amelia. I look forward to seeing the results," I said pleasantly.

"Don't be too long, darling," she said to Richard and then turned and began to elegantly step across the rough courtyard.

I inwardly sighed with relief, but I was seething at Richard.

He was smiling at me, obviously highly amused. "Well, how did you two get on?"

I decided to be honest, as I always had been with him. "Like two rocks falling off a cliff." He suddenly roared with laughter. Amelia glanced back to wonder what he was laughing about, and then she continued towards the door.

"Who is she?" I asked, staring at her back with blatant dislike. I didn't bother to try to hide it.

Richard was grinning and watching my expression with interest. "She's someone I've known for a while. She's very good at organising parties and I thought you had enough on your plate with turning the castle into a home."

"Richard!" I exclaimed, as Amelia disappeared through the doorway. "It was so unfair of you to drop me in that! Why did you do that to me? Look at the state of me and I wasn't prepared for… that!"

Richard lifted my hand and kissed it, his eyes holding mine. "Je suis désolé! It was a test and you handled it really well."

"Pourquoi?" I was confused.

"You've been on dry land for so long and you needed to dip your toe in the water, mon angélique. You haven't met your mother, yet."

I gasped in shock.

Richard kissed my forehead. "Don't worry, Angel. I said I would be with you to hold your hand. You were fine. Amelia clearly isn't happy so you must have stood your ground with her. You survived! She didn't eat you alive, did she?"

I shook my head.

"Voilà! I must go now. Au revoir."

"Bye," I said faintly, as he turned on his heel and left me. But you didn't want to hold my hand or affectionately kiss me in front of… her! I thought, sadly.

I stood, rooted to the spot, overwhelmed by feelings of anxiety and jealousy. Jealousy is a sin and I'm still coveting a man who obviously belongs to another woman. A very possessive and dominant woman!

The helicopter warmed up and then lifted off and headed for the coastline. I was still standing there, imagining how Amelia would be telling Richard about her ideas for the party and fawning over him on the way home!

I had to overcome this! I must! The only thing I could think of to do was work! Work as hard as I could so that there was no room for those thoughts in my head.

The dawn

I woke up at four o'clock and could not sleep at all. I think I dozed, for I remember nothing until... a twitter came to my ears, and another, then one thousand voices of birds that seemed to say,

> "Look hence! Look hence!
> The dawn! The dawn!"

I looked out of the window and what a sight met my eyes! The mountains in the distance, then the peninsular and then the lake, the sky flooded with light, and the sun came out, and that was the dawn.

Sophie Large – aged fifteen.

Chapter Fifteen

CROUCHED down on the path to smell one of the pink roses. I lifted its glorious head and breathed in the wonderful perfume and, for a moment, I forgot the organised mayhem around me. The sun shone, the perfume filled my senses and there was a wonderful scrunching sound of fine gravel when I moved my foot back and to.

"Joy!"

Moment over! I took a deep breath and stood up. Lisa was looking at me with great concern. She was wearing jeans and a white T shirt, her hair casually worn up in a clip. She was standing with her hands on her hips and didn't look very happy.

"Joy, I am so worried about you. You have lost a lot of weight, and you didn't have any weight to lose. You have dark shadows around your eyes and you look really tired. You're working much too hard. Give it a break! Take a rest!"

I picked up my baseball cap from the path and then straightened. I didn't tell her that I was aching from my head to my toes. "I'm fine. Don't fuss. We have a deadline and we have to meet it. Only eight weeks to go now, and there is still so much to do."

Lisa was really cross with me. "You won't live to see it if you keep working at this pace. And you don't stop when you leave here! You're the first to arrive here in a morning, the last to leave, and then you go home and sit at your father's desk with all the paper work until goodness knows what time. Don't step on any cracks in the pavement or you'll disappear through them."

"Lisa," I complained. "Stop being so melodramatic. I'm fine, honestly. I just have to get through the next eight weeks and then the job will be done and I can relax, can't I? I promise I'll put my feet up then."

"You'll be putting your feet up long before that, for good, if you're not careful" Lisa said, dourly. "You can't carry on working at this pace. Take a day off, for goodness sake!"

I smacked the dust off my baseball cap and put it on, then looked down at my dear friend, who was ready to box my ears because I wasn't looking after myself. "I cannot afford to take a day off and the paperwork has to be done. People and suppliers need to be paid and as the work has progressed, the paperwork has increased, as well as the business back at home, which has obviously gone well this season. Thanks to you and the girls."

"You're welcome. We have been busy."

"If I don't work at it every night, I won't be able to walk into Dad's study because of the mountain of paper. I'd have to fight my way into the room."

"Better that than having to fight for your life. Your father is ill. We don't want you ill as well."

"Joy, we're ready to put the chandeliers back up!" Gary shouted from the doorway of the ballroom.

"I'm coming!" I looked at Lisa. "See?"

"I do, but you don't," she muttered. "Okay, I want to watch this and hope that you don't have a smashing time."

In the ballroom a scaffolding had been set up. It was on wheels so that it could be moved around the room, but had brakes to lock it into position. Next to it was a winch system to lift the huge, heavy and ever so delicate chandelier up to the men who were waiting to fix it into place. A clever wiring system had been fitted so that it could now have fake candle power, but, for the ball, we wanted it to be used for its traditional purpose. There were ten to be put in place. This was the first. The crystal sparkled in the site lights, which had been used to aid the work teams. We all held our breath as the winch began to take the strain and lift the fragile item. Slowly, inexorably, the chandelier began to rise. You could have heard a pin drop because no one was making a sound. All eyes focussed on the task.

The men on top of the platform were wearing white overalls and white gloves. One of them was an electrician, the others were assistants. Slowly, it went up until it was level with them. My heart was in my mouth as they moved it into position and fixed it on to hooks and cables which hung from the elaborate gilt rose on the ceiling.

The electrician lifted his hands away from it and so did the others. "Done," he said.

After a moment's pause of almost disbelief, everyone clapped and cheered.

We had to go through the agony another nine times before we could actually relax and the team congratulate each other. The house was now becoming a home. The courtyard garden was now done and the rooms were almost ready for the return of their contents.

Now I would have to get my head into gear to create a really special home. The pressure was now increasing. Not only would it have to be right for Richard and his wife-to-be, but on its opening night it would be viewed by Richard's crowd of friends who included royalty, aristocracy, movie stars, pop stars, actors, writers and super models. A scary group of celebrities!

When I got home that night I sank into Dad's favourite big armchair and rubbed my tired eyes. I stretched my aching limbs and looked at the pile of unopened envelopes and documents on Dad's desk. It was the last thing I felt like doing but it had to be done.

The nights were becoming cool now. I put some more logs and coal on the fire and made myself a mug of coffee and a cheese sandwich, then sat at Dad's desk to start work.

I paused before I began and rubbed my eyes again. I felt shattered. Lisa was right. I was tired and I knew that I had lost weight, because my clothes were now hanging off me, but I didn't know how much because I never weigh myself.

What Lisa did not know was that there was method in my madness and it was working. I seemed to be waking at six o'clock every morning. The moment I woke, I got up and dressed and went to the site. I worked until everyone had left, then came home, ate sandwiches and did paperwork until I could no longer stay awake, then I had a hot shower with lots of lavender gel, and crashed out on my bed.

This meant that I didn't have time to think of anything other than the job and all thoughts of Richard had been pushed out. When any thoughts tried to sneak back into my head, I simply worked harder and pushed them away again. I was going to survive this and then I was probably going to leave and start a new life somewhere else. I didn't know where. God would have to decide that when the time came. Anywhere as long as it was far away from Richard settling down and having a family next door.

I ate my sandwich and sipped my cappuccino. Caffeine helped me to work late into the night, every night.

Tonight, I seemed to be more tired than ever. Lisa was right. The tiredness was starting to get to me and I wasn't feeling very well, but this pile of paperwork had to be done. I took another sip of coffee and then used Dad's silver paper knife to open the first envelope.

I stacked invoice after invoice as I opened the envelopes on my left and transferred them to become a pile on my right. I took a deep breath and picked up my calculator. The room seemed to be spinning. I took some more deep breaths and closed my eyes for a moment.

Cooneenawaun Bay

As the very first streaks of light came over the horizon, he went down to the beach by the bay. As he got his boat the bay looked like a sea of glass. When he rowed out, the very first ripples were made. The sun peaked over the hills as he moored his boat and walked up the peninsular. A handsome sight was he sitting on a rock at the very end by the light of the sun, staring out to sea.

Sophie Large – aged fifteen.

Chapter Sixteen

THE sun shone on my face. I turned my head over and breathed in lavender. I was confused. I opened my eyes to find that the sun was shining through my bedroom window and I was lying in bed, wearing my camisole top and briefs.

I blinked and thought back to the night before. I couldn't remember going to bed, but I must have been so tired that I hadn't showered and undressed properly. I must have just crashed out in bed.

I was a bit shocked. I tried but simply couldn't remember getting into bed. I had been exceedingly tired, but it was a little unnerving to have suffered a memory loss. Lisa's words of warning rang in my ears.

I sighed and picked up my watch from my bedside table. Eight o'clock! The work teams would be arriving on site! I gasped and sat up. Ouch! My head ached. This must be what it is like to be really drunk with tiredness!

I put my bathrobe on and decided to go down and make a mug of cappuccino to wake me up properly. I walked down my attic stairs and pressed the latch to open the door onto the landing. It wouldn't budge. I was stuck! The door was jammed.

"Help!" I called out. "Is there anyone there?" Perhaps one of the girls was making beds. "Can anyone hear me? I seem to be locked in! The door has jammed!"

"Yes, you are locked in."

I heard Lisa's voice. "Oh, Lisa, thank goodness. I'm stuck. The door seems to be jammed and I need to get over to the site. People will be arriving now and I'm so late. Can you let me out?"

"No!" came the reply on the other side of the door.

"Pardon?" I was shocked. "What's the problem? Can't you open the door?"

"Richard won't let me," came the reply back.

I was stunned. "But... I have to work!"

"No, you don't. You're in big trouble, young lady. Richard is furious."

This was ridiculous, having a conversation through a door and me standing in my bathrobe. "Why is he furious? What have I done?"

"Not taken care of yourself. I've never seen him angry before and boy are you in trouble. He is fuming!"

My head was aching and I tried to take on board what she was saying.

"Why... why should he be angry with me?"

"He came to visit you last night, and found you slumped over the desk, crashed out in complete exhaustion. He couldn't believe how much weight you've lost and he banged on my caravan, late at night to ask me to help to put you to bed and asked why no one had thought to stop you working so hard."

I was rigid with shock. "How... how did he know it was your caravan?"

"He banged on the first one he came to, which was Katie's, and asked her to help him wake me up."

"But... I need to work!"

"No way," came Lisa's response. "He brought me back here, in his Aston Martin, which was rather nice, and he carried you upstairs. He didn't want to undress you himself, because he thought you would be embarrassed, so I was the chaperone. We undressed you and put you in bed. You were completely zonked out. Richard had to go back to London but he asked me to stay in the house and I'm under strict instruction to not let you out. I can feed and water you, but he wants you to go back to bed and sleep. He is really, really angry."

"This is ridiculous. I'm fine," I complained, defensively.

"You're not and you know it. I warned you that you were pushing yourself too hard but I didn't realise that it would take the tempest, Richard, to sort you out. If I had, I would have called him myself. Go back to bed and get some sleep. Richard said that he will be here at eight o'clock tomorrow morning to check on you."

I didn't want to admit that Richard was right, but I suddenly felt like a person who is really, really ill, and suddenly has the burden of it lifted from them when someone else takes charge and they allow themselves to be taken care of. I felt faint and the stairs seemed to be moving.

"Okay, Lisa! You win! I'm going back to bed."

"Sleep well!"

I held on to the hand rail for support and climbed back up the stairs, which took a tremendous effort.

I sank gratefully on to my bed and pulled the duvet over me. I couldn't even think about Richard. I just went straight to sleep.

The moonlight horse

I tossed and turned in my bed until I think I dozed, then I woke – I don't know why, to find my room was flooded with silver light. I got out of bed and went to the window. There were funny lights that flitted about, up and down, in the silver sky. Then a shape appeared over the horizon from the silvery moon, a horse – yes, a horse it was, with silver wings. I promise it, I am not fibbing, it was a horse. It came over to my room and I climbed on his back. We sawed threw the air. Every now and then he glanced at the moon his home. I think it was a dream but no – my legs are covered in moon dust. Will they believe me? No! Think again!

Sophie Large – aged ten.

Chapter Seventeen

SOMETHING brushed my face. I sighed and snuggled deeper into my pillow, breathing in the lavender. I didn't want to wake up yet. It brushed my face again. I grumbled and turned over. I was somewhere in the lower levels of wakefulness. I just wanted to drift back into unconsciousness.

It brushed my face again and I grumbled in complaint and tried to open my eyes. They were so sleepy, like the rest of my body, and they didn't want to open.

After a few attempts, I focussed and then blinked in confusion and from the glare. Richard's shirt was as white as my bed linen in the bright sunlight that shone through my bedroom window. He was sitting on my bed and his fingers were stroking my face.

I gasped. "What time is it? I thought you weren't going to be here until tomorrow!"

"It is tomorrow!" He said quietly. "Eight in the morning."

I drew a sharp breath in shock. "I've slept for twenty-four hours!" I noticed his expression. He was looking very stern.

"What have you been doing?" His eyes burned into mine.

I cringed. "Working," I said, faintly, in my defence.

"Working yourself into the ground. When I gave you this job, I didn't realise I would be damaging your health. Look at you, you've almost wasted away and you look dreadful!"

"Thanks for the compliment," I muttered.

"You're welcome and you deserve it," he retorted. "I cannot have you doing this to yourself. Why are you pushing yourself so hard?"

"It's a tight deadline." I was still trying to defend myself. "There's a lot to do."

"Damn the deadline if it's going to do this to you. I was so busy working I had no idea you were doing this to yourself. I was so shocked when I found you last night. You were practically unconscious, and when I carried you, I couldn't believe how light you are. Forget the work. It's not that important."

"It is!" I began to feel tearful. It was tiredness but also a feeling of failure that he believed that I wasn't capable of doing the job. "Please, Richard. Please let me do it. I know I've been pushing myself too hard, and I'm sorry. I just got carried away with the excitement of the project." I hoped he would believe me, because the explanation was based on truth, it was just that I had missed out the bit about not wanting to think of him. Now here he was, my rescuer, and I was allowing him to take control. I don't think I could have stopped him, actually.

"If you've slept for twenty-four hours, you need to consume lots of water and some breakfast. Do you feel like getting up? Try sitting up. See how you feel."

I sat up and winced. My head was still aching and the room wouldn't keep still." Richard's hands gently held my shoulders.

"Are you alright, or shall I rush you to the hospital? I have the helicopter outside I can get you there in no time."

"Where… is the helicopter?"

"On your lawn."

"Don't you ever travel by public transport?"

He gave a glimmer of a smile, for the first time. "It's too slow. Do you feel like getting up?"

"Yes, yes, I'll be fine. I don't need a helicopter ride to hospital, thank you. I need a shower though."

"I'll send Lisa up to make sure that you are alright. I don't want you to collapse and bang your head in the shower. I'll go and make some breakfast. Full English, okay? You need to put some weight on. I'm not sure it's going to fit into that tiny stomach though. Want to try?"

I raised a smile. "Yes, and… Richard…" He paused at the top of the stairs. His eyes looked so very blue. "Merci."

He managed a small smile but he was clearly still not happy with me. "You're welcome. Someone has to look after you."

When Lisa and I joined Richard in the kitchen, there was a wonderful aroma of a traditional English breakfast. Richard was standing next to the Aga with his sleeves rolled up and seemed to be enjoying himself."I haven't done this for ages," he said. "Your kitchen fridge was empty so

Lisa asked one of the girls to get the ingredients for me from the caravan site shop."

"You don't seem to have missed anything!" I commented about the full range. I stopped in my tracks. It was a bit of a shock to see a helicopter parked on the lawn, filling the view through the kitchen window. "I can't believe you landed on the lawn."

Lisa laughed. "Imagine my surprise!"

"Luckily, you have a large lawn. Sit down, Angel, before you faint from hunger." He was dominating the kitchen.

The table was already laid and I sat down at one of the two place settings. There was one on either side of the table. My legs still felt weak. I took a sip of the tumbler full of water.

"I'll go and check on the girls, see how everything's going," Lisa said as she breezed out of the kitchen, but not before she had given me a definite, I-told-you-so look.

Richard put some fresh toast on my side plate and then put two plates piled with the appetising food on the table for us.

He consumed his with relish. It tasted wonderful. I tried to eat as much as I could.

Eventually I sat back, utterly replete. "Richard, merci. That was so delicious. Je suis vraiment désolée… but I can't possibly eat any more. I am stuffed!"

"Your stomach has shrunk with not eating properly, but it's good to see that you managed to eat quite a lot of it."

"I did try!" I looked at him as he got up and put the plates in the sink. "Richard."

He turned. "Oui?"

I felt myself pouting slightly, but I couldn't help it. I was trying to appeal to him. "Are you going to be cross with me all day? I'm really sorry to have made you so worried about me."

His eyes held mine and he still looked stern. "What worried me was what state I would have found you in, if I hadn't arrived the night before last. I dread to think how much more ill you would have become and then I really would be rushing you to hospital in an emergency."

"Je suis désolée," I whispered. I felt tearful again, and still quite tired.

"Now, do you feel up to going out for the day?"

"But I have to work!"

He glowered at me meaningfully. "No, you don't. They can survive for two days without you, or more if necessary. The way you were going they would have had to do without you because you would have put yourself off sick for the rest of the job! So, how do you feel about going out?"

I suddenly caught his meaning and glanced out through the kitchen window. "In that thing?" I asked, faintly.

Richard shrugged. "I don't have a car with me, I'm afraid."

My mouth opened in shock.

"I suppose you haven't been in one before." I shook my head mutely. "Well, there's always a first time."

I looked down at my white shirt and shorts. "What shall I wear?"

I could see amusement twitch at the corners of Richard's mouth. "I don't think you have much choice. You're fine as you are. Bring some sunglasses though. It can get a bit glaring up there.

My heart was pounding. In almost the blink of an eye, before I could think of any excuse, Richard was holding my hand and leading me across the lawn to the helicopter.

I must be dreaming, I really must! He opened the door of the glass that resembled a goldfish bowl, and then secured me in the four-point safety strap. He put the headset on me and showed me how to feel for the volume control and adjust the microphone so that it was in the right position in front of my face. He explained that he needed to communicate with me through the headset, because it was too noisy in the cockpit for normal conversation.

I looked towards the house and saw Lisa and some of the girls by the back door. They were waving at me. I waved back. This was becoming totally surreal. Richard then closed my door and got in to sit next to me in the pilot's seat.

When the engine had warmed up and he had spoken on his radio to someone who seemed to be from air traffic control, the helicopter lifted effortlessly from the ground and I waved again to the smiling, waving girls in the garden.

"Ça va?"

"Richard's voice spoke to me through the headset. "Fine," I gasped.

"Want to survey the work at the castle from up here?"

"Oui, s'il te plaît," I breathed as excitement began to course through me.

What a difference! I was awestruck. The world looked like a living, three dimensional map! That was my first thought. I was looking down on the farmhouse garden. I could see the boundary wall and the door in it. I could see the ground that had been trodden on either side when I had used it as a footpath. Up higher, and I could see over the trees, and there was the castle, gloriously basking in the September sunshine. The trees were turning gold, amber, russet and bronze in the autumn season. It was breathtaking!

"Regarde. Quelle vue fantastique." I heard Richard's voice in my headset. He flew around and around. The helicopter drew the attention of the work teams and they stopped to wave. They must have realised that it was Richard flying it. We waved back to them.

I could see the whole site: the moat which surrounded the castle, the layout of the courtyard garden and the new formal gardens which swept elegantly down to the Broad, huge and edged with trees in their autumn glory and fields with sheep and cattle. From our height I could see the river twisting through the countryside as it linked the vast network of Broads. There were a few boats on the nearest Broad and, just the other side of the sand dunes, a flotilla of yachts appeared to be having a race. Dotted around the countryside, were Norfolk's famous traditional windmills, the new wind turbines on land and those in the sea further down the coast, just off Great Yarmouth.

There were now lovely paths through the woodland and the drive between the gates and lodge entrance and the drawbridge was nearing completion. The stable yard, near to the entrance, was coming up really nicely with its restoration. It looked resplendent in its courtyard. On the far side of the estate I could see the convent school and the little church, the lavish landscape garden, the sports courts and tracks and the beach house.

"Wow!" I was overwhelmed with excitement.

"Want to take the coastal scenic route?"

I heard Richard's voice again through the headset. "Where to?" It was still weird getting used to talking to someone in this way.

"Je voulais que ce soit une surprise."

I sat back in my seat and allowed him to take control of my life for the day. "Okay."

It was the most exhilarating feeling I have ever known, as we swept over the sand dunes and left the coast behind. We swooped over the yachts and white-tipped waves, then headed south. What a life Richard has! I was just going to enjoy it for the day. I sat back in my seat and relaxed, taking in the spectacular view. I felt very privileged to have the opportunity to be with him like this. It was such fun! I looked down at the swell of the sea and the sunlight reflected on it. I felt that I was flying in a bubble.

We flew along the miles and miles of sandy beach and saw tiny, old villages perched on cliffs or nestling behind sand dunes. We flew over Butlins holiday camp, where people were still enjoying the thrills of its water park.

We had to divert out to sea to avoid the giant wind turbines in the water and then we flew over Great Yarmouth with its pier, long entertainment sea front and pleasure beach and, behind the town, the vast network of the glorious Broads stretched all the way to Norwich. Just a little further along we passed along the sea front, level with Admiral Lord Nelson, high up on his column.

I heard Richard's voice. "Do you remember I used to tell you about famous people who had come from Norfolk?

"Yes," I answered. "I loved hearing your stories - like when the Frenchman saluted the man who had died when he led the defeat of the French fleet at Trafalgar. "Bon matin, Monsieur l'Admiral."

I laughed. This was fun. "I recently heard that Anna Sewell was born and died in Norfolk. If she was bed ridden when she wrote Black Beauty, perhaps she wrote it when she lived near Norwich. So many famous writers and artists have been born in or drawn to the area. It must be something in the air."

"Or the water," Richard commented. "There's so much of it! We're entering Suffolk, now. Look, there's the Pleasurewood Hills Theme Park and we're coming up to the old seafront town and harbour of Lowestoft. Do you remember that Benjamin Britten was born there?"

"Yes, I remember you telling me about it. He was one of Britain's most famous composers and his operas were performed by the Sadler Wells, who took them on tour to America with Leonard Bernstein. Very impressive stuff!"

"We'll do a mini diversion and pass over the concert hall soon."

Suddenly I was delighted to see the picture postcard perfect Southwold, dominated by its white light-house and with its string of traditional, painted huts along the idyllic sandy beach. I kept expressing my delight to Richard at all the wonderful places he was showing me, and he seemed to be taking pleasure in showing me. I was enthralled. It was awesome!

"Here's Aldeburgh, the other place that Benjamin Britten loved so much. If we just follow the River Alde there, you can see Snape Maltings. Britten co-founded the Aldeburgh Music Festival which outgrew his little venues of churches and villages halls, so he managed to obtain a building made up of massive grain drying kilns at Snape and converted it into one of Europe's finest concert halls."

Richard flew the helicopter over the gigantic building. It was a perfect setting, next to the river and the traditional little village. The old buildings on the water's edge seemed to have been tastefully converted into a visitors' centre.

From our height, I could see the spread of the landscape. "Suffolk is as beautiful as Norfolk. No wonder Constable painted it."

I was now seeing life from a totally different perspective. We were soon back on the coast and heading south again. Richard took great care when we were in the vicinity of wildlife reserves. He kept a distance, but we did see some wonderful flocks of birds. We flew on over Felixstowe and Harwich Harbour, which was busy with the huge passenger ferry ships arriving, departing and docking from Denmark, Germany and Holland. The string of Martello Towers along that stretch of coast were built as a defence against a possible French invasion and now the Frenchman was flying me over them.

We flew over Clacton, in Essex, with its long beach and amusement pier. Then we were flying over miles of wide stretches of sand in the Thames estuary. Sand yachts were racing along with surprising speed. The sun was sparkling on the water as it wound its way towards London in the distance.

I had a sudden dread. I don't know why, but alarm bells were going off in my head. "Richard," I spoke through the headset.

"Oui, Angélique."

"Why are we heading up the Thames towards London? Is there any particular reason?"

He was silent for a moment, and then said, "We're going to visit your mother."

"What?" I shrieked.

"Ow!" Richard complained.

"Sorry." I had almost deafened him by shrieking through the radio system. "You've tricked me. Why didn't you tell me where we were going?"

"You wouldn't have enjoyed the flight."

We were swooping over the water and London was looming with frightening speed. I could see the Thames barrier. I looked down at our shadow on the sandbanks and suddenly I felt vulnerable. I gulped. My throat felt dry. "I'm not ready to see her."

Richard's voice in my headset was gentle. He turned and smiled at me and put his hand over mine. "You never will be ready. There will never be a right time, so you just have to do it."

"But why today?" I complained.

There was a soft chuckle. "Because you're not feeling one hundred percent so you don't have the energy to fight me over it."

I looked at him with my mouth open, staggered by his logic.

"Do you want to take a quick circuit of London before we land?"

"Where will we land?" I was beyond amazement!

"At the City airport. We're just coming up to it. Regarde!"

I did. The little airport was beside the Thames in Docklands. The smaller type of passenger planes, of the size that operated from Norwich, were taking off and landing. Richard pointed out the planes already in the circuit, waiting to land.

Next to the airport, along the water's edge, the gigantic old dockland buildings were obviously in a major development programme.

"Do you see the gigantic building next to the airport?"

"Yes, I see it." It was dazzling white in the bright sunlight. It had a beautiful series of white iron bridges and walkways and it was obviously on the tube line network.

"That's the Excel - a major exhibition centre and that ship moored alongside it is actually a floating hotel."

Richard gave me a mini air tour of London. I was amazed. "I can't believe how much green there is. I didn't think it would look like this. From down there, you feel that the whole area is so vastly developed that it's a concrete jungle, yet from here there appears to be more park land than houses."

"People need their green spaces. It's important to everyone," he commented. "Okay, we'll go in to land." Richard spoke to traffic control again as he had often throughout the journey.

It wasn't the smooth landing as we came back to earth that caused my stomach to tie itself in knots. It wasn't the fact that we were swiftly escorted through the airport by attendants and before I could reel in shock, I found myself sitting in an enormous, white stretch-limousine that was parked outside waiting for us.

I gasped, feeling the sheer opulence of the cream leather seats and soft cream carpets. "Richard, it feels like I'm in a mobile drawing room. It's huge!"

"I think you need some more water." Richard pulled open a door in a drinks cabinet and inclined his head towards me. "Still or sparkling?"

I was dumbfounded. "Sparkling, please"

He took a still for himself. "Ice and lemon?" he asked.

"Please," was the only response I could manage. He handed a crystal tumbler to me and I sipped the cool fizzy drink. The bubbles fizzed in my mouth and went up my nose a bit. "I think you could have a party in here," I said quietly.

He laughed. "Probably, but it seats eight comfortably. Sit back and relax, okay?"

"Relax? I feel as though I am about to have my head chopped off."

He threw back his head against the huge, cream seat and I watched in fascination as his throat vibrated with laughter. He raked his fingers though his hair. "Oh, Angel, what am I going to do with you? Your mother is not that bad!" He looked at me. "First, we have to get some clothes for you."

"Quoi? Non. Je suis désolée, mais… Richard, if she wants to see me, she can love me for who I am or not at all," I said, rebelliously.

Suddenly, Richard was holding my shoulders, gently but firmly. "Your mother does love you but how hard do you want to make this on yourself?"

I frowned. "Que veux-tu dire?"

"You're deliberately setting out to wind her up. It's going to be hard enough for you to see her again anyway, after all these years, and you're just going to make it worse by doing something that you know will upset her. You know that it doesn't matter to me that you wear boyish clothes and that I've always thought you are stunning, from the first moment I met you. But you know it matters to your mother."

"I don't wear dresses. I don't feel comfortable in them." I felt despondent.

"Try!" he said gently. "You know how upset your mum was, that first day when you took me home, and how pleased she was when you put on one of the pretty dresses she had bought for you, and every day after that, you wore a dress."

"I did it for you," I said quietly.

He kissed my cheek. "I know, but your mother *thought* that you were doing it for her and it made her happy! Do it for me now, to please your mother and earn some bonus points. It doesn't have to be a dress. Just something smart and feminine. Will you, Angel?"

I sighed. "I'm no good at shopping? Lisa is the one who loves shopping. Where will I find a dress?"

"I'll take you somewhere. I'll have to drop you off because I need to change as well. Now sit back and relax. Do you want to watch television? It's useful to catch up on the news." He lifted a panel to reveal a small computer. "If you'll excuse me, I just need to check my emails. TV?"

I nodded and he handed the remote control to me.

"Stop fidgeting and relax," he commented.

"I can't relax," I complained. "Everyone is staring at me!"

Richard smiled. "They're not looking at you. You can see out but they can't see in because of the blacked out windows. They're just looking at the car as it passes and wondering who is inside. You'll get used to it."

Richard was relaxed. He was obviously used to it. He spoke through a handset to the chauffeur a few times. I had been to London before, on the train with Dad, when we had come to some antiques fairs. We had got around on the Underground. I hadn't a clue where I was and it was all passing by in a blur. Occasionally, I saw a recognisable landmark. Marble Arch, Hyde Park Corner, the Royal Albert Hall.

I sat back and tried to appreciate the opulence. Because the streets were whizzing by outside, I tried to concentrate on the television news, but I was quaking inside.

"Okay, we're here," Richard said as the car parked in the street outside a small inconspicuous corner shop. "Just mention Bowes-Lyon. You'll have to press the buzzer and speak through the intercom and they will let you in. They're expecting you for an appointment." He kissed my cheek. "I won't be long, and then I'll join you. Don't look so worried. Shopping can be fun, or so the young ladies I know appear to believe. Shop till you drop…" He stopped himself and looked at me. "Not in your state, but go and have fun and I'll pay for everything when I join you."

The chauffeur opened the door for me. People were staring at me because I had got out of the car. I look worriedly back at Richard.

He smiled. "A bientôt."

The chauffeur closed the door and saluted me, and then the car disappeared into the traffic, leaving me on the pavement. I took a deep breath and did what Richard had told me to do.

I pressed the buzzer. "Hello, can I help you," said the disjointed voice.

I licked my dry lips. "Bowes-Lyon," I said uncertainly. "I have an appointment."

"We'll be down immediately, madame."

There was a flurry of activity in the shop and then the door opened and I walked in. The mouths of the ladies standing before me dropped open in unison.

"Oh," said a very attractive blonde lady. "There must be some mistake. We were expecting the Duchess."

They were staring at me in surprise. I had to struggle to find an explanation. "They made the appointment for me because I need something to wear."

They looked at me, taking in my flat leather shoes, white shorts and white men's shirt and obvious lack of make-up or hairstyling.

"Did an agency send you?" The blonde lady asked. I realised that I had seen her in Lisa's magazines and on television as well, but I couldn't remember her name. I suddenly noticed that they were standing on a red carpet that led from the door to the desk, on which stood a bottle of champagne in an ice bucket and some glasses.

"No, I just need something to wear," I said lamely.

The blonde lady sighed. "There's obviously been a mistake. Look, I'm really sorry, but I'm far too busy to spend any time with you because we're all rushed off our feet, trying to get the collection ready for the show. We just don't have time today. Goodbye."

She turned on her elegant flat heel and walked away from me as one of the assistants opened the door for me to leave.

I nearly burst with anxiety. "But I simply have to have something today or I'll be in real trouble with the Bowes-Lyons. Can't I just look around and see if there is something suitable?"

The lady looked back at me and hesitated. She ran a distracted hand through her shining blonde mane. She had blue eyes and a very pretty face, beneath her fringe. I guessed that she was probably about the same age as my mother, and looked equally stunning, stylish and sophisticated. Her short fine wool dress, which fitted her slim figure to perfection, and opaque tights on her slender legs, created an elegant black column, in striking contrast to her pale blonde hair.

I had just landed on another planet and I would have to learn their language!

The lady sighed. "Yes, yes, alright. If it means that much to you. Feel free to take a look around and let me know if you find something that interests you. We're all up on the top floor, I'm afraid. It's hectic up there. Just press that buzzer on the desk if you need assistance." She smiled. "Sorry. I hope you understand!"

"Thank you," I said gratefully.

They left me and now I had really been dropped in it by Richard! There was a large stylish cream sofa. In front of it was a large glass coffee table that had a spread of fashion magazines. I sat on the sofa. My legs were still feeling a bit weak.

I picked up one of the magazines. They are designed to assist you to get it right, aren't they? I read the front cover. 'Hollywood now: the stars to know'. Help! Were these going to be people at the party I should already know? 'Are you a fashion cliché?' Ouch! 'What do you really wear – we keep watch.' Help! 'The return of the black jacket.' I didn't know it had ever left! 'How to work the grown-up accessory.' Oh, no! 'New Season, New Dress.' Yes! That's what I needed. I looked inside to their feature. 'Seduced by the dark side!' Oh, no! Help!

That wasn't any help. I walked around the small front of the shop. I meticulously looked through what little they had on the rails. They were all beautiful. The materials were gorgeous and fabulous to feel, but they were unwearable.

This was a pointless exercise. All I could do now was wait for Richard to collect me because there wasn't anything suitable here. I sat on the sofa again and waited.

He wasn't long. I couldn't fail to miss the limousine park outside the shop. It filled the view through the window and passers-by were looking with interest.

The chauffeur got out and then opened the door for Richard. I hurried to meet Richard at the door. He indicated to me to press a particular button, and that released the door. He walked in, smiling and closed the door behind him.

"Well, have you been enjoying yourself and bought lots of clothes?"

I grimaced. "Can we just go now please?"

He frowned. ""Pourquoi? Where are your clothes?"

"They're too busy and I couldn't find anything suitable."

"Quoi?" His eyes narrowed and his face flashed anger. I noticed for the first time that he was back in the custom of his own planet with these people. He looked incredibly gorgeous in a spectacular black – probably handmade – suit, black, shiny leather shoes and a sophisticated white shirt with a pale blue, silk tie. He turned swiftly and walked towards the back of the shop. He moved beautifully. Now that we were on his planet, I could see that we were worlds apart.

He seemed really angry. "Amanda!" he shouted up the staircase.

There was a faint reply from up the stairs. "Richard? Is that you?"

Richard walked back towards me and took my hand in his. I stood there helplessly, my insides quaking as there was a thunder of feet down the carpeted and creaky old staircase.

The lady appeared breathlessly at the foot of the stairs, closely followed by her assistants. "Richard!" She smiled and then noticed that he was holding my hand. She looked from one to the other of us and her face fell into an expression of horror. "Oh, no!"

I felt sorry for her. She was really embarrassed and Richard was obviously cross. "I made an appointment," he said, with a deliberate calmness that actually accentuated how angry he really was. "I left Joy here, and when I return to collect her and pay for whatever she wanted, she tells me that you're too busy."

I tried to divert his attention from poor Amanda, who looked really crestfallen. "Richard, they are obviously busy," I said quietly. "Look, there is hardly anything on the rails and only one of each. They're so busy that they haven't had time to finish the clothes."

Richard began to laugh. I was confused. He looked at Amanda and she began to smile.

Richard squeezed my hand in his. "Angel, this is not an off the peg shop. You cannot walk in here, purchase something off the rail and walk out."

I frowned. "Pourquoi?"

He smiled and looked at Amanda. "I don't know what has gone on here but I think we'd better start all over again. Joy, I would like you to meet Amanda."

Amanda stepped forward and shook my hand. She smiled apologetically. "I'm sorry about the confusion." She kissed Richard on both cheeks. "Hello, Richard."

Richard turned his attention back to me, still holding my hand tightly. "Amanda is one of the top designers in the world. She has won heaps of awards for her glamorous evening and bridal wear and she even won the award for Best British Newcomer when she first started in business. She is the tops, Angel."

Amanda was smiling at me. "The reason there is only one of each item on the rail and they are all unfinished, is that if someone would like to buy one of the outfits, we finish it by fitting it to them on the seams and length of sleeves, trouser legs and skirts. We always make them too long, and then they can be trimmed to size. Apart from that, we normally make clothes to specific order and work with our clients on getting it right. I don't know if you've ever heard of tailor's dummies, but we make one for the measurements of each of our clients and then we do proper fittings closer to the occasion."

"Do you make clothes for my mother?" I drew a sharp breath and looked in anxiety at Richard. Why did I say that?

He squeezed my hand. "It's alright. I can trust Amanda." He looked at Amanda. "Joy is the daughter of the Duchess Elizabeth."

Amanda's mouth fell open. "I didn't know the Duchess has a daughter!"

"Nor does anyone else," Richard said quietly, "yet! I know that I can trust you to keep the secret."

Amanda smiled at me. "We keep a great many secrets in this shop. I'm pleased to meet you. I'm so sorry about earlier." She turned back to Richard. "We're trying to get the collection ready for the show."

"Can you spare the time?" he asked carefully.

"Yes, of course, I'll make time, Richard." Something registered in her expression and she looked again at me and then back at Richard. "Is this…"

Richard nodded. They exchanged glances that I couldn't read. "I'll make time," and then she gasped. Her hand flew to her mouth and her eyes widened. "Oh, no!"

"What's the matter?" Richard asked worriedly.

"It's like Audrey!" she exclaimed.

Richard frowned. "Who?"

"You know about that?" I intervened.

"Doesn't every designer?" she said emphatically. "Oh, I am so sorry. I shall be kicking myself for this for the rest of my life."

"It's alright. You weren't to know," I reassured her.

Richard was looking from one to the other of us. "What are you talking about?"

I kissed his cheek shyly. "Girl talk. I'll explain later."

Richard looked at his watch. "Now can we please get on with buying some clothes? Amanda, she's in your hands and, not a trouser suit thank you. She's seeing her mother this afternoon and the Duchess will be hoping for someone very feminine."

"Champagne?" Amanda offered.

"No, I'll just have some plain water please and Joy will probably want sparkling, is that right?" Richard looked at me.

I nodded. "Sparkling, thank you."

Richard sat, with remarkable patience on the sofa, while Amanda and her team fussed over me.

I think they must have tried most of the contents of the shop on me. Amanda kept asking Richard for his opinion and he seemed to be making some quite useful comments about the nip of a waist or the length of a skirt.

I had walked in there, thinking that I was going reluctantly to buy a dress, then thought that nothing would be suitable. I was now going to have an entire wardrobe of clothes. I lost count of the amount of times I was in and out of that elegant changing room and paraded in front of Richard to seek his approval. Finally the choice was made.

I stood there in the last outfit, which was a fabulous dress and jacket, in my bare feet.

Amanda shrieked. "Accessories! We forgot about the shoes and bags!"

Richard and I looked at each other and both groaned simultaneously, "Oh, no!"

I looked at Richard. "Do we have to?"

He looked at my bare feet. "I think you better had, Cinderella. You can't go to the ball with no shoes on."

He and Amanda suddenly exchanged glances. "The ball!" she whispered and shot up the stairs.

When she returned, she was carrying what appeared to be a massive ball of white silk. "We'll sort you out with appropriate shoes and bags. I would like you to try this on. It's the star piece in my collection for the show. I want to see how it looks on you."

It was quite complicated to put on. The assistants, it seemed, were also dressers who helped the models at the shows backstage.

When I walked out, barefoot, Richard had the same expression of awe that I remembered from my dream, when he had found me on the beach and thought I was Venus.

I gasped as a thought struck me. I walked to the nearest mirror, which filled a section of the wall, and looked at myself.

I turned back to Richard. "I look exactly like the painting in the chapel!"

"You do," he said, his eyes vibrantly blue. He had removed his jacket and laid it over the back of the sofa. His shirt was dazzling white. He was much too handsome for my sanity. "You planned this!" I looked from Richard to Amanda and back. "This is too much of a coincidence."

"I'm sorry, Joy, about when you arrived. I just didn't connect you with Richard."

"How?" I was utterly baffled.

Richard was smiling at me. "Sorry, Angel. It just had to be done. I took a digital photograph of the painting and gave it to Amanda and guessed your approximate measurements."

"But, why?" My heart was pounding.

"I realised that, not only is it your twenty-first, but also, you are a debutante in the truest and purest essence of the word and I want you to shine. I would like you to wear this dress as a present from me for your ball. Amanda is famous for her work with silk and I thought that she would be the one to come up with an ethereal creation."

I was overcome. I looked at myself in the mirror again. I really did look like a live version of the painting. Somehow she had managed to create a column that accentuated the length and slimness of my body, but with an ethereal quality that whispered over my shoulders and seemed to fan out behind me, fluttering like transparent butterfly wings. It sparkled, with the hand-sewn diamonds and pearls that seemed to have been scattered at random over it.

"I love the dress, and I would have liked to use it in the show in the finale," Amanda said. "I will not charge you for the dress, Richard, if Joy will wear it in the finale and be my latest muse."

I gasped. "Oh, but I couldn't! I don't know how to walk or stand in a dress. I especially wouldn't know how to do it on the catwalk!"

"It's easy, "Amanda said soothingly. "I used to be a model before I was a designer. I can teach you. You're a natural. I can tell by looking at you, and you already have a physique and bone structure equal to any supermodel."

"When is the show?" Richard asked.

"Thirty-first of October for my slot, this year."

I breathed a sigh of relief. "We can't make it, then. The ball is the night of the thirty-first."

"What time is your slot?" Richard seemed interested.

"Mid-day."

"We can do it!"

"Richard, we can't make it," I protested.

"We can with a helicopter, or jet if necessary. Joy, do it. Will the Duchess be there?"

"Front row as always," Amanda confirmed.

"Richard, I can't do it, not in front of all those people! I've always felt that modelling was something I definitely would not like to do."

"Angel, if I were to ask you to taste test a new dish, would you hold your nose, pull a face like a child and say that you didn't like it before you had even tried it?"

"Non," I said, a little sulkily.

"Voilà. Don't say that you don't like something before you've tried it. Portez ça? I'll make sure to get you back for the ball."

"Will you be there?" I asked hopefully.

"Certainement… but I had better be in disguise."

"Pourquoi?"

"If the press see me with you, they may jump to a conclusion I don't want them to have."

"Oh." Ouch! That reminded me to not get carried away. He was still going to be married to someone else and didn't want the press to go barking up the wrong tree and upset the real love of his life. Amelia, obviously. He didn't mind being affectionate with me in front of Amanda and her staff. It was only in front of Amelia that he behaved differently.

"Amanda," Richard said, as something suddenly occurred to him. "Can we not name Joy. Just keep her as a mystery model in your show and I'll whisk her off immediately afterwards so that she doesn't need to give any interviews?"

"Sure! That will be good publicity, actually. The mystery model vanishes!"

"You'll earn some bonus points with your mother. She will be thrilled to be sitting there, watching you."

Richard was on a roll! How could this possibly be happening? "I know someone else who would love to be there, watching me."

"Qui est-ce?" Richard asked.

"Lisa. It would be her dream to be sitting there."

Richard looked at Amanda. "Have you space for one more on your front row?"

"I can squeeze in an extra chair."

"Okay. One more then. Her name is Lisa and she's been very helpful to Joy. She will need something to wear as well. Can it be arranged?"

"Definitely. If Joy comes for a final fitting on the morning of the show, we can sort something out for Lisa, if you let me have her measurements and preferences in advance."

I squealed and threw my arms around Richard. "Thank you, thank you. Oh, I love you…" A strange, strangled choke came out of my throat, the moment I realised what I had said. I looked at Richard in horror, my mouth open. I didn't know what to say. Why did I say that? Amanda seemed to appear deliberately busy with the clothes.

Richard raised an eyebrow. "You mean that you think I am tasty?" he queried.

His eyes held mine and we both remembered our childhood joke.

"Umm... yes."

He smiled and kissed my forehead. "I love you too, Angel. Now what are we going to do about all these clothes? Presumably they all need to be finished?"

"Yes, we pinned and tacked her into them, so I need a bit of time to get them finished."

"Richard," I protested. "Why am I having all these clothes? I won't have the occasions to wear them."

He grinned. "You can always trust your mother to come up with an occasion to wear a dress. Speaking of which, Amanda, you have neglected to show us a dress in the window and I'm intrigued by it."

"Richard, I have more than enough, here!"

He put his finger to his lips. "Ssh. Be patient. I rather like the look of this one."

Amanda removed it from the chair it was draped over in the window and carried it back to us.

"Try it on," Richard urged.

I stepped out, after all the fuss and performance of getting out of the complicated one and into this one. No wonder their changing rooms were enormous!

I looked down at the almost see-through garment. "Sorry, Amanda. It looks like an oversized Victorian nightgown on me."

Amanda was holding the corset. "Come and stand in front of the mirror and I'll show you the trick."

Her assistants positioned the corset on me. Amanda laced it up and then began to tighten it as she looked at my reflection to see the transformation. All that material now hung, beautifully, having been cinched in at the waist.

"There," she said with satisfaction.

Richard's face lit up and I really wished that he could see me as more than a sister and the best friend he had as a child.

He beamed in appreciation. "Tu es magnifique."

I looked in the mirror and I was still finding it hard to recognise what I saw in my reflection today. This simply was not me. But he was right. This dress was so beautiful. It was the most romantic creation I had ever seen. He was right about Amanda. She was a talented artist. It was ethereal. Layers of the finest transparent silk and delicate embroidery in tear drops, forming a broken handkerchief hem which swayed and lifted with the lightest movement. It, too, looked as though tiny pearls had been scattered over it. The top was gathered and off the shoulder, with miniature effects of the skirt on the sleeves. The whole dress was now held in place by a pale blue suede corset that pulled in on my tiny waist and lifted what little bust I had. It was like a fantasy version of Cinderella's ragged clothes.

"We'll take it," Richard said.

"I won't wear it," I assured him.

His eyes held mine. "Je sais." He turned to Amanda. "Right, I think we are there. How much time do you need?"

Amanda looked at me and chewed on her lip. "May I point something out?"

"What?" we both answered.

"Joy, Richard obviously thinks you look great in anything, but… well, do you have any make-up?"

My mouth dropped in shock. "I hadn't thought about that. I don't possess any and I haven't ever worn it!"

Amanda laughed. "She really is a deb, Richard."

"What does she need? Where do you suggest I take her?"

Amanda looked at him. "Annoushka, at Cobella. If I can get hold of her. She may not even be in the country."

Amanda quickly made a telephone call and made a booking. "We're in luck. She was supposed to be on a television slot but it's been postponed because of something that's happened in the city, so she'll do the favour for us. I've actually already booked her to do the hair for my show as well."

"Yes, there has been a big train crash. It's on the news," Richard explained.

"That means she's now available. You normally have to wait six months to have an appointment with her."

"Six months?" I was astonished.

"Well she is the tops in hairdressing and she told me that she doesn't like to look in her diary. Someone else fills it in for her and she's normally booked up six months ahead with bookings for television appearances all over the world and shows and whatever."

"Hairdresser?"

"Don't worry," Amanda reassured me. "She's a friend and she'll keep your secret as well. She's won lots of awards and she's one of the best hairdressers this country has ever produced. Cobella Aqua is an amazing beauty salon with some fantastic treatments. By the time you're finished there, the clothes will be ready here."

Richard looked worried. "Don't let her cut your hair up to your chin, will you? I've heard what hairdressers are like when they get hold of a girl with long hair."

"She'll be in safe hands. Okay," Amanda said, "You'd better whisk her over there." She gave Richard the address.

The chauffeur parked the limousine outside a very stylish, large salon. Richard came in with me so that there could be no confusion this time. He seemed to know Annoushka as well, and just like Amanda, Annoushka was probably the same age as my mother. I realised that I had also seen her on television advertisements and programmes. She had big brown eyes beneath a rich brown shining mane and she had fantastic bone structure. Her personality turned out to be as sweet as she looked.

"Don't worry, Richard. I'll take care of her. We'll see you later and I promise I won't take any length off her hair."

I later realised that I was being given the VIP works! In the hushed sanctuary of the spa, I lost all track of time and reality. I had top to toe treatments which included an aromatic head massage, non-surgical face lift, oxygenating facial, exfoliation, massage, body wrap, reflexology, pedicure, manicure. I was wrapped in foil, like a turkey, covered in warm towels, as soothing, hypnotic music played through the stereo system. They told me it was usual for the clients to fall asleep during treatments and I did! I was completely zonked out!

Later, after my hair had been thoroughly washed and conditioned, Annoushka quietly sat down on a roller stool behind me, and styled my hair. I was so nervous about it. I didn't really want anything to be done to my hair, but I was amazed at the transformation.

Annoushka trimmed it and put in long layers. I had to trust her judgment, but the result was stunning. With using lots of products and careful layering, my hair shone in smooth cascading and twirling curls to my waist, without the frizz that it sometimes had. She said that she had wanted to emphasise the separation of the curls.

I was finished off with a professional make-up. Annoushka had insisted that it must not be too heavy for me. The girl also explained to me how to apply it. I was beginning to reform my ideas about the occupants of this distant planet. Amanda and Annoushka had proved that there are people living here who are as genuinely kind and nice as they are beautiful. There was nothing brittle or false about these two ladies at all.

Richard was waiting at the desk when Annoushka took my hand and led me over to him.

"Well?" she asked.

He shook his head, staring at me and then his eyes held mine and my heart missed a beat.

"Words fail me." He kissed Annoushka's cheek. "Thank you."

I kissed Annoushka's cheek as well and she hugged me. "You look beautiful. Good luck."

I smiled at her. "Thank you."

As I walked outside into the brilliant, autumn sunshine, I couldn't help but be aware that people were staring at me. I tried to pretend that I hadn't noticed. The chauffeur opened the door for us and we retreated into the quiet opulence of the interior of the limousine. I put my head back against the seat and really began to appreciate the comfort of it. What a privilege to be sitting here in this car and transported around London in the hushed privacy of pure luxury.

Richard was watching me. "Well? How do you feel?"

"Unbelievable! I feel like I have slept for a week. I can't believe I have only been in there for a few hours. It was like a luxurious health spa and I was so far removed from the real world I totally lost track of time."

"Have you eaten?"

"Yes, I didn't know those places had chefs who create the most amazingly delicious and healthy food. I've said no to champagne twice now today. It's mind boggling."

Richard squeezed my hand. "Just relax and enjoy it. You certainly look better than the groggy girl I woke up this morning. I honestly thought I was going to have to rush you to hospital."

I smiled at him. "Je suis désolée... and I have to say that your kind of therapy is working. I don't think the treatments in hospital would have made me feel this much better."

We arrived back at Amanda's shop. All the clothes were ready, in stylish and very large bags. Amanda had even chosen the clothes that she felt would look best for my visit to the guillotine, this afternoon. We were now going to have tea with my estranged mother. I noticed Amanda discreetly slip a piece of paper to Richard and he signed it. I couldn't even begin to imagine the amount it was costing him. How did you thank someone for that? It was beyond!

I stood and looked at myself in the mirror. I looked as if I should be going to a wedding, instead of tea with my mother. I was wearing a full-length, navy coat dress, of the finest wool, shaped to every delicate curve of my body that I didn't know I had. Jet buttons fastened from the mandarin collar down to the middle of my shins. It forced me to walk in a very different, elegant manner, on the low navy court shoes. I was wearing little silk gloves that were navy with white polka dots, and on my head was a navy, shallow-crowned, flat-brimmed, Spanish type of hat.

"This isn't me," I said softly to the mirror.

"Oui, c'est ça." Richard looked at the reflection of my face.

"Why am I wearing these clothes?" I asked his reflection.

"It's a uniform, just like any uniform that anyone puts on to do a job. You adopt the uniform, adopt the role and it helps."

Amanda smiled. "Richard is right. That's all we're doing. When we go home, we can kick our shoes off and slop around in jeans."

"I'll bet the Duchess doesn't do that," I said sourly.

Richard laughed. "Actually, that's true, but life would be dull if we were all the same. Let's get you into the car; we need to go."

The chauffeur opened the boot of the car and he and the assistants filled it with my bags of shopping. In an instant we were off again as the car travelled through more, unfamiliar areas of London.

The limousine parked in a street outside an enormous, elegant building. The chauffeur opened the door. A doorman in full uniform was standing beneath a canopy. He opened the shining glass and golden door for us and saluted. We walked through a large marble lobby, our footsteps echoing. Richard pressed a button and spoke to a disjointed voice then he pressed another button and doors opened to a large lift. The walls were lined with tinted mirrors and golden hand rails. The carpet was soft and we were suddenly in hushed opulence again, far removed from the busy street outside.

I was now quaking with nerves again. I hadn't seen my mother for ten years. It was too much! It was too much of a gap! The damage couldn't be repaired! Richard held my hand tightly.

I wasn't sure how far the lift went up. It was travelling smoothly and swiftly and seemed to go a long way.

Effortlessly it came to a stop and the doors opened. A uniformed butler was waiting for us in a large marble entrance hall.

"Good afternoon, sir," the butler said.

Richard smiled. "Good afternoon, Owen. Is my mother around?"

"She's in the garden, sir."

"We'll go through and join her. Thank you, Owen."

I turned to Richard. "Garden?"

"We're on the top floor. Penthouses often have roof gardens. This way."

Richard led me along a wide corridor and into a staggeringly huge sitting room, which was like a warehouse space. It was a relaxing haven of stylish, modern chic. Ultra minimalist, it had a pale, polished wooden floor, occasional rugs and, thoughtfully grouped, cream leather settees of huge dimensions.

The whole room celebrated the light from large windows, which spanned the walls. Richard was leading me towards some full-length windows with a sliding door that was open. We stepped into the garden and I stopped, rooted to the spot in shock.

I looked at Richard in amazement and then looked around. I wasn't in London. Somehow, I had been transported to another country.

I gasped. "Where are we? What country is this?"

Richard smiled. "Spain, actually, although many people think it looks Italian."

"I'm on a different planet," I croaked.

The dimensions were beyond imagination. There seemed to be acres of it, and I felt totally disorientated.

Running along the length of the penthouse was a covered walk way, just exactly like the castle, except that, like Norwich cathedral, it was on one level. It looked medieval, and yet we were on top of a modern building. It was a medieval walled garden with cloisters and lots of little avenues that seemed to lead to yet more secret parts of the garden. There were ponds, streams, fountains and little medieval waterfalls, and there were ducks and flamingos walking around.

I looked around, still disbelieving. "You've transported me to a different planet."

Richard laughed. "No, this is just a piece of Spain, high above the Kensington traffic."

I couldn't hear the traffic. It was totally peaceful up here. Suddenly, I noticed that my mother was walking towards me. The Queen of stylish society, high up here, the closest thing to heaven. She was utterly elegant in a winter-white, sleeveless, wool dress, high black crocodile leather court shoes and fabulous gold jewellery. I knew enough about fashion to recognise the quality of the Hermes silk scarf that was tied with French flair around her neck. I suddenly had a mental picture of the last time I had seen her, wearing an apron and baking in our farm house kitchen.

I felt Richard squeeze my hand tightly and I took a deep breath. "Here she is, Elizabeth. Your beautiful daughter."

"Darling, look at you! All grown up, my gorgeous girl."

My mother walked towards me with her elegant arms outstretched. My fingertips parted from Richard's and I stepped into her arms. My first thought was the recollection of Dad's description of her, "like a tiny, fragile and exotic bird." She was chic, from the smell of her expensive perfume and the elegant French pleat of her red hair - identical in colour to mine- to her immaculately polished nails.

"Hello, Mum," I said quietly as she enveloped me.

Mum stepped back to take another look at me, her hands on either side of my small waist.

"You were taller than me the last time I saw you, but not this tall. It's rather unnerving to be looking up at one's own child. You obviously take after your father for that." She looked me up and down. "Oh, you do look beautiful, my darling. Is that by Amanda? It has her stamp all over it. Oh, clever Richard. Did you take Joy shopping this morning?"

"I did."

"Oh, I wish you had told me, I would have loved to have come with you. Never mind, we can have lots more shopping trips now that we're together again. Oh, I'm just going to love dressing you up and taking you out. We'll have such fun! What a beauty you are!"

I glanced over at Richard, begging him to help me, but he just stood there smiling.

Mum linked her arm with mine. "Now, I thought we'd have tea in the garden because it's such a lovely day. Oh, excellent, Emma's bringing the tea now."

Mum led me along what appeared to be an ancient flagstone path and through an archway dripping with roses, into a secluded area. Richard walked behind us. There was a large iron and glass table and iron chairs with thick upholstered pads on the seats.

It's hard to know what to say to a mother you haven't seen for so long. I let Mum take the lead in the conversation. She seemed happy to, anyway. Emma, who apparently seemed to be the maid, put the pot of tea on the table which was already laden with a fabulous porcelain tea service and a tiered plate with a variety of cakes.

"That will be all, Emma, thank you."

Emma left us and Mum began pouring tea. Richard was reclined indolently on one of the chairs and had removed his jacket and put it over the back of another. He helped himself to a cake and winked at me. I took my gloves off and put them on the table.

Mum squeezed my hand affectionately. "Darling, I've missed you so much. Thank heavens Richard has managed to bring you back to me. We have so much time to catch up on. Richard tells me that you have full responsibility for the restoration of that castle. How is it going?"

I glanced at Richard, making sure that he realized that he had kidnapped me when I should have been working at the castle today, but he seemed totally relaxed about it.

I was glad to have a familiar subject that I could discuss with my mother. "Really well, it's all going according to plan and we should easily meet the deadline of the thirty-first of October." Again I looked meaningfully at Richard, but he just winked back, totally impervious.

"Your birthday! Yes, of course! It will be your twenty-first."

"Well, Richard plans it as a joint celebration for the rebirth of the castle as a home, and my twenty-first."

"And who is doing the catering?"

"It's all in hand, Elizabeth. Amelia is making all the arrangements for the party."

"Oh, excellent! She's a clever girl. She knows what she's doing!"

She does! She's stolen Richard's heart, I thought.

"Oh and we must have a ball gown made for you and you must have a complete make-over. I don't know if Annoushka can fit you in."

"It's all arranged, Elizabeth. Amanda is making the gown and Annoushka will arrange the beauty therapy and hair."

"Richard, you are quite spoiling my fun!" Mum complained.

Richard laughed. "Don't worry, you'll have plenty of opportunity to fuss over Joy in the future. We do have a surprise for you, though."

Mum raised an elegantly arched eyebrow. "What is it?"

Richard smiled at me. "Angel, I think you ought to tell your mum."

Mum turned to me expectantly. Richard just kept dropping me in it lately. "I am wearing the gown for the finale of Amanda's show and I believe that you will be sitting in the front row."

Mum literally shrieked with delight and hugged me. "Oh, my darling, how wonderful! I'm so excited, that is thrilling news!"

Richard exchanged a glance with me that said, told you so, bonus points!

"It's going to be a bit tight on time but we will make it. Amanda's slot for British Fashion Week is mid-day on the thirty-first. Joy will have a friend with her for the day. They will go for a fitting first thing in the morning, then Annoushka's salon for some pampering, then back to Amanda. Annoushka is doing the hair for Amanda's show. Then we'll whisk Joy away before the press can catch her and we can be back at the castle in time to greet the guests for the ball. Packed day, but it will be fun!"

"Richard you are so clever. I'm so proud of you. Well done!" my mum cooed.

I didn't miss the note of affection in her voice. She had taken the place of his mother and he had taken my place in her life. It wasn't his fault but there was a little stab of pain, because my mum had also stolen him from me and now he was beyond me, marrying someone else.

I made a mental effort to recover and try to repair old wounds. "Mum, I am pleased that Richard brought me to see you. I have missed you."

Mum hugged me tightly to her again. "Oh, darling, of course you have. It must have been terrible for you, growing up without a mother. You needed me and I couldn't be there for you, but it doesn't matter now. Let's put the past behind us. There are so many places that I want to take you and so many experiences I want to share with you. We're together again now."

"You look fantastic, Mum. You're very beautiful. Sister Ruth says you are shining in the constellation of stars in this world."

Mum smiled, warmly. "Dear Sister Ruth. How is she?"

I smiled with affectionate thoughts for the nun. "She doesn't seem to change."

I chewed on my lip and took a deep breath. I glanced uncertainly at Richard and he understood. His eyes silently gave me the security and confidence I needed to speak. My throat felt dry. I felt like a ten year old child again.

"Mum, can I ask a question?"

Mum saw the look on my face and she put her hand over mine. "Yes, darling."

I hesitated, and then said, "Why didn't you say goodbye?" I saw the pain and emotion in her elegant features.

"I didn't know how to tell you. You were always closer to your father, and I felt that you would understand if he explained it to you."

"Didn't you want to take me with you?"

Her expression urged me to understand. "Yes, but then I would have been taking you away from the father you adored and I felt that you would be happier with your father."

"You could have asked me," I said softly.

"And asked you to choose between two parents? That would have been a terrible burden to put on a child."

"I'm sorry if you felt that I took you for granted. I did love you."

Mum hugged me. "I know, darling. I know."

These were painful questions, but I simply had to ask them. "Why did you leave, so soon after the funeral?"

Mum's expression was full of compassion. "Don't you think that it would have been wrong for me to stay, knowing that I didn't want to be with your father? I felt that would have been cruel, and your father wouldn't have wanted me under those circumstances."

"Did you love Daddy?" It was the plaintive question of a wounded, ten year old child.

Mum smiled gently. "Yes, but I had married your father when I was young and had no experience of life. It wasn't until I met Robert that I knew how it felt to truly be in love." Mum looked affectionately at Richard and then back at me. "Richard's mother had been ill for several years, so they had not had a... normal relationship, and, your father and I had sort of drifted apart. He seemed to think it was just normal family life, but I felt neglected, sad and lonely, sort of like a spare part really. It was soon after the funeral that Robert and I started our life together, but it just seemed right to do so. Richard has told me that Alfred is planning to marry Ruby. It hadn't taken me long to realise that she was in love with him and I realised that he had a great deal of affection for her. I'm sure they will be happy together now."

I frowned. "How did you know?"

Mum smiled. "A woman's intuition. Your stomach can tell you a great deal."

I hesitated. "It makes me feel… very strange, that I was born to two people who didn't really love each other."

Mum hugged me tightly. "Darling, we thought that we were in love when we had you. We both loved you and we still do. That bond will never change, no matter what has happened."

I looked steadily at her. "I think I understand," I said hesitantly. "It's almost the opposite of two people who were obsessed with each other, had a daughter and didn't want her. Sister Ruth told me that you were an orphan of parents who had neglected you."

"Putting it like that, I suppose a reaction between opposites was inevitable," Mum said gently.

"I've been thinking about it. Did you use clothes to win approval, like Audrey Hepburn?" I ventured.

Mum was thoughtful. "I suppose I did. I wanted to be liked and I wanted to please others. My parents hadn't wanted me and I then found myself in a different environment, where I had thirty loving and adoring mothers. I think I learned, from an early age, that the way I looked pleased people and clothes were a sort of tool that could get me anything I wanted - which was to be liked and approved of by others."

I took a deep breath and decided to be honest. "I thought that your focus on image meant that you were superficial and shallow. I wanted you to love me for who I was, not how I looked, which was why I reacted against you and didn't want to be 'dressed up' for you. I rebelled and you always seemed… disappointed."

"Like a magnetic field," Mum said softly. "The repelling reaction of total opposites." She gently squeezed my hand. "So very many years we have lost because we didn't understand the problem, and it is Richard who has made us face up to our errors." Mum smiled gratefully at Richard and then her eyes searched mine. "Can we make up for lost time now?"

I nodded, unable to speak because my lips were pressed firmly together in an effort to prevent the tears that were welling up inside me from overflowing.

"The thing is, my darling," Mum continued, her voice slightly croaky with emotion, "you are so much stronger inside than me. I need to hide behind the clothes, but you don't, because you are wonderful inside and out. I do have to say, however, that you are stunningly beautiful and your beauty is enhanced by these fine clothes. I am so very proud of you, with or without the clothes. I loved you as your mum, and I'm still your mum."

I couldn't speak. I felt so emotional and I was about to dissolve. Richard rescued me.

"Elizabeth, Angel is potty about gardens. May I show her the rest? She thought she was on a different planet when she stepped into it."

Mum squeezed my hand affectionately. "It's a shock to most people. Yes, Richard. Do show your Angel around."

Richard took my hand and led me around the garden. It was breathtaking. The covered walkway, with its ancient stone archways, had a low shelf of stone which was like one long seat. We sat in the cool shade and I tried to take it in.

We walked along narrow paths that led to secret little gardens with different themes. In some there was a pond, in others a surprise seat, tucked into clipped box hedging, or under a stone arched recess. Turn a corner and there was an interesting statue, sometimes on a stone shelf. The whole garden was enclosed by an ancient stone wall which was high, but at intervals there were roundels so that you could peek through, looking down on the rooftops of London, just to remind yourself that there was another world out there.

We walked back, still with Richard holding my hand, to rejoin my mother. I had relaxed now. I had to. This had totally thrown me off balance. A dream world - and my mum was the Queen of it!

She walked towards us and put her arm around me. "Well? What do think of our world? Do you think you could live in it?"

She and Richard were watching my expression very carefully. I shook my head in awe. "I don't know. It's beyond imagination. I knew that you lived in luxury, but this is something else!"

Mum turned suddenly, her attention distracted. "Robert!" she exclaimed. "Look who's here!" My stomach immediately cramped. I was about to come face to face with my step-father. I felt Richard's arm around my shoulder as he gently turned me, and it stayed there to support me.

The Duke walked forward swiftly, a beaming smile of delight on his face, and he enveloped me in a tight hug. He stepped back to look at me and held both my hands. Richard's arm was still comfortingly around my shoulders.

"Oh... Richard, your Angel is just as stunning as you described. My dear, you are so beautiful. Elizabeth, look at your daughter!"

"I know," Mum was radiant. "Isn't she gorgeous?"

The Duke kissed both of my cheeks. "Bienvenue."

I was in awe of the Duke and felt rigid with nerves. He was like an older version of Richard, but not as tall, and his hair was dark brown. His eyes were not so large, and a paler blue, but he was very handsome and he and Richard still looked very much alike.

It wasn't his looks that made me nervous. It was his whole presence. Whereas Richard emanated a film star presence and an aura of wealth, his father emanated a presence of sheer power and success in life. The aura oozed from every cell in his body and every stitch of his obviously hand-made clothes.

This man had achieved some awesome things in his life and I could tell just by looking at him, even though he was just standing in front of me. His whole being commanded respect. This was what Richard had meant when he said that he had taken over the reins from his father and had a lot to live up to.

The Duke then turned to his wife and embraced her fondly. "My dear, I'm sorry that I am late. Can you forgive me?"

"Always, my darling." She kissed him on the cheek. "Shall I ask Emma to bring a fresh pot of tea?"

"I already asked Owen. Ah, here's Emma now."

We returned to the tea table. Richard urged me to have another cake. "I don't want you to faint from hunger on the way home."

"Are you trying to fatten me up?" I asked him.

"Yes." He grinned.

"If you succeed, I won't fit into those clothes."

He shrugged. "I'll buy some more." He was impossible! I tried to focus on my mother. I noticed that she and the Duke were holding hands and he several times kissed her cheek affectionately.

"They can't keep their hands off each other," Richard commented.

"And why not? We are still very much in love." Their expressions showed complete adoration for each other.

"One day, I hope you will know such happiness," the Duke said to his son.

"I already do," Richard replied evenly, "and when I am married I will be as fortunate as you."

Ouch! Ouch! I had a stabbing pain in my chest. I looked down.

"And do you know what the key to my happiness is, Joy?"

I looked up. "No, your Lordship."

"Robert," he insisted. "Please call me Robert. The key to my happiness is to let your mother organise my life. She plans everything and just tells me what to do, where we will be, and when. She completely runs my life for me, don't you my darling?" He kissed my mother's hand and the look he and my mother exchanged showed that they were, indeed, very much in love.

"Joy, I think we need to go. I have to get you back home and you've had a long day," Richard said quietly.

My heart felt like a lead weight as I picked up my gloves.

Mum enveloped me again and then so too did the Duke. I had been welcomed like the prodigal daughter.

"Goodbye, darling. I'll see you very soon," Mum said.

"You must visit us again, soon," the Duke reaffirmed his wife's sentiments.

"Bye, Mum. Bye... Robert. Thank you. It's been lovely to see you."

Mum kissed Richard's cheek and his father shook his hand. "Merci beaucoup. This has meant a lot to Elizabeth."

We left them standing in their idyllic garden and returned to the real world. Well, almost! First, there was a journey by chauffeur-driven limousine to the City airport. Then a helicopter flight back home to the farmhouse lawn and I couldn't help thinking about my shirt, shorts and shoes packed somewhere in the pile of stylish bags on the seats behind us.

That night, I lay in my bed and looked up at the beams in the apex ceiling of my attic room, feeling disorientated. My body felt numb with shock and my mind was a whirl of emotions.

How could it have happened so fast? This morning, I had been woken by the man I am in love with, sitting on my bed in my little room, in my ordinary farmhouse and in my ordinary life. Tonight, I was lying here, with a wardrobe full of clothes, created and fitted by one of the world's top designers, my hair had been styled by one of this country's greatest ever hairdressers and I was now back from a whirlwind day trip to another planet. I was going to have to visit the planet again as I was expected to participate in the finale of one of the most prestigious fashion shows. I was almost shell-shocked. I had stepped out of my ordinary life and into the top drawer, just like that!

Now I had another problem. I had avoided wanting to see Richard, because I didn't want any contact with my mother. Suddenly, that had up-ended, because I now didn't want to see my mother because I wanted to avoid contact with Richard. He was marrying someone else and that was much too painful to bear!

It seemed that all aspects of my life were moving and switching at the moment. Like the earth's tectonic plates, the constant force of one against another meant that if I took my eyes off one aspect, and then looked again, it was different. Nothing was staying the same, when all I had wanted on the first day of spring was for my life to remain unchanged.

I thought of my mother in her medieval garden on top of a modern building, high above the streets of London. It was like a surreal castle tower for the high living Queen.

Everything in my life had become bizarre. There was no solid ground for me to stand on. Nothing I could be certain of.

I closed my eyes and remembered the leap of faith that Sister Ruth had asked me to take. There was literally nothing I could do except give it all to God to sort out for me.

I prayed fervently and gave all the responsibility for my life to God, and then I had a feeling of complete release, of letting go of everything. It was a blissful moment of sheer exhilaration. All burdens and pressure suddenly evaporated as I gave them away.

I had a vision in my head. I leaped off a cliff, but I didn't fall. I didn't panic. I was just floating. I couldn't get back to the safe ground on top of the cliff just a few feet away, but I didn't want to. I didn't go down and I didn't go up. I just floated, level with the top of the cliff, and there were golden balls floating around me. I couldn't reach them. They just stayed, nearby and I felt the Holy Spirit, as a warmth spread through me and tingled every nerve-ending on my body with a wave of emotion. No wonder nuns gave their lives to God, if this was how wonderful they felt.

I snuggled deeper into my pillow. I felt like a child, safe and secure in the knowledge that someone was looking after me and so I could relax into a deep and peaceful sleep.

AUTUMN – A fine Autumn Day

Go for a walk in a beech wood & catch 12 leaves & put them in your boot. 12 leaves for 12 lucky months of the year.

Sophie Large – aged nine.

Chapter Eighteen

ON a Sunday morning, in the middle of October, I woke, with the bright sunlight pouring through my window. It was now two weeks before the deadline and I knew exactly what I wanted to do that day. It would be my last opportunity.

When I had showered and had breakfast, I stood in front of the full length mirror in my bedroom and slipped the ethereal, handkerchief petal dress over my head. The pale blue suede corset was difficult to put on, but I managed it. I looked at myself. With my bare feet, I did indeed look like a fantasy Cinderella.

I had borrowed one of the original Georgian ladies' hooded cloaks from the castle, because I had planned this. I put the pale blue ballet shoes on, which matched the corset, pulled the hood over my head and felt like Meryl Streep, in the 'French Lieutenant's Woman,' as I left the farmhouse to walk to the castle.

It was now out of season for the tourists so the girls were not coming to the farmhouse today, and no-one would see me, apart from the security, patrolling the castle grounds and they wouldn't take much notice of me. I wanted to be alone in my dream castle, just once more. It now looked like a home, and I wanted to enjoy one more fantasy before the rush started on the big build-up to the party.

I walked through the shrubbery and opened the door in the wall. I walked along the woodland path towards the parkland. The path was now knee deep in fallen leaves. It was a sea of gold and rust and brown, which scrunched in a satisfying way, as I waded through, leaving a parted trail behind me. My long cloak rustled as it spread over the leaves. The sky was blue and the air was still. Occasionally the silence was broken by the echoing call of pheasants, which were wearing their own autumn glory.

The cloak swooshed over the grass as I walked across the parkland towards the castle. It bathed resplendent in the golden autumn sun.

I acknowledged the patrol guards who saw me and then entered the castle and breathed a sigh of relief to be alone here, just once more.

I walked along the paths in the courtyard garden, as ladies would have done more than two hundred years before. My feet scrunched on the fine gravel and my cloak rustled and swooshed in the movement. The garden would be glorious next spring. For now it had been trimmed ready for its winter sleep, but the herbs and lavender still gave a blissful aroma when I rubbed them with my hands and breathed in their sweet smell.

I used the matches and taper, which I kept in the chapel, and lit the candles. I knelt on one of the two needle point cushions in front of the altar and I prayed, to say thank you to God for helping me over the last seven months to achieve the task which had been set for me, and to ask him to please help me through the next two weeks to the deadline and most particularly, the last night. I just didn't see how He was going to get me through that, but I trusted Him to help me. When I had finished my prayers, I looked up at the writing on the walls. The gold letters glistened in the flickering candle light.

The first proverb that I focussed on was the twentieth, and in modern translation it said, 'Homes are built on the foundation of wisdom and understanding. Where there is knowledge, the rooms are filled with valuable and beautiful things.' I know that God does this sort of thing and gives you messages, but I couldn't work out what he was trying to tell me with this one.

I left the cloak in the chapel and wandered through the house. Room after room now had exactly the tone of faded French chic which I had been aiming for. There was no dust. It was impeccably clean. Oak floors shone with polish, showing off their wonderful patina. Glass panels in the huge French windows sparkled. Elegant table lamps and wall lights illuminated with a soft glow and reflected off mahogany and cherry wood tables.

The sumptuous materials of the upholstered furniture and drapery now showed off the glory of their finery with soft, delicate tones and glistening, gold thread. The gold leaf on the furniture and picture frames shone with a subtle ambience and the paintings, having been expertly cleaned, were even more exquisite, now that their occupants could show off their beauty and the finery of their clothing. The modern, but classic style cream sofas blended with the old furniture beautifully. Large vases of white and burgundy-striped lilies filled the home with their incredible perfume.

One room had been left almost empty, except for a couple of antique sofas. We had been told that the magazine people would be needing this for a studio to photograph all the guests.

I had wanted the giant kitchen to retain the charm of a French farmhouse, with individual armoires and chests, and keep the feature inglenook fireplace, ironwork, range, bread oven and deep ceramic sinks, but it now had the modern convenience of electricity and a plumbing system linked to the sinks, with a useful waste disposal.

One of the giant tables was retained for its usefulness as a work surface and another for family dining, illuminated by lighting suspended from the high ceiling. I didn't want to think about a family enjoying the splendour and homeliness of this kitchen. This had been one of my favourite and most painful aspects of the project. The other was the bedrooms, with their now luxurious bedding and en-suite bathrooms. I didn't know which room Richard would select as his marital master bedroom, and I didn't want to. The stabbing started in my chest again.

I left the kitchen and walked through to the ballroom. The marble floor shone in the light through the long diamond leaded windows. I found a box of matches and a lighting taper. I slowly walked around and lit the candles on the wall lights. The room became illuminated with a soft flickering glow. The light danced and sparkled in the mirrors and crystal, and gleamed on the gold leaf frames.

Rags and bottles of cleaning solution had been left on the floor by the girls who had been polishing the mirrors. I picked up a rag and bottle and began to polish. It was silent in the vast room. I hummed to myself and then noticed a portable hi-fi with a CD player. I pressed the play button and the music from the powerful little unit filled the room.

I polished the mirror and swayed to the music. I noticed the ethereal lightness of the fine silk of my dress as it moved.

The music was Latin American, powerful and evocative. I felt the rhythm of the strong beat and I couldn't help myself. I felt a connection with the lyrics and the rhythm, and I put down the rag and bottle.

The music invaded my senses and I gave myself up to release the uninhibited stir of emotions that had lain dormant within me, until now. My dress was sensual and feminine and moved beautifully as I responded to the pulse of the beat. The music was fast, fierce, powerful, dominating. It filled the entire room from the small but powerful speakers and it pounded through my body.

It was seductive and it drew me into a world I hadn't known before. The art of seduction. My senses swam with a new sensation. I lived for the moment. It was entrancing. This was different from two children trying to learn to waltz, in antique clothing, to the sound of a wind-up record player. I didn't know that I could dance. I didn't know that I was capable - but I just let go of all inhibitions. I danced in front of the mirror, enjoying the thrill.

The lyrics were sung by a man in praise of a woman who was just beginning to understand her power over men. She was starting to become aware of the pain and pleasure that she could arouse in men when she had drawn them into ecstasy. She was learning to play a game. He had closed his eyes for a moment, revelling in the emotion, and then found that she had vanished, leaving him reeling from shock and wanton longing for her tantalising mystery.

I was lured by the rhythm and lyrics into becoming that woman. I felt her exquisite beauty and power and the heady experience of realising that you had that power over men. It was hypnotic and alluring.

I pounded, gyrated, swayed and stretched, sensually and suddenly found myself caught and pulled against something long and hard. I gasped and my eyes opened wide in astonishment to find Richard's face so close to mine - and I realised that he was holding me against his body. He must have been watching me! I blushed and tried to step back but his powerful arms held me closely against him.

I struggled to breathe. His eyes were intense, on fire, and his mouth was much too sensual and much too close. This was like Sleeping Beauty, the Princess Aurora. She was dancing and singing in the forest, completely unaware that she was being watched, until the Prince caught her and pulled her against him.

As our eyes locked, I became aware of the lyrics. The singer was asking if we remembered summer days and did we remember how we were? His hands moved inexorably over my body, over my bare neck and shoulders, leaving a trail of fire on my skin. They moulded to every curve and taut sinew. I became fluid in his arms, like hot molten lava. I felt a need for him in the core of my body, and its searing heat coursed through me, rushing through my veins, making my skin tingle in anticipation. I had not experienced this before, but I instinctively knew what it meant. He had ignited a flame in me and I wanted him. I now had a deep, burning desire that only he could assuage.

I was also the seductive temptress in the lyrics. I had her power. He was moving me but I felt the power that I had over him. I wanted him to be mine and I had the power to have him.

My eyes told him that I knew how I was arousing him as we moved, in perfect rhythm. I twisted, moved and flowed to his direction.

The music changed. Richard and the singer interfaced and I was lost in the arousing lyrics and provocative rhythm. I was the innocent girl in the song, trying out her power on the man and unaware of just how much need for me I was creating in him. He found me incredibly sexy and wanted to make love to me. He wanted to draw me out, break down my walls of inhibition and see me totally break down in his arms.

Richard's hands moved me so that I arched and stretched to his touch, with muscles I didn't even know I had. I didn't know that he could dance so rhythmically - but then I didn't know that he could play golf or fly a helicopter. In many ways, he was a stranger to me. I completely gave myself up, in uninhibited pleasure. I was a musical instrument in his arms and he played a tune on me, extracting notes that I didn't know I was capable of.

The music changed and the rhythm became slower, even more sensual and seductive. The music and Richard had control over me, but I used it as I felt the power that I had over him as our bodies entwined in the dance.

We lived in the moment because the lyrics were astounding. I became the woman in a darkened room, feeling lost and lonely, and Richard was the man, standing in the shadows, wanting me and waiting to love me. Hoping that I would hear the serenade that he was using to try to get me to respond to him, so that my heart could find him. He was singing that time is precious and it's slipping away and he had been waiting for me all his life.

He sang that no one wants to be lonely and no one wants to cry and that his body was longing to hold me so much that it hurt inside. He was singing to me, hoping that I could hear him and respond to his need for me. He envisioned me flying down the stairs into his waiting arms. He was pleading for me to hear him and begging me not to walk away.

I arched and flowed and lived through every rhythm and sentiment. It was me. It was us and we were here. I loved Richard so much and I felt the need and aching desire.

Our eyes locked. Both of us seemed to be struggling to breathe. Richard kissed my left cheek, then my right cheek and then my forehead. I ached for his mouth on my lips. I suddenly realised that my corset had come loose. I hadn't been able to fasten it quite correctly on my own this morning and now the bow had come undone.

Richard's hand found its way under the garment and I could feel the heat of his hand against my back, through the gossamer thin silk of my dress. I trembled with desire and anticipation, drawing in a sharp breath of exquisite delight. I arched against him.

Suddenly, he released me like I was a hot coal, too painful to hold and he stepped back from me.

Without his support, my legs felt too weak and I crumpled to the floor, my dress a pool of silk on the cold marble, my corset in disarray.

He raked a distracted hand through his hair and my fingers itched, wanting to do that for him. Now, there was a definite barrier between us.

"Il faut que j'aille," he said, shakily.

My heart was pounding. "Richard!" It was an agonised plea.

The emotions etched on his face were as agonised as I felt. He saw the tears in my eyes. "Angel, don't cry. I'm sorry. I…I shouldn't be here. Something has just occurred to me. I… I have to go."

He turned on his heel and walked away across the marble floor. As I watched him, the profound lyrics filled the room, "Run to me, run to me cause I'm dyin', I wanna feel you need me, just like the air you're breathin', I need you here in my life, don't walk away, don't walk away don't walk away, no, no! Nobody wants to be lonely, nobody wants to cry."

Tears poured down my cheeks as he walked towards the door and I closed my eyes with the sheer agony of my emotions. I was shaking. I opened my eyes again and he was gone.

Princess Aurora and Prince Phillip had fallen in love when they were dancing, once upon a dream. Was this a nightmare? What had I done? I had lost him, for sure. But then, he wasn't ever mine, and now I had lost him completely and my heart was breaking. I took a deep, shuddering breath but the tears just kept pouring down my face.

My life was such a mess and now I had just made it worse! Why did I do that? Why did I imagine that I had a seductive power that could win him away from another woman, cast a spell over him and make him mine?

He could obviously dance, so he had only been playing the role. I had seen 'Dirty Dancing' and those dancing competitions on television. They just played to the role, but I had got carried away, with the lyrics so closely relating how I felt, and imagined that I had a seductive power over him. I had made it clear to him that I wanted more and now I had embarrassed him and embarrassed myself.

I realised that when faced with the temptation of being so tantalisingly close to the man I wanted, I had tried to use and abuse the power of the legendary redheads. The power that my elevated morals had shunned was what I had obviously, secretly yearned for.

Now I was faced with the dismal truth that I wasn't in their league. I didn't have their beauty or their power but the reality was that I had actually wanted to be like them and if the opportunity had been there, just how far would I have taken it?

I hadn't wanted to have any contact with Richard in the future because it would be just too painful when he was married to another woman and now he would feel too awkward to ever be in my company again. This was humiliating, excruciating agony and I just lay in a heap, my life in tatters and the bleakness of my future without him, evident. All that was left was a physical aching need for him that wouldn't leave me.

Why did I have to try to take control to get what I want? Why couldn't I have just left it to God to handle?

A good party needs:

Nice hosts – to make you feel welcome and comfortable.
Old faces for reassurance and new faces for interest and
potential.
A marquee, because of the smart party atmosphere.
A good band and dance floor so everyone can dance as much
as they want to.

Munchies, so no one is ever hungry, even at midnight.
A smart dinner is just really, really nice.
Lots of booze at appropriate times, i.e. champagne
beforehand,
white/red/pudding wines with dinner, etc.

No curfew – so everyone can stay the night in relative
comfort and enjoy a complete party experience, not just
an incomplete, mildly unsatisfying short one.
Speeches. Um. Why? Speeches add atmosphere and
common talking ground.

Dressing up makes one feel more attractive and thus
confident.
A warm place to go – without which one would feel
unwelcome/uncomfy/cold.
A party needs to be organised down to the last detail. Voila!

Sophie Large - aged eighteen.

Chapter Nineteen

ISA and I were on a friends' VIP morning in Cobella. We lay side by side on our beds in the hushed sanctuary, both wrapped up in tin foil with hot towels over us. There was no way I would fall asleep today. I felt much too anxious.

"Now I know what it feels like to be trussed up like a turkey," Lisa said as she looked at me. "The things we women do to ourselves in the name of beauty. I can't imagine a man having the patience to go through all this palaver."

"Are you enjoying it?" I asked. I breathed in the smell of the aromatherapy oils the beauty therapists had used.

"Mmm." Lisa gave a deep sigh of satisfaction. "This is heaven."

The two beauty therapists left the room so that Lisa and I could have a few quiet relaxed minutes while our treatments were working on us.

The moment they had closed the door behind them, Lisa said, "What is it with you and Richard today?"

"Nothing," I lied. I tried to appear casual, but failed completely.

"Something is wrong. You two normally set the room on fire when you're together with loads of electric pulses going on. I've never seen you both so quiet and it's like you're avoiding eye contact. What's wrong?"

"Nothing is wrong." I tried to sound calm.

"Well you two had better get your act together before tonight. It won't be much of a party if the two hosts can't even look at each other. What is the problem?"

"Richard is marrying another woman and he is planning to announce his engagement tonight."

"And you're in love with him." Lisa hit the mark.

"No, I'm not," I said, defensively.

"Liar," Lisa said softly. "So what are you going to do?"

I hesitated, dreading the night that now faced me. "I'm going to be brave and stand there, while he makes his announcement, and I won't show any emotion apart from pleasure for him finding happiness."

"Doesn't sound like much of a prospect for happiness for you on your twenty-first. It's supposed to be a night of fun for you."

"I'll get through it, somehow. I've prayed a lot about it and I don't know how He's going to manage it but somehow God will get me through it."

"And then?"

I sighed. "I don't know. My job is over, I just have to get through tonight and then… I'll take it a step at a time. We're supposed to fall asleep during our relaxation now, by the way."

"I can't sleep! This is too exciting! I've had a helicopter ride into London, limo to a beauty salon that I've only read about in magazines and didn't imagine I would ever see the inside of. I've had clothes made by one of the world's most famous designers, my hair will be done by one of the major, award-winning television hairdressers, and then I shall sit, with my legs elegantly crossed, on the front row, drinking champagne along with the richest, most famous and beautiful women in the world and watching my best friend on the catwalk in a show for British Fashion Week!"

"How do you know you'll be drinking champagne?"

"They always drink it! Champagne companies sponsor these shows and then sponsor the special magazine extras that people like me read, dreaming of the impossible, and now I'm here and I'm getting shoes and a bag as well!"

"Okay, okay! Enjoy the moment. I'll probably trip and fall flat on my face, so I expect this will be the first and last time."

"Now that would be funny," Lisa laughed.

"Lisa!" I protested.

"I'm only joking, Sweetie! You'll be brilliant, I know it. You were made for this life, I've been telling you that for a long time. I didn't expect the transformation quite so soon, though. You were such a dark horse, keeping the connection with all this a secret from me. Oh, by the way, that book you gave me…"

"Yes," I answered carefully.

"Once I actually sat down to read it I couldn't stop! It's the most exciting book I've ever read. Gary was so tired with all the hours at the castle, and I drove him nuts because when he wanted to sleep, I just wanted to keep reading.

I smiled. "I'm so pleased you enjoyed it."

"I thought it would be hard-going but I couldn't put it down. Mr Thornton is *gorgeous* – he's so sweet and so emotional and he carries such heavy burdens in his life. They're both so much in love but it just doesn't seem possible that they will end up together. When they did, I cried buckets! Gary said I was stupid to get into such a state about a book."

"You should try another," I suggested. "What about Pride and Prejudice? The BBC version is incomparable, but even five and three-quarter hours of glorious drama can't cover the wit and humour of Jane Austen. Books are always better than films because the inevitable editing or adaptation can change the whole concept of the original. 'North and South' is Richard's favourite, incidentally, should you ever get into a discussion on English literature with him."

"Ah," Lisa said, meaningfully. "I see. Well, I didn't imagine I would ever get into *high-brow* conversations about English lit, but now, who knows? Move over, Bridget Jones!" She sighed, deeply. "Now, if you don't mind, I am just going to take your advice and sink into peaceful delirium and get some beauty sleep before tonight. I have a party to go to and the guests include all the movie stars, actors and pop stars I have ever dreamed of meeting!"

I closed my eyes, dreading the day and evening ahead.

Later, Richard was waiting for us in the reception area. He urged us to hurry into the limousine because we were on a very tight timescale. It was yet another whirlwind visit to this strange and distant planet.

The car parked in front of the entrance to the venue and the chauffeur opened the door for Lisa to get out. She was literally beaming with pleasure. I was about to follow her when Richard reached out for my hand and held me back.

He took hold of both my hands and his eyes held mine. He seemed to be feeling as much discomfort about our closeness today as I was.

"Angel," he said softly. He hesitated. "I'm sorry about... what happened."

I tried to appear casual and shrugged. "It's no problem. It was my fault, anyway."

He shook his head. "I had to leave. I wanted to explain to you, but there isn't time now." Suddenly he cupped my face in his hands. His eyes were intense. "Stop fidgeting and don't be scared. You'll be fine. Get on that catwalk and bowl them over, okay?"

My heart was pounding. I still felt the aching need for him and it was much too painful to even look at him, let alone be so close that I could feel his soft breath. I couldn't tell him that I was more scared of tonight than I was of the show.

"Will you be there?" I knew my eyes were beseeching him. I couldn't help it.

"Bien sûr! I'll be at the front, cheering you on."

I frowned. "How will I recognize you?"

He grinned. "Look for the French man! You'd better go." He kissed my forehead. "Good luck, Angel. À bientôt."

As we walked towards the entrance, Lisa said, "You two made up?"

I shrugged. "Sort of." My stomach was churning.

We offered to show our passes to the security guard but he seemed to remember us from this morning and waved us through. We walked into the building, wearing only our jeans and T shirts, because Amanda had said that is what most of the models wear between shoots and shows. Lisa was excited, in anticipation of her transformation.

We found Amanda, the calm in the middle of a frenetic storm. There was an astonishing number of people in a surprisingly small space and it was a hive of activity. She was in her signature column of black, which seemed to be the normal uniform for every designer and award-winning hair stylist when they were working.

Amanda's face lit up when she saw us. "Hello, girls! Enter the madness!"

"Are you nervous?" I asked.

She smiled. "I've been doing this for years, but I still get nervous."

"But you look so calm!" Lisa commented.

"Someone has to hold it together. It would be bad news for the crew if their captain lost it! Where's Richard?"

"He'll be out there in the crowd. I just have to work out which he is in his disguise."

Amanda laughed. "Any clues?"

I pulled a face. "He told me to look for the French man."

"Good one! We'll have to see if we can spot him. Now there's a production line going on over there for hair and make-up. If you would like to go and see Annoushka, I've happily left her in charge of that section."

I hugged Amanda. "Good luck and… thank you."

She hugged me back tightly. "You're welcome, and I look forward to seeing you and that dress in my show. Actually, there's just something I need to show you first."

She walked over to one of the racks and came back, carrying what appeared to be a very long bridal veil. It was scattered with pearls and diamonds and had a crown of white roses for a head dress. "Will you wear this?"

My mouth dropped open. "It's a bridal veil!" I shook my head. "No… I couldn't!"

"Every little girl likes to dress up as a bride to play the role," Amanda said gently.

"Wow," Lisa gasped in awe. "That is magnificent. Go on, Joy, wear it."

"But… it isn't a bridal dress!" I was trying to find a reason to get out of what appeared to be the inevitable.

"It would easily adapt to a bridal role. You are my star in the finale and, well, I am known for my bridal and evening wear." Amanda was studying my pained expression. "It's just part of the show, but it's the finale that leaves a lasting impression."

I touched the cloud of incredibly delicate material. It was totally breathtaking. "What will Richard think?" I asked myself, aloud.

Amanda smiled. "He thinks you look great in anything. Will you do it?"

I chewed on my lip and nodded. This was merely a job, like any other job, and I was required to wear what was necessary for the advancement of Amanda's business.

Amanda squeezed my hand. "Thanks. Now pop over to Annoushka and she'll sort you out."

"Is that Jemma?" Lisa asked in amazement.

"Yes," Amanda confirmed. "She's helping me out with the make-up."

As we walked towards Annoushka and Jemma, Lisa was wearing the expression of awe that you might expect to see on a child at the circus. She was in total delirium at being thrust into the world of high fashion, beauty and celebrities that she had only ever dreamed of.

"Lisa! Come back down to earth!" I said quietly. "What is Richard going to think when I walk out there, dressed as a bride?"

"He will think that you are the sensational star of the show," she said. "It's just like Audrey!"

I frowned. "What do you mean?"

"Audrey, in Funny Face! Remember? She was plucked from obscurity and didn't even want to be a model. She wasn't even interested in clothes, but they whisked her off to Paris and created a fashion show with just her. In the finale she was a model bride, but didn't want to be. It was too emotional for her because she had already fallen in love with Fred Astaire's character and thought that she had lost him because they had an argument prior to the show. When she was on stage, the audience commented that the bride had tears in her eyes. You're not going to cry, are you?"

I took a deep breath and made a resolution. "I'll try not to."

Lisa gasped. "Look! I don't believe it. Wow!"

"What's the matter?"

She was rooted to the spot in awe. "It's Kate, Erin, Amber and Jodie. I can't believe I'll be sitting with them to have my make-up done. I normally see them on the covers of my magazines, and Jemma used to be one of them before she began to concentrate on make-up!"

"Well, we'd better hurry," I urged her.

Annoushka asked us to sit among the line of beauties in front of a long, illuminated mirror and make-shift bench dressing table, which was covered in an array of pots of make-up, hairdryers and brushes. I had to behave like a professional because I was amongst the elite professionals who were here to do a job, which was to give the best possible impression for Amanda's work.

The make-up, this time, was a little stronger, because of being on the catwalk, under the strong lights. Annoushka put lots of products on my hair and created a romantic mass of separated curls that fell in waves to my waist.

Annoushka smiled at me. She was as much of a relaxed professional as Amanda. "Don't worry. You'll be fine! Amanda has told me that you will be the finale bride, so I'll fix your veil and finish your hair just before you go on, okay?"

I smiled, gratefully. "Thank you."

Lisa did a twirl in front of a mirror when she was wearing her new dress. It was a wrap around, fine red wool, that emphasised her petite, curvaceous figure. Her silky mane of dark hair had been pinned up and she was wearing a little black cap with a veil and black silk gloves. I don't know whether she was more pleased with the dress or the fabulous black glittery, high-heeled court shoes and matching bag that completed her look.

"What do you think?" Her face was split by a beaming smile and her eyes were sparkling.

I hugged her. "Very elegant. You look as beautiful and stylish as any other woman who will be sitting there on the front row. Go knock 'em dead, kiddo! I think you'd better go and take your place, it looks like we're ready to start. You realise that there are women who would kill for a place on the front row!"

Lisa grinned. "Lucky me! And, not only do I have this outfit, Richard has arranged for a gorgeous, white, strapless ball gown for me to wear tonight. Your man is so adorable."

I smiled sadly. "He isn't my man."

Lisa kissed my cheek. "He's your step-brother, anyway. What a brother! Must go." She looked at her watch and sighed, dramatically. "Almost noon. I think I need champagne now! Good luck, Sweetie!"

I was pleased for Lisa as she disappeared through the backstage crowd. She was having the time of her life. My insides were quaking and I had to focus. It would be a disaster if I messed up for Amanda.

It was like a military battle plan. Everyone now knew their place and in a short time, it would all be over. The girls were lined up and Amanda was at the head of the queue to check every girl before she stepped out into the limelight. We did have a mini-rehearsal this morning, and practised some routines on the catwalk, while the lighting crew and sound people were putting the finishing touches to their part of the overall show.

The dressers all had their appointed sections and appointed models, with each themed item in order on the rails. I was only required to do the finale so I was lucky to be only wearing one dress. They had many changes to make.

As the show progressed, it was a tightly run ship. There were semi-naked girls everywhere backstage, but with the flow of the performance, there was no time for embarrassment. Besides, it seemed to be such a normal part of the routine that no-one blinked an eye and it all seemed so very natural and innocent.

Annoushka came up to me carrying the veil and a dramatically large bouquet of white roses, freesias and lilies. It smelled wonderful. "Ready? You'll be on soon."

I took a deep breath and took the bouquet. "I'll be fine." I was just being swept along on a wave that was beyond my control, so I allowed it to carry me.

"Come and stand in front of this mirror."

I followed Annoushka and stood, while she arranged my hair and the veil. It was like a huge, ethereal cloud that spread out behind me and I realised that I now looked exactly like Venus in the painting in the chapel. The flowers were like the rose petals that were being cast over Venus, to hail her arrival on the shore. I thought of Audrey, as a tearful bride, and I was determined not to cry.

Annoushka stood back and smiled. "You are truly exquisite, my dear."

Amanda joined us and cast a professional eye over me, then smiled, her blue eyes sparkling. "Ready?"

I nodded.

As I walked through the staggered screens and onto the stage, I felt like a swan. All the frenetic energy and engine that powered the show was backstage, out here it was calm and peaceful. In fact, it was silent!

I faltered slightly, and took some deep breaths, focussing on what I needed to do. When the other girls had stepped out, there had been continuous clapping and shouts of approval. With my entrance, they had fallen silent.

The barrage of spotlights from the cameras almost blinded me. I hadn't thought about those. Suddenly, an almighty roar went up and everyone began clapping and shouting. They stood up! It was a standing ovation! I was supposed to appear calm and not show any emotion, but inside I was in a whirlpool of emotion and I couldn't help it.

Then, something amazing happened. It was like a switch flicked inside me and I adopted the role that I knew I had been born for and had so long avoided. I was astounded, but certain. I looked at Mum and Lisa who were beaming with pride and happiness as they stood and clapped with everyone else.

It felt so natural to be there. Like an instinct that I was born with. I didn't need to remind myself how to walk, stand and turn. It just flowed because I knew exactly how to behave in that role. I felt the power that I had tried to use on Richard. This was the same, but it was a necessary part of this play. It was my job to draw the audience into this fantasy world, so that they would want to wear these fabulous creations by this so talented designer.

Richard! I tried to keep my middle distance gaze, and not focus on any individuals, but I surreptitiously scanned the audience, trying to find the French man. I couldn't see him.

I concentrated on my role, but kept looking for him. I noticed an unusual man at the front of the stage. There was something familiar in the natural elegance of his tall frame. He was obviously French, by his clothes, but he didn't look a bit like Richard. He looked like an artist who had just stepped off the Rive Gauche. He had jeans, a white shirt, an oversized black leather jacket, and a French beret, worn at an angle. He looked so completely French and wore sunglasses, but couldn't possibly be Richard, because he had a rough-looking beard. The man raised his glasses and winked at me, then replaced them. I had recognised the blue eyes. It was Richard! I was staggered! He spread his arms and mouthed, "C'est magnifique!" I couldn't help but smile, before I recovered myself.

I was standing in front of him, dressed as a bride who couldn't be his. My chest tightened, painfully and I blinked back the tears that suddenly stung my eyes.

Someone caught hold of my hand and held it tightly. I turned to find Amanda beside me. We were allowed to smile now because the show was over and we could show our appreciation to our hostess. Everyone was still standing in the audience and the other models gathered around us to hug and clap and congratulate Amanda. She was there in the spotlight to take her bow of honour.

"Did you spot Richard?" she whispered to me.

"Take a look at the weird-looking French man in front of us, down there," I whispered back.

The French man grinned and blew a kiss to us between clapping. Amanda's jaw dropped in astonishment and she had to quickly recover. "What a joker!" she said as she clapped her girls and waved to the audience.

We all breathed a sigh of relief when we stepped backstage. Champagne corks were popping. A party was about to start. Suddenly I was surrounded by the girls Lisa had been so in awe of. Kate, Erin, Amber and Jodie hugged me and I was taken aback by their enthusiastic response.

"Is it true?" Jodie asked. "Amanda told us that was your first time!" I nodded.

"Wow," Kate said. "You were brilliant! A natural! Welcome to the club!"

They hugged me and made the greatest fuss of me. I was agog! These girls were so genuinely nice and friendly. I felt a hand on my shoulder. I turned to see the French man.

"Are you ready?" he asked.

"I just have to remove my veil and put this, somewhere."

"Richard?" Amber asked in astonishment. "Is that you in there?"

"Ssh," Richard said. "It's a secret."

Suddenly Amanda was beside me and she was busy unpinning my veil and Annoushka took my bouquet.

"But we're at your party, later. What are you doing here?" Kate asked.

"It's not really my party," Richard explained. "It's Joy's twenty-first today, and we're keeping her a secret until tonight."

The girls squealed with delight, causing several heads to turn. "Girls!" Richard admonished them.

"Sorry," said Erin. "This is so exciting! It's your birthday! Oh, what fun! Congratulations!"

"Don't worry," Kate assured me. "We'll keep the secret and we'll see you later!"

I kissed Amanda's cheek and then Annoushka's. "Thank you so much. I didn't expect to, but I really did enjoy the experience."

Lisa joined us at that moment. One of the dressers handed some bags to her, but Richard intercepted and carried them. "Allons," he said. He led us through the crowd of party people and photographers and out to the waiting limousine.

Once we were back in the hushed privacy and opulence of the car, Richard took off his hat and sunglasses. He just didn't look like the Richard I knew, but I had to secretly acknowledge to myself that the rough beard did suit him.

He kissed my cheek and the beard tickled my face. "Well done, Angel. "Tu étais fantastique! You enjoyed it, didn't you?"

I couldn't help smiling. "Yes, I have to admit that I really did enjoy it, once I had settled into the role. How on earth did you manage to look like that?"

He was beginning to peel the beard off and it seemed that he was pulling off a second skin. "I have a friend who's in theatrical make-up. He does movies and theatre. He thought it would be fun to help disguise me. It's amazing how they can make it look so realistic. I've seen him do make-up for supposed victims of serious accidents and it's so convincing, you feel that at any moment an ambulance will turn up and really take them to hospital. Clever stuff! Now are you girls ready for a party?"

"Are we ever!" enthused Lisa.

Richard's eyes held mine. "Feeling okay?"

I nodded. The stabbing had started in my chest again. I tried to deflect his attention. "I will feel a little strange arriving at an airport, though, and travelling in a helicopter, wearing a ball gown."

We were soon at the airport and the chauffeur opened the door for us. "One could get used to this lifestyle," Lisa joked as we entered the foyer.

We were whisked through to the waiting helicopter. I had noticed heads turn in curiosity and I couldn't blame them. We did look a strange sight with Lisa in stylish day clothes, me in a ball gown and Richard in jeans.

As we sped over the English countryside, it basked in the golden glory of an autumn evening sun. I watched our moving shadow and thought about the evening ahead. I had been glad to be away from the house all day. Glad to avoid Amelia, who was putting the finishing touches to the home that would become hers for the party that would really turn out to be hers.

My chest felt so tight and the stabbing pain just wouldn't leave me. I steeled myself for the inevitable. I just had to be strong and show no emotion.

Lisa was sitting behind me, and I pulled myself together to make the journey pleasant for her.

This is now

We were all outside
And I, lingering, came last.
The night air caressed me
And held me in its balmy embrace.
I heard you all laughing ahead,
And, unafraid, I felt alone.
And I looked at the lights
Sparkling on the sea. And I
looked long at the clear moon,
Almost full, silver and remote.
And suddenly I felt a huge
sense of the present.
The feelings flooded through me:
I felt that I had so nearly
Touched the untouchable.
I shrugged away the feeling of loss,
And contentment, like wine,
Smooth and clear and sweet,
Filled my soul,
And I said, as I followed you,
A long way behind:
"This is now."

Sophie Large – aged seventeen.

Chapter Twenty

A S WE arrived at the castle, it was still light, but I could see the rows of ground lights which now illuminated the drive from the castle drawbridge to the gates. In the distance, by the gates, I could see a line of coaches, each pulled by four white horses. They were waiting to bring the guests in convoy up to the castle. As we landed, I noticed on the turning area that a gigantic red carpet was now laid over the fine gravel and up over the drawbridge to the castle. This was obviously so that the ladies with their delicate shoes would not have to set foot on the gravel or have the embarrassment of getting their heels caught in the slats of the drawbridge. Good thinking, Amelia!

As we landed, there was a group of people waiting for us. It was Gary and all the caravan crowd. When the engine died down and the blades stopped spinning, Gary walked over the grass towards us. All the men, including Gary, were looking handsome in white evening jackets and white bow ties. All the girls were wearing white ball gowns and looked really pretty. Richard helped Lisa out and Gary carried her and her packages over to the red carpet and then set her down.

Richard swept me up in his arms. "This isn't necessary," I protested.

He grinned, incorrigibly. "Yes it is, Cinderella. We can't have you getting grass stains on those beautiful slippers."

"They're not made of glass, you know!"

He made an attempt to be serious. His mood was much lighter, now. "Je le sais. If they were I would be drinking champagne out of one of them tonight!"

I laughed. "C'est ridicule!" I sighed inwardly. He was the best friend I had ever known. The best friend anyone could ever wish for, and tonight, I was going to lose that special relationship with him that had begun, ten and a half years ago, with a chance encounter on the beach.

Meeting him had, literally, changed my life. I allowed myself just once more to feel the thrill of being held in his powerful arms and breathing in his wonderful smell. I relaxed and allowed him to carry me, etching this moment onto my memory, so that I could look back in quiet moments in future years, and relish the feeling.

Richard put me down, gently, on the carpet. He held my hand and his eyes searched my face. "Ça va?"

I took a deep breath and nodded. I wanted to stay with him forever, but at the same time I needed to escape from him and control my emotions, ready for the countdown to the end of my life. "I need to freshen up. I'll use one of the bedrooms."

He kissed my forehead. "Don't be too long. The guests will start arriving soon."

There were squeals from the girls around Lisa and I realised that she must be telling them about her exciting day. I had to escape. I took my ballet slippers off and fled across the drawbridge into the castle and didn't stop until I was safely alone in a room with the door and curtains closed behind me.

My heart was pounding. I had to get a grip on myself, otherwise I would show Richard up in front of his friends and that wouldn't be fair. It wasn't his fault that I was in love with him and he had a right to find happiness in marriage with the love of his life.

I washed my hands in the new en-suite bathroom. I had chosen the highest modern specifications for these facilities. I wished that I could step into the power shower right now and wash all my cares away with blasts of hot water and the aromatic gels I had put in there, and forget about everyone out there.

I walked back through to the bedroom and sat on the upholstered stool in front of the dressing table. I still looked okay and I didn't have any make-up with which to make any improvements anyway. This was just an excuse to escape for a while.

I was lost in my thoughts when the door opened. My heart missed a beat when Richard walked in, parted the curtain, and closed the door behind him.

He smiled. "Hello. I guessed I would find you in here."

He looked incredibly handsome. He had already showered and changed. He was wearing immaculate black trousers and polished, black shoes. A wide, ivory silk cummerbund bound his waist, beneath an impeccable, ivory jacket and a beautifully tied, white silk bow tie enhanced his white evening shirt.

His eyes held mine as he crossed the room. My heart was pounding and I struggled to control my breathing.

"Tu es vraiment beau," he said, softly. "Il ne tu manquè qu'une chose."

I frowned. "Quoi?"

He was very serious. "Come and stand in front of this full length mirror and I'll show you."

I was trying not to show that I was shaking. I did as he asked. I stood in front of him and his eyes held mine in the reflection. He took something out of his pocket and I didn't realise what it was until he was fastening it around my neck and I gasped in shock.

"Richard, no! I can't! No, you mustn't!" My fingers touched the necklace and his eyes still held mine.

Richard smiled. "You are wearing exactly the same expression of alarm that you had when I put this on you ten and a half years ago. Met-le ce soir. Qui est la déesse, maintenant? You are Venus, are you not? My Angel of Joy, the lady of the waves. Ton collier. Ces beaux diamants."

It was the elaborate necklace of diamonds and sapphires that were in tiers, looking like the sparkling blue and white of the waves breaking on the shoreline and he had said those same words to me.

Being so close to him was agony and I was trying so hard not to show it, but this was becoming increasingly difficult.

He held my shoulders and gently turned me to face him. His mouth was so close. He ran a distracted hand through his hair and he seemed to be searching for words. He hesitated. "Angel… there's something I need to explain to you."

"No!" I cried, too loudly, and bolted for the door. I couldn't hear it from him. Not now!

"Angel, listen," he pleaded.

I shook my head and opened the door. "No, we have to go. You said that people would be arriving." I shot outside, through the French window, before he could say another word. I hadn't prepared myself yet.

I ran along the balcony, down the tower steps and into the courtyard garden. I looked up at the strings of lanterns which spanned the distance between the castle walls high above me. When Richard caught up with me, he was slightly out of breath. "There are some people I want you to meet."

"I don't want to talk to magazine people now." I tried to dash away, again, but he caught my hand. I hadn't mentally sorted myself out yet, to meet journalists and photographers.

"Viens avec moi, maintenant." Richard had a firm grip on my hand

and would not let go. He led me to a drawing room and opened the French window. When we walked in, I stood rooted to the spot with my mouth open in shock.

There was a crowd of people. I screamed and ran into the arms of the first person I laid eyes on. My father!

I was shaking and I felt tears welling in my eyes. I didn't want panda eyes, so I struggled to hold them back. I was overwhelmed with emotion. I clung to him, breathing in his wonderful smell, and he held me tightly. I was conscious though, of how frail he still was. "Oh, Daddy! I'm so happy to see you," I said as I kissed his cheek.

Finally, I found the strength to step back and saw that Ruby was with him. "Ruby, you didn't say anything on the phone!" I kissed her cheek as she crushed me against her ample bosoms. "Dad can't be better yet!" I turned to look at Dad again. "Are you?"

He shook his head and his rough hand rubbed my shoulder. "No, I'm not supposed to leave the hospital, but Richard persuaded the doctors to allow me to have a couple of days off. The jet brought us back this morning and it will return us to New York tomorrow morning."

I turned to look at Richard. He was grinning. He seemed to be enjoying my pleasure. I was thrilled to see my father but what a secret to keep from me! I was staggered that Richard had taken so much trouble to create the surprise for me.

I looked a little further around the room. "Mum!" I rushed into her waiting arms. "Your Lordship... I mean... Robert!"

"Oh, darling, I am so proud of you. You looked wonderful on the catwalk. You were the star of the show! Everyone was commenting about you and wondering who the mystery model was who had vanished!"

Mum looked stunning in a glittering white, strapless ball gown, probably made by Amanda, and a spectacular diamond necklace with drop earrings and a cuff bracelet. She literally did look like a million dollars worth of mum. Robert looked very handsome in his hand-made white clothes which were similar to Richard's.

"Wow, what a necklace!" Mum commented. "Someone is a lucky girl!"

Robert enveloped me in a huge hug and then took something from his pocket. "I wanted to give you your birthday present," he said quietly.

I stared at the object in shock and shook my head in rejection of it. I knew what it was and I guessed what it contained. It was an identical, jewelled box to the one that I had seen in the photograph, when the Duke had given it to his son for his twenty-first birthday, and there had been a twenty million pound cheque inside.

I continued to shake my head as I stared at it. "No, I... I couldn't possibly accept…"

He reached for my hand and squeezed it in his. "Joy, you are now a member of my family, so I am giving you equal to what I gave Richard."

I gasped. "No! No, I can't. You mustn't… you can't do that!" The Duke looked hurt and I kissed his cheek. "I'm not being ungrateful, Robert. I do appreciate being a part of your family, now but… it's just too much. I don't deserve it. I'm not worthy!"

Mum hugged me and I breathed in her expensive perfume. I noticed that Richard was looking at me with concern.

I felt tearful and tried to not let them spill down my blushered cheeks. I stepped back and felt in agony. I held tightly on to Mum's hand and I glanced at Robert. "Mum, Robert… I'm so sorry that I hurt you, that I cut you out of our lives when you still wanted to be my mother. I didn't understand that you were in love. I mean, it's obvious, now… but I didn't want to have any further contact with you and that was mean of me. Can you forgive me, please? Pride is a terrible thing. It blinds you and makes you prejudiced."

I could see tears in Mum's eyes and she hugged me tightly. I could feel her shaking with emotion. "Not the sort of pride that we have for you. Darling, it's we who should ask your forgiveness. You were terribly hurt and we just didn't realise how badly you had been wounded by what we did. Will you forgive us? Please, my darling, and we'll spend the rest of our lives making up for it."

I held my mum tightly. I didn't realise until that moment just how much I had missed her. Robert kissed my cheek and I could see tears in his eyes, too. I realised that Dad was standing beside me and I looked up into his tearful, blue eyes.

Dad stroked my hair. "That goes for Ruby and me too, Precious. This has all been a bit of a mix-up, hasn't it, and I've realised, while I've been lying in that hospital bed, that you've been hurt more than any of us."

I smiled at him and Ruby who now stood beside him. "Are you better?"

Dad smiled. "Seems to be working on me. I've been doing a lot of praying and God seems to be answering me. The doctors say it is in remission, but there is a long way to go yet."

Richard touched my shoulder and whispered in my ear. "Angel, there are some other people in this room."

I stepped back, trying to keep the tears from overflowing, and noticed Sister Ruth and Father David. It seemed that everyone in this room was tearful now, even Richard's eyes had looked watery.

I flew across the room into the waiting arms of dear Sister Ruth, whom I had adopted as my mother for the last ten years. "Oh, Sister Ruth," I whispered in her ear as I bent to hug her. "I have prayed and prayed about this night. I didn't realise it would be so wonderful, so emotional and so painful. Please, please, pray to God to get me through this. I don't think my legs will have the strength to last for the entire evening."

"He is already watching you, my child. God has truly blessed you and He will give you the strength to face up to the inevitable." She took my face in her hands and kissed my forehead. "Bless you, my child."

Father David seemed just as overwhelmed with emotion. He hugged me tightly and then kissed my cheeks. "Bless you, child." I kissed his cross and he blessed me.

God was certainly bringing in the allies but I didn't see how it was going to help me to remain standing for the night. I still had a plan in the back of my head. If Richard made his announcement, then the focus would be off me and I could escape. No one would notice!

Richard put his arm around me and kissed my cheek. I threw my arms around his neck and hugged him tightly. His arms held me closely against him.

Being in his arms was exquisite agony. "Thank you so much, for all of this," I whispered in his ear. "Thank you for doing this for me."

He kissed the top of my head and released me, slightly. He took an envelope from his pocket. "I wanted to give my birthday present to you."

"But, you've already given me my present! This dress, and all the other clothes. You've done more than enough for me!" I protested.

"This is something special."

I shook my head as he placed it in my hand. An envelope. It could only mean another cheque. More birthday money. More reasons for me to feel guilty! I couldn't cope with this.

Richard whispered in my ear. "I want to talk to you. There's something I need to tell you."

"No," I shrieked and then struggled to recover. "I mean… I'm sorry, everyone. I'm overwhelmed that Richard and you have all done this for me but… um… there is a party out there and it's very remiss of us to leave them. Excuse me."

I shot out of the door before Richard could say anything else. He was obviously trying to break it to me gently, as his best friend and step-sister, that he was going to announce his engagement and I just couldn't bear to hear it from him. He was trying to get me alone, so that he could tell me in private, so I needed to be in the middle of a crowd, and then he couldn't talk to me.

I hurried into the ballroom and the first people I met were Alexandra, Portia and Georgia. I inwardly screamed, but it was too late, they were standing in front of me and they surrounded me, squealing with excitement.

"Joy!" they shrieked, almost in unison as they hugged me.

"Oh, Joy, look at you!" said Georgia. "You look gorgeous!"

"It's so wonderful to see you've come out of your shell," said Portia.

Alexandra hugged me tightly again. "Oh, it's so good to see you, Joy. We so wanted to be friends with you at school, but you were so shy and we just couldn't get through to you. It was like you were in a shell and we just couldn't crack it open, no matter how hard we tried!"

I was astonished. "You... you wanted to be friends? With me? I... I didn't realise!"

"You were so busy studying," said Georgia, and we thought you would be fun if we could get through to you, but you just wouldn't let us get close to you. You were so shy! And now look at you! Wow, you've really come out."

"Is this your Deb. Party?" Portia asked.

I was still trying to take in the shock. "Sort of. It's my twenty-first, today!"

"Oh, you must have a glass of champagne!" said Alexandra as she grabbed one from the tray of a passing waiter, who was in elegant, period, white French costume.

"Can we be friends, now?" Georgia asked.

I smiled in amazement. "That would be lovely."

"Let's drink to that!"

They all raised their glasses and clinked them to mine. Wow! This was another shock for me. At that moment, I was suddenly surrounded by Jemma, Jodie, Amber, Kate and Erin. They knew Alexandra, Portia and Georgia and they all hugged and squealed with delight to see each other. The models then told the other girls what I had done earlier that day and there were even louder shrieks of delight that drew attention from around the room.

"What a day!" Georgia enthused, her eyes dramatically huge with amazement. "What a way to celebrate your birthday!"

Because of the support of the girls, I felt more comfortable when they introduced me to famous guests that they already knew. The conversation was so much easier when others were involved in the banter and they made introductions so much less hassle. I wouldn't have dared to speak to various movie stars and pop stars, if it weren't for them. I wouldn't have known what to talk about, let alone who half of them were! The girls were so kind to me and it was fun. What was most noticeable was that everyone was so natural and so friendly.

Occasionally I looked around and connected in a glance with Lisa who rolled her wide eyes in sheer delight because she was in conversation with one of her dream movie or pop stars.

Sometimes I saw Richard in the distance, looking heartbreakingly handsome and mingling with his friends. He stood taller than others and notable in his unconscious elegance. He would stand out in any crowd, even in this room filled with the crème de la crème of celebrities.

My plan was working. If I could avoid him for the night, I could get through this and then collapse in a heap on my bed and not have to get up tomorrow.

The party plan and theme had worked. The house looked beautiful. Everything, everywhere was white and light. A myriad candles flickered, the light sparkling off everything. The security system was in tight operation. The jewellery company was registering and loaning necklaces, bracelets and earrings to every female guest and the light sparkled on probably millions of pounds worth of diamonds and precious stones. Because of the jewellery policy, everyone was wearing jewellery, so, apart from commenting on what a fabulous necklace I was wearing, I didn't have to answer any awkward questions about it because people assumed it was one of the loan items. Diamonds, pearls and sequins shone on white dresses. The men looked handsome in their white jackets and bow ties.

People literally flowed through the house, the garden and up on the balcony and ramparts as I thought they would. Everyone seemed to be having a wonderful time. Waiters were busy filling glasses and offering tempting morsels of exotic tastes.

The ballroom was the most spectacular, with the trails of white silk and flowers cascading from the chandeliers, down to the gleaming marble floor. Wooden pillars held arrangements that trailed to the floor and the house was filled with the divine perfume that emanated from them. An orchestra was playing and the music wafted through the house and garden. Some people were dancing in the courtyard and it was an utterly beautiful sight. A band was preparing to play more modern music later. I hadn't seen Amelia, and I really ought to thank her for the fantastic arrangements. As Mum had said, she really is a clever girl, but I just couldn't face her right now.

"Ohh," said Kate, with dramatic emphasis. "That's gorgeous!"

Her well-photographed mouth savoured the flavours. I felt as though I was watching her in an advertisement and I had to remind myself that this was real. I was actually standing here with these famous people.

"Mmm!" She enthused, again as she turned to me. "Usually, I don't eat at these sort of parties, but this food is fabulous." She looked around. "Problem is, the waiters are having to work twice as hard because everyone's looking for more. I hope they don't run out."

She was right. I had seen the same reaction from others all evening. Intense conversations, suddenly interrupted by the distraction of their mouths experiencing the wonderful, delicate flavours.

"Who's the caterer?" Kate asked. "I hope they've printed enough business cards. Everyone is going to want their number."

"Galton. Michelin Star chef," Georgia supplied in her aristocratic drawl. "Local hotel, TV star. Fabulous! We're staying there tonight, darling."

"Really?" Kate's delicate brow raised. "For the first time in my life, I'm looking forward to breakfast!"

I smiled at my thoughts. Even supermodels were willing to throw away their diets for Galton's food. Clearly, he was impressing the guests with his ingenuity and insistence on using only the finest local, in-season produce. My smile faded as my thoughts turned to Richard. The food was delicious, I had tried some, but my stomach was in turmoil and I could barely manage to eat anything. I just hoped I could avoid Richard for the rest of the evening.

I was startled as I felt an arm slip around my waist. I gasped as Richard held me close to him. He had come for me. He was determined to make me face up to the last thing that I didn't have the courage to face. I saw the girls literally melt in front of him. I had noticed that he had that effect on women. Part of it was his devastating charm.

"Would you mind if I borrow this gorgeous young woman?" Richard asked the group.

"Only if you bring her back soon," said one of the handsome men, who I think was a young movie star.

Richard took my glass and put it on the tray of a passing waiter. He took my hand firmly in his. "Viens avec moi."

Heads turned as he led me across the dance floor and up the steps on to the stage. He held my hand, tightly and drew me to stand close to him by a microphone.

I panicked and looked helplessly around the room. The nearest form of support, the allies that God had sent for me, were standing in a group together at the side of the room, by the door. They were too far away to help me, but I focussed on the door.

"Your Royal Highnesses, ladies and gentlemen," Richard said. "My dear friends. I have an announcement to make."

I screamed, pulled my hand out of Richard's grip and bolted. I didn't care what people thought of me, I had to escape. I ran down the stage steps, and across the room, as people murmured in wonderment at the sight of me, and I paused to hug Sister Ruth, who was standing by the door. I was crying now, but I couldn't help it.

"I'm sorry, Sister, I can't do it," I whispered in her ear. "I don't have the strength for this."

I fled through the door. I needed sanctuary. I needed to be alone. Tears were pouring down my cheeks now. Instinctively I ran to the chapel. My chest was almost bursting with the pain. I opened the giant oak door and slipped inside, then closed it behind me.

The chapel was illuminated with the numerous candles but, as I had hoped, no-one else was in here. I ran to the altar and dropped on my knees onto one of the two needlepoint cushions. I looked down at my hands and realised that I was still holding the envelope that Richard had given to me. I must have been clutching it all evening! I dropped it on the flagstone in front of me. I was racked with sobs and tears poured down my cheeks. I was desolate. I couldn't even begin to repair the damage I had done by embarrassing Richard in front of his friends. My life was just a big void now.

I heard the heavy iron door latch being lifted. The door creaked quietly and then the door latch fell back into place. I heard footsteps and then someone knelt on the cushion beside me. Richard lifted my face and cupped it with his hands. I looked into the face that I loved and I didn't hide the devastation that was tearing my insides apart. His expression showed his anguish for me and that just made it worse.

"Please, please, Richard, leave me alone. Please just go back to your guests. I'm really sorry I embarrassed you. Just please go." My voice was absolute desolation.

"Angel, I can't bear to see you like this. Qu'est-ce que c'est? Qu'y a-t-il? Why did you run?"

I decided to be as honest with him as I almost always had been. "You were about to announce your engagement."

He looked stunned. "But I haven't asked you yet!"

My eyes flew to his in shock. I must have misunderstood his meaning. "Comment ça?"

He was watching my expression, carefully. "I said, I haven't asked you to marry me, yet."

My mouth dropped open. "But… you're marrying Amelia!"

He looked totally confused now. "How did you work that out?"

"Well, it was obvious. You behaved differently with me in front of her than when you were with me in the company of others."

He raised astonished eyebrows. "And that is evidence of my undying devotion and love for her?"

"Isn't it?" I asked, hardly daring to breathe with the glimmer of something that I couldn't quite grasp.

"Amelia is the hottest party organiser and she is also the hottest gossip-monger. I didn't want her to have any indication of my feelings for you or she would have spread it through all the gossip columns and blown my plan out of the water!"

"And that is?" I asked, carefully, not quite daring to pin any hope on what he was saying to me.

"To marry you," he said, bluntly. "I told you that I didn't want speculation to spoil my moment."

I reeled. "But... when I asked you if your wife would want to participate in creating your home, you said that she will trust my judgement and my skill as I much as you do."

He raised an enquiring eyebrow. "And you do, don't you... trust your own judgement in what you've created?"

I shook my head in disbelief. "But... Amelia was so possessive and affectionate with you."

"She's like that with all men. She drapes herself over any man, it's just her way."

"But she seemed to have strong feelings for you and intimated that she was the one you had chosen for a wife."

Richard frowned. "If she did, those feelings were neither encouraged nor reciprocated." He smiled. "I think she was playing a game with you. Testing the water to see if you were the one, and you obviously didn't give her any satisfaction. In fact, you appeared to distinctly put her nose out of joint."

"I didn't mean to!"

Richard grinned. "It's okay. You stood up for yourself. Now, is there anyone else that you have dreamed up for me?" I shook my head. His eyes burned into mine. "Have I ever said that I don't love you?" I shook my head again. He kissed my cheek and whispered in my ear. "It was your pretty head that chose to imagine that I was referring to someone else. I'm going to have to have a little chat with that imagination of yours, later."

I gasped at his inferred meaning and felt myself blush scarlet. I looked in amazement into his eyes and there was the same smouldering intent that I had seen when he was dancing with me, but now there was something more. It was almost as though a guard had been removed and now he was revealing a naked passion that made me tingle from my finger tips to my toes in response. I was astonished.

"But... when we danced, you walked away and left me crying on the floor. You didn't want me!"

Richard took a deep breath and raised his eyes to look at the statue of Mary and the baby Jesus, then he looked back at me and the desire that I saw in his face shocked me to the core.

"I had to leave you. I had to walk away, because I got to the point where I almost lost control. I wanted to make love to you so badly, it hurt, but you weren't ready. A man has a responsibility to protect women, even from himself."

"But I wanted you, desperately!"

His hands held my face and his eyes burned with desire. "Angel, you hadn't a clue what you were doing or where it was leading. You were playing with fire and you could have got burned. I had to leave to protect you."

I was hardly able to comprehend what he was saying to me. "Are you saying that... you love me?"

"Haven't I already said so?"

I frowned. "When?"

He smiled. "In Amanda's shop, when you told me that you love me, I responded by telling you that I love you. I thought that had given the entire plot away."

"I thought you meant it in a brotherly affection."

Richard raised an eyebrow meaningfully. "The feelings I have for you are in no way brotherly. They are much more serious, I'm afraid."

I gasped and frowned. "But you've never even kissed me! You kiss my face, I've longed for you to kiss my mouth but you've always noticeably avoided it!"

He studied my mouth and traced it slowly, inexorably, with a finger, and then his eyes burned into mine. "I've always known that if I kissed that incredible mouth of yours, I wouldn't be able to stop myself making love to you, so I've always made a point of avoiding it." His eyes were focussed again on my mouth. "Ta bouche - un autre monde m'y attend."

I reeled. My head was spinning. I couldn't believe this was happening to me. "Since when?"

He looked at me, very seriously. "Since I was fourteen years old. That's a big responsibility to carry. You've always been much too young and I've waited ten and a half years."

"But why didn't you say something? Why didn't you tell me how you feel? I've been going doolally, thinking that you wanted someone else. I've idolised you for all this time. I've wanted you and wanted you to kiss me, desperately!"

He chewed on his lip and hesitated. "Just as your mother idolised your father. She was convinced that she loved your father, until she met my father and found true love for the one and only time in her life. You were in exactly the same position as your mother. No money or home of your own, no chosen career, no experience of life. Your mother made her choice, based on her experience of life and circumstances, which added up to a big, fat zero. She thought she loved your father, until my father came into her life. I couldn't face that prospect with you. I had to know that you were really sure."

"I am sure!" I urged him to believe me. "I do love you. I've loved you from the moment I met you!"

"Moi aussi, but you can only make a real choice, based on your experience of life, and you had none when I called on you seven months ago. You were still so very much a child and I couldn't interfere in your growth. I couldn't influence you. The only true choice you could make would be if you came to it totally of your own volition. You had to make your own mind up, without any help from me. I stayed away from you, trying to give you space."

I was confused and overwhelmed with a mixture of emotions. "But you've done so much to help me, over the last seven months."

He shook his head. "All I've done is give you the opportunities to gain experience, face up to any truths that you needed to and discover who you are and what you want out of life."

I frowned. "I thought you went to enormous trouble to reunite me with my mother because you felt that you wanted me as your sister and a close member of your family."

Richard drew a deep breath. His hand stroked my hair. "Angel, I wanted you as my wife and we were in the unusual situation where we would share the same in-laws, your mother and my father! You know the jokes about in-laws, but I wanted to smooth everything so that you would be on good terms again with your mother and mother-in-law. I wanted a close family and I was hoping that you two could be friends again."

I was bewildered. "This is all so difficult to take in. I've thought of you as my best friend for such a long time and, tonight, I thought I was losing you but it seems that it's my stupid head and my pride that got in the way of seeing the truth, about a lot of things that you have made me face up to."

"Think about it," Richard said, gently. "Think about what you have now that you didn't have seven months ago, that your mother didn't have when she met your father. I'm very glad that your mother did meet your father, by the way, otherwise I wouldn't have you, but just think about what you have. Money, if you take the money from my father, two families who love you very much, three careers if you count modelling, interior design and restoration, and you have a home of your own."

I shook my head. "If Dad survives, which I pray that he will, he and Ruby will probably live in the farm house, and I can't live with them!"

Richard picked up the envelope and handed it to me. "You still haven't opened the present from me."

I opened the envelope and struggled to comprehend what I was looking at. "This is the deed to this castle and its contents. It's in my name... and it's dated the twenty-first of March! But... this is your birthright! You can't give it to me!"

"I wouldn't want it without you," he said quietly.

I was absolutely staggered. "What do you mean? You've wanted this castle for so long!"

"But, I only saw the castle for the first time on the day I met you and from that moment, I only wanted it if I could have you, too. I'm giving it to you, with my love, but I'm hoping that you will accept me with it, because I want to love you and live with you in this home. I gave you the task of creating this home to your entire taste, because I wanted it to be your home and I wanted to share it with you. I couldn't contemplate having this home if you didn't want me as well so, in that eventuality, I wanted to give it to you because I could not conceive having this as a home without you. I would have... I don't know! Probably gone off to some far, distant place and tried not to think about you. It would have been too painful to see you with someone else!"

My mouth dropped open in shock. Our feelings for each other were identical! The realisation suddenly dropped on me like a bomb and for the first time, I felt my eyes light up and I looked at him with all the love for him that I truly felt.

"When did you plan on asking me?"

He grinned. "I've been trying to ask you all night, but you just kept bolting every time I tried to talk to you alone."

I couldn't help the smile that had now spread across my face. I had been such an idiot, with so many people, for so long! "What were you going to announce then?"

"You! You had obviously met many of the people, thanks to the girls. I was watching, by the way, noting if you were responding to any flirtatious men."

"I didn't!"

He grinned. "Je le sais. I hardly took my eyes off you. I felt that as you had met so many people, it was time to introduce you, formally, and wish you a happy twenty-first birthday!"

Realisation dawned on me about how much of an idiot I really was and how much I always seemed to jump the gun and jump to the wrong conclusions. "And asking me to marry you? Where was that going to come into it?"

He sighed. "I don't know! I'd already asked your father's permission. I thought I'd better wait for my opportunity and pin you down, if necessary, to stop you from bolting again so that I could actually get the words out."

I frowned. "When did you ask my father?"

"The second day that I called on you, when your father and I talked for ages, while you and Lisa were in the kitchen, before you and I came here for the first time in ten years."

My mouth had now completely dropped open in shock.

The iron latch lifted on the door. Richard and I both turned to see Amanda burst in, carrying the veil and the bouquet, followed by a man who had a camera around his neck.

She looked at the two of us, kneeling at the altar. "Am I too late?" she gasped. "Are you already married?" She looked at the shock on my face and then at Richard, who was grinning. "Uh, oh! Have I done it again? Have I put my giant foot in it?"

More heads popped around the door. "Well, has she said yes yet?" Lisa asked Richard.

"I haven't had chance to ask her yet!" Richard said with clear exasperation.

I looked at Richard and then back at the small crowd of people in the doorway. "You'd better come in," I said, "as you all seem to be a part of this."

The crowd entered the chapel and Dad closed the door behind them. Along with Dad, standing there with anticipation, were Ruby, Mum and Robert, Sister Ruth and Father David, Annoushka, Lisa, Amanda and the man with the camera.

"Amanda, who is the man with you?" I asked.

"This is Mario. He saw you at the show and he was desperate to photograph you."

"I was entranced by the emotions on your face," Mario explained. "I saw innocence, a child, a woman, desire, sensuality, naivety and love. Emotions seemed to be waking up inside you and battling each other. It was fascinating to see those expressions. You disappeared so quickly! I looked outside for you but you had gone!"

"When I told Mario that you might be married tonight, he was desperate to photograph you because he says that tomorrow, you will look different and the beautiful bloom of innocence will have been replaced by the knowledge of womanhood." She looked at me and then at Richard and she grimaced. "I've done it again, haven't I? I'll just shut up."

I looked at Richard, questioningly. "Wedding? Tonight?"

He exhaled deeply and took my hands in his. He hesitated. "Okay. Here's the picture. If you didn't want me, I was just going to disappear. However, if you did want me, I've waited ten and a half years to have you. The last seven months have been particularly hard to get through. If you did want me, I couldn't wait a moment longer to make love to you, but I couldn't do that without making an honest woman of you first! So, I asked Father David if he would make the arrangements for us to be married, tonight, if… you wanted it to work out that way!" He looked at me uncertainly, waiting for my reaction.

I looked at the crowd and frowned. "Is this a conspiracy? Is everyone in on this?"

"Angel," Richard said gently. "These are the people who are closest to us and… it was obvious to everyone how I feel about you… apart from you, it seems."

Everyone watched me with baited breath, waiting for my response. I didn't know what to say.

"There's something else." He chewed on his lip. "I'm Catholic and you are not. There is only one God and our title of religion shouldn't come between us. This bone of contention has cost lives and torn people apart in the past. I don't want it to come between us. I am willing to give up my religion if it would make the decision of marrying me easier for you."

I was completely shocked. "You would give up everything for me? Your dream of this castle, your religion, everything? For me?"

He nodded. "It wasn't an easy decision, but I don't want birthright and religion to continue to come between a Bowes-Lyon and the woman he loves. My family history is plagued with such stories."

"Richard… I am overwhelmed that you would do this for me, but it isn't necessary."

He looked worried and studied my face. "Pourquoi?"

I smiled, loving him. "Because, having spent months in your company, as Sister Ruth observed, you had a great deal of influence on my life, and when I started at the convent school, just before I was eleven, I soon converted to become a Catholic."

He was amazed and glanced at Sister Ruth and Father David as he obviously realised that they had known he would not have to make a choice over his religion. "This seems like a day of revelations for both of us. Look, there's a crowd of people out there who will wonder what is going on. We'd better go and inform them there will be a surprise wedding tonight." He tried to read my expression. "You will marry me, tonight, won't you?"

I smiled and felt the power of the woman in the song, who knows she has her man if she wants him. I raised an eyebrow, questioningly.

"Marriage, Richard? You haven't asked me!"

I felt a thrill course through me at the look he gave me for playing games with him and drawing out his emotions. In that moment, we shared the same memory, from the words of a fourteen year old boy and a ten year old girl.

Richard looked up at the painting of the Angel of Joy, the original legendary redhead, illuminated by candle light behind the altar table, and then he turned to me. He held both of my hands, tightly. I could hardly breathe and he seemed to be experiencing the same difficulty.

His eyes held mine with a searing passion that told me in no uncertain terms what would be happening later. "Be my Angel of Joy, toujours... forever," he whispered.

"I will if you never leave me," I whispered back, my heart pounding in my ears.

He kissed my hand, his eyes holding mine. "I swear to protect you, milady, till death us do part," he promised.

"Was that a proposal?" Amanda asked in total confusion. "Or did you two just get married?"

"I know you two would like to be married here in this chapel," said Father David, "but we're not going to fit three hundred people in here and your guests would be rather upset if they discovered that you had left them in the lurch to have a wedding without them, so I think you had better get in there and tell them what is happening."

"I suppose I'd better give you this." Richard removed a diamond engagement ring from his pocket and placed it on my third finger, left hand. The diamond was huge and the ring fitted, perfectly.

I frowned in confusion. "How can it possibly fit so well? Let alone the fact that you have been walking around with an engagement ring in your pocket."

"I tried to give it to you but you kept running away," he complained. "Okay, confession! It fits because when Amanda was sorting a pair of gloves out for you, I had her pretend that she needed to measure your fingers to get the size right, and... she particularly measured that finger."

I was stunned by the duplicity. "And I suppose the elaborate cake you asked for was intended for the wedding?" He grimaced. "And if I had said, no?"

Richard made a cute, puppy expression that he knew I found irresistible. "I was rather pinning my hopes on you saying, yes."

I breathed in, etching this moment on my memory, and glanced up at the walls. My attention was caught by the twentieth saying, again, and this time, I knew what God was saying to me. My new home was built on the foundation of wisdom and understanding. The knowledge I had gained over the last seven months, would be the basis for the wonderful life I was about to begin.

God had been there for me all the time. He was just trying to open my eyes to the truth!

"Now, are there any more buts?" Richard asked.

I smiled and shook my head.

Richard and I were still holding hands as we walked towards where Sister Ruth stood and I had a sudden intuition. "Sister Ruth, if you have been confidante to both Richard and me, over the last seven months, then you have known that we are in love and would marry."

Sister Ruth smiled and shook her head. "Not necessarily. I am not a matchmaker. That is not my role."

"But you told me that God would give me the strength to face up to the inevitable!"

Her smile was serene. "And you did, didn't you? I felt that it was inevitable that you would be together, but I couldn't interfere. God set you on the path to self-discovery, and when you take a journey like that, no-one knows what the outcome will be. The person you are at the end, and what is right for you, may be entirely different to the person who took that first step. Richard was right to stay away from you and not try to influence you. It was up to God to sort you two out and decide if you were right for each other. Luckily, he seems to have been thinking along the same wavelength as me!"

We hugged everyone in there. There wasn't a dry eye in the chapel. Even Mario felt the emotion. This small group were now the dearest people in our lives. The journey God had set me on was now almost complete.

"Joy, Mario needs to photograph you, before you marry. Is that alright?" Amanda asked.

Richard raked a hand through his hair. "Can it not take too long, please? I've waited long enough to turn this girl into my wife."

Amanda smiled. "Wedding photographs, Richard! Every bride is photographed before she gets married, as well as after! Be patient, man!"

Richard almost glared at her and she laughed. "It won't take long, honestly! We'll have to prepare her first, though. A bride should look her best."

Richard looked at me, his eyes blazing passion. "I'll take her exactly as she is, if it means I don't have to wait a minute longer!" He sighed. "Very well, but for heaven's sake, don't take too long. Allons, Angel. We'd better inform everyone what they were really brought here for." He winked at me and I was shocked at the audacity of his large scale planning for my life.

Richard held my hand tightly and led me back through the ballroom to the stage. Everyone clapped when they saw us and gathered to see what was going to happen.

Richard returned me to the microphone. "Okay. Hello, everyone. I have retrieved a gorgeous girl and I have to explain what is happening tonight." People clapped and whistled and then listened to what Richard had to say. "Right, this is Joy. This is rather complicated, but I will endeavour to explain the situation to you. Joy, as you might have noticed, is rather stunning…" The crowd clapped their agreement and I blushed. "Obviously, by the way she bolted out of here, earlier, she is also rather shy. You may also have noticed the strong resemblance between Joy and the Duchess Elizabeth, my step-mother. That is because the Duchess is Joy's mother." More claps and whoops of delight. "It was obvious that Joy would be very much a focus of interest to the press so she has remained a secret, allowing her to grow up away from the public glare. Joy is a true debutante, in every sense of the word. Today is her twenty-first birthday and today we also celebrate the completion of the renaissance of this wonderful home. Joy had total responsibility, carte blanche, for the entire project. So you see, this evening is really all about Joy. Earlier today, Joy made her debut as the mysterious model in Amanda's fashion show. Tonight we celebrate Joy's birthday, her debut into society and this home that she has created. I would like to propose a toast, if you would all raise your glasses, to celebrate, Joy!"

Everyone shouted almost in unison, "Joy!" and then they cheered and clapped.

"There's more!" Richard announced. He was holding my hand and his fingers stroked my skin affectionately. Everyone fell silent to listen. "Joy and I have been best friends since we were children and we've been in love for a very long time." More claps and cheers. "I proposed to Joy, a few minutes ago, and she has accepted." Loud cheers and whistles. "However, I cannot wait a moment longer for the love of my life to be my wife, so I am asking if you would all be witnesses at our wedding in this room, tonight?" The roar of approval and shrieks of excitement were deafening. Everyone obviously thought it was a wonderful idea. When the noise had died down, Richard said, "Now, Joy has to go off and do whatever it is that brides do to prepare for the ceremony and she'll have to have some photographs taken by Mario there. I have begged them to not take too long because we're keen to see a wedding here, aren't we?" Another roar of approval indicated the crowd's agreement.

As I descended the steps, I was surrounded by Annoushka, Amanda, Jemma, Kate, Erin, Amber, Jodie, Alexandra, Portia, Georgia and, most dearly, Lisa.

They all made the greatest fuss of me and were in sheer excitement. I really was grateful to them for helping me to get through the night. Now, I felt more relaxed with Richard's friends because I had been properly introduced to them.

"Girls, thank you so much. Tonight was going to be so difficult for me. I really felt scared about meeting people and you have made the party fantastic for me."

"Annoushka and I will sort out your dress and your hair. Mario is waiting to take the photographs," Amanda explained.

"I've volunteered to do your make-up," said Jemma. "I have an idea! If you're getting married, do you have any bridesmaids?"

Not having known I was getting married until a few minutes ago, my honest answer was easy. I shook my head. "No, I don't."

"Well, why don't these eight beautiful girls stand for you as bridesmaids?" Jemma suggested.

There were loud shrieks of excitement and agreement, causing people to turn and look at us.

"Joy? How do you feel about that?" Amanda asked.

I looked at the beaming faces of these glorious girls. "Honoured," I said simply.

"Right, let's get moving or we'll be in trouble with Richard,' Amanda urged. 'We have a bouquet for Joy and, to be honest, Richard anticipated Lisa, hence the dress and a bouquet for her. I saw Paul and Marie, earlier, they did the flowers and there are so many around here, I'm sure they won't mind if we recycle some into seven more bouquets. I'll see if I can find them."

As the girls fussed over me, getting me ready, my mind was free to consider my situation. I was totally overwhelmed. Here I was, wearing a wedding creation by one of the world's top designers, hair being styled by one of the world's greatest hairdressers, make-up being done by an ex-supermodel who was now one of the world's leading make-up artists and four of my eight bridesmaids were world-famous supermodels. I had a new set of friends and Richard's friends would now be my friends and I would feel comfortable and bond with them because they were going to be witnesses at our wedding.

My brain was reeling with the enormity of it. The whirlwind Richard seemed to have swept me off my feet so fast and entirely changed my life. At the same time, he said that he hadn't interfered and changed my life, he had merely given me the opportunities to do so. And now, in one day, Lisa was achieving everything that she had day-dreamed of as we sat on the beach, debating over her magazines.

I had changed so completely in seven months but I was still going to have what was fundamentally important to my life, beyond all else, and that was Richard and this home that we had discovered together and wanted to share forever. Staggering! God had organised my life and was blessing me in a way I could never have imagined.

On my way to be photographed in the studio room, I managed to see Amelia and thanked her for the amazing party she had created, but then I was whisked away.

Richard sat in on the photographic shoot and I knew that some of the photographs, where I was smiling at him with all the love in my heart, would look like those in 'Somewhere In Time', when Jane Seymour was smiling in the same way at the love of her life, her Richard, played by Christopher Reeve.

Mario took a lot of me on my own, quite a few with Richard with me, some of Richard alone, and quite a lot of me with the bridesmaids, four of whom had worked with him on photo shoots many times before.

"Right. Are you done, now?" Richard asked with quiet exasperation.

"Patience, Richard," Amanda whispered.

Richard looked as though he was far from being patient. "J'ai faim ma fiancée."

Mario put his hands up. "She's all yours!"

"Almost," Richard muttered. "Okay, do whatever you have to do, because I'm going to announce to everyone that we're ready."

Richard reached for my hand and I could see the blaze of passion in his eyes, undiminished from earlier. He kissed my cheek. "A bientôt, mon Angelique," he whispered.

My stomach churned as he left me. I was thinking of what would happen with the promise of, soon!

When we returned to the ballroom, everyone was standing, but there was now a central path left, leading through the room and up the steps, on to the stage, where Richard and Robert were waiting. The guests were no longer holding drinking glasses. They each held a candle and a hymn sheet.

My father was giving me away and Richard's father was his best man. I could see Mum, Ruby, Sister Ruth, Amanda, Annoushka and Jemma at the front, with tears filling their eyes. I knew I looked like Venus, in my ethereal cloud, and my bridesmaids were my beautiful hand maidens, helping me to start a new life.

Father David married us. Richard held my hand tightly throughout the entire ceremony, and he seemed to not want to ever let go of me again. The band sang well known hymns and celebratory religious songs and everyone joined in. We said prayers and it was a spiritually uplifting service. Everyone seemed to be affected by the poignancy of the occasion. I had to keep blinking to stop the tears from rolling down my cheeks. I was crying with happiness! I was in awe of what was happening. I was marrying this wonderful man and we were so incredibly in love!

I wasn't aware that a rigging had been created above the stage, until Richard and I turned to stand and face our guests, as a newly wedded couple, and rose petals fell like confetti from above. The guests cheered loudly.

Amid the gentle shower, I looked at Richard with all the love I felt. "You can kiss me now," I said softly.

He studied my mouth, and then looked at me with a deep, burning passion glinting in his eyes, and shook his head as he smiled. "A bientôt," he whispered. "Not yet. I can wait... just a little longer."

My heart pounded in anticipation. Richard led me down the steps and there were many tearful embraces. The lead singer announced that the 'happy couple' would lead the first dance and that Richard was dedicating this song to his new wife. The crowds parted and Richard led me to the centre of the marble floor.

I looked at him with suspicion. "Just how much of all this did you plan?"

He grinned. "Every last detail, with a little help from God, and allowing for the fact that you would actually marry me."

I was stupefied. "Did I have any choice?"

His eyes held mine and I almost stopped breathing. "What do you think?" He paused, his eyes intense. "You did give me a scare though."

I frowned. "When?"

His powerful arms held me even more closely against him. "On that first day, when I called on you, for a while, you led me to believe that you were already mother to another man's child and I thought that I must be too late. I was knocked completely off balance."

I remembered the shock on his face and I kissed his cheek. "I did notice," I whispered in his ear.

"So you weren't oblivious to the fact that I wanted you," he murmured as he kissed my forehead.

I looked into his eyes and shook my head. "No, just... hopeful, and I prayed, a lot."

Richard smiled, with all his love for me. "Moi aussi. God seems to have truly blessed us."

As the powerful voice of the singer, racked with emotion, filled the room, my eyes widened in amazement. The lyrics of the Bryan Adams song were an astonishing message as Richard moved me to the rhythm. "You might stop a hurricane, Might even stop the drivin' rain, You might have a dozen other guys, But if you wanna stop me baby, don't even try. I'm goin' one way, your way, It's such a strong way, let's make it our way. Can't stop this thing we started, You gotta know it's right, Can't stop this course we've plotted. This thing called love, we've got it, No place for the broken-hearted, Can't stop this thing we started, no way, I'm goin' your way!

You might stop the world spinnin' round, Might even walk on Holy ground, I ain't Superman and I can't fly, But if you wanna stop me baby, don't even try. I'm goin' one way, your way. It's such a strong way, let's make it our way. Oh, why take it slow? I gotta know, Nothing can stop, this thing that we've got!"

Tears filled my eyes. This was his very public declaration of love for me. "Now, will you kiss me?" I asked.

His eyes held mine and he smiled as he shook his head. He kissed my forehead and held me close in his arms and I had to be content with that, for now.

At midnight, everyone stood on the ramparts to watch the massive firework display that was synchronised to music. It was incredible. Loud bangs shook the sky and even the walls beneath us seemed to vibrate with the shock wave. Light filled the sky and it was glorious.

I was snugly wrapped in Richard's arms and I looked at him, illuminated by the flashes of light. "Now, will you kiss me?" I couldn't breathe in anticipation.

He kissed my cheek and his soft breath fanned my skin as he whispered in my ear, "A bientôt."

I was trembling. "I've never been kissed before," I whispered against his face.

"Je le sais," he whispered back. "That's why I want to wait."

The waiting was exquisite agony. My body was tingling and trembling with an aching need for him. We stood in the giant doorway and waved as the last coach left. There had been tearful partings, particularly with my father, but not as traumatic as the previous time, and now everyone had left except us.

Richard pressed a button and the drawbridge began to rise. His arm was still around me, as it had been since we married. His eyes were on fire as he looked into mine and we both seemed to be struggling to breathe.

I frowned. "What are you doing?"

"This is my equivalent of the do not disturb sign on the honeymooners' door so that you and I can be alone, in our castle, cut off from the outside world."

My heart was pounding in my ears. "Does that mean I'm going to be kissed?" The answering look in his eyes caused a great big metal clamp to grab hold of my stomach and twist it into knots.

"I think there is every likelihood." He swept me into his arms. "I did say that I was going to have a little chat with that vivid imagination of yours as well, didn't I?"

I couldn't breathe! It came in shallow gasps as my entire body trembled. I loved being in his arms, feeling securely wrapped and supported by his strength. I nuzzled my face against his neck.

"Have you ever wondered why there is no family coat of arms on this castle?" Richard murmured against my hair.

I shook my head, breathing in his wonderful smell. "I hadn't thought about it." My voice was muffled against his skin.

"It's because of our family motto. I think that the Duchess Annette was so devastated by what Antoine did that she had someone remove it from the face of the building."

"Pourquoi?"

"Because, our family motto is, 'To Love Is To Honour.' That's what I want to do to you, tonight, mon Angelique. I want to honour you. I think we should name our home, Maison St. Honoré. House of the patron saint of honour."

I sighed and snuggled against his shoulder. "That sounds wonderful."

He carried me up the steps in the tower and along the balcony to the bedroom where he had found me earlier. He easily opened the door and then closed it, still holding me in his arms.

Richard laid me carefully on the bed and sat beside me, looking at me with the same awe and wonderment that he had when he had first found me on the beach. His eyes searched my face and then held mine intensely. We both seemed to be holding our breath. He reached out to a bowl on the bedside table and took a handful of fresh, white rose petals. He held his hand high above me and let them fall, like a shower. His gesture held more meaning than a thousand words.

"You wanted to put history straight with your family and this castle that was built for love, and you've done it," I whispered.

"Not until I've made you mine," he said, softly.

I frowned in confusion. "But I am yours!"

He kissed my hand, his eyes never leaving mine, and then he pulled me, gently into his arms. He kissed my left cheek, my right cheek and my forehead with delicate, butterfly kisses. He left a trail of fire as his kisses traced my jaw line, down my neck, along my collar bone to my shoulder and I arched against him.

My fingers did what they had been longing to do. They raked through the depths of his hair and traced his bone structure as I held his head close to me. After an eternity, his mouth descended on mine and I discovered heaven.

He kissed me slowly, gently, tenderly, inexorably, taking a very, very long time, arousing a need in me until it became an excruciating fever of burning desire and I melted. I became molten lava in his arms as I surrendered completely to him. "Now, you're mine," he whispered softly, his voice muffled against my neck.

He showed me how much he honoured me and that he knew, exactly how I wanted to be honoured which, until that moment, I hadn't actually known for myself.

Sunglasses

In an attempt to escape reality
I put on the sunglasses,
Because my eyes were dazzled by life.
I grew used to their comforting dimness
And it was only when, many years later,
I remembered I was wearing them,
And found the courage to take them off,
That I realised what I had missed.

Sophie Large – aged fifteen.

Chapter Twenty-one

THE suspended lights illuminated the domestic scene in the huge, French farmhouse style kitchen. Although it was large, it was a very cosy room. The logs crackled in the inglenook fireplace and the black ironwork gleamed.

Lisa had her magazines spread over one end of the huge table, while Annie and I were busy baking on the rest of it.

Annie was revelling in her important jobs and was stirring some white chocolate muffin mixture with great concentration, her dark curls flopping over her big brown eyes. We were covered in flour and chocolate, but we didn't care.

"The Bowes-Lyon wedding was most definitely the society wedding of the year," Lisa read, aloud.

Richard was helping himself to a fresh warm chocolate chip cookie from the spread of cooling racks on the other table. "Does it mention the beautiful bride?" he asked and winked at me.

I felt my face warm. I was still a blushing bride with the constant new discoveries in my life.

"You two are on the cover and more than half the magazine is taken up with the feature about your wedding. There are loads of pictures of famous gorgeous people, and I don't look too bad either!"

"Lisa, you looked equally gorgeous," I commented. I assisted Annie to stir some more chocolate chips into the mixture.

"Did you know that they did a much bigger print run, to allow for selling extra copies with their exclusive feature on your wedding?" Lisa asked.

"They always do that when they have paid a huge amount of money to have the exclusive on the story," Richard explained.

I frowned. "They paid?"

Richard shrugged. "Bien sûr. We always let the magazines bid against each other for the exclusive rights to our parties, and then we give the money to Sister Ruth for the convent's charity work."

I shook my head in wonderment. "I'm still new to this planet."

Richard grinned. "You'll get used to it

"Childhood sweethearts, Joy Bennett and Richard de Bowes-Lyon kept their wedding plans a secret. The guests were transported in a convoy of coach and horses to the couple's romantic castle. Guests believed that they were attending a fabulous celebration of the restoration of the ancient building. Miss Bennett is an accomplished interior designer and she has transformed the castle into a wonderful home."

"That's true," Richard observed as he looked over Lisa's shoulder at the pictures.

"It was also the occasion of Miss Bennett's twenty-first birthday and debut into society. The shy beauty had stunned the fashion world, earlier in the day, when she had been a star attraction on the catwalk for British Fashion Week and had then vanished without trace. She was formally presented at her debut ball that evening, when it was revealed that she is the daughter of the celebrated icon, the Duchess de Lyon, second wife of the Duke, Robert de Bowes-Lyon. Richard and Joy chose to use the occasion to surprise their friends by asking them to be witnesses for their wedding. It was obvious to everyone that the couple are deeply in love and guests were amazed that Richard de Bowes-Lyon had managed to keep the wedding plans such a closely-guarded secret."

"Especially from the bride!" My eyes connected with Richard's across the room but I had to look away quickly, as I registered the passion that was still there from earlier this morning. I focussed on helping Annie instead.

"Guests were concerned to see Miss Bennett take flight during the evening, but it was only pre-wedding nerves for the shy debutante and she returned later, happy and relaxed with her fiancé. Miss Bennett's closest friends were her bridesmaids. These included Miss Bennett's PA, three society beauties, who had been her friends at school, and four of the world's most famous models," Lisa continued.

I shook my head in bewilderment. "They make it all sound so straightforward. So… inevitable!"

Richard's eyes held mine. "The power of the press, Angel. If you don't put out a story, the press will speculate and make one up. We used the magazine to put out the story that gave the impression we wanted, so that you and your mother wouldn't suffer from any awkward and embarrassing speculation. You are now Madame de Bowes-Lyon. There is no other story for them."

Lisa laughed. "I love these captions! Joy captures the Lyon's heart. The Lyon's pride. Richard's pride and Joy, Richard's joie de vivre. Did you know that Mario is one of the world's greatest ever portrait photographers? His work has been exhibited at the National Portrait Gallery. Everyone in society wants to be photographed by him and he's very selective with his subjects, but he came chasing after you, Joy."

I hadn't realised that Richard was behind me until he pulled me back against him and wrapped his arms around me.

"That's the modern day equivalent of Reynolds and Gainsborough painting my ancestors," Richard said. "We must hang your portrait with the other beautiful Madame de Bowes-Lyon, in the traditional manner."

"Yours, too," I insisted.

"Those chocolate fingers look very enticing, may I suck on one?" Richard asked as he lifted my hand to his mouth and began to suck on one in a manner that was much too evocative for my current state of sanity. I felt the tingling in every nerve of my entire body and he knew exactly what his gesture was doing to me.

"They're already speculating on when you two will be having a pride of your own!"

"Vraiment?" I gasped. "That's jumping the gun a bit, isn't it?"

Richard pulled me back against him, his arms wrapped around me, and he nuzzled my neck. "Mmm, sounds like a good idea to me. I want lots and lots of Joy in my life. Perhaps we ought to keep the photographs for the family album."

"Don't forget little Richards," I responded as I felt the warmth tingle through my body, again.

"I think I hear the patter of tiny feet," Lisa said, meaningfully. "Remember that your mother probably conceived on her wedding night."

"Is that so?" Richard murmured against my neck. "In that case, the press may have a story on the way."

"Are you a practising Catholic?" Lisa enquired.

Richard wrapped his arms more tightly around me and I could feel his desire for me.

"Mais, oui. Mon Angelique et moi... we're having lots and lots of practice, aren't we?"

I felt myself blush scarlet and a tremor of sheer happiness flowed through me. My life is complete. So this must be the end of the story... or is it the beginning?

Merci, Sophie! Merci, mon Dieu!

I have found my God!

I have found my God! I went to the Family Church today, and it was there I found Him.

The first thing that struck me as I entered was the number of people that were there. Usually there're about fifteen to thirty people huddled in the pews, while the rather dull organ drones on. Here people were laughing and calling. And the room was high and full of light from two enormous windows. There was a form of altar, but it was ignored through most of the service.

Oh, Arion, the hymns of praise we sang! We sang so loudly, so joyously, so fully, dancing and clapping in the love of God that we felt in and among us, us a whole, a single being. I cried, Arion. For here people openly professed their love of God so other people heard. Instead of hiding away within themselves, they were calling and loving and singing praise.

It was not like the forced singing of everyday hymns, whose words have little meaning. It was singing of the joy God gave us, and we were so thankful, Arion. So grateful I could have burst with the overwhelming new feeling of the truth.

Some people came and read pieces from the Bible or told of events that had moved them during the week, and some had come to ask for the prayers for others.

One man said we all bore fruit, but that fruit was not for us to keep, it was for others to enjoy. We had to give it away. A girl said God handed to us what we were meant to have, and it was not right to try and get at what was behind it just because it looks better – but to take up a friendship or gift or opportunity and not try to get what was not offered to us.

The preacher said how we find it difficult to understand when God 'prunes us', when he chops away our fruitful branches along with the dead and the bad, festering ones, and how it's hard to understand that; but God has a reason for everything that happens and if you look, you could see this. It was amazing.

The communion really meant something – it meant remembering Jesus's love and compassion for us, and there was a cup about the size of a thimble full of Ribena and a piece from a real loaf of bread. It was beautiful, Arion, and ten sincere people, as they handed you the bread, said, 'bless you, forever' or something. I felt that I couldn't care what happened next – I had learned more from this service than anything else I have ever done.

Sophie Large – aged fifteen.

The end...or is it the beginning?

Sophie Large
1978 - 1998

For their help, support and encouragement
through some very difficult years,
I would like to thank

Family: Rose – my brother Ian, Christine, Basil, Jill, Duncan, Fiona, Andrew. Robertson – Kathleen, Kara, Kylie. Benson – Jack, Kathleen, Shaun, Melanie, Gavin, Fiona. Palmer – Phil, Cerys. Rowlands – Chas, Jenny. Sergison – Chris, Amanda. Jones – Kevin, Karen. Most especially – Elsie Jones, for her incredible love and support! Having been the local post mistress for many years the whole area knows her as 'Auntie Elsie' but she really is, *my* Auntie Elsie! West – Ralph, Margaret. Pearson – Rod, Di, for fun and wonderful hospitality in Morzine!

Friends: Chesney – Anna, Katrin, Jack and, most especially, Allan, for profound insight and advice. Carrdus – Susan, Head Teacher of the Carrdus School. Burrell –Paul, Maria. Malthouse – Janet, Ray, Louise. Knott – Julie, Simon. Wilby – Karen, Roxy. Matcham – John, Melanie. Berger – Rob, Jane. Crouch – Colin. Jones – Chris, Claire. Diana Davenport. Councillor Janet Bearman, of the Green Party. A special thank you to Tim Moore. Broomhall – John and, my dear friend since we were children in Pony Club – Angela for insisting that she wants to be the first person to buy a signed copy of my book!

Special people:
Amanda Wakeley. When I needed a character who was a stunning and talented, award-winning British fashion designer with a particular creativity in silk and renowned for her evening and bridal-wear, with Royal, aristocratic and celebrity clients - Amanda was the only choice and she kindly allowed me to base my character on her.

I have to say a very special thank you to Amanda and her PA, Bridget Bowen. As this novel was about to go to press, Sacha and I were invited to Amanda's show at London Fashion Week. In life, we were following in the footsteps of my fictional characters and we were treated as VIPs.

Galton Blackiston. When I needed a Michelin star chef, capable of stunning the jaded palettes of celebrities, with an award-winning, country house hotel, who celebrates life in Norfolk and claims his success is due to fantastic, local, in-season produce - the only choice was Galton. Many famous people have been born or drawn to Norfolk. Galton is the latest national celebrity and he very kindly allowed me to include him in my story.

Anestis Kyprianou, owner of Cobella spas. When my characters needed VIP pampering in a luxury spa, with the latest state of the art technology treatments, relentlessly sourced from all over the world - the only choice was Cobella Kensington in London and Anestis very kindly allowed me to use it in my story.

Ian Gould, manager of the Costa cafes in Waterstones and Chapelfield shopping mall, Norwich, for many wonderful mocha flakes piled with cream and chocolate, and for allowing me to include him in the story.

John Davies, Curator of the Norwich Castle Museum – for kindly allowing me to include him in the story.

John Horsewell, local artist, for allowing me to use his original oil painting for the cover of my book and David Koppel of St. Giles St. Gallery, Norwich, for supplying it.

Canon Philip Leonard-Johnson – for proof-reading my manuscript: particularly my French.

Ricky Martin – for the words of 'Nobody wants to be lonely,' Sony Music Entertainment. Bryan Adams – for the words of 'Can't stop this thing we started,' A&M Records.

I would like to wish Norwich City Football Club the very best wishes for a successful season. The City is behind you and your owner, the nation's favourite television cook, Delia Smith.

Last, but definitely not least, my printers, Biddles of King's Lynn, for creating this beautiful book for me.

Information List

Art gallery – David Koppel, St. Giles Street Gallery, 51 St. Giles Street, Norwich,
NR2 1JR. email: info@sgsgallery.com www.sgsgallery.com (01603) 630794

Beauty spa and hair salon – Cobella, 5 Kensington High Street, London, W8 5NP.
email: info@cobella.co.uk www.cobella.co.uk 020 7937 8888.

BBC – British Broadcasting Corporation, The Forum, Millenium Plain, Norwich,
NR2 1BH www.bbc.co.uk/norfolk (01603) 667865

Book printer – Biddles Ltd., 24 Rollesby Road, Hardwick Industrial Estate, King's Lynn,
Norfolk, PE30 4LS. www.biddles.co.uk (01553) 764728.

Book store – Borders UK Ltd., 146 Merchants Hall, Upper Ground, Chapelfield
Shopping Centre, Norwich, NR2 1SH. (01603) 664538

Book store –Waterstones, 11 Castle Street, Norwich, NR2 1PD. (01603) 767262

Book store – Waterstones, Units 21-24 Royal Arcade, Norwich, Norfolk, NR2 1NQ.
email: enquiries@norwich.waterstones.co.uk www.waterstones.co.uk (01603) 632426

Coffee – Costa within Waterstones, 11 Castle Street and 306, The Dining Terrace,
Chapelfield Shopping Centre, Norwich, NR2 1SY. (01603) 766326

Computers – Colin Crouch, Computer and Technical Services, 58 York Street,
Norwich, NR2 2AW. email: colin.cats@clara.co.uk (01603) 619121

Council – The Green Party, 15 Connaught Road, Norwich, NR2 3BP.
www.greenparty.org.uk (01603) 623223

Country House Hotel- Galton Blackiston, Morston Hall Hotel, Morston, Holt,
Norfolk, NR25 7AA email: reception@morstonhall.com www.morstonhall.com
(01263) 741041

Department store – Jarrold, 1-11 London Street, Norwich, Norfolk, NR2 1JF.
www.jarroldthestore.co.uk (01603) 660661

Fashion - Amanda Wakeley, 80 Fulham Road, London, SW3 6HR.
www.amandawakeley.com 020 7950 9105

Norwich Airport – Norwich Airport Travel Ltd., 60 Castle Mall, Norwich, NR1 3DD.
email: mall.enquiries@travelnorwichairport.co.uk www.travelnorwich.com

Norwich Castle Museum – Castle Hill, Norwich, NR1 3JS. email:
museums@norfolk.gov.uk www.museums.norfolk.gov.uk (01603) 493625

Norwich City Football Club – Carrow Road, Norwich, NR1 1JE. www.canaries.co.uk
(01603) 760760

NSPCC – For all child welfare concerns. Weston House, 42 Curtain Road, London
EC2A 3NH. www.nspcc.org.uk 020 7825 2505. Childline 0800 1111

School – Carrdus School, Overthorpe Hall, Banbury, Oxfordshire, OX17 2BS.
email: office@carrdusschool.co.uk www.carrdusschool.co.uk

Questions about life and God – The Alpha Office, Alpha International, Holy Trinity,
Brompton Road, London, SW7 1JA. email: info@alpha.org www.alpha.org
0845 644 7544

Sophie's Silver Lining Fund – 17 Silver Street, Chacombe, Banbury, Oxfordshire,
England, OX17 2JR. email: office@sslf.org.uk www.silverlining.org.uk
(01295) 711155

Visit Norwich Ltd. – 2 Millenium Plain, Bethel Street, Norwich, NR2 1TF. Tourist
Information Centre – email: tic@visitnorwich.co.uk www.visitnorwich.co.uk
(01603) 727927